D0644541

Praise for *New York Times* bestselling author Lindsay McKenna

"McKenna provides heartbreakingly tender romantic development that will move readers to tears. Her military background lends authenticity to this outstanding tale, and readers will fall in love with the upstanding hero and his fierce determination to save the woman he loves."
—*Publishers Weekly* on *Never Surrender*

"Talented Lindsay McKenna delivers excitement and romance in equal measure."
—*RT Book Reviews* on *Protecting His Own*

"Lindsay McKenna will have you flying with the daring and deadly women pilots who risk their lives… Buckle in for the ride of your life."
—*Writers Unlimited* on *Heart of Stone*

Praise for *New York Times* bestselling author Joan Johnston

"A guaranteed good read."
—*New York Times* bestselling author Heather Graham

"Joan Johnston does short contemporary Westerns to perfection."
—*Publishers Weekly*

"Joan Johnston continually gives us everything we want… fabulous details and atmosphere, memorable characters, a story that you wish would never end, and lots of tension and sensuality."
—*RT Book Reviews*

NEW YORK TIMES BESTSELLING AUTHORS

LINDSAY McKENNA

& JOAN JOHNSTON

A MEASURE OF LOVE
&
HAWK'S WAY: BILLY

If you purchased this book without a cover you should be aware that this book is stolen property. It was reported as "unsold and destroyed" to the publisher, and neither the author nor the publisher has received any payment for this "stripped book."

ISBN-13: 978-1-335-03998-9

A Measure of Love & Hawk's Way: Billy

Copyright © 2019 by Harlequin Books S.A.

The publisher acknowledges the copyright holders of the individual works as follows:

A Measure of Love
Copyright © 1987 by Lindsay McKenna

Hawk's Way: Billy
Originally published as The Temporary Groom
Copyright © 1996 by Joan Mertens Johnston

Recycling programs for this product may not exist in your area.

All rights reserved. Except for use in any review, the reproduction or utilization of this work in whole or in part in any form by any electronic, mechanical or other means, now known or hereafter invented, including xerography, photocopying and recording, or in any information storage or retrieval system, is forbidden without the written permission of the publisher, Harlequin Enterprises Limited, 22 Adelaide St. West, 40th Floor, Toronto, Ontario M5H 4E3, Canada.

This is a work of fiction. Names, characters, places and incidents are either the product of the author's imagination or are used fictitiously, and any resemblance to actual persons, living or dead, business establishments, events or locales is entirely coincidental.

This edition published by arrangement with Harlequin Books S.A.

For questions and comments about the quality of this book, please contact us at CustomerService@Harlequin.com.

® and TM are trademarks of Harlequin Enterprises Limited or its corporate affiliates. Trademarks indicated with ® are registered in the United States Patent and Trademark Office, the Canadian Intellectual Property Office and in other countries.

Printed in U.S.A.

www.Harlequin.com

CONTENTS

Lindsay McKenna is proud to have served her country in the US Navy as an aerographer's mate third class—also known as a weather forecaster. She was a pioneer in the military romance subgenre and loves to combine heart-pounding action with soulful and poignant romance. True to her military roots, she is the originator of the long-running and reader-favorite Morgan's Mercenaries series. She does extensive hands-on research, including flying in aircraft such as a P3-B Orion sub-hunter and a B-52 bomber. She was the first romance writer to sign her books in the Pentagon bookstore. Visit her online at lindsaymckenna.com.

Books by Lindsay McKenna

Shadow Warriors

Running Fire
Taking Fire
Never Surrender
Breaking Point
Degree of Risk

Jackson Hole, Wyoming

Out Rider
Night Hawk
Wolf Haven
High Country Rebel
The Loner

Visit the Author Profile page
at Harlequin.com for more titles.

A MEASURE OF LOVE

Lindsay McKenna

Chapter 1

"Jessie, we need your help."

She was working on the latest figures that had been called in by her ranchers for the Colorado-Wyoming mustang population. No one ever needed her help. Or if they did, it wasn't often. They had stuck her away in a small cubicle at the end of the hall of a huge federal building in the heart of bureaucracy in Washington, D.C.

Raising her head, she pushed the thick, heavy strands of blond hair across her shoulder and looked up. Mr. Humphries, second-in-command of the Bureau of Land Management, stood before her.

"Yes, sir?" Immediately her palms became damp, and she tried to inconspicuously pull them off the desk and into her lap, where he couldn't see them.

Humphries cleared his throat. "Er, well, that is…come with me. This is most urgent."

Jessie's heart began to pound in her breast as she hesitantly rose. Something was wrong. Mr. Humphries, who normally looked like a pit bull waiting to bite someone, was shifting from one foot to the other, looking uncomfortable.

As Jessie followed him down the brightly lit halls, her curiosity got the most of her. She had been working for the BLM since her divorce. Part of the Department of Interior, the BLM dealt with anything having to do with mustangs. At the time she had applied, they had been looking for someone who could oversee the important project of assigning newly captured mustangs to people who wanted them. They had promised her travel, excitement and field work. That had been five years ago. She had never left her small, dingy office, but it didn't matter. Placing the unseen mustangs with good, loving homes had become her focus in life. That and coordinating investigations into anything having to do with the wild animals. From her office, she sent the BLM's agents out all over the U.S.

"In here, Jessie," Humphries said, holding open the door to a conference room.

Jessie smoothed her light wool heather skirt against her hips as she entered. At one end of the twenty-seat conference table was Joe Allen, one of her field representatives. He didn't look happy, and barely gave her a nod of recognition when she entered the room. Jessie managed a weak smile, knowing something serious must have happened. She automatically flexed her fingers, realizing it was her head, not Joe's, that was on the chopping block if Joe had fouled up his assignment in some way.

"Sit down, Jessie. Over there."

She sat, giving Joe a warm smile of welcome. Joe

raised his hand, but his hazel gaze was on Humphries, who remained standing in front of them.

"Now, Jessie, a situation of grave importance has come up." He cleared his throat, his gray brows falling into a V over his narrowed brown eyes. "You sent Allen here to investigate a rancher out in Colorado after we received an anonymous phone call that Mr. Kincaid, owner of the Triple K, was shooting mustangs."

Jessie's lips parted. "Yes, sir, I remember the incident." Her cinnamon-colored eyes widened slightly as she prepared for Humphries's blustering tirade.

Humphries glared over at Joe. "To say the least, he and Mr. Kincaid didn't get along. As a matter of fact, Kincaid had the gall to literally throw him off Triple K property. Isn't that right, Allen?"

Joe, who was a slender man of thirty-five, nodded quickly. "Yes, sir."

Humphries cleared his throat again. "Well, go on, tell her the rest."

"Yes, sir." Joe turned his attention to Jessie. "I treated the Kincaid case like any other. When I got to the ranch, Mr. Kincaid was in a foul mood. When I discreetly asked him to let me investigate the matter, he turned ugly. He started questioning me and making allegations that the BLM was acting like a jackass."

"Mr. Kincaid did that?" Jessie interrupted. She had talked to Sam Kincaid on several occasions several years before and had liked the terse rancher.

Joe nodded weakly.

Jessie couldn't contain her surprise. "But Mr. Humphries, the Kincaids have been staunch supporters of environmental protection, and they've always worked with us on the mustangs. According to my files, and

I've got a thick one on the Triple K, Mr. Kincaid is on our side."

"That was Sam Kincaid," Humphries corrected. "This is his son, Rafe, who's running things now. And obviously a lot differently. Well, go on, Allen."

"When I asked for Kincaid's cooperation, he asked if I had a search warrant. I said no. He demanded to know what the investigation was for. Well, naturally, I couldn't tell him. I just told him that we wanted to inspect the northern boundary of his property, where it butts up against the federal reserve. He didn't trust me or my intentions. Instead of allowing me to go up there to see if I could find any mustang carcasses, he threw me off the ranch and told me that if I came back I'd be staring down the barrel of a thirty-aught-six rifle."

There were a few moments of silence, then Humphries said, "Allen, you can leave now."

"Yes, sir."

The door closed quietly behind him. Jessie tensed as Humphries circled her like a buzzard. Was he going to fire her because of Joe's disastrous encounter with Rafe Kincaid?

"Your boss, Nicholas Van der Meer, seems to feel that you have the right combination of talent, resources, knowledge and diplomacy to deal with Rafe Kincaid." He sat one ponderous hip on the table, and it creaked accordingly. "Van der Meer feels your assets could be invaluable to this case. Right now we're getting a lot of pressure from environmental groups to treat the mustang as a natural resource. I can't afford to have the damn papers blaring with news headlines that some bullheaded rancher is picking them off like crow bait just because they're on his property. I want you to leave this evening for Denver, Jessie. My secretary has already made a plane reservation for you, and there'll be a rental car waiting for you there. I want you personally to deal with this problem. Do you understand?"

Jessie stared at him, feeling the blood draining from her face. "Me?"

"Why not you?"

"Well, uh, because, Mr. Humphries, I've never stepped out of this office. I don't know the first thing about being a field rep—"

"Nonsense. You have five hundred ranchers that you take care of in connection with the mustangs. You've had contact with these men and their families for five years, plus you assign our agents all over the country. No one's more familiar with the intricacy of investigating than yourself."

Her knuckles whitened as she gripped the chair. "Well, yes, sir, that's true in one sense. But I've only done this over the phone and through the mail; I've never actually set foot on a ranch."

He gave a negligent wave of his hand. "Doesn't matter."

Jessie rose, her eyes wide. "I've never been west of Pittsburgh, Pennsylvania. I know nothing about the West."

"You've got more knowledge about the mustangs, the land they live on and wander across, and the ranchers than anyone else in this office."

Panic was setting in, and Jessie began to pace, using her hands to punctuate her words. "But, sir, I'm an office manager! A paper pusher! I've never seen a horse except in a parade along Pennsylvania Avenue. My knowledge is through the books and reports I read. I only know the ranchers through minimal phone contact or letters." She compressed her full lips, wondering if they were trying to fire her.

Humphries rose, scowling. "You have your orders, Ms. Scott. We feel your diplomacy and ability to humor Kincaid will do the trick."

Humor? Sure, people had always commented on her ability to see humor in every situation. And some of her friends even called her Sunny. That was all fine and dandy, but she still didn't see how she could persuade someone like Rafe Kincaid to cooperate with the BLM.

Jessie stood there as Humphries opened the door and disappeared. Her hands were damp and cold, and she rubbed them on the sides of her tailored wool skirt. This couldn't be happening! Were they trying to get rid of her? She couldn't stand still a moment longer and headed down the hall with swift strides.

"Nick!" she stage-whispered, sticking her head inside her immediate superior's office door.

Nick Van der Meer looked up and smiled, then motioned for her to come in. "I see you've talked with Mr. Humphries, Jessie."

Jessie closed the door and pressed her back up against it. "Get me off the hook, Nick. I'm not cut out for this assignment. I'm strictly office material."

Nick smiled from beneath his full gray mustache, and set down his pen on a stack of papers in front of him. "No, you're not. I've been saying for years that you'd be good out in the field."

"This is crazy, Nick." Her voice quavered, and Jessie waited for a moment, gathering her fortitude before she went on. "I'm no more a field rep than that mouse that lives in my office!"

"You still feeding him every day?"

"Of course I am. Nick, I'm being serious."

"So am I. Come on, sit down. You look like you're ready to explode, and really, there's no reason for your panic."

Jessie sat, with her hands gripped in her lap and her jaw set in a stubborn line. "You did this, didn't you? You put Mr. Humphries up to this."

"Yes, I did," he admitted slowly, leaning back in his expensive leather chair. "I felt it was about time you started seeing something of the world, Jessie, instead of spending your life back in that dark little office you fondly call your second home." He held up his hand. "I know you love your job. That's obvious from the long hours and care you put into it. But there is life outside these walls."

Her nostrils flared, and she avoided his gaze. Nick had been her boss for the five years she had been with the BLM; he was like the father she had never had and always dreamed of having. But right now she wasn't feeling particularly like a daughter toward him or his attitude that he knew what was best for her. "I happen to like my office, my mouse, my job, my little apartment and Washington, D.C."

"No question about it." Nick sighed, becoming serious. "Look, we're both in a spot. Joe Allen is fairly new at being a rep, and sometimes he gets a little too eager. Even you have to admit that. I know you've dealt with Sam Kincaid and you're familiar with the Triple K, its resources and the mustang reserve that borders it. Rafe Kincaid, the son, is now the owner. I find it hard to believe that he would cold-bloodedly kill mustangs when he was raised by a father who respected the land and wild animals."

Jessie frowned. "From the way Joe talked, he didn't exactly level with the rancher, and it's obvious he should have. Why not just send him back and have him explain the whole thing?"

"Because, Jessie, he's done too much damage already. And somehow I don't doubt Rafe Kincaid's coming out with a rifle. We need you to repair the damage he's done. The Kincaids have been long-time friends of the BLM, and we want to smooth over the waters with them. Joe should have leveled with him. My personal feeling is that Rafe Kincaid isn't shooting mustangs." He gave Jessie the fatherly smile that always got to her. "There isn't a rancher under your jurisdiction that doesn't have something good to say about you, Jessie. Right now, I need your gift of human relations to heal this rift with the Kincaids. This'll give you a chance to broaden your experience with the ranchers, see some mustangs and travel, all at the same time."

Worriedly Jessie stared down at her interlaced fingers, which were bunched in her lap. Her fingers were as cold as the drizzle of freezing rain that fell outside the window behind her boss. "I thought maybe you were trying to get rid of me, Nick."

His laughter was rich and he sat up, resting his elbows on the heavy walnut desk. "Not a chance, Jessie. Take your time on this assignment. You know from handling the reports that this kind of thing can take from a week to a month to solve. If you need help, I'm always here. Just call." He smiled warmly. "Knowing you, however, I think you'll do just fine, you always have. Stay in touch. And enjoy the experience. It won't be all that bad."

All that bad, Jessie thought. She closed her eyes and tried to sleep on the plane. The entire day had been a blur. She had managed to catch her next-door neighbor, a college professor, at home. Susan Prigozen had agreed to water her many plants while she was away. Other than racing through the motions of packing items she thought she might need, there had been little else to do. Jessie felt alone. And scared. Right now, all she wanted to do was ask the captain to turn around and head back to D.C.

She opened her eyes and stared pensively out the window into the blackness. She could see lights of small towns far below them. They looked like jeweled pendants twinkling on the velvet setting of the earth. It was a beautiful sight.

There had been so many firsts that day: first airplane ride, first time to leave her hometown, first assignment. Why had Nick chosen her? He knew she lived a cloistered existence that ranged from her apartment to her job with the BLM. But so what? She was happy.

You're a mouse, Jessie. Just like the one that lives in your office and you feed. Mice are frightened little creatures. They scamper away at the first sign of danger. Her mouth went dry, and she took a long drink of the white wine she had ordered from the flight attendant. *And where you're going, there's a great big lion who eats up little mice like you.* She scrunched down in the seat. Her life had just been uprooted. A tornado couldn't have done a better job. She was a walking disaster, and Nick and Mr. Humphries expected her to be successful with Rafe Kincaid.

Jessie shut her eyes tightly. In another hour they would land in Denver. She would get a hotel room for the night and in the morning rent a car and drive out to the Triple K. As she pried open one eye, she noticed the luminescent full moon in the sky. Wonderful. Dracula and the vampire came out with the full moon. What effect would it have on Rafe Kincaid?

* * *

Rain was pouring out of a slit in the gray underbelly of the sky that hovered over the valley. Rafe's black brows were dipped ominously beneath his felt cowboy hat of the same color, and his narrowed blue eyes were barely visible beneath the brim. He pulled his gunmetal-gray Arabian gelding to a halt on the muddy road, motioning with one gloved hand at his cowhands to start bringing the cattle across. His mouth compressed as he sat on the horse. The black rain slicker he wore was shiny with water and draped over his body like a huge tent. The cattle moved slowly; they didn't want to leave the lowlands and begin their trek up through the valley to the high pastures that were still dotted with snow. Grass was easier to forage where there was no snow. Cattle were basically a lazy lot, Rafe thought.

He watched his four men, on sturdy, small Arabians, going about the business of moving the hundred balky, bawling steers across the ranch road that was now little more than a brown ribbon of quagmire. As he sat on his restive mount, Rafe fumed. If he had had extra money, he would have bought the necessary gravel to lay on the road earlier, before the late April rains had come. But he hadn't, and so four-wheel drive was the only type of vehicle that could negotiate the ten-mile stretch between the Triple K and the asphalt highway.

Water followed the hard line of his jaw, gathering on his stubborn chin before dripping off. His thin deerskin gloves were soaked. Water was leaking down the back of his neck, soaking into his cotton shirt, making his skin itch. But he wouldn't have traded any of the minimal discomforts for the world as he looked toward the small valley below him. The valley was a favorite of his sister

Dal. It was ringed with ponderosa pine, blue spruce, fir and tamarack, all darkly green, silver or blue, depending on the species silhouetted against the lead-colored sky. Buffalo grass grew thick and tall on the valley floor, providing a rich, vibrant background for the more somber trees.

Rafe gazed appreciatively over his land.

Then his blue eyes clouded. If he hadn't been so preoccupied with the past, if he had been more alert to the changes in the fluctuating stock market, the ranch might be in better shape than it was presently. He shifted position in the saddle, and the leather creaked pleasantly. The past was dead and gone. Let it go. Let it go…

His alert gelding heard it first. The rain had intensified, sending sheets of torrential water down from the sky, nearly obliterating visibility. Suddenly, a small red car burst over the crest of the steep hill as if it had been shot out of a cannon. It was aimed directly at him. The engine was screaming, the wheels spun, and mud flew in every direction. A shout rose in Rafe's throat and time seemed to slow down to single frames of a movie. He saw the car land with a thunderous *clunk* on the rutted road, then slew sideways to avoid hitting him, his horse and the milling cattle.

To his horror, he watched helplessly as the car swerved over the edge of the soft earthen bank and slid down the hillside. With a shout, he sank his spurs into the gelding. The horse lunged forward in a few strides and went over the edge. Rafe rode the sliding, slipping animal down the precarious bank. It was a hundred-foot incline to a wall of pine below. He twisted and turned in rhythm with the animal and bolted to attention as he saw the car crunch into the densely packed trees.

   With a curse, Rafe brought his horse to a halt and
leapt out of the saddle. Steam was rising from beneath
the hood of the car. Miraculously, there seemed to be
little damage, except for dents on the passenger's side,
where the car had come to rest, lodged up against some
bushes and the stand of pine. He slipped in the sucking mud and cursed again as he made his way toward
the driver's door. He'd better have worn a seat belt, was
Rafe's only thought. Rafe heard the steers bawling far
above him and a shout from Pinto Pete, the old man who
was in charge of the drive. Clutching the handle, Rafe
pulled on the car door. It wouldn't give. Then, with a
more powerful yank, he wrenched it open.

   His eyes widened. The "he" was a "she." And she
hadn't worn a seat belt. A kaleidoscope of impressions
assailed Rafe as he stared at her unconscious figure lying
prone before him. She looked to be in her early-twenties,
and as Rafe leaned over the steering wheel to see the ex-
tent of her injuries, the delicate scent of her perfume surrounded him. A heady, almost spicy fragrance… Rafe
shook his head, muttering to himself.

   The poncho he was wearing smattered water all over
the interior of the car as he reached forward to lay his
hand on her camel-colored wool blazer. It was impossible to get to the other side of the car since the door was
barricaded with a huge pine tree trunk. As gently as he
could, Rafe brought her into a slumped sitting position,
pressing her gently back against the seat. Her blond hair
was pulled into a tight bun at the nape of her neck; a neat
and severe look that was marred by the crimson line trailing down her temple.

   He heard another horse and rider approaching, and

pulled out of the car. Pinto Pete, with his grizzled gray mustache and beard, sat astride his bay mare.

"You need help?" the old man called, his voice drowned out in the thunderous downpour.

"Yeah, get on the walkie-talkie and see if you can locate Mel. He's got the four-wheel drive. There's a woman hurt in here. While you're at it, raise Millie at the ranch and have her call the doctor."

Pete nodded, pulling the plastic-encased walkie-talkie from the safety of his saddlebag.

Rafe glanced back over his shoulder, the adrenaline pumping through him making him a bit shaky. The damn woman. Who the hell was she? Didn't she know any better than to drive like a kamikaze pilot down a dirt road like that? He grudgingly admitted that at least she had had the presence of mind to veer away from him.

"Hey, Boss," Pete called.

Rafe lifted his head, rain slashing at his face. "Yeah?"

"Mel's clear up by the first line shack. That's fifteen miles away."

Damn! They had the first herd of the year to move up to the high pastures. He couldn't afford the costly time out to take care of the woman himself. "All right, tell him to stay put. I'll take her back to the ranch myself. What about Millie?"

Pete dipped his head, his dark chocolate eyes mirroring his worry. "Said she'd call the doctor and prepare a room for the little lady."

"Good. Come on down and give me a hand," he ordered.

Pinto Pete was only five feet nine inches in height, but he was wiry and amazingly agile for his sixty-five years. The old mustang wrangler had joined the Triple K forty years before and had stayed ever since. He watched as his boss jerked off his hat and then pulled off the huge poncho, leaving himself to be soaked by the rain.

"You want her in that?" he guessed.

Rafe nodded, settling the hat back on his head. The late-April temperature was in the forties, the rain cold and bone-chilling. "Yeah, I've got to ride with her for two miles. I can't have her getting pneumonia on top of whatever else is wrong with her. Here, help me, and I'll put this over her."

Pinto Pete squeezed in between Rafe and the car door to lend a hand.

They managed to get the poncho over her head, but it snagged on the bun at the base of her neck. Jerking off one deerskin glove, Rafe leaned across her and fumbled with an array of bobby pins. Her feminine scent assailed his nostrils, and automatically he inhaled it. The almost forgotten perfume of a woman's body unconsciously pleased him, and he pulled the remaining pins out of her hair more gently.

"Okay, let me pull her clear," he said to Pete.

Rafe braced his shoulder against the frame of the car door as he slid his arms beneath her, taking care not to snap her neck back and possibly cause her more injury. The fact that she hadn't awakened in the past ten minutes bothered him. A bump on the head was one thing—a concussion another. Usually, if a person was knocked out, they could be expected to wake up in five or ten minutes.

After some jockeying, Pinto Pete lifted the woman back into Rafe's rain-soaked arms after he had mounted. At least she would remain reasonably dry. Something old and hurting wrenched free in Rafe's chest when her long blond mane fell starkly across the slippery black surface of the poncho as her head came to rest against his chest.

He made sure she was comfortably situated across the saddle, and he kept both arms around her. He guided his gray gelding down through the pine with pressure from his legs. Like all good ranch horses, the animal had a long, swift walk. Rafe didn't dare go any faster for fear of hurting the woman even more. He tried to protect her face, which was nuzzled beneath his chin, from the rain. Her blond hair quickly became soaked by the rain, lying in vivid goldenrod colored sheets across the poncho. Rafe had never seen anyone with hair that unusual blond before, and he was transfixed by it.

The ride took a good twenty minutes, and he tried to ignore how good it felt to have a woman in his arms again. How long had it been? Then he snapped the lid shut on those memories that still burned in his heart like a painful branding iron. Pete had stuffed her black leather purse into one of the saddlebags. He'd find out who she was in a while. What was she doing out here? Had she gotten lost on the back roads of the Rockies? Was she looking for directions on how to escape the mountains and get back to civilization? A bare hint of a smile tipped one corner of his mouth as he gazed down at her. His initial anger had abated, and he studied her curiously. Maybe it was the soft fullness of her parted lips that made him feel less antagonistic toward what she had done. Maybe it was the thick mane of blond hair she had tried to capture into a bun that made him a little more inclined to ease up on her stupidity. He wasn't sure. She looked like a city girl, with her fancy tailored suit, black heels and hair tamed into a sophisticated style.

Too bad, Rafe thought, his blue eyes glittering. His hands tightened against the slippery poncho, keeping her balanced as he guided his horse between the barns and to the back porch of the ranch house. He saw Millie, the housekeeper, come flying out to the enclosed screened porch, and a ranch hand, Carl Cramer, came to help.

Rafe lowered the woman into Carl's waiting arms and then dismounted. The rain was easing. That figured, Rafe thought with irony. He took the woman back into his arms and mounted the wooden stairs onto the porch. Millie's plump face was pinched with worry as she opened the door to the house.

"What happened, Rafe?" she asked, waddling quickly through the kitchen and down the hall.

"Car accident," he muttered, his boots squishing with each step he took across the polished brick floor of the kitchen. "She came over the hill like a grand-prix racer, saw us and then took to the hill. Ended up in some pine."

Millie clucked sympathetically, hurrying as fast as she could make her sixty-year-old body move as they went down the darkened hall. "Doc Miller is on his way. But you know what the weather and roads are like. He said it'd be at least an hour. Said to treat her for shock and a possible concussion, from the description Pinto gave me."

Rafe slowed his stride, frowning. He'd hoped Millie had given the woman the guest room. Instead she swung the door open to another bedroom: the one that hadn't been used since Mary Ann's death.

"Can't use the guest room," Millie said, as if reading his mind and the objections he was going to voice. She hurried over to the bed. "I'm busy spring-cleaning it."

"I see." Rafe had given orders that this room never be used again; it hurt too much to be in the room because of the memories it dredged up. Swallowing hard against the past that still haunted him, he gently laid the woman on the bed, took off his drenched hat and let it drop to the highly polished cedar floor. He glanced up at Millie. "Can you handle her by yourself?" There wasn't another female around to help the old housekeeper.

Millie's face puckered. "Of course I can't, Rafe! Now don't go giving me that moon-eyed look! You've seen a woman before. Land's sakes! Come on, help me get her out of this poncho."

Properly chastised, Rafe took the poncho off her. And then Millie found the woman's clothes were damp despite all he had tried to do to protect her from the wet weather.

"We'll have to undress her," Millie muttered. "I can't put her to bed like this. She'll catch her death of cold."

"I'd like to paddle her," he growled.

"You ought to be thankin' her for not hitting you! Now stop your growling like an old grizzly."

Rafe helped Millie gently remove the wool blazer, then the pale peach blouse. They left her full-length slip on, and Rafe was momentarily transfixed by the sight of her slender, gently contoured body outlined by the ivory silk.

"She's built like an Arab," Rafe muttered, picking her up while Millie pulled back the bedding. He laid her on the mattress, and the housekeeper tucked in the crisp sheet and covers around her.

Millie raised one eyebrow. "Is that a compliment or an insult, Rafe? You're just like your daddy, always comparing women to horses. I swear."

"It was a compliment," he said, bending down to retrieve his hat.

The housekeeper leaned over and studied the lump on the woman's head. "Well," she said sternly, "you'd better hope she's tough like an Arabian, Rafe Kincaid. This isn't good; she should be waking up."

"Yeah, I know."

Millie examined the bluish-purple lump that was now the size of a hen's egg. "What if this is serious? Doc Miller ain't gonna be able to do much for her here at the ranch."

He walked to the door and then hesitated. "Then I'll take her and the doctor down to Denver by helicopter. There's no place closer." Grimly Rafe turned, thinking that his day was turning into nothing but mud. "I'm going to get her purse. Pete put it in the saddlebag. Maybe we can find out who she is and contact her family. I'll be in the study after I get some dry clothes on, if you need me."

Rafe sat at the huge cherry-wood desk, the stained-glass Tiffany lamp near his elbow providing the necessary light in the dark paneled library and study. Her purse was small and dainty, like her. He felt a twinge of guilt as he rummaged through the contents, locating and pulling out the slender leather billfold. Unsnapping it, he found her driver's license, made out to Jessica Scott. His brows drew down as he read her address: Washington D.C. He'd just gotten rid of a BLM guy two weeks earlier from the same damn city. Was he cursed with people from D.C.? Rubbing his jaw, he studied the plastic license. She couldn't be a government official; she looked too young and...fresh.

He set aside the license and rummaged through the rest of the contents: a social security card, a YWCA membership and a Visa card were all that were enclosed. Rafe glanced again at the license, offhandedly noticing her birthdate. Surprise flickered in his dark blue eyes. She couldn't be twenty-eight! She barely looked twenty-three.

Intrigued, he slowly went through the pictures on the

other side of the wallet. The first one was of a much older woman, probably in her seventies, bound to a wheelchair with a colorful afghan across her lap, smiling. Must be her grandmother, Rafe thought. The second photo was obviously cut from a magazine. Jessie was turning out to be quite a surprise. In the magazine photo was a picture of a rare medicine hat mustang running free. Did she own the horse? Or did she know who owned it? He lifted his head, peering out through the gloom toward the hallway. Jessie Scott. Interesting…

Jessie heard rain drumming in a staccato beat around her. She moved her head slightly, but the pain kept banging away inside her brain. She heard the faint movement of cloth against nylon and then softened footsteps gradually fading away. Forcing open her eyes to mere slits, she became aware of the smell of her damp hair, of the warmth surrounding her and the muted light pouring in through large-paned windows to the right of the bed. Bed…she was in a bed. She pulled her hand from beneath the heavy goosedown quilt and touched her brow.

"Ouch!" She winced as she carefully felt around the lump on the side of her head. The light hurt her eyes, making them water. The effort to lift her hand drained what little returning strength she had, and she dropped her arm across her stomach, trying to think, to remember.

The sound of heavy, steady footfalls snagged her groggy awareness, and she looked toward the opened door. An older woman slipped quietly through it, and then a man. He was much younger than the woman, and powerfully built. Jessie's eyes widened as they both approached her bed. Despite the toll of agony it took for her to speak, she said, "What happened? Where am I?"

Rafe placed his hands on his narrow hips, studying her. "You don't remember? You damn near hit me and my herd of cattle up on the road earlier." He hadn't meant for his words to come out quite so clipped, and he saw hurt register immediately in her wan features.

Millie glared across the bed at Rafe as she moved to Jessie's side. "Don't pay him no mind. I'm Millie Martin, the housekeeper. Now, we want you to just stay quiet until Doc Miller arrives. You took a nasty bump on the head in that car accident." She reached out and patted Jessie's cool hand.

Jessie remained staring up at the rancher. She was too groggy to sort out the impressions he was making on her. His features were so weathered by the seasons that he looked as if he were hewn from rock. Deep crow's-feet at the corners of his intensely dark blue eyes told her that he squinted a great deal. His forehead was broad and lined, as if he frowned more than he smiled. Jessie noticed that his nose, which had once been clean-lined and aquiline, had several bumps on it, indicating he'd broken it more than just a few times. Harsh lines bracketed his mouth, but the corners curled softly upward. His full, flat lower lip gentled his rugged features, yet didn't deny the stubbornness of his jutting chin.

Rafe relented a little, pleased that she had fearlessly met his gaze and not shrank back from him. "You're at the Triple K, Jessie Scott. I'm the owner, Rafe Kincaid. Do you remember what happened?"

Jessie gripped the edge of the bedcovers that were draped across her shoulders. "Oh, no…" she croaked as the entire sequence of events came back to her. Heat swept up through her cheeks, and she shut her eyes tightly. She had nearly killed the man who was standing in front of her, the man she had come to see. This was his ranch, and his bed. And she was in a lot of trouble. What about the car? And how had she gotten here…?

She tried desperately to sort out her priorities. Her knuckles whitened against the quilt as she struggled to think clearly. Finally she opened her eyes and forced herself to look at him. "A-are you okay? I mean… I could have killed you…"

A slight hint of a smile shadowed his mouth as he heard her concern, not for herself, but for him. "I'm fine."

"A-and your horse?"

"The horse will survive. More importantly, how are you feeling?"

Jessie shivered on hearing the warm timbre of his voice and was momentarily arrested by the change in his face. One moment he was glowering at her, the next his blue eyes lightened, the corners of his mouth eased, and his voice caressed her like a gentle touch.

Rafe waited patiently for her to speak, well aware of how slowly her mind must be functioning. As he gazed at her, a sharp ache moved through him. She looked so fragile in the large bed, so delicate, and he wondered what it would be like to tunnel his hands through the thick honey hair that framed her face. And those lips… He scowled. What was he thinking of? She was hurt, and all he could do was think of getting into bed with her and pulling her close? Was he that starved for a woman? He didn't look too closely at the last question.

Jessie saw him scowl, and she blurted out, "I'm fine… I think. Just an awful headache. Really, I'm okay. Honest."

"Now, now," Millie soothed. "You just stay lying there. Doc Miller should be arriving shortly. You're not taking up much space, and we don't mind helping you, so stay put."

Properly chastised, Jessie remained still. Why was Rafe scowling at her? Then she remembered that her identification and file on the Triple K had been in her briefcase in the car. If he knew her name, he had to have gone through her luggage. Joe Allen's vivid description of the rancher came back to her. She'd made an even bigger mess of things: she'd wrecked a car, nearly killed Rafe Kincaid and hadn't mended any fences. In fact, she had made the rift between him and the BLM worse.

"Mr. Kincaid," she began in a scratchy voice, "I'm deeply sorry for what happened. I can assure you that the BLM didn't send me out here to make things worse. I—"

"The what?"

His voice cut like a whip through the room. Jessie's eyes became round, and she pulled the quilt up to her chin, caught in his glare.

"The BLM," she croaked. "You looked through my attaché case. You must have seen I was the field representative from the BLM."

Rafe's brows shot up, and he allowed his hands to fall from his hips. "*You* are from the BLM?"

Her mind whirled. Hadn't he gone through her briefcase? Her purse! He must have looked in her purse. Biting the bullet, she said in a clear, calm voice, "Mr. Kincaid, I've been sent by the BLM to straighten out the misunderstanding between us."

"I don't believe it," he ground out, looking first at her and then at Millie.

"Now, Rafe," Millie said, "don't you take your anger out on this poor girl. She's been injured." She wagged her finger at him. "Go on. Ain't you got anything better to do right now? Let's get Doc here, first. Everything else can wait."

He ran his fingers through his black hair, then glared at Jessie. "If that doctor gives you a clean bill of health, you'd better hightail it, Ms. Scott," he said through clenched teeth, before he stalked out of the room.

Millie patted her hand. "Never mind him."

"That's easy for you to say," Jessie mumbled, feeling almost physically hurt by his anger.

"Rafe's got a lot on his mind of late. This is a busy time of year at any ranch with calving, foaling and all. Let him cool down. He'll be in a better frame of mind later."

Somehow Jessie doubted that. And then she closed her eyes. What a mess she had made. How was she ever going to rectify the situation? Judging from Kincaid's murderous looks, she had lost not only the battle, but the war, as well.

Chapter 2

Rafe tried to concentrate on the numbers staring back at him. Red—they were all in the red. His large hand clenched and then slowly unclenched. If, and it was a big if, all the Herefords produced healthy calves, it would be a bumper crop this year. The biggest "if" was the weather. It might be mid-April, but that didn't mean a thing up in the Rocky Mountains. A spring blizzard could come tearing out of Canada, dumping four or five feet of snow in its path. His eyes clouded. If that happened, many of the newborn calves would freeze to death. Just as they had last year. He had planned on the last year to bring the ranch back into the black after—Quickly he shut his mind to the past.

Rubbing his furrowed brow, he got up and headed to the liquor cabinet, where he poured a shot of whiskey. It wasn't like him to take a drink in the early afternoon.

Late at night, of course, after a good day's work had been put in, there was nothing like a bit of whiskey to warm his insides as he watched the sun sink behind the rugged mountains he had grown up with. But now... Rafe turned and moodily stared around the study that doubled as a library. Why the hell was he thinking of her?

When he looked down at the figures, all he could see was the ripe color of her hair and her huge cinnamon-colored eyes. And her mouth. He threw the potent whiskey into his mouth, grimacing as the heat curled down his throat and into his knotted stomach. With the back of his hand he wiped his mouth, then set the shot glass back down on the cabinet. Jessie Scott was burning through his mind and his daily work schedule like a branding iron.

Muttering a curse under his breath, Rafe strode back to the desk. The whole day was a complete loss, and he didn't like the way his routine had been upset. Especially by a blond-haired filly who—

"Well, looks like you're up to your hocks in paperwork," Doctor Miller said by way of a greeting, ambling through the door, black bag in hand. He flashed Rafe a smile.

Bringing his mind back to focus around him, Rafe hesitated only a moment before greeting the doctor. "Sit down, Doc. Has Millie fed you yet?"

Dr. Miller patted his flat stomach, then sat down. "Fed, primed and ready for packaging," he said with a chuckle.

Rafe leaned back in the huge leather chair. "Good. So, how's Ms. Scott?"

"Doing fine. Oh, she's got a roaring headache from that bump, but all in all, I'd say she'll survive." Dr. Miller smiled fondly. "She has the normal collection of bruises here and there."

"No concussion, then?"

"No. Should have, but doesn't." He laughed. "She said she had a hard head, and I believe her."

"Did she tell you she's a BLM agent?" Rafe asked suddenly.

The older man nodded, his hazel eyes dancing with amusement. "Yes, she did. Matter of fact, she told me the whole story of how you two met."

"Well, she's going right back where she came from as soon as she's ready to leave. When will that be?"

"Give her a couple of days. She's not too steady on her feet yet. A little dizzy. If it isn't putting too much of a strain on Millie or yourself, let her stay in bed for the rest of the day. Tomorrow is the earliest she should be up and walking around."

Rafe grunted and rose. "Thanks for coming, Doc."

"My pleasure." He rose and shook Rafe's hand. "You're looking tired."

He shrugged it off, walking the doctor out of the study and toward the front door. "It's usual for this time of year."

"I s'pose it is, Rafe. Calving and all. Hear you got a bumper crop of Arabians planned this year, too."

"Yeah, I do. The best of the lot will be sold at some fancy sales down in Arizona and back East this fall."

"Hope it brings in a bumper crop of cash," Dr. Miller commented with a chuckle, shrugging into his coat.

Rain was still falling, but at a lesser rate as Rafe opened the door for the doctor. "Makes two of us, Doc. See you later."

He watched as the doctor climbed back into his four-wheel drive pickup. After closing the door, Rafe shoved his hands into his jeans pockets and wandered aimlessly through the house. Eventually he found himself at the door that used to be his and Mary Ann's bedroom. The one that Jessie now occupied. Millie knew it was never to be used—just like the nursery directly across the hall. Of course, with the guest room all torn apart from spring cleaning, where was Millie going to put Jessie? In her room? Or his? There hadn't been a lot of choices in the matter. Dal's room, which was next to the unused nursery, had been turned into a sewing room for Millie. Cathy's room was the one that long ago been turned into a nursery…one that would sit empty forever.

Grimly Rafe swung open the door in front of him. He scowled. "What the hell are you doing up?" he demanded.

Jessie gasped and turned toward the thundering voice. She had managed to sit up, slip into a white chenille robe and walk to the couch that was adjacent to the windows. Now Rafe Kincaid stood blocking the doorway, his face set in an angry cast and his large hands on his narrow hips. The throbbing ache in her head intensified accordingly.

"Don't shout at me!" She gripped the back of the couch with one hand, and pressed her other against her temple.

"Doc Miller said you were to stay in bed," Rafe rumbled. Dammit, why did she have to look like a waif? The robe was too big on her; the sleeves were below her fingers and the bottom of it dragged around her bare feet. His anger began to dissolve as he took in her slender form, graceful carriage and her proud look. Her hair was dry and had obviously been combed. It was shimmering and glossy even in the murky light of the rainy day. He wondered what her hair would look like out in the sun. Would her eyes also sparkle and dance in the light, and not look as they did now, dark in her narrowed gaze?

"I was looking for my clothes," Jessie told him, forcing her voice into a more neutral tone.

"Millie's taking care of them. They were wet."

She allowed her hand to drop and faced him squarely. He had harsh features, broad shoulders and a barrel chest. But Jessie lived more on her instincts than on what she saw initially in any person, and she switched to that internal radar. Perhaps it was the color of his eyes, their dark blue cast that carried hidden pain in their depths. Or the wry twist of his mouth. Jessie couldn't be sure. She felt that he was a man who was carrying tremendous burdens; some, if not all of them, sad. Rafe Kincaid was not happy outwardly or inwardly, and that struck Jessie's heart.

"I wanted to leave, Mr. Kincaid. I don't feel I've started off on the right foot with you. What I'd like to do is find the nearest motel, spend a couple days recuperating from the accident and then come back to the Triple K." Her voice became more firm, and she held his stare. "There's unfinished business between us. I was sent here to straighten it out, not make more of a mess for you." She slowly sat down on the arm of the flower-print couch, her hands in her lap.

"What do you know, an honorable agent." Rafe crossed his arms.

Jessie's lips compressed, and her eyes turned a dark cinnamon color. "Sarcasm is not going to help the situation, Mr. Kincaid."

"You should have told that to the first agent, Ms. Scott."

"Joe Allen is new. And young. He was just a little too eager, that's all."

With a snort, Rafe circled the room, never allowing his gaze to leave her. The backlight from the window outlined her in radiance; almost as if she were ethereal. "So why'd they send you, Ms. Scott? To dodge my questions by putting a pretty face in front of me?"

Jessie gasped and then winced as her head began to pound. Gently she rubbed her temple, holding on to her anger. "What are you implying?"

Rafe smiled, but it didn't reach his eyes. "That's obvious to me. It should be to you, too," he drawled.

Color heightened in her pale cheeks, and this time Jessie wasn't embarrassed—she was mad. "Mr. Kincaid, I could lower myself to your level of needling me with innuendos, but I'm not going to. One of us has to conduct themselves in a professional manner. I know you had words with Mr. Allen. And judging from what he told us, he wasn't honest and up-front about why he came to you in the first place."

Rafe came closer until he stood directly in front of her. Ruthlessly he stared down at her, yet she didn't pull back. A grudging admiration shot through him. "And you're honest?" he prodded.

She held his stare. "Yes, I am."

Rafe turned abruptly and walked back toward the door. If she had been snippy or pushy, he'd have wanted to throttle her. Instead, the inner calm he felt around her had appeased him. He halted and turned. "You aren't going anywhere."

"What?"

He nodded. "You're staying here. The closest motel

is sixty miles away. The doctor said you were to stay in bed until tomorrow."

Jessie's lips parted. "But—my car. I can drive to the motel."

"Really?" he goaded softly. "I haven't seen many cars with a broken axle travel very far."

"Oh, no. Are you serious? A broken axle?" She closed her eyes. Nick and Mr. Humphries were going to have her head on a platter.

"I'm having some of my men drag it out of the pines. The rental agency has already been contacted, and they'll be bringing out a tow truck to have it taken back to Denver."

Jessie opened her eyes. At least he wasn't a total bastard. No, he wasn't one at all. Millie had told her earlier how he had rescued and carried her back to the ranch. She owed him for that. "I see… Thank you for calling them."

"Look," Rafe said gently, his conscience needled by the bleakness in her eyes and voice, "why don't you get back to bed and rest? Millie will bring you dinner around six." Then he disappeared as quietly as he had come.

A quiver moved through Jessie. Rafe's voice had dropped into that dark, low tone again, and she had felt as if he had reached out and physically stroked her. Touching her breast, Jessie breathed deeply, trying to still her fluttering heart. Rafe was more of a man than she had ever met. Of course, how many men had she met other than her ex-husband? Not many. With a determined look on her face, she slowly stood, allowed the dizziness to pass and then walked back to the brass bed. She would have to call Nick and tell him what had happened. But not now. First, she somehow had to persuade Rafe Kincaid to allow her to investigate the mustang killings. She lay down and almost immediately fell asleep.

Rafe's eyes smarted and he blinked. The figures swam before him. It was nearly one in the morning. Time was a robber when he tried to balance the budget: rob Peter to pay Paul, and practice a form of financial wizardry that would get them through the spring. Suddenly Rafe found himself wondering about Jessie. Dammit, he'd done it again. He'd had a hell of a time concentrating on the budget: his mind was always wandering back to her, her soft but firm voice and the glimpse of fire he'd seen flash in the depths of her eyes. *God!* He dropped the pencil, rubbing his face wearily.

A sound caught his attention. Was Millie up? Impossible. She always went to bed around ten every night. Rafe hauled himself to his feet and walked quietly into the hall toward the direction of the noise. At the entrance to the living room, he halted. Jessie was standing near the open flames of the stone fireplace. His breath jammed in his chest as he saw the way the molten gold of the fire bathed her long thick hair as it fell in careless abandon over her small shoulders. A warm feeling trickled through his heart; she looked like a waif in the huge robe she had on. Then he noticed how drawn her face was, and the tired way she put her hand on the mantel to support her weight. "Are you all right?"

Jessie's head snapped up, and she whirled in his direction, her mane of hair flying about her shoulders. "My God, you scared me to death! Do you always go sneaking around like that?"

A sour grin tugged at his mouth as he walked toward her. "I heard a sound and came out to investigate."

Her heart was banging away in her throat, and she pressed her hand against the pulse there. "I thought everyone was asleep."

"So did I."

She grimaced, placing her hand back on the mantel. "I thought ranchers went to bed early and got up early," she muttered, managing a slight smile to match his.

Rafe leaned his elbow on the mantel and studied her more thoroughly by the firelight. The room was dark and quiet, with the exception of a few cattle lowing now and then, out in the paddocks near the barns. "Most ranchers this time of year are up early and go to bed late."

"Why?"

"It's calving and foaling season. My men take shifts around the clock checking on the cows and mares to see how they're doing."

She watched as shadows and light emphasized certain planes of his exhausted features. "Calving?"

He gave her a long look. "You really are a city girl, aren't you?"

"Is it a sin?"

"No. It's just that—"

"What?"

Rafe grimaced. "You look wild and free. Like that picture you carry in your wallet of that mustang."

She smiled softly, pleased by his compliment because she had never expected anything like it from him. "Thank you." She touched her hair. "I think it's my mane of hair that gives me that look."

His face grew still, and longing briefly showed in his eyes. "You have beautiful hair."

A shiver flowed through Jessie, and she stood transfixed by the sudden flame she saw in his dark eyes. His voice was like melting butter, and she felt an ache begin deep within her. What was happening? She had to get a hold on herself. "Th-thank you."

Seeing her sudden shyness, Rafe changed the subject. "Why were you up?"

Jessie breathed a sigh of relief upon hearing his casual drawl again. "I had a bad dream about the accident. Doctor Miller said I might have a few afterward. Something about trauma, or whatever."

"I see. Did Doc Miller say anything about giving you some apricot brandy?"

"Why—no."

"Stay here, I'll be right back."

Jessie watched him disappear around the corner. One moment he could be so hard and cold, and the next, almost gentle with concern. The man was confusing. She rubbed her arms with her hands, suddenly aware of the night chill in the house.

Rafe came back as silently as he had left; only this time Jessie was prepared for his approach. He held out the shot glass filled with amber contents. "Apricot brandy. My sister Dal would sometimes have a shot before going to bed. She went through a pretty traumatic divorce a couple of years ago and said it always helped her when she had problems going to sleep sometimes."

Their fingers touched as she took the small glass, and both withdrew quickly, as if the contact had been electric. "I wish a shot of brandy could have helped my marriage," she finally said in jest, sipping the liquid cautiously.

"I'm afraid it's not a miracle cure. Down it all in one gulp," he advised.

She looked at him doubtingly, but followed his instructions. The fire hit her stomach, and she took in a deep breath. "Now I see why it would help her sleep," she whispered hoarsely, handing him the glass.

Rafe managed a slight smile. "Yeah, that's over hundred-proof homemade brandy. You'd better get going, or you won't make it to bed before that hits you. Come on, I'll walk you down the hall." Although there was no real reason to reach out and slide his hand beneath her elbow, he did it, anyway. Merely a precaution, he told himself as he guided her down the hall, extremely conscious of her delicacy next to his large frame.

"How much do you weigh?" he asked.

"A hundred and three pounds."

He chuckled. "You're nothing but a feather."

"Don't let my size deceive you," she warned him with amusement in her voice.

Rafe halted and opened the door to her bedroom. Reluctantly he dropped his hand from her elbow as she turned and faced him. "There's an old Western saying: never underestimate a banty rooster."

"What does that mean?"

He smiled as she fearlessly looked up at him, the darkness playing across her soft features. Rafe wanted to reach across the inches that separated them and slide his fingers across her hair. For those precious few seconds, he realized that he was actually happy. Happy. An emotion, a feeling, that had died two years before, with Mary Ann. He scowled, unable to cope with the discovery and Jessie's nearness. "I'll tell you about it some other time," he muttered.

"Well, we'll see how much talking you'll do to me tomorrow morning after I tell you about the reason why I'm here," Jessie said in just as somber a tone. She saw the longing in his eyes, and pain. Somehow, she wanted to erase whatever Rafe was carrying around inside him. "Good night, Rafe. And thank you for the brandy. I think it's doing its job."

He watched her turn and enter the bedroom. Frowning, he quietly shut the door and headed down the hall to the study.

Sunlight was streaming through the bedroom windows when Jessie awoke. Swathed in the large robe, she went in search of the housekeeper. When she entered the kitchen, she found Millie hard at work kneading bread on the table.

"Good morning," Jessie murmured.

"Morning." Millie turned and smiled, then resumed the kneading, flour staining her hands and wrists. "Rafe said to let you sleep in. Said you were up late last night."

Jessie rubbed her eyes, still drugged from the good eight hours of rest. "He told you about that?"

Millie tittered. "Said you about jumped out of your skin when he found you in the living room. Let me get this dough in the pans, and then I'll fix you breakfast."

"Please, don't go to the trouble."

Millie arched an eyebrow. "You ain't trouble. Rafe had one of his men get your luggage from the car. It's sitting right inside the bathroom between your two rooms. Why don't you get a nice hot bath, dress and then join me out in the dining room? Doc Miller said to feed you good."

Smiling widely, Jessie said, "You're a dear. I won't be long."

"Now, don't go hurrying. There's no reason to. Rafe ain't gonna be back until noon. That's three hours from now. He said you were lookin' mighty peaked last night. And Doc told you to rest today."

Smiling, Jessie trailed out of the kitchen. At the entrance, she stopped and turned to Millie. "Did anyone ever tell you that you're a good mother?"

The housekeeper beamed, her apple-red cheeks shining. "Ask Rafe and those two sisters of his, and they'll tell you they had two mamas—their real one and me. Now scat! I'll see you in a little while."

Jessie stood at the rear porch window, watching the activity in the back of the ranch house. She had finished a huge breakfast of whole-wheat pancakes, maple syrup and fresh fruit earlier. Millie had stuffed her like the proverbial turkey. Now, her curiosity of ranch life held her in its magical embrace. Mesmerized, she watched as the wranglers, mounted on small, delicate Arabians, moved bawling cattle from holding pens. She almost couldn't contain her excitement. Finally, after twenty-eight years, she was getting to see real cowboys at work on ranch horses!

"You know, you can go outside for a while if you're getting cooped up in here," Millie said, coming around with her feather duster. "There's a jacket in that hall closet that might fit you. Dal keeps one out here for when she and her husband, Jim, visit. Don't think she'll mind you using it." Millie stopped by her side, pointing to the red barn. "If you like good horseflesh, go to that barn. That's the stud barn where Rafe keeps his three stallions. The green barn next to it is the broodmare barn. If you like the foals, you might want to go there, instead."

Jessie brightened. "I'd love to see the new babies."

With a chuckle, Millie nodded. "Figured you would. You look like a mothering type."

With a smile, Jessie went to the closet and donned

the heavy wool coat over her apricot turtleneck sweater and brown wool slacks. "Just to babies," she amended, "not to men."

"Amen to that! I think Pinto Pete's out in the brood-mare barn. Rafe always keeps him hoverin' around when one of the mares is gonna foal. You might see if you can't scare him up. Pete'll give you the grand tour."

"I'll do that," she promised. Going out the door and stepping onto the screened porch, Jessie smiled to herself. The Colorado morning was crisp with brilliant sunlight. Between the snorts of the horses, the lowing of the cattle and the panoramic splash of colors that surrounded her, her senses were overwhelmed. The odors ranged from pungent to pine as Jessie walked down the stairs. She'd plaited her hair into one long braid, and the wind played with the wispy bangs across her brow. She inhaled deeply, staying on the sidewalk of red brick that led her safely past the lawn and muddy areas to the barns.

The huge doors were open on one end of the broodmare complex, and Jessie stepped into the well lit, immaculate area. Rows of large, roomy boxstalls stood on either side of the aisle, a horse in each one. A few stablehands were cleaning some of the stalls, putting water in others, or simply passing through on their way to other duties. The smell of sweet alfalfa and oat straw was like a perfume. No wonder Westerners loved their ranches so much!

How long she stood at the first stall watching a wobbly-legged bay foal walk stiffly around her mother, Jessie didn't know. The beauty of the Arabians was breathtaking. She'd seen photos of them, but had never seen one in person. They were beautiful. And it was Rafe who had an eye for such art in a living animal. That made her feel good about him. Beneath that dark, brooding mask he wore, there was a human being who not only saw beauty, but reveled in it.

Jessie wasn't sure when Rafe walked up behind her, she only knew that in a moment she was aware of his powerful presence. She had been torn between watching the foal cavort awkwardly around in the straw, and turning toward the feeling of warmth radiating from behind her.

"The foals are my favorite part of the day," he confided, looking down at her.

Jessie nodded, and her voice was hushed, even though her heartbeat had quickened appreciably. "She's so cute."

"It's a he." Rafe walked up to the stall, leaving only inches separating them.

"Of course," she said, blushing.

Rafe rested his arms on the edge of the stall. "Kind of hard to tell, though, at this age. He was born last night."

Jessie was grateful that Rafe allowed her error to pass. As she looked up at him, she saw that his features had softened. "I don't know how long I've been standing here," she admitted. "I love babies. This is the first time I've ever seen a little foal…"

"Oh?"

She wasn't going to lie to him. There was too much to lose by doing so. "When I joined the BLM five years ago, Mr. Kincaid, I was stuck away in a cubicle. My job was to stay in touch with the ranchers who were capturing and penning up the mustangs. I coordinated finding owners for these mustangs all over the U.S." She walked to the stall and rested her hands on the cool bars. "I did a lot of study on the mustangs, even though I've never been near them. In fact, the closest I've ever come to a horse is watching one go down the parade route of Pennsylvania Avenue in Washington, D.C." She twisted her head to see what kind of a reaction her confession would have on him.

He held her steady gaze, noticing how clear her eyes were this morning, and how the strain around her mouth had disappeared. "Why?"

"Because I'm afraid of them. They're big."

"If I were a banty rooster, I'd be respectful of them, too," he said with a slight smile.

"You aren't upset that I haven't had a lot of experience with horses?"

Rafe shrugged. "You're out here this morning, aren't you? If you were really afraid, you wouldn't be here. I think you're ignorant, not scared of them."

"Is that supposed to be an oblique compliment?"

"Yes, ma'am, it is. Come on." He slipped his hand beneath her elbow, drawing her to him.

Jessie trusted Rafe, for whatever that was worth. As he slid the bolt back and opened the door to the stall, she figured he was either going to help her overcome her fear, or he was about to embarrass her. She didn't know which, and she stood uncertainly in the ankle-deep straw, waiting as he shut the door.

"Now, stay at my side and do as I tell you," he told her in a low voice.

With a nod, she walked forward with him, her throat tight with fear. The mare looked awesome to her. Crooning to the mother, Rafe crouched down in front of the animals. Jessie followed suit. As soon as they knelt, both horses walked over to them.

"There's a trick in getting a horse to come over to you," Rafe told her quietly, his eyes never leaving the mare. "The eyes of a horse are constructed so that we appear almost twice our normal height to them. We look like giants. So if we crouch down, we become much smaller and less of a threat. Since they're real curious animals, eventually they'll come up to investigate."

The mare's velvet muzzle found Jessie's cheek. Prickles of pleasure went through her as the mare sniffed her, fanning her moist breath across her cheek. "This is wonderful!" she whispered. "Her nose is so soft. Like a baby's bottom."

Rafe smiled at Jessie, enjoying her first experience with a horse almost as much as she. He rested one hand on the mare's front leg to make sure she wouldn't accidentally bowl Jessie over as she continued her investigation.

Laughter gurgled up through Jessie. "She's so friendly! I can't believe this. I never knew…"

Her bubbling enthusiasm was contagious. Rafe glanced at her again. She was beautiful. Her eyes danced with a golden flame, her cheeks were flushed scarlet, and her lips were curved into a delightful smile. He wanted to reach out, draw her into his arms and kiss her and to drink in the absolute happiness that radiated from her. It was only in that moment that he began to understand how depressed he had been. Jessie's laughter had lifted him out of the abyss of grief, and for a split second he felt like living again.

The bay foal came bounding around the rear of his mother and with a little grunt, crashed headlong into Jessie. With a gasp of surprise, she fell back into the straw, the foal sprawled across her.

Luckily the broodmare was a relatively calm mother who didn't consider humans harmful to her baby, and she just stood there, watching. Jessie's arms closed around the winded foal. His fur was soft and fuzzy, and she reveled in it. She saw Rafe get slowly to his feet and with a broad smile, she allowed him to pick the foal off her. His hand was firm on her arm as he guided her to her knees.

"He's so silky," she whispered, petting the foal lying across her thighs. "Look, Rafe, he loves this! He loves me petting him."

Kneeling beside her, Rafe felt an ache sweep through him. His name had rolled off her lips like a husky prayer. "The colt's got sense," he murmured, picking bits of straw out of her hair. "I'd lie in your lap, too, if I got the chance."

Jessie lifted her face and stared up into his dark blue eyes, lost in their sudden intensity. Longing rippled through her as he continued to pull out straw that had collected on her braid when she had tipped over backward. When his callused fingers grazed the nape of her neck, her lips parted. A bolt of fiery pleasure nearly unstrung her. He was so close, so male and so virile. Her breath caught in her chest as she felt herself responding to an unspoken, primitive message.

The colt whinnied plaintively, breaking the tenuous silence that stretched between Jessie and Rafe. She helped the colt back to his feet, then watched the baby forge headlong to the rear legs of his patient mother, in search of his noonday meal.

Giving Rafe a shy glance, Jessie started to get up. His hand settled on her shoulder.

"Stay put. He'll come back to you," he said.

"But—"

"This is the way we gentle the babies, Jessie. A wrangler will sit in the stall, talk to the foal, handle him, and generally make friends with him. The sooner it's done, the more accepting the foal is of people." He slanted a glance down at her and reluctantly removed his hand. "You did want to get to know horses, didn't you?"

"Well—I didn't want to get in the way."

"You aren't in the way, believe me."

In silence they remained where they were. Without touching him, Jessie was vividly aware of his strength and the power that emanated from him. The scent that was vividly his wafted over to her, mixed with the damp odor of his sheepskin jacket. Something raw and elemental inside her moved, stirred to life by the unique amalgam that was Rafe. No man had ever made her feel like a caldron of simmering, explosive emotions. And she was out of her league. Completely.

The foal quenched his thirst then leapt back on his hind legs, nearly bowling himself over. His huge dark eyes focused on Jessie, and he toddled toward her. With a nicker, he thrust his tiny muzzle into her chest, nudging at the wool coat she wore. With a laugh, she curled her arms around the colt, petting him gently.

"I've got to tell you," she confided, "this is the greatest experience. I love babies. All babies. I never knew a foal could be so loving."

"Normally foals aren't this friendly at first," Rafe said with a nod toward the colt. "It's you. The foal senses something good about you. He feels safe, or he wouldn't have come back." Hell, he'd feel safe, too, if he were wrapped in her arms.

Frowning at the sudden thought, he gave himself a mental shake. He had to stop thinking about her like that. He got down on both knees and pushed his black felt hat back on his head. He was genuinely curious about her and her unusual combination of strength and warmth, and he also wanted to steer his mind to a safe topic. "Tell me about yourself," he ordered.

Chapter 3

"I'm afraid I'm a very boring subject, Mr. Kincaid."

"Call me Rafe. And I don't think there's anything boring about you."

Jessie shifted uncomfortably beneath his stare. "I can assure you," she began, concentrating on petting the foal because she couldn't stand how his cobalt-blue eyes melted her, "that I've lead a very quiet, limited and uneventful life."

"Where were you born?"

Jessie groaned silently. He obviously couldn't be dissuaded from the topic. With a small sigh, she answered, "In Washington, D.C."

"You lived there all your life?"

"Yes. I'm a survivor of the street system of D.C. That in itself is a feat," she said, managing a smile.

"That explains why you're not good on muddy roads," he drawled.

Recalling the fiasco on the ranch road, she grimaced. "It's pretty obvious, isn't it?"

He picked up a straw and chewed on it thoughtfully. "Most people don't take their faults as gracefully as you do."

"I've had a lifetime of learning that I'm far from perfect."

"Sounds serious."

"I think it's a virus I picked up." Jessie smiled fully into his relaxed face. "Every once in a while, it flares back up, and I make a total fool out of myself."

One corner of his mouth twitched. "Think there's an antidote?"

Her laughter pealed through the stall. "How I wish there was! I'd be first in line for it."

"I like your style, Jessie Scott. Instead of pointing out your strengths, you point out your weaknesses. Why, I wonder?"

"Let's just say I had five years in a marriage that pointed out my defects and deficits instead of my strengths," she murmured, resting her head against the foal's fuzzy neck.

"It takes two to make or break a marriage," Rafe said, leaning his broad back against the stall and studying her.

"To hear Tom's version, it was more my fault than his."

"Tell me about it."

Jessie gave him a wary look. "Why all this sudden interest, Mr. Kin—"

"Rafe," he corrected. "I'd like to hear your side of the story if you're willing to share it with me."

Jessica weighed the sincerity in his voice. She had never talked about her reasons to anyone. Neither Tom nor his family after the divorce had expressed any kind of sympathy, or extended a friendly hand. Now Rafe, with his soft words, was willing to listen. To care.

She took a deep breath and allowed the foal to wander back to his mother. Clenching her hands into fists she rested them on the long curve of her thighs. "I was married just after I turned nineteen, while I was in college," she began hesitantly. "I was young, idealistic and naive at the time. Tom was a senior, had lived and partied hard, and was ready to settle down. He was the son of a blue-collar family and believed that men should be the bread-winners and women should be barefoot and pregnant.

"I grew up wanting only one thing in life: a family of my own. I wanted to marry and have babies. Maybe that's old-fashioned for today's modern women, but I didn't care. Looking back on it, I fell in love with the idea more than with Tom. But I had thought that it was real, a binding love that could last us a lifetime. So I married Tom and quit college to become a happily married housewife."

Jessie leaned over, picked up a straw and moved it nervously through her fingers. "The first year I didn't conceive. Tom's family said not to worry, that it was normal for a newly married couple who really wanted children badly not to have them. The second year, no difference. They started saying I was trying too hard, to relax and everything would be all right and I'd get pregnant. The third year, Tom's family was pressuring us to the point where I went to five different doctors trying to find out why I couldn't get pregnant. They didn't have any answers, either. Technically, I was given the seal of approval to be able to have children." She glanced up at Rafe, noticing his face was grim. "I couldn't stand Tom's mother calling me every week, or his sisters dropping over to give their advice. Of course, they each had one or two children themselves. I took a clerk's job with a small company just to escape the pressures, the phone calls and visits."

Tossing the straw away, she took another deep breath and looked up at the ceiling of the barn. "By the fifth year, Tom's family was against me. I couldn't produce an heir for their family. Tom was the only boy. He listened to his folks, who said I was taking contraceptives, when I wasn't. He accused me of so many terrible things. His sisters all had little girls. There was no one to carry on the long family tradition.

"God," she whispered, "looking back on it, I was too young and green to be my own woman, or to set Tom's family in their place. No one wanted a baby more than me. But that didn't matter. I accepted the fact that it was my fault, and Tom agreed to a divorce. By that time, we'd both realized our puppy love was only that. We didn't have the kind of love we needed in order to stay together. 'Irreconcilable differences' was how the divorce read. Were there ever…"

Rafe studied her clean profile, the way pain pulled in the corners of her mouth and darkened her eyes. As if sensing her sadness, the foal came tottering back to Jessie, nuzzling her hair and then sucking noisily on the end of her braid, which had slipped across her shoulder. Watching, but not really seeing the colt's actions, Rafe was experiencing his own personal agony. Jessie's hurt-filled voice had opened bolted doors, within himself. He remembered the nursery that would never hear his baby's cry or laughter. The strong woman he had made his own, who would never smile for him again.

Clearing his throat, he slowly got to his feet, feeling

awkward with not knowing what to say or how to handle Jessie. It was his fault for practically forcing her to tell him about her past. *Damn your need to know.* He held out his hand to her.

"Come on," he rumbled, "it's noon. Millie will be calling out the back door for us any minute now for lunch."

Jessie stared at his hand. His fingers were long and large knuckled, callused from work. It was the hand of a man who loved the earth. She tried to swallow her pain. Rafe was embarrassed enough, and there was no need for her to say anything more to him. He knew how much she hurt. As she gripped his hand to stand, she felt anything but hunger.

Rafe pulled her to her feet. The foal remained at her side. Jessie's hand felt small and fragile in his. He searched her face for any remnants of the laughter or pleasure she had felt before he had stolen it away from her. But there were none. As she turned toward him, her face pale, eyes large and expressive, something broke inside Rafe. The walls he hid behind came tumbling down, exposing his vulnerable position. He framed her face with his hands, feeling the delicate strength of her jaw in his palms. His gaze searched her sable eyes, then moved down to her parted lips.

The breath jammed in Jessie's throat as she saw Rafe lower his head. A wild fluttering of her heart matched her sudden panic. His breath was moist against her cheek. It had been so long since she had been kissed by a man. And Rafe wasn't just any man: he was a sleek, sensual animal who sent an ache so intense through her that she placed her hand against the wall of his chest to stop him—because she was afraid of her own reactions.

"No... Please don't—"

His mouth claimed hers gently, clinging to the contour and shape of hers. Jessie's eyes closed as shock bolted like lightning through her. Somewhere in her stunned mind, she had expected savagery to match his harsh looks. Instead Rafe molded his mouth tentatively against hers, as gossamer as a butterfly alighting on a flower. His solid male scent entered her flared nostrils, and she tasted the pine on him, the salt of his flesh and the clean outdoors. Shock melted into an awakening awareness as she realized that the kiss was his way of apologizing. He was a man of few words. A soft moan slid from her throat as she swayed against his hard, solid body. With aching tenderness, she shyly returned his kiss.

Slowly Rafe drew away from her. Jessie stared up into the stormy blue of his eyes, still lost and floating in the fiery splendor of his kiss. She saw so much in those precious seconds afterward, saw him without the barriers he had constructed. She saw a man, as naked and vulnerable as she—as shaken to the core by the unexpected tenderness and fierce wanting.

His hands tightened on her arms as she swayed unsteadily before him. "Are you all right?" His voice was thick and unsteady. God, how he hungered for her! Her mouth had been yielding sweetness beneath his. And when she had hesitantly returned his kiss, he had nearly come unstrung.

"Y-yes," she answered faintly. She took a step out of his grip. "Excuse me." Edging past Rafe, she shakily slid the bolt back on the door and escaped.

The sun was blindingly bright, and she squinted against it as she hurried toward the ranch house. *Why did I let him kiss me? Why?* She climbed the steps, fighting to ignore the confusion of emotions assaulting her.

"Millie, I'm not very hungry," she apologized when she found Millie in the kitchen. "I think that walk made me tired. I'm going to lie down for a while."

"Well, of course. You're lookin' mighty peaked."

With a wry smile, Jessie touched her flaming red cheeks. "I'll be okay."

In the bedroom, she shut the door and walked over to the bay windows. The view was gorgeous: the emerald green carpet of the valley flowed out to the blue mountains, which were covered by pine, spruce and fir. Snow was draped across the tops of the mountains as casually as a cape wrapped around a regal woman. She stood in silence for a moment, drinking in the calm. She started as Rafe's deep voice faintly penetrated the closed door. *Please don't let him come in here.* To make good her excuse to Millie, Jessie nudged off her shoes, laid down on the bed and drew up the rainbow-colored afghan over her shoulders. As time passed, she began to relax, convinced that Rafe wasn't going to pursue the matter. Her lashes drifted closed, and she fell asleep.

"Rafe?" Millie poked her head into his study.

"Yes?"

"I'm worried about Jessie. You know she came in right at lunch, sayin' she was feelin' a little tired. She's been sleepin' for six hours straight."

Rafe put down his pen. After lunch, he had driven to the southeast pasture, where most of the cows were calving. As he'd moved through the herd, checking the new babies for any sign of health problems, he'd automatically thought of Jessie and her love of newborns. Their conversation was indelibly imprinted in his mind, and no matter what he did the rest of the day, he hadn't forgotten it, or the anguish in her voice.

"Have you checked in on her?" he asked.

"A number of times." Millie wiped her hands on the towel she was carrying and wrinkled her brow. "Seems to be sleepin' awful hard. You don't think she's gone into a coma, do you? Doc Miller said to watch for signs of her sleepin' too much."

Rafe rose to his full six-feet-four-inch height. "I think I'd better see if I can wake her up."

"If she's awake, see if she's up to eating. I saved enough of that pot roast and dumplin's for her."

The hollow sound of his boots on the cedar floor echoed through the hall. He opened the door to her room and stood for a moment, allowing his vision to adjust. At 6:00 p.m., there was only a bare hint of dusk. The afghan had slipped off her shoulders. She lay on her side, the thick, golden braid frayed and coming loose at the end. The dim light was kind to her soft, unlined features and parted lips. Rafe stared hard at her mouth, remembering the yielding softness of it, her natural sweetness.

He walked quietly to Jessie's side and sat down on the edge of the bed, his hip resting near her thigh. Against his better judgment, he reached out and smoothed several tendrils from her cheek. Her flesh felt like velvet beneath his fingers. She stirred. He sat there, watching her awaken.

"Jessie?"

Rafe saw the effect his low voice had on her as she stretched like a cat that had been sleeping on a sunny windowsill. Her arm moved over her head, her slender fingers curled inward. He smiled to himself, watching as her lashes slowly opened, and her sable eyes clouded as they came to rest on him.

"Millie got a little worried about you," he explained quietly. "She said you've been sleeping for over six hours."

Groggily Jessie stared at Rafe. "I have?" she murmured, her voice husky with sleep.

He nodded, relishing the quiet, tender moment with her. Is this how she would wake up every morning? Would her voice be that throaty sound that sent a raw yearning through him? "She thought you might be suffering the effects from that blow to your head." He leaned over, gently pushed strands of hair from her brow and studied the lump. "Looks better. How do you feel?"

The feel of his hand on her forehead woke her slumbering body and brought her mind to quick attention. Struggling into a sitting position, she rested her back against the brass headboard. "I'm okay," she mumbled, rubbing her face. "I overslept, that's all."

Rafe sat back, watching her, his eyes drawn to the braid that hung between her breasts. The urge to release her hair and stroke it was strong. Her clothes were rumpled, her hair was mussed, and she was sleepy, but that didn't take away from her natural beauty, he thought. Jessie would look good dressed up, down, or wearing nothing at all...

"First time I've kissed a lady and put her to sleep."

Jessie heard the wry amusement in Rafe's voice and looked up. He appeared almost shy about admitting it. There was so much sensitivity beneath that granite exterior of his, she thought. In an effort to make him feel less awkward, she murmured, "The last thing on my

mind was sleep, believe me." And then she realized her
faux pas. "I mean—"

"I know what you meant," Rafe said as he stood, a
smile lingering in his eyes. "Do you always dig yourself
into a deeper hole?"

She grimaced and swung her legs over the bed and
sat up. "The first half hour after waking I'm not held
accountable for what I say or do. Take my word for it."

"Maybe some coffee is in order?"

"Please?" She looked up at him as he towered above
her and felt her entire body respond to the pure male
strength he emanated. She imperceptibly swayed toward
him as he reached out for a brief second and touched the
crown of her head.

"Millie's got supper warming in the oven for you. The
coffee will be waiting." Then he was gone.

She sat there and watched him leave, a lonely, retreating figure swallowed up by the shadowed hall outside
her bedroom door. Jessie was aware of some incalculable
pain that was known only to him that was evident in his
sad gaze. Automatically she touched her hair. She must
look a sight! When she got to the bathroom and looked,
that much was confirmed. "You look like Raggedy Ann,"
she muttered at the image in the mirror.

As she unbraided her hair and brushed it until it shone
with gold highlights she thought about Rafe's kiss. When
had anything like that seared her like wildfire? Tom's
ardor had been lukewarm in comparison. And thinking
about the sparse dates she had with men after her divorce,
she couldn't remember one man who had equaled Rafe's
appeal, who had stormed the doors of her defenses and
forced her to confront her fiery desires. Jessie pondered

the effect he had on her as she applied some lipstick and a bit of blusher to hide her paleness.

The emotions, the feelings he had released in her were surprising and scary. It was if he had reached deep inside her and pulled from the very depth of her being hungers and needs that she had thought dead. He'd brought out within her desires to match the ones she glimpsed in him. And Jessie didn't know how to resist. Rafe was like the wind: when he caressed her she responded like a slender shaft of wheat before him. As she walked out into the hall toward the kitchen, she realized just how vulnerable she was.

Millie fussed over her like a mother, and Jessie welcomed the attention. The fact that she was going to have to face Rafe about the mustangs after dinner squashed her appetite. The kiss they had shared played on her mind, and she knew it was going to hinder rather than help the situation. After thanking Millie, she got up and wandered through the living room toward the study.

Postponing the inevitable for a few minutes, Jessie took her time crossing the living room. The warm cedar floors, dark leather furniture and fieldstone fireplace, where a fire crackled pleasantly, all appealed to her, and gave her the sense of coming home. Pausing to look more carefully around herself, she noticed the handwoven Navajo rugs on the walls, and the way the plate-glass window allowed the sun to splash color into the room. The browns, tans, and brief touches of orange gave the room a distinctly masculine tone, as if the whole room were a reflection of the man of the house. Rafe.

Girding herself, she walked through the room and knocked on the partially open door.

"Come in."

Jessie took a deep breath and opened it. Rafe sat at a desk, ledgers surrounding him. There was a blue glint to his black hair, and a few strands dipped over his furrowed brow. His light blue cowboy shirt emphasized the richness of his eyes as he lifted his head and held her captive in his stare.

"Am I interrupting?"

"No. As a matter of fact," Rafe said, leaning back in the creaking leather chair, "I can use a break. Come on in."

Disregarding a leather couch near the wall, she chose a wing chair near the desk. Sitting down, she stated, "I need to discuss the BLM problem with you."

Rafe placed his hands behind his head. He was having a tough time not staring like a gawking teenager. Her hair lay like a golden cape around her shoulders, thick and shining, begging to be tamed. "Okay. Looks like problems are the order of the night."

Jessie glanced at his desk. "Bill-paying time?" she guessed.

"Twice a month. Twice too often."

"I'm just beginning to realize what it takes to run a ranch," she admitted. "Millie started telling me about some of the problems you have, and how you have to juggle your loans and bills."

He nodded. "That's just the tip of the iceberg. Anyway, let's talk about this mustang thing. When Allen came here, he accused me of shooting them. It was the first I had heard of it."

"Our office received an anonymous phone call, Rafe. The caller said you were shooting mustangs that had drifted down off the federal land that's connected to your property."

"Who was the caller?" Rafe demanded, his eyes glittering dangerously. His body had tensed with barely checked anger, and he leaned forward on his elbows.

"We don't know. He wouldn't give his name."

"What proof did he offer to you that I was supposedly doing the shooting?"

"None."

His nostrils flared. "Pretty flimsy evidence, wouldn't you say?"

"Yes, I would." Jessie shrugged. "Allen should have made a study, gone up into the area in question and investigated. Mustangs usually stay on the lower plains during winter and migrate to the mountain areas only during the summer, for grass. The snowfall was lighter this year, so it made the mountain valleys available to them earlier than normal. The horses may have come off the Red Desert area of Wyoming because food was sparse."

"So do you think the call was a hoax?"

"I don't know. Let me ask you this—is there a local rancher who has an ax to grind with you?"

The smile on his lips didn't quite reach his eyes. "One. Bryce Darley. He's been wanting to buy a thousand acres of my land that sits next to his. He's expanding his beef operation and wants my grazing area for his herd. I won't sell it to him because that's where I run our cattle every summer. Darley's an Easterner come West with big corporations backing his efforts. I guess he thinks that with financial acumen, running a beef herd can turn into a gold mine of sorts." Rafe snorted softly and shook his head. "I was born and raised on this ranch and I've seen a lot of ups and downs in the beef business in thirty-five years. With the price of grain skyrocketing, you're never going to make big money. Hell, you're lucky just to get into the black every few years."

"I see. How often do you get mustangs on your ranch? Or do you know?"

"Right now, according to Pinto Pete, we got five studs with their own individual broodmare bands up in the northwest corner of my property. That's the area that connects with the federal reserve." Rafe stood and went to a large, Plexiglas-covered wall map of his property. "My guess is similar to yours; the plains didn't give the mustangs good forage over the winter, and they've come farther south earlier than usual, trying to find grass."

Jessie stood and went over to the map. "Where did Pinto Pete see these herds?"

He traced a triangular area with his finger. "Right up in this corner, which is where Darley's land, the federal lands and mine converge."

"A stud with a broodmare band could mean as few as two horses or maybe as many as fifteen," she murmured.

"Right. Pete said there were close to fifty-five of them when he went up there to check out the pasture and spring runoff three weeks ago. The studs are protecting their scraps of territory. The only problem is, that's my prime cattle grazing area. I can't afford to have those mustangs up there, or to have any more drifting down from the reserve."

The problem was an obvious one. There weren't many ranchers who took kindly to mustangs eating the grass meant to fatten their own beef for market. She turned to Rafe to say something, then stopped as she caught him studying her. Her heart thumped quickly as she, herself, stared at his firm, but generous mouth. She forced her attention back to the map.

"There's only one way to solve this, Rafe. I've got to go into that area and investigate."

He frowned, moving across the study to the liquor cabinet. "Can't you just take my word that I haven't been shooting mustangs? I admit they're a problem, and there's been times when I'd like to have shot a couple of those studs when they went after my broodmares." He poured some amber whiskey into a tumbler and turned. "Want some?"

"No, thank you," she said as she sat back down in the chair and crossed her legs.

"What do you mean by 'investigate'?" he asked, then sat down at the desk.

Jessie held his gaze as she leaned forward earnestly. "If you can loan me a horse and a guide, I'll go up there. If those herds are on your property, I need to know how many there are, and then get the BLM to take action to protect your grazing rights. And, of course, I'll have to search for any evidence to back up that phone call."

Rafe set his mouth in a grim line and stared down at the whiskey in his hand. "If a mustang was killed, you aren't going to find anything but bones by now. If the coyotes didn't eat the carcass, then the cougars would."

"I know it's a long shot, Rafe, but it has to be done."

He gave her a dark look and took a sip of his whiskey. "Do you realize what you're doing? You're a tenderfoot. Hell, you've never been on a horse, much less camped out. A study like that is going to take at least ten days. It's nearly sixty miles one way up there, and you're telling me you're going to rough it, try to find those mustangs plus locate nonexistent bodies?"

"Someone has to do it, Rafe," she said in an even voice. "If not me, how about Allen?" Secretly she was thrilled with the adventure. "With the right guide to help, it shouldn't be much of a problem."

"I don't believe you," Rafe muttered, getting to his feet. He dragged his fingers through his dark hair. "This is late April. Spring runoff has made small creeks into raging rivers up in that area. There's still a lot of snow up there, and it's colder than hell. And if you get real lucky, there could be a late-spring blizzard that could kill you!"

Jessie clasped her hands in her lap. "There's no sense in trying to scare me, Rafe. I appreciate your concern, but someone from the BLM is going to have to do it. And soon. We've got environmentalists clamoring for action, and they're putting pressure on us through the media. This has to be investigated and resolved as quickly as possible. The BLM will pay for the use of your horses, any equipment and a guide."

He stalked the perimeter of the study. "That's not what I'm worried about. We've worked with the BLM on other projects before. I know they'll compensate us." He halted, putting his hands on his narrow hips, and pinned her with his smoldering gaze. "A greenhorn has no business making this sort of trek. It's dangerous."

Coming here was a risk, Jessie thought, in more than one way. "Living is dangerous, Rafe."

"Some types of living need someone who has the experience to negotiate it properly and safely."

"If I have a qualified guide, someone from your ranch, I'll be fine." She brightened. "Why not Pinto Pete? He knows where those mustangs are."

Damn her, she didn't know when to back down. "Pete isn't going anywhere. For the next month he's got foaling duties here at the ranch. I've got twenty mares carrying purebred foals. Of those twenty, I have five broodmares whose foals are already consigned to fall sales. If everything goes as planned, I can make close to a million dollars, which will finally put us back in the black. If you think I'm letting a man with forty-five years of wrangling experience take you on that little jaunt, you're mistaken."

"All right, then send me with someone else. Anyone."

He clenched his fists. "Dammit, Jessie, not just 'anyone' will do. I'd send my brother-in-law, Jim Tremain with you, but my sister is pregnant and expecting soon. He should be with Dal, not trekking into the high country looking for mustangs. You know," he added, "he's the regional director for the Department of Interior in Denver."

"Yes, I know of Mr. Tremain. I didn't realize he was married to your sister. Anyway, that wouldn't work, because technically, this is a BLM problem and must be handled solely by us."

Rafe drummed his fingers on the desk, while looking into the distance. "You're putting me between a rock and a hard place."

"I don't mean to. I'm sorry. But I've got pressure on me to solve this case. Based on your past record with the BLM, my personal opinion is that you didn't shoot any mustangs. I could understand that if one of those studs came down and tried to take some of your prize mares you might be tempted. But that isn't the case."

He grimaced. "Oh, there's one stud who's taken a few of my good mares. Two years ago a medicine hat stud tore the hell out of one of my board paddocks, stole four of my best Arabian mares and took off with them. If we had seen it happen, that stud would be dead with a bullet between his eyes. As it was, one of my wranglers coming in from the high country recognized the mares in a meadow, heading north, toward the reserve. That stud wasn't stupid. He knew he was safe if he got those mares off my property and onto the reserve lands."

Jessie tried to look properly concerned over the loss of the mares. But a medicine hat! That type of mustang was the purest of their bloodline, and at first glance resembled a pinto. But on closer inspection they had particular markings that the Cheyenne Indians considered magical. A distinctive bonnet of dark color covered the mustang's ears and the top of its head, and a 'shield' of the same color was located on its chest. Crow, Sioux and Blackfoot all preferred the specially marked mustangs because the blood that flowed through them was wild and hot. If only she could actually see one!

Stilling her excitement, she addressed Rafe's concerns. "I could hire a guide, providing you give me permission to launch the investigation."

Rafe studied her. "And if I don't give you permission, you'll get a damned court order, won't you?"

"I wouldn't like to think either of us has to go to that extreme."

A plan formed in his head; one he should have felt guilty about, but didn't. Maybe there was a way to short-circuit the whole business, get the BLM out of his hair at the busiest time of the year and get rid of her. The last thought didn't sit well with him. Jessie had been an unexpected bright spot in his dark life. He would miss her, not her assigned duties.

"All right," Rafe said slowly, measuring his words, "I'll take you into the interior. I can't spare the people who know both mustang behavior and have a thorough working knowledge of that northwest quadrant. I can fill in for Pinto."

Jessie's eyes widened. "You will? I mean, are you sure? You're so busy here."

"I am busy. Taking ten or fourteen days out of my schedule is more than just a slight inconvenience to me, Jessie. If there's a problem at the ranch, I won't be here to deal with it." Rafe emphasized the problem with the slight hope he could make her feel guilty enough to back down.

"I'll make my study as quickly as possible. I won't keep you away from the ranch any longer than I have to."

"Do you realize what you're doing? How many hours a day you're going to be in a saddle? You've never ridden, much less packed into rugged country. What if one of those mustang stallions decides to charge you? What will you do? We have to cross some pretty powerful rivers that are gorged with fallen trees and other debris. It's dangerous for anyone, but downright stupid for a greenhorn to even attempt it. Plus, there's always the threat of a late blizzard. You ever been caught in one?"

Jessie shook her head solemnly.

"If you were, do you know how to survive it?"

She shook her head again.

"Do you know what saddle sores are?"

"I've heard of them."

"You're going to have them. And I've seen dudes get them so bad they get infected and have to go to the hospital. Do you want to wind up in the same way?"

Jessie set her jaw and held Rafe's black gaze. "All right, you've spelled out the worst that can happen."

"Only some of what might happen. We have grizzly up in that area. And black bear. If one is hungry enough coming out of his hibernation and smells our food, he's going to wreck the hell out of our camp trying to find it. And they'll attack humans, if provoked."

"I won't provoke a bear," she promised, wiping her damp hands on her thighs.

Rafe leaned back in his chair. "Hell, you don't even know what to do if one starts after you."

Jessie bridled beneath his scathing tone. "Now look, I know I'm a greenhorn, as you put it, but I've got a job to do, and I'm going to do it. I feel guilty about taking you away from the ranch right now. I'm scared, but I've been scared before and went on to do what had to be done." Taking a breath, she continued in a less strident tone. "I'll deal with the saddle sores, the bears, the mustangs—"

"Don't forget rattlers and copperheads while you're at it," he drawled. "Up at that elevation, as cold as it still is, they're always hunting for a warm spot at night. It's not unusual for one to crawl into your sleeping bag with you. You wake up in the morning with it coiled around your feet."

Jessie shut her eyes. *Snakes! God, they were the worst of her fears. That and spiders. Ugh!* Between clenched teeth, she said, "I'll do it, come hell or high water, Rafe. Now will you quit scaring me to death? It won't work!"

He swallowed a grudging smile. God, but she was beautiful when she lifted her chin and stared down that elegant nose of hers at him. And she had that petulant set to her lips again... Despite everything, Rafe respected her. "Fine. We'll start tomorrow morning. Set your alarm for 5:00 a.m."

Five in the morning? She started to protest. It was still dark then! But she thought better of it and nodded. "All right, five."

"Tell Millie to get you some riding clothes. Those

slacks and shoes aren't going to cut it. Dal is the smaller of my sisters. You can wear some of her old clothes. I hope you've got big feet."

"Why?"

"Because Dal has a pair of old cowboy boots here you can use. That is, unless you brought a pair?"

Jessie held on to her temper, realizing Rafe was trying to goad her into quitting before they started. Well, he was going to be sadly mistaken. "No. I didn't bring anything like that."

He grunted and got to his feet. "Millie will fix you up. I'll take care of the rest." And with that, he left her alone in the quiet confines of the study.

Well, she'd asked for it. Closing her eyes, Jessie rubbed her brow, trying to ignore the headache that had come because of the confrontation. Could she do it? Standing up, she shoved her hands into the pockets of her slacks and started in search of Millie. If Rafe's look and voice were any inkling of what was to come, she was in a lot of hot water. Could she stand the heat in the kitchen, so to speak? And then Jessie smiled to herself. She'd scraped through far worse circumstances in her life than those thrown at her by Rafe. If she'd learned nothing else from her life, it was that she could survive.

Chapter 4

Rafe had the entire plan set and ready to execute the next morning when Jessie followed him to the barn after the 5:00 a.m. breakfast. He felt like a bully trying to ruin another child's birthday party. The glow of excitement in her eyes forced him to experience things anew, from the choosing of a good mountain mustang for the trek to the bare hint of a salmon-colored dawn as they rode out at a slow trot. Her smile made him feel warm and good inside and dissolved his plan in the process. Was it because she had braided her hair into two long braids, which made her look like a young girl off on a lark? Or the fact that although she had never been on a horse, she mounted as if she had done it hundreds of times before, and was ready to take on the world from her perch?

Rafe angled the party, which consisted of his Arab mount and packhorse and Jessie's mustang, into the pine and spruce above the ranch. The sun had broken clear of the fog and illuminated the lush grass meadows, and slanted through the trees around the group. Only the wispy jets of steam from the horses' nostrils, an occasional snort or the warning cry of a blue jay broke the silence. Rafe didn't have to keep looking back to tell Jessie to keep up. She was right on the packhorse's tail, clinging to the saddle horn, a dogged look of determination on her face. Rafe smiled sourly and pulled his hat down a little lower across his eyes. Jessie wasn't going to give up easily.

By mid-morning, they had climbed over the first set of hills and ridges and found themselves in a high meadow. Jessie had tried to remember all the instructions Rafe had given her, which ranged from how to hold the reins to how to sit properly in the saddle. After four hours' of walking and trotting, her legs were rubbery from being bounced around so much. But she refused to complain, knowing Rafe would consider using it as a lever to get out of the expedition. Once she had seen him smile, though it hadn't been much of one. Was he happy she was in misery? Would he really sink that low? She mulled over the logic and her head said yes. Her heart emphatically said no!

Halting at a small stream, Rafe dismounted and hobbled his two horses.

"Dismount," he told her.

Jessie took a deep breath then struggled off the saddle. The dun-colored mustang gelding that she rode stood patiently while she went through the contortions. Her feet hit the ground, and if she hadn't been clutching a part of the horse's mane, she'd have collapsed into a heap.

Rafe looked over. "You okay?"

"Fine, just fine. A little winded, that's all," Jessie lied, leaning heavily against her mount. She managed to pat the tolerant mustang, which was small in comparison to the two Arabians. Forcing her tortured body to do what she wanted it to do, she hobbled her horse after several unsuccessful attempts. Rafe had warned her that he wasn't going to babysit her; she either pulled her weight or they would turn back.

Watching her struggle out of the corner of his eye, Rafe turned away once she had finished the chore. "Hungry?" he asked, pulling out a plastic bag that Millie had given them.

"Starved!" She got up, dusted off her jeans and gave him a wide smile.

He motioned to several logs near the stream. "Let's sit and eat, then."

"Do you know how good it feels not to be on something moving?" Jessie groaned as she sat, then laughed at her predicament.

"You won't be laughing by tonight."

They both launched into the fried chicken, their appetites whetted by the fresh air and physical exertion. After a few minutes of eating in silence, Jessie asked, "I meant to ask you why I got that little dun mustang."

"You want one of those big Arabians? You're the one who said you were afraid of horses, remember?"

"I think I'm losing my fear. Fred's a wonderful horse."

"'Fred'?" Rafe arched one eyebrow.

"Sure. That's what I call him." She motioned to the mustang, who was nibbling on the grass. "Doesn't he look like a Fred?"

Rafe's eyes glimmered with amusement as he glanced

at the horse and then at her. "Are you always such a child?"

She grinned and polished off the chicken. "I asked you his name at the barn, and you said he didn't have one except for Jughead." She wrinkled her nose. "And that's not a very complimentary name."

"And Fred is?"

"Sure."

"I guess it depends upon your point of view. I sure as hell wouldn't want to be called Fred."

Jessie dug into the plastic bag, took out an orange and began to peel it. "Rafe is a good name for you—it's a strong name. It sort of reminds me of an English word: rakehell."

"It sounds derogatory."

She bit into a juicy slice of orange, relishing the fresh tang. "It means someone who's a free thinker, who will do as he pleases, no matter what anyone else says. I'll bet you were a real rascal when you were a kid."

"Oh?"

"You probably went around pulling little girls' braids and ponytails when you were a boy. Not to mention pestering people just for the pure pleasure of it."

A smile tugged at the corners of Rafe's mouth. "You're a tart little thing this morning, aren't you?"

Warmth flowed through her as he gave her his first genuine smile of the day. How could she tell him that his entire face had changed? That the harshness was softened in an indefinable way? "Blame it on the mountain air," she tossed back. "Well, am I right? Were you like that as a boy?"

"Yes," he admitted, grinning. "And so was my sister,

Cat. If there wasn't any excitement, we'd create some. At home or at school, it didn't matter."

"Dal wasn't like that?"

"No, she was the careful one in the family. Dal wouldn't jump a horse between two cliffs, or ride her horse over a ten-foot drop into a lake like we would."

"I like your baby sister already," Jessie said dryly. "At least she had some common sense."

Rafe nodded his head in agreement. "Dal didn't end up with a broken arm or leg like we did, either. She never rode hell-bent for leather."

Jessie got up and knelt down at the icy stream and washed her hands. She could feel Rafe's eyes on her, watching her with an intensity that took her breath away. "I take it you didn't respect Dal much for her choices," she said, making an effort to continue the conversation.

Rousing himself from his sitting position, he went to the stream to wash his hands. Turning his head toward her, he said, "Until recently, I treated Dal like a baby sister and not the woman she had become. Her husband, Jim, helped me see her in a different light. A better one. The past year I've appreciated Dal a hell of a lot more than before." He rose, wiping his strong fingers across the dark leather of the chaps he wore.

"What made you change your mind, Rafe?"

He stood towering over her. Jessie was as natural as the woods that surrounded them: she had no makeup on, her cheeks were flushed pink, and her eyes were a brilliant sable with brown flecks. She looked so happy, so fresh and healthy and filled with an enjoyment of life. And she made him want to live again. That lightning bolt of knowledge shocked Rafe. Maybe he was past grieving for Mary Ann and the baby. It took but a second for him to recover, and before she could read anything in his expression, he answered her. "Dal grew up while I wasn't looking. Jim pointed that out." He scowled as they walked back to the horses, which were resting beneath the shade of the pines. "She's pregnant now, and that worries me."

Jessie glanced up at him. "Isn't it the prospective father that's supposed to do that?" she teased.

Rafe knelt down, released the hobbles on the dun and stuffed them back into the saddlebags. "I guess it is."

Jessie mounted and swallowed a grimace as she swung her leg up and across the saddle. Rafe picked up the reins and handed them to her. "Is this the first baby in the family?" She saw an undefined darkness come to his eyes as he stood facing her, his gloved hand resting on the wither of the horse.

"Yeah, it is."

"That it explains it, then. How long before Dal delivers?"

"About two and a half months. And I could strangle her."

"Why?"

"Because she wants to have the baby at home, that's why," he grated through clenched teeth as he mounted his horse.

Jessie frowned as she rode beside him. "Why are you so upset about that, Rafe? A lot of women are choosing to have their babies at home instead of a hospital. Frankly, if I could have children, I'd have them at home, and not in some impersonal hospital. I think it's just as safe to deliver at home."

"What the hell do you know about it?" he snapped at her with a fierce glare, then spurred on his horse. The Arabian grunted at the unexpected action and leapt forward. The packhorse followed suit. Jessie stared open-mouthed at Rafe. What had she said?

The distance between them grew as he galloped his horse down the meadow. Afraid that he'd leave her behind, Jessie coaxed her mustang into an identical pace. She'd never cantered a horse before, and nearly fell off several times before she got the hang of the three-beat motion. Once she found it, she unceremoniously bumped along in the saddle, the wind tearing at her, her eyes watering as they flew down the length of the meadow.

For the next four hours, Rafe set a blistering pace. Jessie was bumped, bruised and chafed endlessly in the saddle as they climbed hill after hill, moving through a succession of flower-filled meadows. Rafe would not look back, and all she saw was the breadth of his shoulders and how ramrod straight he sat in the saddle. Anger began to replace her shock over his actions. Clinging stubbornly to the saddle horn, she kept up the pace, trying to ignore her tortured legs and hips. She was damned if she was going to give up because Rafe had suddenly developed an ugly mood. Was he always moody? No wonder he wasn't married!

Suddenly she remembered the nursery she had found across the hall from her room. Had Rafe had the room converted for Dal's baby? It had to be, since he was single. Perhaps his family was closer than she realized, but it still didn't give him the right to fly off at her. Frustration boiled inside her. All right, if Rafe wanted to be moody that was fine by her. She'd ignore him and go about her business—with or without his help.

Rafe pulled his gelding to a stop and turned back toward Jessie. Some of his initial anger had abated during the long ride. If he hadn't ridden ahead, he'd have ripped her head off for the ignorant remarks she had made. Now his anger merely simmered, as it always did, on the back burner of his conscience, where he could deal with it once again.

"Get down," he told her, "we're taking a break."

Jessie clenched her teeth and dismounted. She refused to let Rafe know how much pain she was in. Her inner thighs were cramping sporadically, and the insides of her knees were raw from all the chafing. She watched as he turned his horse around and began to head toward the top of the next hill without her.

"Where are you going?" she shouted.

"I'll be back."

"I should be so lucky," Jessie muttered to herself, testing her legs. With a groan, she walked around a bit. After hobbling Fred, she stood back and drank in the view. The grassy hillside was peppered with huckleberry bushes, and a gentle pine-scented breeze caressed her face. Despite Rafe's unexplained anger, she could still enjoy the glory of the mountains. "To heck with you," she said, thinking again of Rafe's actions.

Spotting a carpet of newly blossomed daisies, she went to investigate. Kneeling on the damp, spongy ground, Jessie gathered a few flowers and sniffed their less than winsome scent.

"Here," Rafe growled from behind her, "smell these."

Startled, Jessie twisted around. In his gloved hand he held out a bouquet of blue lupine toward her. Her lips parted as she stared at them, and then at Rafe. Touched by his thoughtfulness, she took them.

"Thank you."

He shrugged, as if embarrassed by the sudden catch

in her voice. "It's nothing," he muttered and turned to head back to the horses.

Jessie winced as she got to her feet, clutching the blue lupine in her hand. "Rafe, wait!"

He halted and barely turned his head in her direction. "What is it?"

"They're beautiful." She drew abreast of him and held his gaze.

"Are you always so easy to please?"

"What do you mean?" Her heart took off at a galloping beat as he stared down at her with a hungry look in his eyes. Jessie felt herself responding automatically to him. She knew he was trying in his own way to apologize for his actions, and the combination of strength and vulnerability made him irresistible.

"Just that it takes so little to make you happy."

"And it takes a lot to make you happy?"

Rafe held her honest sable gaze. The blue lupine against her chin and cheek brought out her flush and the velvet texture of her skin. "I've forgotten what it's like to be happy, so let's drop it," he said gruffly. He started to walk away, but felt Jessie wrap her small hand firmly around his lower arm.

"Oh, no you don't, Rafe Kincaid. You're not going to scare me off that easily. I'm going to figure you out yet, whether you want me to or not."

"Quit trying. If you're smart, you'll stay out from under like everyone else."

Jessie fearlessly met his stormy gaze. "Is that a threat or promise?"

"Take it any way you want," he growled softly.

"I forgot to tell you that I'm at my best when a challenge is thrown my way."

"Yeah?"

"Yes."

An unwilling smile curved Rafe's mouth. "I would never have thought there was so much dynamite in such a little package."

Warmth tingled through her, and Jessie reluctantly dropped her hand from his arm. "I think you want everyone to think you're unapproachable."

"Nothing wrong with that."

"Yes, there is."

"Like what?"

"It says that you don't want to get close to people. That's not healthy, Rafe. There are people who care for you, and you just can't go around snapping their heads off because they make a mistake." Jessie tilted her head and gave him a knowing look. "Like before. I know I said something that hit a raw nerve, and I don't mind paying my dues if I know what I'm paying it for. But you haven't even given me the consideration of telling what I did wrong."

Rafe inwardly bristled. He knew he owed her an explanation, but he wasn't used to one being demanded of him.

"I know this is your way of apologizing to me," Jessie continued, "and they're beautiful. But I still need an explanation from you, Rafe. Do you realize I'm black and blue? Haven't I paid enough?"

Tension drained from his face, and he reached out, barely touching her golden hair. "Yes, you have..."

"I'm not asking for an apology, Rafe."

He squirmed beneath her calm gaze. "I should be giving you that, too."

"An explanation is all I ask."

Just the husky sound of her voice coupled with the understanding flame burning in her large eyes triggered an avalanche of emotions through him. If Jessie had been strident, demanding or imperious, it would have been easy for him to flick aside her request and ignore her. As he had ignored so many things lately. Running his hand over his hair, he sighed deeply, then began.

"Two years ago, my wife, Mary Ann, was pregnant with our first child. We'd been married seven years, and she'd desperately wanted a family. When she found out she was pregnant, I don't know who was happier, her or me. Everything was fine throughout the whole pregnancy…then, two weeks before she was due, I had to leave for Denver on banking business. Millie was over at a neighbor's ranch helping an old friend who had broken her hip.

"Mary Ann was all alone when a blizzard hit the ranch. Snow was six feet deep, and the temperature was fifty to sixty below. The storm tore out all the electric and telephone lines." Rafe took a deep, unsteady breath. His voice was strained, and tears shimmered in his eyes. "I was stranded in Denver when I got this feeling something was wrong. When I tried to call Mary Ann, I found out the phone lines were dead, and I couldn't contact Millie or the doctor—I couldn't get ahold of anyone to check up on her."

He paused and looked past her, although his mind didn't register the peaceful, scenic meadow. All he could see was the devastating past. Focusing back on Jessie, he said, "I took the helicopter back the next morning and damn near crashed because of the wind and ice. When I finally reached the ranch, everything was in total chaos.

Pinto Pete met me at the chopper pad." Rafe closed his eyes. "Mary Ann had died, and so had the baby."

Jessie inhaled softly. "My God, no…" Words were inconsequential to the pain she saw in Rafe's face. Automatically she reached out and touched his arm. "I'm sorry Rafe. So sorry…"

He gave a broken shrug. "Everyone was." Then he grimaced. "That's why Dal has me worried. This is her first baby. She ought to be in a hospital to have it, not at home. Mary Ann died at home—alone and with no one to help her, or hold her…"

Tears of sympathy rose in her eyes, but she held them back, knowing Rafe would be embarrassed. "Listen to me, Rafe. Dal lives in Denver. She's close to all kinds of hospitals, and I'm sure Jim will be there for her."

"And I wasn't."

"I didn't mean to imply that, Rafe. How could you know Mary Ann would have the baby two weeks early?"

He lifted his craggy head, staring blindly toward the mountains. "She died in that bed you slept in. Alone."

Without thinking, Jessie went to Rafe and slid her arms around his waist. She held him with all the strength she had in her arms. The ragged pounding of his heart beat against her ear, and she heard and felt a low groan come from deep within him.

Sweeping his powerful arms around her, Rafe held Jessie hard and long, drawing from her strength and understanding. So many old, withheld emotions came tearing up through him that the anguish rooted him to the spot. Only her scent, the thick silk of her hair and the awareness of her soft form molded to him kept him from losing all control and giving in to the pain that engulfed him. His throat tightened, and he felt hot tears slide down his cheeks. How long he kept Jessie in his embrace, he didn't know. The small act of holding Jessie seemed to draw the pain away from his grieving heart, which had borne the burden far too long by itself. Finally, taking a ragged breath, Rafe picked up the reins of his unleashed emotions. This time, he gently put them back in his heart instead of cruelly ignoring their existence.

"You're healing," he said, his voice thick and unsteady. "Like the sun. The sun will warm away the coldest night."

Jessie shut her eyes tightly, content in his arms. "You've seen too many cold nights alone."

With a bare nod of his head, he agreed. Slowly Rafe began to release her. He kept his hands on her small shoulders as he stared down at her serene face. The woman who stood before him shook his foundations as no other had before. In that spinning, poignant discovery, he realized how easy it would be to love her. And then he laughed at himself; he was like a violent, destructive thunderstorm to her sunlit beauty. Twice now he had wounded her with his cruelty. What was it inside him that made him so damned abrupt when he wanted to be tender instead? Could he trust himself to open up to her warmth? "I'm used to the cold."

"No, no one gets used to the cold. I never could. To say you're used to it is to say you've barricaded yourself against feeling again, Rafe, or reaching out to live."

He caressed her shoulders gently. "You're an idealist, Jessie."

"I'm a realist."

"Then what does that make me?"

Her lips parted as she raised her hand and gently caressed his face. "A man who has been deeply wounded by life. Wounded and scarred. But not dead, Rafe. You're trying to live your life as if you'd died."

"I died when Mary Ann and the baby did," he said in a low voice.

"Yes, a part of you did," she agreed softly. "But we're all walking wounded, Rafe. It's only how we handle our wounds that counts."

He closed his eyes, tempted by her husky tone and the rich offerings of her heart. Wasn't she aware that he could take her beliefs and twist them? That what she offered in sympathy he could ridicule and turn it against her? Rafe tasted bitterness in his mouth and gradually allowed his hands to slide from her shoulders. "Come on, Jessie, we're done riding for today." His voice was devoid of emotion. "We've both been through enough today; it's time to stop and rest."

They set up camp in silence. Jessie tried to carry her weight by gathering wood for a fire, and unsaddling her mustang and brushing him down. It was obvious that Rafe's mind was still on their conversation. He went through the motions of preparing camp without seeming to pay attention to anything. Jessie quietly kept out of his way, knowing that Rafe needed to deal with his memories in his own way.

Sitting by the fire, above which he had suspended a small black kettle filled with soup, Rafe cut chunks of beef jerky with his hunting knife and tossed them into the pot. He had covertly watched Jessie as she'd gone about her chores, and guilt had nagged at him when he'd seen the way she winced from pain. Only hardened wranglers could stand eight hours of solid riding in the saddle, and he had forced her to do it on her first day on a horse.

Taking a larger kettle, he suspended it over the fire and filled it with cold stream water.

"Jessie, come and sit down for a while. We've got plenty of wood."

She dumped her last armload on the pile and brushed off dirt and bark from the stained sleeves of her blouse. "I didn't know how much we'd have to have for tonight."

Rafe forced a smile as she sat next to him on the log he'd dragged near the fire. He handed her an onion and his hunting knife.

"Here. Peel this, chop it up and throw it in the kettle."

"But I haven't unsaddled your horse yet. You said—"

"I know what I said," he cut her off, "but from the looks of it, you need to sit down and rest."

She grimaced. "I'm just sore, that's all."

Rafe took off his hat and ran his fingers through his dark hair. "You're more than sore," he said as he motioned to her jeans. The inner part of her knees had been rubbed so badly they had bled, and the material over her legs was darkened and damp from drying blood. "Why didn't you say something sooner?"

"I didn't want to slow us down, Rafe. I agreed that I'd keep up with you and do this the way you wanted to. You've taken time off from your work to come up here with me, and I knew the responsibilities I had to take." Seeing his face darken with anger, she added defensively, "I was going to take care of them when I was done with my chores."

"Stay put," Rafe warned her. "As soon as I get the horses bedded down for the night, we'll take care of you."

A warmth passed through her, and despite the aggravating pain in her legs and hips, Jessie smiled. "Going to slap some horse liniment on my legs?" she teased.

Rafe smiled back at her bravado. "No liniment tonight. Just some precautionary doctoring."

As Rafe took care of the horses, Jessie peeled the onion. Placing it on a flat stone that Rafe had used before, she carefully cut it. Tears were streaming down her face when Rafe returned.

"Is it that bad, Jessie?" he asked, misunderstanding, as he crouched beside her.

Jessie dropped the final handful of onion into the pot. "It's awful! I've never cried so much."

"Damn! You're worse off than I first thought. Come on, climb out of those jeans. Maybe you tore a muscle in your thigh or something."

Startled, Jessie looked at Rafe. "What?"

"You're crying."

"Well, of course I am!"

"Then strip down. I want to look at those legs," he growled.

"Now just a minute!" She rose and put her hands on her hips. "I'm crying because of those silly onions, Rafe Kincaid!"

His face went blank for a moment. "Oh. I thought—"

"My legs are killing me and, okay, so I bled a little at the knees. No big deal. Believe me, I've weathered a lot worse than this, so don't go getting all jelly on me."

"You're such a hellion, Jessie Scott," he said with a grin. "Go wash your hands off; you smell like an onion." As she turned, Rafe added, "And change behind that big pine over there. Get into the pair of shorts Millie packed for you. I want to look at your legs."

Disgruntled, Jessie gave him a parting look that said volumes, then made her way to the stream. After rinsing off her hands, she crossed the camp and went behind the pines that surrounded the small, open space. Changing as quickly as she could with her stiff legs, she walked back to the fire a few minutes later.

"They look pretty bad, don't they?" she asked, wrinkling her nose at Rafe.

Her thighs were covered with bruises and swollen, and the insides of her knees were raw and bloody from gripping the horse.

"Sit here," he muttered. Retrieving two white towels, he dipped them in the water he had set over the kettle to warm. Hunching down in front of her, he made her hold the moist towels around each of her thighs.

Jessie sighed. "That feels wonderful."

"Thought it might." Rafe gently placed his hand on one of her knees and examined the damage. "Dammit," he breathed, "I pushed you too hard."

The instant Rafe's hand settled on her leg, all Jessie was aware of was the feel of his touch. The throbbing in her legs receded as she concentrated on his nearness. He was so close and so achingly male. "It's all right," she whispered, her eyes large and dazed with tiredness.

Rafe glanced up. "It isn't all right, Jessie. You could get blood poisoning from this mess. Dammit!" He reached for his saddlebags. "I'm going to have to clean these wounds off, and it's going to hurt like hell," he warned.

The tiredness that she had been able to keep at bay crept up on Jessie. Between Rafe's comforting touch and the soothing warmth of the wet towels on her legs, she grew drowsy. "Can't it wait, Rafe? I'm so tired I feel like I'm going to keel over."

He gave her an alarmed look. "Okay, hold on." In a matter of minutes he put down a plastic ground cover and her sleeping bag, then led her over to it. "Lie down," he ordered.

"But—"

"Now."

Biting down on her lower lip, Jessie sat on the sleeping bag. Rafe had brought over her saddle and covered it with a blanket so it could be used as a pillow. Once down, she felt heavenly. She closed her eyes. "I don't think I should lie down, Rafe."

"Why?" He knelt by her knees, the first-aid kit next to him.

"I'm going to fall asleep."

"Not while I'm tending these knees you won't," he warned her grimly. "All right, if you want to cry or scream, you'd better do it now."

One moment her knees had been a dull ache, the next, they were on fire. Jessie jerked upright and grabbed at his hands as he held iodine-soaked gauze to each knee. The pain was so great she thought she was going to pass out. Rafe was talking to her, but his voice sounded very far away. She felt his iron grip on her shoulder as he laid her down. For a few minutes she skirted the edge of faintness, the odd, floating feeling lifting her above the pain.

Rafe watched as Jessie's lashes fluttered closed. He knew the agony she was feeling; he had blanched at the same time her face had gone white with pain. He knew what agony he was putting her through, but he had to do it. It was bad enough he had caused this to happen to her, but it would be worse if he didn't take the proper— but painful—precautions.

Out of years of experience wrapping injured horses' legs, he quickly and thoroughly cleaned, washed and dressed Jessie's knees. In a matter of a few minutes, stark white bandages covered the seeping wounds. Throughout his ministrations Jessie had had her fists clenched at her sides, and her body had been stiff and unyielding. Perspiration stood out on her brow and upper lip.

"It's all over," he told her, briefly caressing her cheek. "You can relax."

Jessie released a long-held breath and slowly opened her eyes. "Thank God. I've never had anything sting so badly."

Rafe got up and put the saddlebags aside. He retrieved a heavy wool blanket and laid it across her. "It's better than blood poisoning. I want you to lie here and rest. Dinner will be ready in another half hour." He studied her for a long moment. "You're a pretty courageous lady, you know that?"

"Courage?" she joked, as she stared wearily at him. "I'm a big chicken at heart. You're lucky I didn't start squawking."

"No," he murmured, lightly stroking her head. "I don't think you realize your own limits. Yet."

Jessie closed her eyes, soaking up the warmth of his voice and his touch. "Believe me, I know my limits," she said, her voice slurring. "Rafe?"

"Yes?"

"I'm so tired."

"I know you are, honey. Go to sleep. You've put in a hard day."

She resisted the exhaustion that tugged at her. "But—the food—"

"It'll be there when you wake up." He brushed several tendrils of blond hair away from her cheek. "You've earned a rest."

Honey...he had called her honey, was the last thought Jessie had as she fell into an exhausted sleep.

* * *

The dancing firelight changed the shadows across Rafe's pensive face as he watched Jessie sleep. It was a cloudless night, and the stars were a bright, sparkling quilt thrown across the cobalt heavens. He held a tin cup filled with coffee between his hands as he gazed at her.

Color had gradually come back to Jessie's cheeks, and the tension had dissolved around her eyes and mouth. Rafe sipped the hot liquid, allowing himself to savor her natural beauty. The wind was picking up out of the northwest, and he had taken his own sleeping bag and placed it over her to make sure she wouldn't get chilled. She looked like a lost waif beneath all the blankets. There was a refreshing innocence to Jessie. And yet, she was all woman. Rafe couldn't define her strength; he simply knew it existed in her, and he was reaching out toward her because of it. Or was it more?

He stared darkly at the flames, pondering the question. Rightly or wrongly, he was drawn to Jessie just like that fire was to the wood. Was it her beauty? Her sense of humor? The way she was able to look life in the face and laugh at it? He wanted to know everything about her, to understand what had made her the strong, yet gentle woman she was. Tomorrow, he promised himself.

Rubbing his brow, he threw the remains of his coffee on the fire, then added large logs to the flames, to insure that the fire would burn throughout the night. Taking his plastic ground wrap, he placed it next to Jessie. There were two wool blankets, which he wrapped himself up in. He didn't have the heart to wake Jessie or move her into her own sleeping bag. He laid down next to her, his back against her. He wanted to sleep with her cradled in his arms. For now, he would settle for just being near her.

Chapter 5

Jessie wasn't sure what woke her up; the only sounds she could hear were the call of a magpie, the soft snort of the horses and the crackle of the fire. Then the smell of fresh coffee brewing and the salty tang of bacon frying made her eyes widen with appreciation. She lay snuggled under the covers, warm despite the chill in the air. Rafe was crouched by the fire, with a skillet in his hand. He was clean shaven, his hair was neatly combed, and he looked ruggedly handsome to her. The dark blue denim jacket he wore hugged his broad shoulders, outlining him to perfection.

She was about to give him a cheery "good-morning" when she moved. A low groan tore from her throat as pain shot through her legs.

"You okay?" Rafe asked, concerned.

"Yes…just cranky, sore muscles." She slowly sat up

and began to unbraid her hair. "Whatever you're cooking smells great."

He watched for a few seconds more, reassuring himself that she was all right. "It'll be ready in about five minutes. I want to use the fresh bacon up before we reach bear country."

She smiled, running her fingers through her hair. "I'd better like bacon for breakfast."

"Right." Rafe stared at her, arrested by the site of her long hair shining in the sun. He remembered caressing her hair and how good it had felt. Tearing his attention back to her, he asked, "How are your knees?"

The air was chilly, but Jessie pulled the sleeping bag off her lower legs. "They look fine."

"Any throbbing or unusual pain?"

"No, not anymore."

He nodded, satisfied. "Good, that means we caught the infection in time. I'm going to wrap them in flannel before we ride, so don't go changing out of those shorts just yet."

Covering back up, Jessie looked at him. "It's too cold to be running around in shorts, Rafe Kincaid!"

His smile was genuine. He cracked five eggs into the emptied skillet that still contained some bacon grease in the bottom of it.

"So take your breakfast in bed," he said as he set aside the bacon and began preparing eggs.

Jessie laughed. "This is a first! I've never had breakfast in bed." She stretched and gazed around the quiet meadow. Everywhere she looked, there was beauty. A light coating of frost covered the lush expanse of the meadow, and the sky was a clear sapphire blue. "Rafe…"

He glanced over at her. "Yes?"

"This has to be the most beautiful place on earth. You can feel the silence. And the grass is gorgeous! There are so many colors and shades! It's nothing like D.C."

The reverence in her voice struck a responsive chord in Rafe. He finished the eggs and divided them between two tin plates. Scooping up the bacon and some warm pan bread he had made earlier, he stood up and walked over to her. "You're a country girl at heart," he told her, sitting next to her. He handed her a plate. "And you're beginning to find that out."

She smiled and thanked him for the food. There was a relaxed camaraderie between them this morning that seemed to stem from the beauty of the day and the magic of the mountains. Sitting close to each other, they concentrated on their food, content in listening to the sounds of nature and being near each other.

Jessie was sipping her coffee afterward when she asked, "What time is it?"

"Seven-thirty or so."

"I thought you said we'd be getting up at five every day."

"I changed my mind," Rafe said curtly.

Was he feeling guilty about her knees? Had he allowed her those extra hours of sleep to mend properly? Whatever his reasons, she was grateful. "I'm glad. I was never so tired as last night."

"Mountain air and long hours in the saddle will do that to you." He allowed a hint of a smile. "You slept like a baby all night."

Somewhere in one corner of her mind, Jessie vaguely remembered turning over and strong arms holding her. "How would you know that?"

"Because I held you most of the night, that's why."

The drawl in his voice sent a quiver surging through her. "So, it wasn't a dream after all. You were holding me!"

His eyes gleamed with laughter. "At least you didn't call it a nightmare."

She blushed fiercely, aware of the heat sweeping up her neck and into her cheeks. "I thought it was only a dream…" she began lamely. A wonderful dream! she wanted to add.

"I didn't have the heart to wake you up and make you climb into your own sleeping bag. I threw mine on top of you to keep you warm and settled down next to you with a couple of blankets." He looked across the silent meadow. "Out here, you sleep close for body heat. I put my plastic liner down and laid with my back to you." He shot her an amused look. "About two hours later, you turned over, snuggled into my arms and stayed there the rest of the night."

Jessie gulped unsteadily. "I see."

"You were probably cold and turned to the nearest source of heat. People become elemental out here in the mountains."

It was a few minutes before she spoke again, as each of them was occupied with their own thoughts. First, Jessie remembered, he had kissed her in the box stall. And then she had held him while he had hurt for the loss of his family. Now Rafe had held her against the cold darkness of the night. So much was happening between them so fast, yet everything seemed a natural extension of their blossoming relationship. She couldn't explain the chemistry that was setting off reactions within each of them, but she knew it was right.

I should be scared. I should try to stop what's happening. She knew he could mortally wound her; he had that powerful an effect on her. There was nothing compromising about Rafe either physically, mentally, or emotionally. He was a survivor. But so was she, in a different way. That was why, she reasoned, she wasn't retreating from him. She had the ability to penetrate the walls he'd erected. She saw the naked and vulnerable man behind them, the man her heart hungered for…ached for.

Lifting her chin, she looked at him and said softly, "I think the thing I missed the most after I divorced Tom was sleeping with a man. Not just any man…"

Rafe nodded, his mind back on the night. He hadn't slept well after Jessie had nestled against him. He'd been too aware of her molded against him, and there had been moments when his tender feelings had threatened to change into an overwhelming need…to have her… claim her…and make her his woman.

"I understand," he said softly. "That was—still is— the hardest thing for me to get over when I go into the bedroom at night."

A tender smile touched her lips and eyes. "For whatever it's worth, Rafe, thanks for holding me. I never slept better."

If he didn't stand, he was going to reach out and take Jessie into his arms. He was beyond reasoning why she affected him; he only knew he had to have her. She made him burn like a hot, hungry fire each time he was with her. His mouth quirked and he rose.

"Come on," he said gruffly, "time to get moving. We've got a long day ahead of us."

The moment Rafe helped her into the saddle, Jessie encountered a wall of pain.

"Here," Rafe said, "take your right leg and hook it

around the saddle horn. Keep your left foot in the stirrup." He saw immediate relief on her face as she did as he instructed.

"I never realized I could hurt so much," she admitted with a shaky laugh meant to hide her real feelings. "This is like riding sidesaddle."

Rafe kept his gloved hand on her thigh, watching her closely. "Every hour switch positions. The mustang won't mind. And we'll be going at a walk today."

"Sounds great," Jessie murmured gratefully.

He gave her a gentle pat and went over to his Arabian and mounted. "There won't be any more mountain climbing. We're as high as we need to be. Today we'll be doing nothing but crossing meadows and ridges, providing there isn't snow clogging them." Looking up into the clear sky, he observed, "And we'll have good weather for most of today."

Jessie nodded. She didn't know how Rafe knew about the weather, she simply trusted his judgment. They fell into a brisk walk, their legs occasionally brushing against each other. The morning was cold, and streams of breath were visible from their horses' nostrils. Her ears were freezing, so Jessie placed the looped reins on the horse's neck and unplaited her hair. The thick strands fell gracefully over her shoulders, tumbling down across her wool jacket. She looked up and saw Rafe staring at her.

"My ears were cold."

"I'm glad. You look beautiful with your hair down."

She swallowed, caught in the fire burning in his dark blue eyes. Rafe made her feel more of a woman than she had in her entire life. "I—thank you." She wished she hadn't sounded like a breathless child. She had been married and divorced—she was long past those kind of reactions. Then the thought struck her that perhaps she had never met a man until now, because he made her feel so inexperienced.

The horses labored up and out of the small stand of pine. They rode the ridge of the hills, which still had patches of snow here and there. Rafe was having a hard time keeping his eyes off Jessie. Her hair was a halo around her head, and the cool air and exercise had brought a flushed pink to her cheeks and her rosy, parted lips.

"So tell me," he said, doing his best to sound casual, "what was it like when you were growing up? Were you raised around concrete, glass and steel?"

Jessie's heart pounded abruptly. She tried to evade Rafe's question. "There's a lot of that in D.C."

"How about family? I saw a photo of an older woman in your wallet when I was looking for your ID. Is she your grandmother?"

She chewed on her lower lip. She didn't want to lie to him, but the truth was so hard. Taking an unsteady breath, she said in a low voice, "I'm an orphan. That picture was of my last foster mother."

Rafe's gaze sharpened. "Orphan?" He felt his heart wrench in his chest. No wonder she wanted a family and children of her own…

"Yes." Jessie shrugged, trying to make light of it. "Don't give me that distressed look, Rafe. There are lots of orphaned kids around, believe me." Her voice shook with undeniable conviction.

He swore softly. His eyes were narrowed and shadowed by the brim of his cowboy hat as he held her gaze. "Who the hell would give up someone like you?"

"It's a question I've asked myself many times."

"I'm sorry," he said abruptly, realizing that he had just blindly stomped like a bull in a china shop into a very painful part of her life.

"Don't be. Every situation has its good side, too."

Rafe snorted. "I don't believe that."

"I do. Maud Scott, the woman in the photo, turned me from a very bitter teenager into someone who could cope." Jessie's eyes softened, and she smiled gently. "Maud was sixty-three years old when she took me out of the orphanage. I was thirteen at the time, and after being shuttled between six homes, I hated everyone. I was angry, Rafe. Angry at the world for what it had doled out to me. Maud had the wisdom and the years to persevere with me. She turned me from a bitter kid into someone who believed that rainbows always followed the rain in your life. Maud gave me hope."

"She must have been damned influential to have turned you around like that," he muttered, finding it hard to accept how much pain and rejection Jessie had suffered. She was so incredibly extroverted and idealistic, the opposite of him, and he had had all the breaks in life.

Jessie laughed. "Oh, Maud had her hands full with me for a while."

"Why were you so angry, Jessie?"

She sobered and avoided his searching look. "Let's just say that some of the foster homes I was in weren't very nice."

"In what way?" he probed darkly.

With a shrug, Jessie said, "The last foster home I was in, the husband's cure-all for his problems was wife abuse."

His fist clenched at his side as he stared hard at her. "He beat you up, too?"

"Don't make it out as something it wasn't, Rafe. He mainly took it out on his poor wife. He only went for us kids if we were stupid enough to get under foot when he was in one of his ugly moods." She cast him a grim smile. "I learned a lot in the two years I was with them. I learned how to be seen, but never heard. I learned how to hide and live for the hours I'd spend at school. No, John Ballentine taught me more than anyone else how to survive."

The mental and emotional cruelty had taken its toll on Jessie, Rafe realized as he looked into her challenging sable eyes, which were flecked with dark shadows from the past. "That's why you told me earlier that what you were going through now was nothing compared to your past."

She nodded. "Right now, I hurt physically, but somehow it doesn't compare to what I had to deal with mentally, when I was growing up." A tender smile tipped the corners of her mouth. "I'm happy now, Rafe. With you. With the land. Frankly, I've never been happier, and I'm glad I was chosen for this investigation. Maud had always read to me about the West and about the cowboys, Indians and the mustangs. She was a well-traveled woman who was crippled with rheumatoid arthritis. Maud may not have been able to travel much when I was with her, but we did, through books. The richness of life, the reveling in it came from Maud." Her voice quavered, and her eyes were bright with unshed tears. "I owe Maud my life. She took a scared kid who had learned to survive at any cost and turned her into someone who could embrace life instead of hate it. I loved her as I've never loved anyone else in my life."

"From the way you're talking, she's no longer living," Rafe guessed, touched by her confession.

"She died two years after I married Tom." With a sigh, Jessie murmured, "I always call that the year it rained in my life. That was one of Maud's euphemisms. There were rainy years, fertile years and sunshine years. The rainy ones were when your life cycles brought losses of some sorts. Fertile years were years of learning and growing and reaching out. Sunshine years were few and far between, but when they came, she told me to soak myself with their happy radiance. They were reward years to her, and they made up for all the suffering, pain and growth we'd persevered through."

"I think I'd have liked your Maud Scott," Rafe commented after a moment.

"You'd have loved her, Rafe. Everyone she touched was better off for it."

"Well," he said huskily, "you're a spitting image of her, Jessie. You bring that smile of yours and that laughter into my life anytime you want." He scowled. "I've been through two hellish, rainy years. I'd like to believe there was a year of sunshine out there somewhere for me."

Her laugh was lilting, and she reached out to touch his shoulder. "There will be, believe me. I've experienced all three types of years. So does everyone else."

He met her winsome smile with one of his own. Jessie's touch was like a heated brand, and a hungry ache uncoiled deep within him again. "So, what year are you in now?"

She gave him a wry look. "Definitely a fertile year. My sedate life is pulled out from under me, and suddenly I'm out in the wilds, investigating a possible crime. If that isn't growing, nothing is."

A smile lingered in his smoky blue eyes as he drank in the sight of her. "Not to mention a sour rancher who goes around barking and snarling all the time, giving you more trouble than help."

"No, Rafe," Jessie said, an understanding look on her face. "You've been grieving. I know what that's like. And maybe you're starting to come out of it after two years. It took me three years to get over Maud's death. She was my mother. Maybe not my biological one, but she had my heart, and that's all that counts. You've lost much more than that, and whether you want to believe it or not, you're starting to live again. Sometimes I think you're just fighting it."

"Tell me, Jessie Scott, where did you get your PhD in psychology?" He put his hand over his heart melodramatically. "I think you're looking right through me and into my soul."

She laughed delightedly. "Maud's coaxing, believe me! She taught me to watch, listen, and most importantly, feel with my heart. She said the head would lead me wrong, but my feelings never would." Jessie sobered. "When I married Tom, I was listening to my head. My logic said that I loved him and so I could have the babies and the family I'd always wanted. Obviously, my logic was flawed. Maud had tried to talk me into waiting a while before I married, but I didn't listen. The rest is history."

Rafe reached out, catching her hand as it rested against her thigh, and squeezed her fingers. "We all make mistakes, Jessie. Yours might have been painful, but you were still able to get through it. Just remember you're special. Very special…"

She returned the squeeze, her heart filled to overflowing in that moment. "I think everyone is special, Rafe. You, me…we all have our own gift we can share with others."

Reluctantly he released her fingers. "If we can share at all."

"Are you saying you can't?"

"I shared a part of myself with Mary Ann, and then that was taken from me."

Jessie met his bitter stare. "I think you're capable of sharing, Rafe. Losing your wife has hurt you, and you've withdrawn. That doesn't mean you won't ever reach out again to live."

He gave a shake of his head. "I won't," he said flatly. "It hurts too damn much. I'd rather not feel at all than put myself out on the line again for someone else."

She ached for Rafe and for the suffering he had gone through. "Well, maybe one day when you get one of those sunshine years, you might want to try again," she said softly.

Rafe pulled his gelding to a stop at the end of the ridge. "All it seems I've done in the past two years is inflict pain on others." He rested one arm on the saddle horn and stared at the forest and meadows below them. "I gave Dal all kinds of hell because she was falling in love with a half-breed Navajo man. That was a year after Mary Ann's death, and at that time, I couldn't recognize how much Dal loved Jim. She finally had to call me on the carpet about it." He pulled the brim of the cowboy hat lower on his brow, his eyes narrowing. "Cat's been having her ups and downs in life, too, and all I'm able to do is commiserate with her. You'd think I'd be able to give her some helpful or positive advice. All I can do is say, 'Yeah, life's tough, and it ain't going to get any better.'" He glanced over at Jessie. "And with you…well, let's just say I've been a first class selfish bastard. I can't seem to stop hurting you."

Jessie's lips compressed. How could she make him see that he was just fooling himself? He felt things so deeply, yet insisted on seeing himself as a cruel, unfeeling man. Then, remembering his apology the day before, she opened her saddlebag and pulled out the wilted blue lupine. "Look, Rafe," she coaxed, holding his wavering gaze, "you gave me these. A man who didn't care or who was insensitive wouldn't have made an effort to pick these flowers to apologize to me."

He couldn't stand the compassion on her face or the tenderness in her husky voice. Yet at the same time he wanted her in his arms, close to him, holding that flame of life he saw burning so brightly in her wide, trusting eyes. Denying himself that brief respite from his self-directed anger, he said, "I'm just as cruel as that foster father of yours was. The only difference was in the way I carried it out, that's all."

Jessie moved her mustang closer until their legs met and touched. "Now hold on, Rafe. Let me decide who is or isn't cruel." She reached out and gave his arm a good shake. "Look at me!"

He raised his eyes. Her gaze was fiery, her lips were set in a stubborn line, and her nostrils flared with anger. "What?"

"Stop thinking of yourself in such negative terms! My God, you're not an ogre. You're not a murderer. You care so much about the people and animals on that ranch of yours. Don't you think I saw you handling that foal? The tenderness was in your eyes, Rafe. In your voice. Everytime Millie comes to you, your face softens, and you lose that hardness you wear like armor. And what about me? After I nearly hit you and your cattle on the road, you had every reason just to call an ambulance and have them take me to the nearest hospital instead of to your ranch. You cared for me, got a doctor and even allowed me to stay under your roof after you found out I was a BLM agent. I don't call that cruelty. I call it humane." Her voice cracked. "I see you differently, Rafe. I see the man. And he's basically kind and well-meaning. And perhaps even too sensitive for his own good, but he hides that part of himself from everyone." She held the flowers out to him. "Look at these and tell me you don't feel."

Rafe looked down at her, a tumult of violent, longing emotions tearing loose within him. He blindly reached out, gripping her by the shoulders and pulling her hard against him. Out of instinct, out of need for her warmth and love, he crushed her to his chest. He saw the startled look in her eyes as he leaned over to capture her lips. A driving ache sheared through him as he molded his mouth possessively to hers, wanting, taking her softness, her very self. A low animal growl reverberated through him as he felt Jessie suddenly relax against him, her hands shyly coming to rest upon his chest. Her touch was so hesitant and light. Hungrily he parted her lips, his breathing ragged as he absorbed all of her taste, smell and goodness into his starving soul.

She moaned, and immediately Rafe lessened the pressure of his mouth upon her. He felt her tremble violently. Her breasts were round and soft against the wall of his chest, and her moist breath fanned raggedly against his cheek. Her hands moved up and around his neck, and sent a burst of elation through him. Tenderly Rafe moved his lips over hers, trying to soothe and give, when just a moment before he had fiercely taken.

How long he kept her captive against him, he had no idea. Jessie's scent, her yielding lips upon his mouth and her fingers caressing his nape had caused a firestorm to break loose within him. No woman had ever made him feel the blistering liquid fire that now raced through his throbbing, hardened body. Rafe's need for Jessie went beyond hunger, beyond starvation. He wanted her body, her heart—he wanted to bury himself in her and bask in the radiant love that poured out with such force. As he gradually released her, his dazed mind registered what he had thought and felt. Love? That word didn't exist. And if it had, it had died with Mary Ann. Rafe opened his eyes and drowned in Jessie's languorous sable gaze. She was breathing hard, her lips were wet and glistening from his ravenous assault, and her fingers trembled against his chest.

He kept his hands upon her shoulders as he lowered her to sit back on the saddle of her horse. God, how he wanted to kiss her again, take off his gloves and feel the thick texture of her hair through his fingers, and then love her totally. "I'm not good with words, Jessie," he rasped. "I can show you how I feel. It's the only way I know how." He glanced down and saw the flowers scattered beneath the horses' hooves; Jessie must have dropped them when he had kissed her. An odd smile came to Rafe's mouth, and he dismounted. Pushing the horses apart, he bent down and picked up the bouquet. When he straightened up and handed them to her, he said, "Your ex-husband was a fool not to know what he had when he married you."

Within moments they began a long, winding trek off

the ridge toward a sunlit meadow in the valley far below. Jessie clutched the blue lupine in one hand as they began the steep descent. Her thoughts were barely coherent, and she could do nothing during the next half hour but feel. Rafe's savage kiss had branded her, made her feel she was his, and then their embrace had turned into the joy of mutual giving...

Four days, Jessie thought as she rode beside Rafe, four wonderful days on the trail... Ever since he had kissed her, their relationship had subtly changed for the better. She stole a glance at his rugged profile, her heart swelling with an incredible sense of elation. Rafe had become her teacher on the trail in every way. He had taught her how to ride, to camp, to cook over an open fire and treat the horses' minor injuries. But he had made no further move to touch her or kiss her, and she accepted his decision.

The sun was beating down overhead as they traversed a ridge that would eventually flow out like a skirt to the valley below. Jessie lifted her face to the sun, smiling. The mountain air was magical. And it had worked its spell over her and Rafe.

Pushing several strands away from her face, Jessie nudged her thick tangle of hair across her shoulders. She saw Rafe give her a yearning look that made her go weak inside. He wanted her. And she ached to have him. It was that simple and that complex. She knew they were diving headlong into an emotional whirlpool that Rafe might survive, but she doubted if she could. Then she remembered Maud's advice to follow her inner feelings. Her mind was screaming at her that too much was happening too soon; her heart spoke differently.

Jessie knit her brows as she concentrated on her

thoughts and feelings about Rafe. She cared deeply for him, and she knew she was helping him out of the dark tunnel he'd crawled through. But inexperience was keeping her off balance; she had never encountered a man like Rafe before. And she had never wanted the chance to know a man more than she wanted to know him. The magnetism that arced between them was so powerful that she could feel when he was thinking of her. Jessie would look up from the campfire and catch him staring at her with a dark stormy look of longing in his eyes. And it automatically triggered her need of him. She bit down on her lower lip. If she gave in to her emotions and to Rafe, she would be giving him the means to either raise her to the heights of heaven or throw her in the pit of hell. Which would it be? Could she deal with his mood swings? His long hours of silence?

Rafe drew the horses to a halt at the end of the ridge. He reached into the saddlebags and withdrew a pair of binoculars. For a few minutes he slowly scanned the valley that sprawled out before them.

"See that river down there?" he asked, pointing with one hand.

Jessie nodded. "Looks wide and angry."

"It's both. A lot of spring runoff in it. It'll be colder than hell, too."

"We have to cross it to get to the mustangs?" So far they had been able to avoid fording any of the rivers.

"Yes." He handed her the binoculars, and there was a smile in his eyes. "As for the mustangs, take a look down beneath that stand of pine."

She gave Rafe a surprised look and lifted the binoculars. "Mustangs!" she breathed excitedly. "Rafe! The mustangs!"

He threw his leg over the horn of the saddle, enjoying her reaction. Pushing the hat back on his head, he soaked up Jessie's smile. "Yeah. Pinto Pete said there was a grulla stud with a band of five mares. That's him down there. From the looks of it, he's going to use those trees to weather the storm that's coming our way." He studied the clouds in the distance that looked bruised and swollen with rain. The front was coming from the northwest, which meant it was swinging out of Canada. He'd been watching the formations build all morning and knew that within the hour it would begin to pour.

Jessie handed him back the binoculars and dug for her notebook from the saddlebag. "This is wonderful!" she whispered.

"You don't have to whisper. They can't hear you. We're five miles away from them."

With an embarrassed smile, she opened the notebook and scribbled down her findings. "They said mustangs had excellent hearing and sight."

Chuckling, Rafe watched the mustangs standing placidly beneath the pine. "They do. But they aren't superhorses."

"Do me a favor and call off the colors, markings and sex of the horses down there. I'm going to have to have this information for later use."

"Sure." As he began to describe the animals, one part of his mind remained on Jessie. Since he had kissed her, they had grown incredibly close. He had never shared so much of himself, or his thoughts with a woman as he did with Jessie. And it was natural, without any hesitation or strain. He had found himself teaching her everything he knew about ranching, and she proved such a rapt and eager student that the hours had sped by. Rafe glanced over at her. She looked so earnest as she concentrated on her task that he had the urge to kiss her seriousness away. But he didn't dare. Next time, if he kissed Jessie, he might not stop.

Jessie put the notebook away. "Thanks. All this will come in handy when I get back to the office."

"We're going to have to hightail it down to the valley, Jessie."

She looked up. "Why?"

Rafe pointed to the angry mass of approaching clouds. "We've got one hell of a storm brewing. I want to cross that river before it starts raining. Otherwise, the water level will rise another two or three feet, and it'll be more dangerous." He held her sable gaze. "Ready for a gallop?"

"You bet!"

Smiling, Rafe turned his horse down the grassy slope that flowed out toward the valley. Jessie had taken to riding like a talented beginner, and with her knees healing, wrapped as they were in protective flannel, she could enjoy a trot or gallop occasionally. The enthusiasm in her eyes over the unexpected gallop made Rafe go warm inside. Her smile simply melted away all his worries, grief and darkness. She was sunshine to his life. And he needed her.

As they swung down from the ridge at a steady pace, Rafe pondered their relationship. Jessie had grown close to him in a way he rarely allowed other people to. Every morning he woke up on the opposite side of the campfire from her, wishing he could be sleeping at her side once again. Every task, no matter how insignificant, became a joy with Jessie. He had taught her how to flip the eggs in a skillet and laughed at her crow of delight when she had accomplished the feat. And when he had helped her learn fly casting when fishing for rainbow trout, it had become nothing less than pure pleasure. He had caught five trout and Jessie one. But her excitement over having fished for the first time in her life and her pride in that one ten-inch trout had made him smile.

The band of mustangs took flight as Jessie and Rafe cantered across the floor of the valley. The grulla stud nipped and circled his band of mares, driving them up into the hills and eventually disappearing in the woods.

"They'll be back," Rafe said, riding easily at her side. "After we've left."

She nodded.

At the bank of the river, they halted. Rafe studied it for a long time before turning his attention to Jessie.

"This river is treacherous under the best of conditions, Jessie. It's deep and the current is swift." He pointed to a whirlpool further down the water. "Stay away from those. If you get sucked in, you may get pulled under. A horse is strong, but in a whirlpool his hind feet can't touch bottom and then bound back up, so he's going to flounder heavily." He glanced over at the dun. "This mustang is plenty savvy about crossing water. Just be sure to give him his head. Don't pull back on the reins or start sawing on his mouth with the bit. If you do, he's liable to go under. And so will you." Rafe pointed to the horn. "Whatever you do, hold on to that horn. If the current pulls you off the saddle, grab the mustang's mane and hold on. Understand?"

She nodded soberly.

Rafe grimaced, pulled his hat down firmly and gathered the reins of his Arab. He leaned over and unsnapped the lead to the packhorse. "The pack will follow me across, so don't worry about him. You never keep a lead on a horse trying to cross a river like this." He gave her a hard look. "I'll go first. Wait until I'm on the other bank before you start to cross."

Jessie stared at the unforgiving river. Some three hundred feet above them, the river curved and was filled with a brief flurry of muddy-looking white water rapids. Below them, at approximately the same distance, was another set of rapids. Rafe had chosen the quietest point to cross. But the river was hardly quiet. "Be careful, Rafe."

He turned and reached out, caressing her flushed cheek. "I will be. It's just you I worry about. If we didn't have to cross this damn river in order to get into the interior, I wouldn't. As a kid, I nearly drowned in this thing once, and Cat lost her horse to it." He dropped his hand. "Just remember that the river's ice cold. Be prepared for the shock when you get in."

"Okay."

Jessie watched as Rafe slowly urged his mount down the grassy bank. After four strides, the Arabian suddenly floundered and was swallowed up by water except for his neck and head. Rafe turned and shouted, "It's a drop-off, so watch it!"

She nodded, holding her breath. Rafe was strong and so was his horse. She saw the current grab them and carry them swiftly downstream. The packhorse followed doggedly, wallowing heavily with his load against the fierce river. At first she thought they would end up in the rapids. To her relief, Rafe had angled his laboring Arab toward a predetermined point downstream. With a sigh of relief, she watched as the Arab hit solid ground. In another minute, drenched and dripping, they were safely on the other side.

"Come on, Fred," she urged, clucking to her horse.

Jessie was so intent on safely entering the swollen river that she didn't hear Rafe's shout. The mustang took four strides, and suddenly she was up to her chest in icy breath-stealing water. She clung to the horn beneath the water, her hands numbing in seconds. The mustang bobbed and struck out with his front legs, angling downstream as the powerful current caught and captured them.

Her heart was pounding. Water was tearing at her legs, and Jessie felt herself losing her grip on the saddle. She panicked and clutched at the mane with her right hand. Then she looked upstream. A scream caught in her throat. A huge pinetree, roots and all, was bearing down directly toward them. The roots stretched toward them, as if they were long gnarled fingers reaching for her and her horse.

The mustang saw the tree come around the bend and through the rapids. With a snort, he tried to change directions, to get out of the path of the hurtling tree. Jessie's eyes widened, and she screamed as the roots loomed closer and closer. The mustang grunted hard as the roots enveloped them, then pushed him beneath the water. Jessie let go of the horse. The tree slewed sideways when it hit them, and bobbed and dipped as its path was momentarily blocked. Water rushed over Jessie's head. Blindly she tried to surface. The hoof of the horse struck her a grazing blow across her shoulder. Stunned, she felt herself being pulled down.

Water funnelled up Jessie's nose, into her mouth and lungs. Terror coursed through her, and she struggled desperately. Her coat was snagged on an exposed root. Her lungs seemed to be on fire as she wrenched out of the jacket. Pushing away from the tree, she stroked toward the surface. Jessie shot up in an explosion of gasping and choking. Air flowed into her lungs. Water blinded her, and her hair fell in heavy sheets around her as she flailed weakly to stay afloat. The cold was numbing, and each time she lifted her arm to try to swim, she felt weaker and weaker. The current swept her toward the middle of the river, and she saw the rapids coming up. Fear caused her to strike out in the direction of her horse. Jessie instinctively knew she'd never survive the raw tumult of the rapids.

Suddenly she felt herself being pulled into a swirling current. She managed half a breath before she was trapped by the whirlpool. Jessie spun around and around, deeper and deeper, until somewhere within her, she found the strength to resist, to survive. Using her last bit of energy, she kicked hard and pulled out of the sucking water.

The second time she surfaced, she could barely move. Maud's words came back to her. *If you're in trouble, float on your back!* Rolling over, Jessie tried to float. To her despair, her cowboy boots, filled with water, kept pulling her back down. Sobbing, Jessie raised one arm upward in a silent plea for help before she went under a third and final time. She was exhausted, and too cold and numb to fight anymore.

A loop settled expertly over her head. Jessie heard Rafe's raw voice above the roar of the river. Flailing weakly, she managed to bring the rope under one arm. The lasso tightened immediately. Water cascaded over her, and she closed her eyes, unable to even cling to the rope as a cold grayness descended on her.

Chapter 6

Rafe's hands shook as he dragged Jessie from the river. She lay against the bank, unconscious. With a strength born of fear, he managed to get her up on the grass flat. His eyes mirrored his terror. He ripped off his gloves and shakily placed his fingers against her neck. He felt a slight pulse. *Thank God!* He turned her onto her stomach and then straddled her to pump the water out of her lungs. Her blond hair was matted about her face and shoulders. He heard Jessie cough and then gasp. Relief surged through him as he leaned down, forcing more water from her. *She was alive. Oh, God, she was alive.* He couldn't stop the scalding tears that burned in his eyes as he worked on her.

Jessie hadn't seen that tree coming, and it was his fault! He should have told her to look upriver before ever entering the water to make sure no debris was floating down toward her. Suddenly the first crack of lightning flashed in the sky, heralding the beginning of the storm. But it wasn't anything like the storm Rafe was experiencing inside. When he had seen the tree hit Jessie and carry her down, he'd thought she was dead. He had lost her before…before…

Rafe took his hands away and got up, moving quickly to the packhorse. He ripped off the canvas and the protective plastic covering over their supplies and jerked several wool blankets out of the pack. He hurried back to Jessie's side as she weakly tried to sit up.

"No," he said urgently, throwing the blanket around her shoulders, "don't move."

Jessie lay gasping, drinking in huge draughts of air. Weakly she opened her eyes and stared straight into Rafe's ravaged face. She began to cry. He tucked both blankets around her and then lifted her to carry her toward a nearby overhang of granite.

She clung to him, exhausted, unable to stop crying. She had almost died. She had come so close. Her fingers, bruised and bleeding from her struggles with the roots, clutched the folds of Rafe's jacket.

"It's going to be all right," he soothed in a raw voice. Gently he laid her down beneath the outcrop. There was just enough room for two people underneath it. He sat her up, making sure she was conscious.

"I—I'm okay…"

Rafe crouched down, moving the damp hair away from her eyes and face. "You will be now. Listen, it's going to storm, Jess. I've got to get the horses hobbled…"

Jessie nodded, burying her head in her arms against her drawn up knees. She was shivering from the cold and shock. "G-go ahead."

Rafe glanced up at the approaching storm. "I'll be right back. I promise. Just stay here."

Making a muffled sound, she nodded again. Time dissolved, and she could only sit huddled beneath the rock, shivering and trembling. She dully looked up once and saw Rafe spreading a shelter half across the overhang and anchoring it on one side. Lightning danced around them, and the wind howled as it funneled though the narrow valley. Jessie buried her head in her arms as the thunder caromed off the mountains, the reverberations drumming through her.

Rafe threw the sleeping bags down as a floor for them and ducked beneath the rock. Grimly he stripped the blankets off her and began to undress her. Jessie's eyes widened.

"W-what are you doing?" she cried hoarsely, trying to stop him from unbuttoning her blouse.

"You're freezing," he growled. "Now stop fighting me, Jess. You'll go into shock if I can't get you out of these wet clothes and get you warm. Just sit still, for God's sakes!"

She sat still as he stripped the rest of her clothes off her. His face was so hard and set that it frightened her. His hands trembled violently as he threw the scratchy wool blankets back around her.

It began to rain. Only it wasn't the soft spring rain that she'd known in D.C. It was a deluge that Jessie had never encountered, a hammering, angry rain that stripped leaves from trees, drilled holes in the soft soil and broke the heads of daisies bowing beneath its onslaught. Nature was so violent; from the ruthlessness of the river that had nearly robbed her of her life to the storm that now broke angrily around them. She had no more tears;

she simply huddled on the sleeping bag, her legs drawn beneath her, shaking.

Rafe got up and started a blazing fire with the help of magnesium heating tabs that had been in his pack. He placed a small black kettle over the fire and poured a can of soup into it. Taking off his hat, he shrugged out of his coat and returned his attention to Jessie. He couldn't still the terror that surged through him at the knowledge that she'd almost died. Feeling helpless, he sat down next to her. Gently he drew Jessie to him and began to briskly rub the wool blanket against her skin. Her lips were blue and so were her fingers. The rain cascaded down around them, and Rafe held her tightly, continuing to force circulation back into her arms and legs, trying to head off the shock he saw in her vacant eyes and chalky face.

The wiry blankets chafed her sensitive skin until it almost hurt. After a while the coldness that had invaded her had been reduced. Shutting her eyes, she clung to Rafe, needing the steady sound of his heartbeat. Every time lightning shattered the roiling heavens, she flinched.

"It's all right, honey. It's going to be fine," he breathed thickly, kissing her damp temple.

Jessie sighed and tried to relax. Rafe's breath was warm and moist against her cool cheek. She needed his body heat. "J-just hold me. I'm so cold, Rafe."

He rocked her. "I know you are. I'll hold you. Forever, if that's what you want. Now just rest. Rest."

Leaning heavily against him, Jessie absorbed Rafe's heat. His strong arms held her tightly to him, and his trembling fingers worked their way through her matted, wet hair. She had no idea how long she lay in Rafe's arms. When she opened her eyes, the storm had passed, and only muddy, churning clouds were left in its wake.

Her fingers curled against his chest, and she felt Rafe shift slightly.

"How do you feel?" His deep voice was like a balm to her.

"Better," she managed, the sound coming out more like a croak.

"I've got some soup heated for you. I want you to drink it, Jess. We've got to get your body temperature up. You're close to hypothermia."

Her brow wrinkled. "Hypo—what?"

Rafe sat her up, tucking the blankets around her as she leaned against the granite wall. He poured the steaming soup into a tin mug. "Hypothermia. Your body takes a sudden plunge in temperature, and you go into shock. If you're not brought out of it and warmed up slowly, you can die from it." Grimly he turned and settled beside her, taking her back into his arms. "Try and drink this," he urged, holding the tin to her lips.

Jessie never thought tomato soup would ever taste so good. The soup was salty, and she felt it warm her all the way down to her toes. Rafe made a satisfied sound when she finished, and put the empty mug aside.

"Good. Now stay put. I'm going to get a few other supplies from the pack."

Jessie looked around the makeshift shelter. Water dripped a few feet away from the overhang. The valley was oddly silent after the ravage of the thunderstorm. She focused on Rafe, noticing for the first time that he was still wearing wet clothes.

"You've got to be freezing," she protested when he returned.

Rafe crouched in front of her, awkwardly wrapping her thick, heavy hair in a towel. "I'll be okay."

"But—"

"I'll change as soon as I get you taken care of, Jess. Now don't start arguing with me."

She lifted her head, her eyes dangerously bright as she reached out for his hand. "I didn't mean—"

Uncovering her feet, he pulled her legs across his and put heavy wool socks on her. "Dammit, Jess! I'll take care of myself when I'm through with you!" Seeing her wounded look, he said, "I'm not used to this kind of care, Jess." He patted her calf to indicate that he was done.

Dutifully Jessie slid her legs off his. Stung by his oath, she retreated into silence. Her emotions were raw. She was frightened by the near-drowning.

Looking into her withdrawn features, Rafe reached out and framed her face with his hands. "I nearly lost you, Jess. And God help me, I almost died with you when you were out there alone." His voice fell into a low quaver. "You're a part of me, Jess. I found that out the hard way." His fingers tightened against her flesh. "I can't let you go. I won't. Just let me take care of you until I'm satisfied you're past the shock. Okay?"

Scalding tears filled her eyes, but Jessie fought them back. "Okay, Rafe," she whispered hoarsely. "I was just worried for you like you were for me."

He leaned over, pressing a kiss on her pale cheek. "I know that, honey. Don't worry. I'm one tough son-of-a-bitch. I'll survive."

Exhausted from the trauma, she capitulated to his request. "A-all right. May I get dressed into some dry clothes?"

Rafe nodded and eased himself out from beneath the shelter. "While you dress here, I'll go in search of more firewood. Hopefully I'll find some that isn't soaked through. What you need is a steady source of heat right now."

She dressed with trembling and numb fingers. Shrugging into a large, lavender fisherman's knit sweater, Jessie didn't worry about wearing a bra. Rafe had provided her with a set of dry Levi's, and she struggled into them. By the time he came back minutes later with an armload of wood, Jessie had brought the blankets around her and was sitting, watching as he worked. There were no wasted motions to Rafe's economical movements. She marveled at his male grace. The power of her feelings for Rafe lay nakedly before her. Was it possible to fall in love so quickly? Or was the trauma magnifying her feelings? Had death brought her closer to the truth or only enlarged the fantasy?

Miserable, Jessie didn't know. She said little and remained close to the fire. Rafe completed the shelter by putting a tarp over the open side, shielding them from the bulk of the wind and the rain that threatened them again. The shelter was like a tent with a rock roof. The soft quilt of the sleeping bags beneath her, the quiet bubbling of a rich, hearty soup on the campfire joined with the warmth she was beginning to feel to make her sleepy. Without a word, she lay down, her hair still wrapped in the towel. The moment she closed her eyes, she fell fast asleep.

Rafe watched Jessie closely. He had changed his clothes, gotten the horses taken care of for the day, and now sat near her. Over the past two hours, her wan features had come back to their natural tones and he breathed a sigh of relief. He glared out of the shelter at the sky above. The weather mirrored how he felt inside—torn and roiling. Every time he thought of losing Jessie to the river, he got nauseated. He held out his hand. His fingers trembled. That was how badly scared he was. And nothing, except Mary Ann's death, had shaken him to the core like that. He stared down at Jessie long and hard.

Her lips were parted in sleep, and he heatedly recalled their pliancy and sweetness. Her fingers lay softly curled near her head, and her knees were drawn up toward her chest. The word "helpless" crossed his mind. She was truly a babe in the woods to this kind of life. But she was far from helpless. He had watched from the shore, trying to shout instructions to her when he had seen the tree hurtling around the bend of the river. He had seen her courage and her indomitable fighting spirit as she had struggled to live. Rubbing his face, Rafe felt exhaustion pulling at him. Following his instincts, he lay down next to Jessie, bringing her into the safety of his arms.

A low groan emerged from him as in her sleep she automatically nuzzled into his arms. She trusted him. And he cared so damn much for her that it was eating him up alive. Rafe gently removed the towel from her hair, which lay in thick, damp tangles that smelled of river water. But that didn't matter as he tucked her head on his shoulder, his hand resting protectively around her. He could still smell the faint scent of her despite the river odor. Her flesh was warm and supple once again, and he breathed in deeply, giving thanks to a God he had quit believing in two years earlier...

Jessie awoke with a jerk. She sat up, disoriented.

"It's all right."

Her eyes widened, and she turned to see Rafe hunkered over the fire, holding a skillet in his hand. Her heart raced, and she closed her eyes momentarily to let the beat settle back to a normal rhythm. "I dreamed I was drowning."

Rafe couldn't protect himself from the terror in her husky voice, so he avoided her eyes and moved the freshly caught trout around in the butter.

"You'll have a few nightmares over that little escapade," he said more tersely than he'd meant to. For two hours he had held Jessie in his arms, and a hot, forging ache had begun in his lower body, fanning out into a nearly uncontrollable hunger. Compressing his lips, he glanced at her out of the corner of his eye. "Hungry?"

"Yes," she answered as she tried to comb her fingers through her hair. She watched as Rafe piled her plate high with steaming kerneled corn, two batter-fried trout and thick slices of pan bread. With a grateful smile, she took the plate from him.

"I think I can eat all of this," she admitted wryly, and then she laughed. "Me, who used to eat like a bird back in my office in D.C."

"Mountain air always makes you hungry. Chances are, you'll lose weight and never gain an ounce on the trail." Rafe settled opposite her, his plate piled as high as hers. The day was dying around them, and the skies were now clear of the marauding thunderclouds from earlier. Only the gray silhouette of the forest surrounding them remained. Firelight danced off Jessie's delicate features and seemed to lick her hair on fire. Thinking of how he had run his finger through it, he lowered his eyes and tried to force his attention to his food.

Jessie relaxed as Rafe did. Perhaps he was just as hungry as she was, which would account for his mood. The flaky white trout melted in her mouth, and she closed her eyes, making a sound of utter pleasure.

"Rafe Kincaid, you are the best cook in the world! This trout is delicious." She smiled over at him. "You'd put the chefs of D.C. to shame with this meal."

A slight smile tugged at his mouth. "Starved people always have kind words for the cook."

Her laughter was clear and melodic. "Another of your pragmatic cowboy insights about people in general?"

"Yeah." Rafe nodded, melting beneath her laughter. Longing fanned through him like a fire igniting. Did Jessie remember him holding her during those precious two hours? He'd never forget them. Scowling, he bent his head.

Darkness stained the dusk, and Jessie found herself pleasantly tired after the meal. The firelight danced on Rafe's harsh features as he collected all the utensils. She reached out, her hand covering his.

"Let me clean them."

Her touch was electric, unexpected. Rafe savored the feel of her warm fingertips barely brushing the back of his hand. "Not tonight, Jessie. You've been through a lot today. I just want you to sit back and rest."

"But—"

He raised his head, his eyes dark and commanding. "You're not a quitter, I'll give you that. But you don't have a lick of sense."

Jessie removed her hand. "I tried," she said lamely.

Walking outside their shelter, he said, "A mustang that's pulled a leg muscle doesn't take off at a run, either. Just remember that." Then he was swallowed up by the night.

With a sigh, Jessie leaned back against the granite. "You want everyone to think you're such an ogre, Rafe Kincaid. Well, you don't fool me." All she wanted to do at that moment was throw her arms around his powerful shoulders and thank him for saving her life. But he wasn't going to have any of that, Jessie realized. If she didn't know better, Rafe was shy when it came to making himself the center of attention and that endeared him even more to her.

A few minutes later, Rafe threw another log on the fire and settled back near Jessie. He took off his damp cowboy hat and ran his fingers through his thick black hair. Jessie had found a mirror, comb and brush and was intent on working the nest of snarls from her hair. He saw her wince a couple of times, and her full lips were pursed as she ruthlessly attacked the tangles.

"Drat!"

"Huh?"

Jessie let her hands fall into her crossed legs. "Oh, I got a terrible tangle at the back of my head."

"'Drat'? Is that a word?"

She gave him as evil a look as possible. "Don't go teasing me right now, Rafe—I'm in an ugly mood."

"Drat," he murmured, his mouth curving upward. "Must be a fancy Easterner's word, eh?"

"Do you enjoy teasing someone when they're down and out?"

"Want me to see if I can't undo the snarl before you rip out all that pretty hair of yours?" Rafe swallowed his own surprise at his request.

Jessie quickly got to her knees. "Would you? My arms are so tired! Here." She eagerly gave him the comb and brush.

With a shrug Rafe motioned for her to sit down between his legs. Without hesitation, Jessie did as he instructed, her back and the long cascade of her beautiful golden hair to him. Rafe swallowed hard, already feeling his body beginning to throb with her closeness.

"Sit still, you're squirming," he ordered, locating the snarl.

"I am sitting still!"

"You're like a little child sometimes," he groused, gently working out the knot in her silky hair.

"Then you're a sulky little boy," Jessie shot back. Each time he touched her hair, she felt a flickering heat move through her, making her warm and wildly aware of her femininity.

"Me? A sulky little boy?"

Jessie twisted around. "Read my lips. You're a sulky little boy, Rafe Kincaid, when you get upset."

He stared at her, thinking how proud and petulant she looked in that moment. "You know what sulky little boys do with spoiled little girls?" he rumbled warningly.

A reckless smile crossed her mouth, and she held his cobalt-blue eyes, which blazed with a dangerous flame. "I know what an Eastern boy would do," she goaded throatily. "What do Western boys do?"

In one swift, single motion, Rafe took her and turned her over his knees so that her rear was well within range of his opened hand. He grinned as she gave an indignant cry and tried to squirm off his lap. "No you don't, wild filly. You pushed too far. Now you can pay the consequences."

Jessie twisted to look at him. "You wouldn't dare!"

"Why not? You wanted to know what a Western man would do with a spitfire like yourself." He raised his hand threateningly.

With a shriek, Jessie twisted and turned. "Don't you dare hit me, Rafe! You have no right!" And then she dissolved into a fit of laughter as she saw him trying to hold back a grin. Without thinking, without analyzing her spontaneous gesture, Jessie turned over and threw her arms around his neck, holding him as tight as she could.

Her breath came in gasps next to his ear as she laid her head on his shoulder. "Thank you…thank you for everything, Rafe. For my life…" She choked with emotion as she felt his arms sliding around her. "For your smile that I never see often enough and—" she stopped to press a chaste kiss on his stubbled jaw "—for sharing your laughter with me. It means so much…"

Rafe groaned as she fit herself against his hard contours. He murmured her name, his voice thick as he eased her from him. Tunneling his fingers through her glorious mane of hair, he framed her face, drowning in her warm sable eyes. He saw the invitation in them; saw her parted lips begging him to kiss her. He couldn't help himself. After two long, desolate years without the feel of a loving woman in his arms, his logic was trampled beneath other, more powerful needs. He might be tough and abrasive, but he had a heart that felt, that needed, and he knew nothing more than that as Jessie's fingers caressed his face.

Jessie quivered as she read the naked hunger on his face as he drew her against him, guiding her mouth toward his. Anticipation sang through her as she felt him mold his mouth possessively against her own, stealing her breath, filling her with his fire, his desire. Uttering a small moan of pleasure, she sank against him, wanting nothing more than to share the joy of being alive.

His rough, callused hands slid beneath the loose folds of her sweater, outlining her slender rib cage, finding and cupping her firm breasts. A gasp tore from Jessie and languor made her weak as he teased the taut, hard nipples. She thrashed her head against his shoulder as she felt a torrent of hunger so sharp and fierce that she was helpless beneath its onslaught.

"Lie here with me," he told her, his voice unsteady.

Jessie barely opened her eyes as she was gently lowered to the sleeping bag. Rafe was outlined above her, dancing shadows from the fire highlighting and emphasizing the unpolished angles of his face. She saw his desire for her, and a flame of unbelievable tenderness deep in his hooded eyes. In one motion she slipped the sweater over her head, and Rafe put it aside. Her entire body tingled as he stared down at her, the hard line of his mouth softening.

"You're perfect," he whispered, lightly caressing her breast, then following the curve of her rib cage down to her waist. "My God, you're so small…" He splayed his hand across the white expanse of flesh.

Jessie placed her hand over his. Light against dark. In that exquisite moment, she wished, as never before, that she could have children. Four years, her mind echoed to her pounding heart. For four years she had avoided men because she could only be half a woman to them. She could have been a bed partner and that was all. She could never bear children or be part of a family. Tears glittered in her eyes. From deep within her came the knowledge that Rafe was the man she had been waiting a lifetime for. Jessie didn't question her heart's knowing.

"Somehow, we bring out the worst and best in each other," she said, sliding her fingers over his hand. "We can make each other laugh again, Rafe, and that's so precious. I love your smile—your whole face changes, and I can see the gentle man underneath." Jessie shut her eyes, taking a deep, ragged breath. "Today I realized something. I realized each day, each hour is important. I could die tomorrow and never know your touch." Jessie opened her eyes and stared up at him, her throat constricting. "I want to be yours if you want me…"

Rafe bowed his head, shutting his eyes tightly against the sudden deluge of emotion pouring through him. "Want you?" he said, his voice was unsteady. He opened his eyes and saw the fear of rejection in hers, as well as the fire of her longing. He leaned down, barely touching her lips. "Let me show you how much I want you."

She sighed, her fears dissolving beneath the aching tenderness of his kiss. This was the man hiding behind the armor. This was the man she loved. Jessie arched instinctively against Rafe as he drew her aching nipple into the warmth of his mouth. A cry of pleasure tore from her, and she became mindless as he showed her how much he wanted her. When his fingers opened her jeans, sliding downward, she sobbed his name as he caressed her. Rafe murmured her name as he eased the last of the clothes from her. She was naked in the firelight, the shadows dancing over each hollow and curve as she lay beneath his hungry inspection.

Rafe saw the languor in her eyes as he took off his shirt, jeans and boots. He felt powerful and protective at the same time, as he came to lay at her side and take her back into his arms. For a brief second, he thought about protection for Jessie, but then recalled just as poignantly that she could never have children. As he buried his face against her breasts sadness overwhelmed him. If anyone deserved children, it was Jessie. Releasing a sigh, he ran his hand across her back and thighs.

"You're so small… I can hurt you," he muttered.

Jessie laughed softly, running her hands across the thickly bunched muscles of his shoulders and back, content to have him hold her. This was what she wanted; the intimacy, the caring that she had instinctively known that Rafe was capable of and yet unable to share with anyone. Until now. Despite her hunger to have him, she waited patiently, savoring each word he spoke, each caress he gave her.

"I don't think that's anything you have to worry about."

He smiled, holding her tightly to him, his skin burning wherever she was pressed against him. "I never want to hurt you or make you cry, honey. You're built like a Thoroughbred with these beautiful, long limbs." He ran his hand over the curve of her thigh. "And like a Thoroughbred, you're strong in some ways and so damn fragile in others." He lifted his head, melting beneath her smile.

"And I've got the stamina and heart of a Thoroughbred," she reminded him tartly.

He leaned over, caressing her lips, feeling her yielding pliancy. "You have the heart," he murmured against her. "You're all heart…"

"And I'm yours, Rafe," she sighed, moving against him, taunting him beyond whatever barrier had made him hesitate with her. "I need you," she whispered softly, "more than I've ever needed anyone…"

Jessie felt him shudder as his hands tightened against her possessively. He was on the verge of losing what little control he had. He knelt before her, his hands on her hips, and leaned down, his tongue relishing each of her nipples. A moan escaped her, and her fingers dug into his forearms. She had almost expected him to take her fiercely. Instead, Rafe was worshiping her, pleasing her, bringing her to such a level of need that she twisted and moved mindlessly beneath his hands. Her breath came in gasps, and a sheen of perspiration made her body glisten in the firelight.

"Easy, Jess," he breathed harshly against her ear, lifting her hips, "easy… I don't want to hurt you."

With a little cry, Jessie clung to him, barely able to stand the ache that was building to a painful intensity. Rafe was trembling; sweat beaded across his brow as he gently brought her to him. A sob tore from her, and she arched her body, wanting, needing more of him; her fingers grasped his taut shoulder muscles. Jessie was beyond speaking; beyond reasoning. Four years without a man left her helpless in Rafe's embrace.

A groan shook Rafe as he slowly entered her slender body. Sweat stood out on his face, and he clung to the last of his control. He wanted to plunge into her; take her as savagely as he felt, but he knew better. His instincts cautioned him to go slowly, and he savored each second. Her breasts rose and fell sharply, and both their breathing was ragged. Rafe buried his head against her thick, silky hair, inhaling her wonderful womanly scent. And when he heard a sound of frustration from Jessie and felt her arch her hips, taking him deeply within her, his world exploded around him.

Slowly he twisted his hips, first one way and then another. A soft sigh escaped her parted, well-kissed lips and told him everything. He wanted to give to Jessie: give back all the beauty, the laughter and the sharing she had given him. Rafe brought her into rhythm with himself, keeping a chain on his own hunger. This time, he thought in a haze of exquisite heat, this time is for you, Jessie. And he gave to her as he had never given to another woman, and in return, she gave him the gift of herself. Only then did he thrust deep into her and gave the ultimate gift to her: himself.

Pleasure filled Jessie, and she met his thrusts as wave after wave of heat throbbed through her. Each powerful movement of his taut body carried her higher and higher. The ache in her exploded into a shower of spun rainbow colors, and Jessie cried out, burying her face against Rafe's corded neck, drowning in an incredible fire that hungrily consumed her. Languor flooded her, and she found it almost impossible to move. She heard Rafe growl her name while his arms tightened possessively around her, and she reveled in his completion.

Weak beyond belief, Jessie sighed his name, pressing her lips to his temple, tasting the salt of his flesh. His mouth caressed her brow, cheek and finally, met and slid across her lips. They kissed deeply, with a hunger not born out of physical needs this time, but out of their shared tenderness.

Reluctantly, Rafe rolled off her and covered her with the blanket. He saw the drowsy fulfillment in Jessie's wistful smile and in her eyes as she looked up at him. He smiled and brushed away the sheen of perspiration from her brow with his thumb. There was no need to ask if she enjoyed him or what they shared. Jessie simply radiated joy through the flush in her cheeks, through her touch as she ran her fingers up his arm, and in the reflection of happiness in her gaze.

Rafe lay next to her, holding her, never wanting to let her go. He nuzzled his face into her hair.

"You smell so good," he said thickly, "like a field of wildflowers. I can smell the pine in your hair and your sandalwood scent." He licked a drop of perspiration from her temple. "You're so damned giving and warm."

Touched by Rafe's love, his halting words, she could say nothing. Pressing a kiss on his jaw, she smiled softly. The night embraced them in pitch-blackness, and the roar of the river continued unabated. She felt light and incredibly drained; but it was a good feeling. At first, her words came out hesitantly.

"I always thought a man took for himself when he made love to a woman, Rafe." She ran her fingers up his arm and came to rest on his shoulder. "Either my former husband sold me a bill of goods, or I'm naive."

There was amusement in Rafe's tone, but he wasn't laughing at her. Running his fingers through her hair, he said, "Why didn't you tell me, Jessie?"

She looked up at him. "What?"

Rafe stared down at her for a moment, looking deep into her confused eyes. "You haven't been with a man in a long time, have you?"

A hot flush stained her cheeks, and Jessie lowered her lashes. "No," she began a little defensively.

"Why? Morals?"

She shook her head. "No..."

"What, then? Come on, look at me."

Hesitantly she opened her eyes and looked up at Rafe. Her throat closed with tears. "By the time I left my marriage, I believed I wasn't worth much of anything, Rafe. My ex-husband made me think that I was half a woman and not a whole one."

"Why the hell did he say that?" Rafe exploded.

"B-because I couldn't give him children. He said all I was good for was as a bed warmer for a man who wanted a one night stand. That was all I was worth." Her mouth trembled. "I—I didn't want to become a toy in some man's life, Rafe. I couldn't bear that. If I couldn't have a long-term relationship, I didn't want the alternative…"

Rafe gruffly pulled Jessie back into his arms and tucked the sleeping bag around her. That bastard of an ex-husband of hers had hurt her as much as Dal's ex-husband had; and in just as cruel a way. He gently pushed the strands of hair from her cheek and cradled her close.

"Listen and listen good, Jessie. There are men who would value you as a wife regardless of whether you're able to bear children or not. Surely you must know that."

Her eyes were awash with tears, and she bit down on her trembling lower lip. "Tom brainwashed me into believing that if I couldn't be a broodmare and produce heirs, I was nothing." Jessie took a deep breath. "I finally figured it out two years ago and started dating again." Her voice turned bleak. "But all they wanted to do was paw me and get me into bed on the first date. I guess I couldn't take it. I guess it confirmed what Tom had told me in the first place about myself. Maud always said that the right man would come along at the right time and not to worry about it. So, I buried myself in my work instead."

Rafe felt rage move through him over her ex-husband's selfish motives. "He only wanted to strike out and hurt you, Jessie. Do you understand that?"

"Yes."

He snorted softly. "I'm just like him. I strike out at you in anger, too."

Jessie's gaze flew upward. "You're nothing like him, Rafe! You were so tender and gentle with me. Tom never was. He never gave me the pleasure you have. I mean, I never realized how wonderful it could be—making love."

The ache in his chest spread as he stared down at Jessie. He could tell she was untutored when he had loved her, but that only endeared her even more to him. Rafe shook his head. He could teach her so much about herself and about him through the silent art of touch. "Come on, my proud, beautiful Thoroughbred," he said. "Let's catch some sleep. We've earned it."

She came into his arms, comforted by the feel of his naked flesh against hers. A little sigh escaped from her as she nestled into Rafe's protective embrace. Sleep claimed her gently as Rafe's moist breath flowed across her cheek. She'd never been happier.

Chapter 7

The bugling cry of a furious stallion startled Jessie out of her deep sleep. Before she could open her eyes or even move, she felt Rafe jerk into a sitting position. The cool morning air hit her as she sat up.

"Damn!" Rafe said, getting to his feet, going for his clothes.

"What?" Jessie asked, rubbing her sleep-ridden eyes. She twisted her head as another bugling sound echoed off the walls of the narrow valley. Her eyes widened. There, no more than three hundred yards from their camp, were two stallions warily approaching each other.

"Jessie, get dressed," Rafe ordered tightly, throwing on his boots. He saw the three geldings, all hobbled, moving back toward the camp from where they had been eating grass earlier. What a hell of a way to get woken up, he thought, sliding the rifle from its case on the saddle.

"Rafe!"

He twisted his head. Jessie's eyes were like saucers as she struggled into her jeans. "Stay there. I'm going to get our horses," he ordered.

Her attention was riveted on the wild stallions that were approaching each other. One was a medicine hat, chestnut and white, the other a big, rangy sorrel. Her heart thudding heavily in her chest, she sat down and pulled on her dry socks and boots. Beyond the two studs was a band of five mares in the distance. Rafe was carrying a rifle. Would he shoot the stallions?

Rafe watched the two studs circling and pawing at each other. At any moment they would begin fighting. He angled off to the left, toward where the geldings were trying to flee with no success, since the hobbles only allowed them to take small, mincing steps. Gripping the halter leads in his left hand, he broke into a jog. He had to catch the geldings before one of the stallions became the victor and tried to add them to his herd.

Pulling on her jacket, Jessie called to Rafe, but because of the river and the screeching stallions, he didn't hear her. She leapt to her feet, running to catch up with him to help him capture their horses. Judging from the way the geldings were frantically trying to escape, he'd need her assistance. Just as she reached Rafe, the fight ensued.

Sheer, icy terror moved up her spine as she spun around, hearing the sickening clash and squeals of rage. Jessie heard Rafe curse and then felt his fingers grip her arm.

"I told you to stay back at camp," he whispered angrily, all the while watching the stallions. "Those studs are dangerous, Jessie."

"Let me help, Rafe," she gasped. "I don't want to lose our horses, either."

Disgruntled that she hadn't obeyed his order, Rafe released her and motioned her to move ahead of him. The valley echoed with the screams of the stallions. "Grab your gelding," he said, handing her a halter lead.

Her fingers trembled badly as she managed to catch Fred and snap the lead onto the nylon halter. Jessie saw the gelding's ears move nervously back and forth, and the whites of his eyes gleamed brightly. Anxiously she looked back at Rafe, who had caught the other two horses. He leaned down, releasing the hobbles, and Jessie followed suit. Just as she unbuckled the one that freed the horse's front legs, she heard Rafe give a shout, but it was too late.

The gelding jerked upward, spinning around in a half circle. Her shoulders felt as though they'd been yanked out of their sockets, and Jessie hung on as the horse dragged her off her feet and pulled her through the wet grass. She hadn't worn her deerskin gloves as Rafe had. The nylon lead sizzled through her hands, burning them. She hung on, realizing that if she let go, they'd lose the gelding to the wilds. After dragging her up the hill, the gelding finally stopped, quivering. Jessie slowly got to her feet, crooning softly to the terrified animal.

Rafe reached her just as she managed to put her hand on the animal. His blue eyes were black with anger and concern as he wrapped his hand around the horse's halter.

"You all right?" he breathed harshly.

"I—I think so." Jessie hid her hands at her sides. "I didn't realize the gelding would try to run off," she added lamely.

Rafe knelt down, placing the hobbles back on the gelding. "Wouldn't you? Those two studs are tearing the hell out of each other." He rose, his mouth grim. "That bastard of a medicine hat has three of my Arabian mares," he said, pointing to the horses eating contentedly in the distance.

Jessie was more concerned with the actual fight. "Rafe, isn't there something you can do to stop it? Look at that sorrel, he's got chunks torn out of his mane and neck. My God..." She had heard of stallions fighting among themselves, but had never thought to witness it firsthand. Although the medicine hat was more compact and much smaller than the rangy sorrel, he was faster. His teeth were bared as he hurtled into the sorrel. Grabbing the sorrel by the mane, the stallion shook him savagely, throwing the other horse to the ground. Instantly the medicine hat wheeled around, screaming. He sank his hooves deeply into the ribs of the flailing sorrel, who was desperately trying to lurch back to his feet.

Jessie cried out, taking a step forward.

"Hold it," Rafe said, "where do you think you're going?"

"But—he's killing him, Rafe!"

"There's nothing you can do."

They were too beautiful to die, Jessie thought in anguish. The sorrel managed to stand, wheeling and planting both hind feet into the charging medicine hat. A huge gash opened up across the chest of the stud, momentarily making him back off and regroup. Jessie turned to Rafe.

"Please, stop them! Can't you do something?"

Rafe kept his hand on her arm. Knowing her the way he did, she'd probably try to run between the horses to break up the fight. "There's nothing that can be done," he ground out.

"Fire your rifle! That will scare them into quitting!" she cried.

"Dammit, they're liable to take more interest in us if I do that. Do you want that, Jessie? You see what they're doing to each other. Think what they can do to us. If I fire this rifle and draw their attention, I'm not going to let them charge us. I'll kill them first. Is that what you want?" His nostrils flared as he saw huge tears well up in her eyes. "Let nature run its course."

Jessie sobbed, watching as the injured stallions slowly circled each other like wary wolves. The sorrel was badly wounded, with blood running and dripping off his neck, and hunks of mane and flesh torn out of him. He limped badly, and the right side of his ribs looked as though they had been caved in with a huge mallet. In that moment, Jessie turned her frustration on Rafe. "There's got to be a way to break it up!"

"There isn't. Now stand still. You aren't going to run down there like Joan of Arc and try to save those two brutes from each other." His eyes flashed with anger. "Take a good look, Jessie; this is real life. Nature at work. One of those two studs will come out the victor. The other will die. That sorrel's too old and too stubborn to quit. He could have run after the medicine hat bested him, but he didn't. There's nothing you or I could do. We can't afford to have either of them turn on us. Do you understand?"

She didn't want to understand as she stood there, watching as the sorrel was finally knocked to the muddy earth. Tears scalded her eyes as she saw the medicine hat squeal in rage, rear upward, then come down. The sickening thud of hoofs smashing into the beleaguered sorrel was more than she could endure, and she turned away. The crunch of bones being broken made Jessie cover her ears in an effort to blot out the screams and the dying cries of the sorrel stallion.

The valley quieted once again. She heard the medicine hat bugle triumphantly, and she turned in time to see the stud cantering toward his herd of mares. The sorrel lay still in an area of mud and torn grass, barely hanging on to what little life was still in him. She ached for the loss of the valiant stallion who refused to bow. Tears fell down her smudged and dirty cheeks.

Rafe glanced down at her, his heart wrenching. "Come on," he said, picking up the halter leads to the horses, "it's time to go."

She was angry at Rafe for not intervening somehow. When he leaned down to release the hobbles on the horses, she took the lead to Fred and headed back to camp without a word. Her hands smarted from being burned, but the pain she felt in her heart far outweighed that of her hands. There had to be a way of breaking up that fight! There just had to be! Jessie watched as the medicine hat circled his band of mares, nipping savagely at their rumps and pushing them into a trot down the valley.

Rafe tied his two horses to a low-hanging pine limb and loaded the rifle. He glanced over at Jessie, and then grimly walked down the slope to the mustang stud. Rafe winced inwardly as he gazed at the stud, who bared his yellowed teeth as he approached him. As he lifted the rifle, aiming it at the sorrel's bloodied forehead, Rafe knew Jessie would hate him. He squeezed the trigger; the sorrel dropped with a final groan. Rafe stood there, feeling the bitterness in his mouth as he stared at the mustang. The stubborn old bastard deserved to die without any more suffering. He turned away, his gaze pinned on Jessie as she stood frozen, her eyes huge, her hands across her mouth. She wouldn't understand and he knew it.

Jessie did everything she could to avoid being around Rafe. While he saddled and bridled the horses, she noted the pertinent information on the mustangs in her journal. The sun was shining brightly, peeking over the crowns of the trees as she finished wrapping up their bedrolls. The sky was an intense blue, and she squinted until she put her wide-brimmed cowboy hat on to shade her eyes. From time to time, she felt Rafe's burning gaze on her, and she tried to ignore that silent communication that was still strung between them.

Her hands shook as she wrapped up the cooking utensils after washing them off in the river. The warmth of the sun felt good on her because she was still damp and miserable from being dragged through the dew-soaked meadow earlier. The inner rage she felt overcame her mild discomforts, and doggedly Jessie carried the parcel over to Rafe.

He glanced down at her as she handed him the neatly packed utensils. Her mouth was set, and her eyes were huge with silent recrimination. Rafe took the bundle, placing it in the supplies that were anchored to the horse. And then he saw her hands.

"Jessie!" He gripped her arm, pulling her back to him. Rafe felt her tense and try to pull away. "Wait."

"What is it?"

"Your hands. What happened to them?" He turned one of her slender white hands over, examining it. He frowned when he saw the burns across her palm.

"It's nothing."

"Yes," he said patiently, "it is." He pulled the first-aid kit from the pack. "Come on over to the rock. I want to clean those out, or you'll get an infection."

Jessie could barely tolerate Rafe's gentle touch as he ministered to her hands. She had expected him to be angry at her; instead, he was concerned and patient. As she sat there, her hand resting on his bent knee, an ache rose in her chest. The night had been so beautiful, like a dream. This morning, harsh reality had woken them up. She risked a look up at Rafe. All of his concentration was on the task of cleaning her wounds.

His deep voice broke through her inner turmoil. "I know you're angry at me, Jessie. What you just witnessed usually isn't seen by anyone except a handful of ranchers. Stallions fighting is serious business." He glanced over at her. "And it can be deadly." Completing the wrapping on her hands, he straightened up. "Death isn't something anyone should witness," he said, then rose and went back to the packhorse.

Rafe's last words had been torn from him in anguish, and Jessie winced. She sat there for a moment, digesting what he had said. Then, getting to her feet, she put on her thin deerskin gloves and walked toward the saddled horses. It was time to move on and try to locate some of the other mustang herds.

By noon they were well out of the narrow valley and moving along another ridge. A larger, far more beautiful valley sat in the distance, and Jessie wondered if another stallion "owned" it along with his small herd of mares. Despite the unexpected storm of the previous day, the weather was turning mild. Everywhere she looked, wildflowers were in bloom. Despite the panoramic beauty, Jessie could only think of Rafe and their shared night. Did she regret it? No, never. He had made her feel more alive, more cherished and wanted than she had ever felt. Was this real love or infatuation? She wished Maud were still alive; she would have someone to confide in and to help her understand. Glancing up, Jessie stared at Rafe's powerful back and broad shoulders. Sadness overwhelmed her as she realized he hadn't mentioned their lovemaking. More than anything, she wanted to share her insights, discoveries and worries with him.

A few hours later, Rafe crouched by the camp fire, watching Jessie as she picked at the plate of food he'd just prepared for their noon meal. Something was bothering her. Was it last night or this morning's fiasco with the two studs? He wanted nothing more than to sit on the log and join her, but he was so damned poor at talking and getting out what really mattered. Now, as never before, he felt the frustration of his own shortcomings. Mary Ann had always accepted his moody silence; she'd seemed to be able to know intuitively what he wanted or needed. She'd been a quiet woman, unlike Jessie, who chattered in comparison.

With a frown, Rafe put the coffeepot over the fire to let the water begin to boil. In all fairness to Jessie, she really didn't chatter. No, he enjoyed her vulnerability and wished for a shred of her ability to communicate. Jessie always seemed to have the right words to go along with her touch. He felt his body hardening in want of her again; a sweet fire spread through him, like the welcoming warmth of the sun after enduring a frigid winter. He mulled over what he should say to her to try to break the stiltedness that had grown between them. Risking a glance, he saw Jessie staring pensively away from him.

Throwing a small handful of ground coffee into the boiling water, he brushed his hands clean. "You want coffee, Jessie?"

She tensed, as if unexpectedly assaulted by him. Licking her lower lip, she nodded. "Please."

"It'll be ready in a few minutes." Rafe tipped the hat back on his head, studying her. "You're being awfully quiet."

She shrugged.

"I'm supposed to be the quiet one of the two of us."

Jessie lifted her head, meeting his dark, searching gaze. She felt a gnawing guilt, realizing he was desperately trying to communicate with her.

"I have my quiet moments, too," she said, keeping the defensiveness out of her voice.

"My sister Cat is like that. Sometimes she's like a broody hen sitting on a clutch of eggs. Step on her the wrong way, and she goes off like a roman candle. I never did know what made her moody like that." He frowned and stared down at the pot over the fire. "Still don't."

"Is that how I seem to you? A broody hen?"

Amusement lingered in Rafe's blue eyes. "I tend to put all women under that label when they're doing something I don't understand or can't explain, I guess."

A sliver of a smile tugged at Jessie's lips, and she hung her head. "And you never show your emotions, right? You just ignore them. Who taught you that?"

"No one."

"Your father, maybe? Was he the quiet, silent type, too?"

"Dad? Yeah, if we got ten words out of him in the same breath, we considered that a real speech coming from him." Rafe managed a bashful smile, relieved that the anger had diminished in her eyes.

Jessie stood and got the tin cups, bringing them over to Rafe so that he could pour the coffee. "Did your sisters follow your dad's silent treatment, too?"

"No. Dal and Cat both are sticks of dynamite with a short fuse."

She handed him one cup and then walked back over to the log, sitting down across from where he was crouched. "How do you see me then, Rafe? Do I fall into the broody hen category or the stick of dynamite?"

Taking a sip of the hot, dark liquid, Rafe eased himself to the ground and sat cross-legged. Maybe trying to talk to Jessie was going to be easier than he thought. "Neither."

"What then?"

"You're a simple woman."

"And you're anything but a simple man, Rafe."

He shrugged, blowing across the scalding coffee to cool it. "I don't see myself that way. I'm pretty black and white, Jessie."

"You're pretty complicated to me because you either can't or won't tell me what's going on inside you, Rafe. That leaves me having to guess where you're at all the time." Jessie opened one hand in a gesture of conciliation. "Right now we're sharing, and I need that."

"I can't read your mind, either, Jessie."

"What do you want to know?"

"If you're still angry over this morning's events."

Smoothing her hand over her hair, she said, "I'm frustrated, Rafe."

"Because of last night? Or the stud fight?"

Jessie smiled tenderly. "Last night was beautiful… unexpected. A gift…"

Rafe felt her voice move through him, stirring him,

making his heart swell. Relieved, he nodded. "Then you're upset over the studs fighting?"

She gripped the hot mug. "I'm upset because nothing could be done to stop them, Rafe."

"Jessie, you ever seen a stallion turn on a domesticated horse and his rider?"

"No."

"You've been working with a lot of ranches who deal with mustangs. Ever hear any stories on it happening?"

She shook her head. "No."

Rafe gave her an intense look, and his voice became low with fervor. "I wish like hell there was something I could have done this morning. I don't like taking the blame for this, Jessie. The smartest thing we could have done was to stay out of the way. But a stud has only three things on his mind: keeping his territory, keeping his band and perpetuating the species. Anything or anyone who gets in the way of doing any one of those three things is asking for more trouble than they ever bargained for. Ask Pinto Pete when we get back for some stories from his wrangling days." He settled the hat more firmly on his coal black hair.

"I didn't like seeing that stud go down any more than you did, Jessie. But the only humane thing I could do was put him out of his misery. He might have got back up after that medicine hat left, but you could bet a year's pay that the wolves would have him as a meal by nightfall. It's not a pleasant way to die, and frankly, the stud didn't deserve that kind of death. In his own way, he was heroic."

Rafe lifted his arm, pointing toward the valley. "You're not in the city anymore, Jessie. Out here, everything lives or dies according to nature—not man. It's a world for survivors, not weaklings."

The coffee tasted bitter, or maybe it was her response to Rafe's explanations. "I can't stand to see animals or people hurt," she whispered tightly. "There's enough pain in this world, Rafe. If you could have fired off a shot from your rifle and made them separate, then there might not have been one of them killed."

Anger flashed ominously in his eyes, and he slowly rose, tossing the rest of the coffee on the fire. The fire hissed violently, steam twisting and rising in the wake. "Don't live your life on ifs, Jessie," he warned darkly. "Ranching isn't a 'what if' proposition. It's black or white. Life or death. Nothing in-between. Come on, I want to make that valley by nightfall. There ought to be a good chance we'll see some mustangs." *Damn her!* No matter how patient he had been or how thoroughly he tried to explain the situation, she wasn't going to accept it. Shaking his head, Rafe moved back to the horses to tighten their cinches. Why did Jessie have to be such an idealist? A dreamer?

The lush carpet of buffalo grass spread before them as they walked their tired horses through the newly sprouted growth. Jessie moved stiffly in her saddle, glad that it was almost time to stop for the day. The afternoon had been spent in abject silence. Except for spotting a black stallion with two mares at the northern end of the valley earlier, they had seen nothing else. Her heart wasn't on her work; it was on Rafe. Rubbing her forehead to will away a pending headache, Jessie closed her eyes.

"You okay?" Rafe rode up beside her, his leg briefly touching hers.

Jessie forced a smile. "Fine. I'm just tired, that's all."

Rafe pointed to three pines near a small stream. "Let's make camp over there. You find the aspirin, and I'll get the camp set up."

Nodding in agreement, she moved her horse toward the indicated spot. Her emotions were all mixed up in a vortex that could only be called love. Desperation interwove with hope as Jessie dismounted. One moment she was lifted onto such an exquisite plane of joy, and the next she tumbled into a hopeless abyss. Rafe hadn't mentioned the past night aside from his one question. Had it really meant anything to him? Did he expect her to bed down with him tonight? She gnawed on her lower lip, unsure of what to do or say.

The stars were brilliant gems studding the ebony heavens. The camp fire crackled pleasantly. Jessie lay on her side with her sleeping bag beneath her as she finished off the last bit of pan bread Rafe had shared with her. She nibbled on it, not tasting it.

"You didn't eat much," Rafe observed, putting the skillet aside and sitting down opposite her. All evening Jessie had been quiet, and it bothered him. She'd barely eaten enough to keep a bird alive. "Still have that headache?"

"No, it's gone. I guess I'm wrung out from everything."

"Why don't you hit the sack? I'll finish the cleanup tonight."

Her heart sank, and she avoided his dark stare. Why had she let herself believe that she meant more to Rafe than a night in bed? Swallowing her disappointment, Jessie got up and pulled her boots off. "That's a good idea," she murmured, "I think I will. Good night."

He slowly got to his feet, his brow furrowed. "Good

night, Jessie." His mouth twitched, and he went about cleaning the utensils. The night was chilly, and his breath came out in white wisps as he walked out of the circle of firelight to go check on the horses. He rubbed his chest, wanting to somehow remove that odd pain that lay there. Jessie... God, how he wanted her again. Last night had been a fluke brought about by dire circumstances. He couldn't just bull his way into her bed and sleep with her again.

There were no easy answers about himself and Jessie, Rafe decided later. He lay under the bough of pine, staring up at the shimmering stars overhead. The fire popped and crackled. Once he looked across it to check on Jessie—she was sleeping deeply. Her lips were parted in invitation, and Rafe groaned to himself, remembering their velvet warmth. Even her scent lingered around him, and he inhaled deeply, wishing he could bury his face in her waterfall of blond hair as he'd done the previous night.

How was he going to keep his hands off her for the duration of the trip? Rafe groaned out loud and turned over, his back to the fire. The need to have Jessie in his arms again was almost a physical ache, and he didn't know how to deal with the desire that flowed through him. Without Jessie's sunlit smile, her beautiful sable eyes sparkling with life, he felt desolate. Where was all this going? He could promise her nothing, and yet, he wanted to give her everything. And then he laughed derisively at himself. Who would want a cold, silent rancher who was barely making ends meet? He was one hell of a booby prize, he decided.

On the tenth day, near noon, they both heard gunshots being fired. Rafe pulled his gelding to a stop along the hill they were climbing. With a frown, he held out his hand, signaling Jessie to halt beside him. Two more shots echoed up from the other side of the hill they were on.

"What is that, Rafe?" Jessie turned to him for explanation.

"Somebody's shooting. Probably a thirty-aught-six," he muttered.

Surprise flared in her eyes. "A rifle? There's no hunting season going on now."

Rafe nodded. "I know. Come on, let's go investigate. We're about five miles from Bryce Darley's property now." He didn't want to say anything further. His gut feeling was that Darley's ranch hands were shooting deer on his land and dragging it back to their property. Anger simmered in him, but he said nothing.

The valley was thin and narrow, and it didn't take Rafe long to spot the problem. Jessie saw one mustang dead, lying in a pool of blood, and another one not far away with a wound in her neck. When the injured mare spotted them, she broke into an uneven trot, heading toward the fleeing band of mustangs that were already far above them in the wooded slopes of the hills to the north.

Rafe dismounted by the dead mustang, and Jessie joined him. Her eyes mirrored her worry as she looked about them.

"Who did this?"

Rafe took the knife from his belt and began to dig for the bullet that had killed the mare. "The same person who's trying to blame these killings on me," he muttered.

Jessie turned away as Rafe worked. "This is awful. Who would want to shoot them? I just don't understand it."

Rafe wiped the blade on the grass and sheathed it. He

took a close look at the bullet, his eyes narrowed. "Whoever is doing this knows his weapons. If I don't miss my guess, it looks like it came from a military rifle. Take a look." He dropped the bullet into her gloved hand, and saw her wince and pale. "A high-powered military rifle can punch a hole as big as this at 400 or 500 yards. When it hits the target, the nose expands. It may make a small hole going in, but it'll tear a gaping hole out the other side, killing anything it hits instantly."

"I'll have it analyzed over at the FBI to try to find out what kind of rifle was used."

"Identify the weapon, and you're liable to identify the man who did this." He frowned.

Jessie watched the bay mare that had been wounded in the neck. "What about the other horse?"

"If she got hit with the same type of bullet, she'll bleed to death sooner or later." Rafe's mouth flattened, and he put his arm around her for a moment. "I'm sorry, Jessie."

Mutely she nodded. "I'm going to take some photos, too."

Rafe stood out of the way while Jessie logged in the incident, took photos and then put the bullet into a small plastic bag. He glanced to the northwest, and a cold feeling ran up his spine. Was Darley trying to frame him? Put him under BLM scrutiny so that he could pressure him to sell his land?

"I think I've got everything," she told him.

"All right. Let's mount up. I want to make it to the Triple K border before we have to start our trip back to the ranch."

Jessie mounted. In four days, they'd be back home. Despite her anguish over what she had just witnessed, a sharper pain plunged through her heart. She thought of the Triple K as home—not her apartment in D.C. She glanced at Rafe's hard features, and her stomach knotted. Had making love with him been a dream? He'd not touched her or made a move to show her any more affection since that night. Jessie tried gamely to put what they had shared behind her, but it was impossible. Four days and they'd be home. And then she'd fly back to D.C., out of Rafe's life forever. She knew that if she had more time with Rafe he would gradually open up to her. But neither one of them could afford that precious time.

The rest of the trip was uneventful. They never found carcasses to indicate previously shot horses, but neither of them was surprised. Rafe had explained to her that it would have been surprising if any of the wild scavengers had left anything for them to find.

Their descent back to the Triple K went quicker than the trip out. They passed the time politely, with long silences and some small talk. Rafe continued to teach Jessie about ranching and the outdoors, and her interest seemed to grow.

To Jessie's disappointment, soon they found themselves entering the ranch area. Both Millie and Pinto Pete were on hand to greet them. Pinto took the reins of her horse.

"How was the trip, Miss Jessie?" he asked.

"It went fine, Pete."

"The gelding here looks a little thinner and meaner. You two must have done some riding."

"We did," Rafe said, coming up and handing the reins of his Arab to the older man. He glanced down at Jessie. "Why don't you go on in and take a long, hot bath and relax?"

"That's the best suggestion you've had today," Jessie

said, managing a slight smile. She excused herself, and Millie met her halfway up the walk and threw an arm around her.

"You came back at the right time. Rafe's sister, Dal, and her husband, Jim, are visiting. They'd like to meet you." Millie wrinkled her nose, giving her a merry smile. "I'd visit with them after your bath, however. I've got clean clothes laid out and pressed in your bedroom."

The whirlwind of activity escalated. After a brief introduction to Dal and Jim Tremain, Jessie excused herself. The hot bath pulled out the soreness in her muscles, and as she toweled off, Jessie noticed that her entire body looked leaner and more fit than before. She knew it was from the riding, the fresh air and exercise. Millie had taken out her burgundy slacks, a white blouse and a pale pink angora shell sweater for her to wear. After brushing her newly washed and dried hair until it shone like sunlight, Jessie took a deep breath and walked toward the living room where everyone was gathered.

Rafe was leaning negligently against the entrance to the living room, still in his riding gear, his hat dangling in his left hand. Jessie moved past him, achingly aware of his solid, quiet strength, and risked a glance into the hard planes of his face. For a precious fleeting second she saw Rafe's blue eyes widen and then thaw. She saw desire like a blue flame leap to life in his eyes. Hope sprang up strongly in her. But just as quickly that hope was crushed as Rafe veiled any other reaction to her arrival, and his features became unyielding and silent once again.

Dal Tremain was decidedly pregnant. Jessie immediately warmed to the tall woman, who stood up and gave her a welcoming hug. Surprised and pleased, Jessie almost felt like part of the Kincaid family when Dal made the extra effort to make her feel welcome among them. She extended her hand shyly to Jim Tremain, the regional director for the Department of Interior. She liked him immediately and it was obvious that he and Dal had a wonderfully happy marriage. A bit of envy dashed through Jessie as Jim put his arm around his wife, smiling down at her with tenderness. If only Rafe could open up to her like that...

Millie brought in fresh coffee, freshly baked chocolate-chip cookies and shooed everyone, except Rafe, to the sofa or a chair while she served them.

"Rafe's too dirty to sit down on anything," she muttered, giving him a look that said volumes.

Dal laughed, taking a cookie. And then she decided on a second one. She looked over at Jessie. "I'm eating for two," she explained and gave her husband a teasing look.

"Looks like you're eating for three," Rafe growled. He took a handful of cookies when Millie brought them around to him. "Sure you aren't carrying twins? Does that doctor you're going to know what he's doing?"

Dal pushed several strands of ginger-colored hair from her cheek. "Rafe, I'm due in two months! I should look like a watermelon."

"Or two," her husband added with a smile, moving his hand gently across her swollen belly.

Jessie watched Rafe's expression closely. She saw the terror in his eyes and heard it leak out beneath the gruffness of his voice.

Dal laughed, covering her husband's hand. "I think it's a boy."

"What do you think, Jim?" Jessie asked, sipping her coffee.

"A girl."

"Is that what you want?"

Jim smiled, sliding his arm round his wife, pulling her near. "I don't care which one it is, as long as the baby is healthy and the mother is fine."

"Then you damn well ought to have her at home, Tremain, and not out gallivanting around the countryside this close to her time."

They all looked up in unison at Rafe. Jessie winced inwardly, feeling Rafe's worry and his anxiety for his sister. She stole a glance at Dal and Jim. They understood, judging from their lack of reaction to Rafe's statement.

Rafe looked uneasy, as if he'd just realized how he'd sounded. "Excuse me, I've got to get cleaned up."

Millie frowned as Rafe lumbered down the hall toward his bedroom. She turned to Jim. "Pinto Pete said he wanted to talk to you, Jim. You've got some time before dinner. Why don't you go and see him now?"

"Good idea." Jim rose and glanced at his wife and Jessie. "I'll leave you two ladies to get acquainted."

The living room eased back to a pleasant quiet, with the fire burning brightly in the fireplace giving the room a comfortable glow. Dal grew pensive and looked over at Jessie.

"What's going on?" she asked softly.

Jessie raised her chin. "What do you mean?"

A faint smile touched Dal's face, and her eyes sparkled. "If I don't miss my guess, and I'm pretty good at being on target, I'd say my big brother likes you an awful lot."

Heat stole into Jessie's face. She knew Dal hadn't said it to embarrass her, or out of spite. She warmed to Dal and felt as if they were old friends. "How can you tell?"

With a laugh, Dal said, "He's acting like a cranky old bear."

"I thought he was acting that way because he's worried about your pregnancy."

Dal's brows moved up in surprise. "Did Rafe tell you what happened to his wife and child?" she guessed.

"Yes, he did. I'm afraid I sort of blundered into the story because he was telling me how worried he was for you."

Dal rose, her hand automatically coming to rest on her stomach, as though to protect the baby she carried. A thoughtful expression was on her face as she walked over to the fireplace. "Rafe's never told anyone about Mary Ann." She gave Jessie a probing look. "You've been out there for fourteen days with Rafe?"

"Yes, and I have the saddle sores to prove it."

Dal laughed. "My brother rides roughshod on everyone, so don't feel that he picked on you."

"Beneath that tough exterior, he's basically a kind man," Jessie defended him.

"I was right!" Dal clapped her hands together, delighted. "You do like him. Oh, this is great. Wonderful!"

Jessie stared up at Dal's animated face, feeling none of her joy. "There's nothing between us, Dal."

"Humph! I saw the look on my big brother's face when you came through that entrance."

She had seen it, too, and didn't want to make anything of it because there was nothing to build on it. "He's a man with a shell around him, Dal. You probably know that."

Dal came over and sat close to Jessie, touching her arm. "But he wasn't like that before his wife died, Jessie. Rafe was more open, more approachable. He can become that again—if you give him a chance."

"Me give him a chance? I have—I mean." She floundered, realizing that she had blurted out everything Dal had suspected all along.

Eagerly Dal gripped her hand. "Don't give up, Jessie! This is the first time Rafe's opened up since Mary Ann's passing."

Jessie shook her head miserably. "Rafe really doesn't care for me that much, Dal. Take my word for it."

"Are you serious about him?" she asked softly, holding her gaze.

Jessie felt Dal's fingers squeeze hers. "Yes."

"How serious?"

With a grimace, she said, "Dal, I don't know what's going on. One moment Rafe can be so caring, the next he's impossible. I don't know how to get past those walls he throws up. It's as if he wants to keep me out."

Gripping Jessie's hand firmly, Dal could barely contain her happiness. "Listen to me! If Rafe didn't like you and if you didn't get to him, he wouldn't be flip-flopping like he is. Don't you see? If you didn't affect him, he wouldn't be running hot and cold. I know my brother—he's even worse than he usually is when something gets to him."

Jessie squeezed Dal's hand. "You're good for me. Almost like the sister I never had but wished I did."

"You're so beautiful," Dal whispered, her voice dropping, "and I can see why Rafe would fall in love with you."

Jessie accepted Dal's compliment, though she'd never thought of herself as beautiful at all. "Rafe does nothing but avoid me. Ever since—I mean—" She blushed and avoided the knowing sparkle in Dal's eyes.

"Rafe's like an old, scarred mustang stallion that's too

used to having his freedom, and now you've come along and settled a lariat around him. And whether he likes it or not, you've captured his heart. It's as simple as that. Oh, I'm so happy for both of you! Rafe's been so lonely and sad for too long."

Jessie didn't dare allow Dal's enthusiasm to sway her. "And like a mustang, Dal, your brother needs his freedom. He can't be corralled. He wants everything his way. I know you mean well, but Rafe won't talk. He won't share, Dal." She gave her a pleading look. "If he refuses to talk to me, to bare his feelings and share what he's thinking, it won't work. And as much as I want something to be there for us, it isn't, Dal."

Patting her hand, Dal smiled gently. "Be patient with him, Jessie. Rafe's just got to get used to needing someone again."

"There isn't time," Jessie said in a strained voice. "I have to go back to Washington as soon as I get all the reports and evidence gathered."

"Well, how long will you be here, then?"

"Maybe another three or four days at the most." The thought of going back to a city of steel, glass and concrete sent a shaft of pain through Jessie. Rafe had shown her the beauty and majesty of the mountains. She wanted to see thick-stalked buffalo grass grow, the wildflowers bobbing their heads in a languid breeze and smell the sweetness of fresh air instead.

"And when will you be back, then?"

"My assignment's finished now, Dal. I'll get stuck back in my cubicle at the federal building."

Dal looked disappointed. "I see."

"It's not a very hopeful picture," Jessie agreed.

"Rafe will call. He hates writing letters."

Jessie gave her a wry look. "Rafe won't even talk when I'm here in person. What makes you think he's going to pick up a phone and call me?"

"You're probably right," Dal conceded, her brow wrinkling. "But let me think about this. Jim's good at talking with Rafe on important matters." She patted her hand again. "Don't worry. This isn't as bad as you think."

Chapter 8

"I fed your mouse while you were gone, Jessie," Nick Van der Meer greeted her as she handed him her reports.

"Thanks, Nick."

He brightened considerably. "We missed you! Our 'Mary Sunshine' went West, and we've all pined away for you in your absence." He smiled, lighting his pipe and leaning back in his thickly upholstered leather chair. "How was it?"

Jessie had to put aside her bittersweet memories to stick to the business at hand. The previous day, her last one at the Triple K, had been both painful and wonderful. Although there were still many unspoken thoughts between her and Rafe, they had spent a beautiful day together. "There's no doubt someone is shooting mustangs up on Mr. Kincaid's property, Nick."

"Question is," he murmured, opening her folder with the reports, "who? Did you find out?"

She shook her head. "No. Although, Rafe—I mean, Mr. Kincaid, feels it might be the neighboring rancher." And she went on to explain the shooting that they had heard and showed him the bullet retrieved from the mustang. Nick listened carefully, occasionally puffing on his pipe, a halo of white smoke around his graying head.

"I'll take your report home with me tonight and read over it. Send the bullet over to the FBI lab for analysis. If Kincaid's right about it being from a military rifle, there are two angles to consider."

"What angles?"

"You're aware we've had a lot of survivalist camps living on federal land?"

Jessie's eyes narrowed in thought. That particular group of people often lived and hunted in the wilds. They believed the U.S. was going to topple beneath a Russian attack, so they had moved to the mountains to be free. The only problem was that they were armed and lived, like the military, in fortified camps and trespassed without regard to laws. With federal lands paralleling Rafe's property, and if the bullet did indeed come from a military weapon, Nick's theory could prove valid.

"That's an excellent idea, Nick. When I get the report back from the FBI, let's talk further about it," she agreed.

"Come to my office at nine tomorrow, and we'll discuss your reports." He winked at her. "And welcome back."

Jessie smiled. "Thanks, Nick."

That night she kept busy by cleaning her small tworoom apartment, which was actually the attic of an older home. Jessie didn't want to think of the Triple K, the fireplace in the living room, Rafe's study, or Rafe. She straightened up, dust cloth in hand, and looked around.

A photo of Maud sat on an antique table near her cherry-wood rocker. Jessie walked over, picked up the picture and stared down at it.

What am I going to do, Maud? I love Rafe. And I know he loves me. I saw it in his eyes, the way his voice trembled when he held me yesterday. Oh, God... Jessie bowed her head, holding the picture tightly to her breast. In her mind she could hear Maud say, *Well, you got five minutes to feel sorry for yourself, then you've got to move on!*

A tremulous smile touched Jessie's lips as she raised her head and stared past the ivory panels across the window that overlooked the sparkling red, white and green lights of D.C. Maud was right; she had to go on. Rafe said he would call her. He hadn't said when. And she hadn't asked. Would he ever ask her to come back out to the Triple K? Taking a shaky breath, Jessie gently sat the photo down after dusting off the table. If Rafe did ask her to come back out, she intuitively realized it would be because he had finally settled the ghosts from his past and put them to rest. He would be ready to get on with his life.

Straightening up, Jessie pushed all her doubts and heartache aside, taking Maud's timely advice to heart. She couldn't live in a vacuum, praying for a call from Rafe. No, she'd have to pick up the pieces and move forward as best she could.

Jessie watched the little mouse as he skittered from behind one of the towering file cabinets in her office to retrieve a morsel of cracker she had placed beside it for his lunch. A soft smile touched her mouth as she sat there, her chin resting in her hands, watching him. A knock on the door startled her friend, and he scurried back to the safety of the filing cabinet.

"Jessie?"

It was Nick. She straightened up. "Come on in," she called.

Nick entered, his pipe clenched between his teeth. "What are you doing in here, young lady? It's lunch-time, the sun's shining outside, and you're wasting away inside."

She forced a laugh. "I should ask you the same question."

Nick walked over and placed a thick folder labeled Kincaid in front of her. "I'm getting ready to leave, that's what. I hope you didn't have any plans for the Fourth of July."

Jessie shrugged, staring at the file. Over two months had passed since she had last worked on the Triple K investigation. She was just beginning to get over some of the pain of Rafe never contacting her. She frowned. "Nick, what's this? I thought you and Mr. Humphries were satisfied that Rafe Kincaid was innocent of killing those mustangs."

The bullet she had brought back with her had proved to be from a military weapon known as an Armalite AR-18. Nick had concluded that the killer of mustangs was probably a survivalist who lived in the mountains, and hunted for food. Bryce Darley, owner of the spread next to Rafe's, denied owning an AR-18. She'd been able to trace down several other rifles and handguns to Darley, but not the weapon used to kill the mustangs. The sheriff had been sent up to hunt for a survivalist camp, but the survivalists had never been found, although there was evidence to point to their presence. Rafe's name had been cleared, and the case closed—until now.

Nick shoved his hands into the pockets of his gray slacks. "Well, we got problems. Again. Humphries is up in arms about it, too."

"Oh, no. What now?" Protectively, Jessie placed her hand on the file. As much as she didn't want to think of Rafe, his face loomed in her memory and her heart.

"We've got unsubstantiated reports that three more mustangs were found killed on Kincaid's property." He shrugged apologetically. "I'm sorry, Jessie, but you're going to have to fly out there immediately and check it out."

Panic seized her. "B-but, can't Jim Tremain, the regional director of the Department of Interior, handle this?"

"You know he can't, Jessie. It's our office's problem." Then he added thoughtfully, "Anyway, with the way you've been feeling lately, I think some sunshine and fresh air is exactly what you need."

Jessie grimaced. The past couple of weeks she had battled a stubborn flu. But the last thing in the world she wanted was to have to go out and face Rafe again. Whatever had been between them was dead. She knew that because he hadn't made any attempt to get in touch with her. No letter. No phone call. Nothing. A knot formed in her stomach, and she felt queasy.

"If the reports are true, do you think that the survivalist angle is viable? Is it possible the group has moved back into Rafe's territory?"

Nick nodded. "Yes, it's beginning to look better all the time. I think you should make a helicopter search of Kincaid's property and see if you can't spot something from the air. If you do, call me first. Then I want the local sheriff called in to assist. I'll go through our superiors in the Department of Interior, and they can contact the FBI to pull them in on this. All I want you to do is snoop around at this point. Tell Rafe Kincaid that we don't suspect him of any foul play." He grinned. "This time, I want him on our side. Use his helicopter and tell him we'll foot the fuel bills."

"I—I don't know if I'm up to it, Nick."

He walked over and patted her shoulder. "I'll look after the mouse while you're gone. My secretary has reserved your airline tickets for you. I've had her contact Kincaid already and told him you'd be arriving tomorrow at Denver International."

She wanted to cry. Lately she'd been very emotional, more than usual, and the news that she had to face Rafe again didn't help her fragile emotions. The only member of the Kincaid family to stay in touch with her had been Dal. Dal had kept her posted writing once every two weeks, filling her in on the details of their life and always devoting a few paragraphs to what was going on at the Triple K. A lump throbbed at the base of her throat as she looked up into Nick's kindly face.

"A-all right, Nick. I'll investigate it and get back here as quickly as possible."

"That's my girl. Hey, you know you've got two weeks' vacation accrued. If you want, after wrapping it up, stay out there."

Jessie nearly burst into tears. "Uh, no, Nick. Thanks, anyway."

He gave her a keen look. "Funny," he drawled, "I could have sworn there was something between you and Kincaid."

Jessie refused to look at him, and instead she nervously moved paper around on her desk top. Nick was speaking as a friend, not a boss, but she still couldn't talk about it. "No," she said in a strained voice, "there's nothing between us. I've more or less been a burr under Rafe Kincaid's saddle blanket all along."

Laughing pleasantly, Nick opened her office door. "I see. Well, when you do get back, Mr. Joshua Randall wants you to call him. He's that friendly old rancher up on the Colorado-Wyoming border."

Jessie's face softened at the mention of Joshua's name. She had worked with the elderly rancher from the start of her tenure with the BLM. His phone calls were always delightful, and she dearly loved the old widower. "Did he say what he wanted?"

"I told him you were going to be away from the office for a couple of weeks, and he said he'd call you when you returned. He has a surprise for you, I believe."

"He's been in and out of the hospital this year. Did he sound okay?"

Nick nodded. "Yeah, just his gruff old self. Said he had about twenty head of mustangs he was taking care of for you."

The old man had been a wrangler and rancher all his eighty-plus years. Because his ranch sat on the border of the Red Desert area, he helped save the mustangs that wandered off their protected domain and onto his. She scribbled a note on her calendar as a reminder to call Joshua when she got back to the office. If she had anything to do with it, it was going to be a very short trip out to the Triple K.

"He'll be the first person on my list to call when I get back," she promised Nick.

"Great. Hey, I'm gone. See you when you get back."
He winked and then disappeared.

Jessie sat there, allowing the tears to rise in her eyes.
She made no effort to stop them as they spilled over her
lashes and streaked down her cheeks. Oh, God, she'd
have to face Rafe again—after three months of silence.
He wouldn't want her there any more than she wanted
to be.

To her great relief, Jim Tremain met her at the Denver International Airport. His smile was genuine as he
came forward with his hand extended.

"Good to see you again, Jessie."

She tried to return his welcoming smile. "Hi, Jim.
How's your baby daughter and Dal?"

He picked up her overnight bag, slid it over his shoulder and led her down the long corridor toward baggage
claim. "Alessandra is doing beautifully," he told her, with
pride in his eyes. "And Dal looks more beautiful every
day. I don't know who's happier, Alessandra or us."

"You're so lucky," she said with a genuine smile. "And
I'm so happy for both of you." And then her smile disappeared. "And thanks for meeting me at the airport…"

"Dal thought it might be best. You're looking pale,
Jessie. Are you feeling all right?"

"You know how the BLM works us to death, Jim,"
she joked.

"I see…" His expression softened. "You love Rafe,
don't you?"

She halted, as if she'd taken a blow to the chest. Val-
iantly Jessie was fighting back the rising tide of tears
when she felt Jim's hand on her arm to steady her.

"I'm sorry," Jim murmured. "I didn't mean to shock

you. Dal and I both feel there's a lot between you and Rafe."

"I'm not very strong, I guess." And then she gave Jim a grateful look. "Yes, I love him. But it's not reciprocated, Jim."

Grimly he led her to the baggage claim, taking her airline ticket. "Sometimes I think Rafe needs to be knocked up alongside the head. He can be deaf, dumb and blind, Jessie."

"I'm responsible for my own actions in this, Jim. I should have kept my distance. I knew what I was up against."

Jim collected her two bags. "Well, before you have to square off with Rafe, we're going to keep you overnight at our house." He brightened. "Dal insists that you stay with us. Besides, Alessandra wants to be held by you."

Two hours later, Dal rocked contentedly on the rear porch of the A-frame house that had been built near a lake. She smiled, watching as her baby daughter cooed and laughed as Jessie took her into her arms. Jim leaned against the redwood railing, a tender look in his eyes as he watched his daughter reach toward Jessie.

"She's so precious," Jessie whispered, holding her close and inhaling that special scent that only a baby had.

"And spoiled," Dal added with a laugh.

"You said in your last letter that the delivery went fine," Jessie said, kissing the baby's velvety brow.

"Like clockwork," Dal agreed, and then she cast a look up at her husband. "I had the best partner in the world there as a coach."

Jessie closed her eyes, relaxing in the peace and contentment of the tight-knit family. There was love here in this house. Love in the eyes of Dal and Jim for each other. And she was holding the proof of their love in her arms. Her heart swelled unaccountably because at least someone in the world had found love and made it work for them.

Dal frowned as Jessie brought Alessandra back to her. "Go ahead, you hold her," she urged. "I know how much you love children, and frankly, Aly is such a little oinko for affection. You give her some for a while. I'm going to put dinner on."

For the next hour, Jessie rocked the baby in the rocking chair. The warm July breeze was cooling off the small lake. Off the back porch and in their own paddock were two dogs that were half wolf, Thor and Akiva. Jim had told her that the female, Akiva, was expecting any moment with her first litter of puppies. Peace settled around Jessie as she was left alone to absorb the beauty of the lake and evergreens. The dogs lay in the shade, their pink tongues lolling out the sides of their mouths. Everything about the Tremains shouted of life; but then, didn't love always create rather than destroy?

She held the baby, now fast asleep in her arms, close, rocking slowly back and forth. The serenity Jessie felt was one of completion; if she could have children, this was how she would feel. If Rafe could only trust himself and her enough to let go of the past and live in the present, they could work toward and share a similar happiness. Didn't he realize that? Did Rafe want to live in the past? Leaning down, Jessie pressed her lips to the round cheek of the child. At least she wouldn't have to see Rafe until the next morning, which gave her time to bottle up her emotions so she could meet him without falling apart. She had no idea where she would find the strength to face him.

The next morning Jim took her out to the Triple K, and Millie met them with open arms. The plump housekeeper gave Jessie a welcoming smile.

"This place has been worse than a morgue since you left, Jessie. Come in, come in!"

Exchanging a shy smile with Jim, Jessie walked into the ranch house. Anxiously she looked for a sign of Rafe as they took her luggage to her room.

"Where's Rafe?" Jim asked.

"Out in the broodmare barn. His best mare is foalin' right now, and he's out there helpin' with the birth. Go on out, lamb. He's expectin' you." She waved them out of the bedroom toward the back door.

Jessie's heart picked up as she walked with Jim down the sidewalk. The ranch was busy—wranglers were riding by, small herds of cattle were lowing in their pens, and there was the feel of a lot of activity in the air. The sun was strong and bright, and the wind soothed her jangled nerves as they approached the busy entrance to the broodmare barn. Jessie had been torn as to what to wear. She'd wanted to look beautiful for Rafe, but at the same time, there'd been no sense in dressing up if he no longer cared for her. She had settled on a pair of jeans, a peach blouse and had allowed her long blond hair to lie about her shoulders.

Jim guided her down the spotless aisle. "Rafe's favorite broodmare, Quilchena, is foaling. He's hoping for a filly." And then he grinned. "Fillys bring more money in the Arabian market," he explained. "Quilchena was bred to a national champion stallion, and Rafe's hoping the combination will make this baby worth a cool quarter of a million once he gets her or him to one of the prestigious Arizona sales."

Jessie nodded, spotting Pinto Pete and another wrangler at a stall at the far end of the barn. Her mouth grew dry as they approached it. If it hadn't been for Jim's reassuring hand on her shoulder, Jessie doubted she could have made it to the stall. They halted, looking over the stout oak paneling and through the slats into the huge, roomy area. Rafe was down on his knees, crooning softly to a gray mare who lay on her side, sweat running off her polished hide. Next to Rafe was a veterinarian, who, Jim had told her, was Dr. John Graves. Together they were helping the mare deliver.

Her hands tightened against the stall, and she hungrily soaked up Rafe's expression. Perspiration stood out on his tense face, and black strands of hair were plastered to his brow as he gently patted the mare on her hip, talking in a low, soothing tone to her. His voice was steadying, his touch calming on the mare as she strained to deliver her foal. Jessie found herself holding her breath each time the mare grunted and twisted, trying to give birth.

"Breach?" Rafe asked the vet, his eyes never leaving the mare.

The older man nodded. "Looks like," he affirmed. "She should have delivered by now. It's been half an hour."

Rafe moved aside so that the vet could ascertain the position of the foal. He ran his long fingers over the mare's neck and mane, calling her name softly. He returned his attention to the vet, who had finished his examination.

"Not breach." He grinned, and sweat glistened on his features. "First foal for a mare can always take a little longer. The baby's positioned correctly."

Rafe shut his eyes. "Thank God," he muttered. Breach

birth of a foal could spell death for it. When he opened his eyes, something told him to look up, and he did. His breath lodged in his throat, and his eyes widened. Jessie stood outside the stall, and her huge sable eyes met his. Rafe started to rise and then remembered he was needed by the vet. God, she looked beautiful! Her skin was translucent, almost radiant. *He loved her.*

"Jess…" he called.

She froze as she heard Rafe call her in a voice filled with undisguised emotion. Her lips parted, and all she wanted to do was fly to his arms. Love was shining in his cobalt-blue eyes as he stared hungrily up at her. Her throat constricted, and tears welled up in her eyes.

Rafe motioned for her to come into the stall. "Come on," he urged her in a quiet voice. "Come and stay at the mare's head. Comfort her. Talk to her…"

Numbly Jessie did as he asked, walking through the almost knee-deep straw to kneel down by the mare. She had never seen any animal's birth, and the experience was new and exciting. Rafe looked up, giving her a heart-stopping smile that took her breath away. This was where she belonged, Jessie realized. Here, at Rafe's side, sharing moments like this. Birth instead of death. Living, not dying. Joy, not grief.

Suddenly the vet let out a sound of pleasure as a dark bundle slid free of the mother. Rafe grinned and cut the sack open, allowing the struggling foal to breathe. He quickly wiped the mucous away from the baby's nostrils and mouth and helped the vet clean and dry the newborn.

"What have we got?" Rafe asked.

"Don't know," Graves said, smiling. "Let's take a look." Gently he turned the coal-black foal on its back. Swabbing the baby's navel with iodine, he chuckled.

"Looks like you got your wish, Rafe. It's a filly. A fine-looking filly."

"Yes," Rafe agreed, his gaze on Jessie and not the foal. His blue eyes smoldered with intensity.

"Got a name for her?" Jim called, smiling as he hung his arms over the stall door.

Graves helped the foal move to his mother, who was craning her head toward her offspring. "Million-dollar baby, maybe?"

"No," Rafe said, getting to his feet, "I'm going to call her Jessie's Girl because she's pretty just like another gal I know by the same name." Rafe held out his hand to Jessie to help her stand. He looked at her more closely than he had at first, and noticed that the translucence of her skin was caused by weight loss and a certain pallor. Her fingers were cool and damp as she slipped her delicate hand into his massive one.

Jim opened the stall door, and the three of them trooped out. From there, they watched as the mother got to her feet, nickering coaxingly to the foal. Jessie's Girl issued a high-pitched whinny and lurched to her front feet. She promptly crashed back onto the straw.

Rafe was wildly aware of Jessie standing next to him. She was nervously licking her lips. Could he blame her? He hated himself for not calling her, although God knew how many times he'd picked up the phone and dialed her number only to set it back down on the cradle before it connected. He longed to reach out and slide his fingers through her luxurious golden hair. But it was neither the time nor the place. Reluctantly he returned his attention to the foal.

Quilchena nuzzled her baby, licking her off with her long pink tongue. The filly whinnied and struggled again. This time she stood unsteadily on all four pathetically thin legs. Jessie wondered how they could stand the weight, much less propel the filly around as she aimed herself at her mama's milk bag. Achingly aware of Rafe's inspection, Jessie concentrated on the baby. Two babies in two days; she felt blessed and humbled by the experience.

"Looks like she's gonna make it," the vet said, stripping off his elbow-length rubber gloves and dropping them into a container in his medical bag. "I've got to get going, Rafe. Any problems, just call."

Rafe shook the vet's hand. "Thanks, John. I don't think there will be; she looks like she's ready to take on the world."

Graves laughed. "Wished I had the kind of spunk that filly's showing. See you all later." He waved goodbye and left.

"I've got to get going," Jim said, putting his hand on Jessie's shoulder. "Nice filly, Rafe. Congratulations."

Rafe shook Jim's hand. "Thanks. How's Dal and the baby doing?"

"Great." He shared a smile with Jessie. "Aly already has a second mother, I think. She took to Jessie yesterday like a duck takes to water. I'll see you later. Dal says to give you her love."

Rafe stood in the aisle, watching his brother-in-law leave. He slanted a glance down at Jessie. "Like a duck to water?" he teased.

She managed a smile. "Aly is beautiful. Like her mother," she answered softly.

Nervously Rafe nodded. "How have you been?" he asked quietly.

"Okay. Working hard." She averted her gaze as her throat constricted with tension.

"It seems like I'm always apologizing to you, Jessie." His mouth quirked, as if he were in pain. "I was going to call."

She placed her hand on his arm. "I understand, Rafe. You don't need to say anything." Taking a huge breath, Jessie shoved on, ignoring the empty feeling inside herself. "All I want to do is investigate this latest incident and get out of your life." She risked a glance at his stoic face. "I know this is uncomfortable for both of us. I won't stay here any longer than necessary."

His mouth compressed into a thin line. Jessie was continually surprising him with her backbone. She didn't look strong, but she was. And in ways he wasn't and probably would never be. "You have a right to be angry," he muttered, taking her elbow and leading her out of the barn.

"I'm not angry, Rafe."

The sunlight was dazzling as they walked out into the yard. "What then?"

"Sad," she admitted, "but not angry."

Rafe pulled her to a halt. He wrapped his hands gently around her upper arms as he stared hungrily down at her. "Don't write us off, Jessie. Not yet. I'm trying to come to grips with a lot of things. Things that I can't put names or words to. I do care about you. God knows how many times I nearly called you, but then I asked myself what the hell could I say to you? I can't promise you anything just yet, Jessie, and I won't lead you on. I know what we've shared has been good. For both of us." He gave her a small shake. "There's no life in your eyes, Jessie, and that scares me. I don't deserve you or what you've given to me without ever asking anything for yourself in return. But I want to make it right between us."

She wanted to throw herself into Rafe's arms and simply be held—to give love and receive it. But she couldn't do that, not yet. "I think I know what you're going through, Rafe," she began hoarsely. "But until you can sit down with me and really talk to me, there's nothing for us to build a relationship on. Do you understand that?"

"I'm trying, Jessie, but it isn't easy," he explained in a torn voice.

"It's not easy for either of us, Rafe." She pulled herself from his grasp. "I'm really tired, and I'd like to take the rest of the morning going over our latest problem. Do you have a couple of hours free to devote to me so I can dispatch an immediate report back to my home office?"

Grimly Rafe stared down at her. She was pale as hell and her eyes were fraught with pain. With a brusque nod, he moved forward toward the ranch house. "I'll give you all the time you need, Jessie. Let's get started."

Each minute, each hour spent with Rafe was a bittersweet misery for Jessie. She forced herself, as never before, to concentrate on the business at hand. By noon, she had outlined to Rafe the possibility of a group of survivalists using his property to camp and hunt on, and had presented the evidence to him.

"I've been missing some cattle up there, too. They could easily be killing some off from my herd," he commented.

It made sense to Jessie. "All the home office wants of you is the loan of your time and helicopter for three or four days, Rafe."

"You've got it. I don't feel like losing cattle or mustangs to that fanatical group."

"If we do spot anything, I'm to call my boss, and the sheriff and FBI will take over."

He nodded, satisfied.

Millie poked her head around the door. "Lunch is on," she called.

Rafe looked up from behind his desk at Jessie, who occupied the wing chair across from him. "Want a break?" he asked, rising.

She wasn't hungry at all, but nodded. All morning her stomach had been queasy and food didn't appeal to her in the least. The dining room was as cheery as she remembered it, and she sat down opposite Rafe while Millie served them. Typically, it was a huge meal, and Jessie picked at the salad, passing up the beef Stroganoff and freshly made rolls.

"Aren't you hungry?" Rafe asked.

"No. Lately, food hasn't set well with me."

"Why?"

She took a sip of her water. "I've been lucky enough this summer to have a long bout of flu, that's all. I think I'm still getting over it."

"We can hold off on that search a day or two if you want."

"No, I'd rather get it done as quickly as possible."

Stabbing at a chunk of beef, Rafe bit back a retort. He knew she wanted to leave as soon as she could. He didn't blame her.

Millie eyeballed Rafe as he entered the back door for the evening meal. She watched as he took off his hat, tossed it on a peg, and then ran his fingers through his coal-black hair.

"Before you go clean up, I want a word with you."

Rafe ambled into the kitchen and poured himself a mug of coffee. "Something wrong, Millie?" He leaned against the drainboard. The day had been a total bust in every way possible. They hadn't located any camps. Using a special search pattern, Jessie had concentrated entirely on the work at hand, and Rafe had missed her natural warmth. He'd felt left out in the cold, and useless.

Millie placed her hands on her fleshy hips and looked up at him. "Somethin's wrong with Jessie. She's in her room right now sleepin'. The girl looks positively like she's ailin', Rafe. Last time she was out here she was perky, had good color to her face and was a heck of a lot happier."

With a grimace, Rafe pushed off from the drainboard. "You heard her, Millie. She said she had the flu."

Muttering under her breath, Millie shoved her hands into a pair of kitchen mittens and went to the stove. She pulled out a juicy ham scored with cloves and topped with pineapple rings. "I don't like it, Rafe. There's more wrong with her than meets the eye; you mark my words."

Rafe flinched inwardly under Millie's accusing stare. "If she isn't feeling any better by tomorrow morning," he muttered, "call Doc out."

Millie placed the ham on the drainboard, eyeing him as he disappeared out of the kitchen. "Stubborn mule," she muttered, tossing off the mittens. "That girl loves you, and all you can do is call a doctor!"

Tension was strung tautly between the three of them at the dinner table. Jessie had deliberately put on some makeup, so she wouldn't look so pale. Even her hair seemed limper than usual and had lost its normal sheen. Rafe's black looks didn't help her digestion, either. Three different times he'd passed her bowls of food that she passed on to Millie without touching. Didn't he understand she was upset? That being in his presence was like a knife pricking her heart? Mercifully dinner ended when Rafe stood and dropped the linen napkin on the table.

"How about some brandy in the study?" he asked her with an ominous undertone to his voice that told her she had better follow him.

Placing the napkin on the table, she looked at Millie. "Would you like some help clearing the dishes?"

"No, lamb. You don't look well. You ain't eaten enough to fill up a bird." She raised her hand, shooing her away from the table. "Go with Rafe. Maybe what you need is a good belt of brandy to bring some pink back into your cheeks."

Her stomach in knots, Jessie walked into the study. Rafe closed the door behind them. She could feel his tightly bottled anger and steeled herself for the coming confrontation.

Rafe moved to the liquor cabinet. "Brandy?"

"No, thank you." She sat down on the leather couch, trying to relax despite Rafe's sharp glance in her direction. He poured himself a shot of whiskey. Jessie didn't blame him; he was just as nervous and upset as she was.

Rafe moved to the couch and stood in front of her. He took a long sip of the whiskey and studied Jessie in the thickening silence. She had gripped her hands in her lap and refused to look at him. Without a word, he sat down next to her, although not close enough to touch. Rafe held the tumbler between his hands and stared down at the golden liquid.

"I've never had a woman get under my skin before," he said in a low tone, cocking his head to catch her reaction out of the corner of his eyes, "but you have, Jessie."

She closed her eyes, tensing. "You make it sound like I'm an infection of some kind."

A slight grin tugged at his mouth and then disappeared. "Mary Ann never minded my quiet spells."

Anger ripped through her, and Jessie turned, her eyes wide with sable fire. "Rafe, don't you dare compare me to your dead wife! That's not fair to me, or to you!"

He sat up as if she'd slapped him. "Look, dammit, I don't have many other women in my life to compare to *you*." He shot to his feet, took a long swallow of whiskey and crossed the room, a scowl working across his tense features. "I did plenty of carousing around when I was a teenager. When I joined the army, out of college, I did a hell of a lot more." He turned, his eyes black. "And in all my travels and in all my experience, I've never run across a woman like you."

Jessie leapt to her feet, her hands on her hips. "Why don't you stop putting women under labels and types and maybe you'd be able to see me for what I am! I'm me, Rafe. Not Mary Ann, not one of your hundreds of other conquests!"

"There weren't hundreds," he drawled.

"Yeah, well, I suppose none of them minded your tight-lipped attitude. I do! Any serious relationship is based upon two people talking to each other, and not on one party trying to mind read and keep up."

"We're talking now," he roared back. "Isn't that what you wanted?"

Helplessly Jessie shrugged. "Not like this." She touched her brow, and her voice sounded strained. "I'm angry with you, Rafe. I try and understand, but I'm human and I'm hurting. I wish I could be a saint like Mary Ann was and put up with your silence and your moodiness, but I can't. I'm used to sharing hopes, dreams and fears."

"You wouldn't want to share what's inside of me," he warned darkly.

"How do you know? Since when was it your privilege to make my mind up for me, Rafe?" She took two steps forward, and there was an ache in her tone when she spoke. "Why don't you give me a chance?"

Rafe spun around, downing the rest of the whiskey and slamming the tumbler down on the cabinet. His knuckles whitened as he gripped the edge of the furniture. "Why can't you be satisfied with what I give to you?" he parried harshly.

"Why should anyone be satisfied with one-quarter of you, Rafe? Put yourself in my place—how would you like me to be the strong, silent type?"

"I wouldn't. Besides, there isn't a woman alive that can be quiet like a man can. You're natural talkers."

Jessie's fists knotted at her sides. "God gave you a tongue, too! If he didn't want the noble male animal to communicate, he'd have made damn sure you didn't get a tongue, Rafe! So stop giving me that macho garbage— you don't believe it any more than I do."

Rafe shook his head. "I can't be what you want me to be, Jessie," he said, the anger dissolving in his voice. "That's partly why I didn't call you. It was the biggest thing stopping me from contacting you." Turning, he saw she was close to tears. A sharp ache centered in his chest, and he wanted to walk those few feet, wrap his arms around her and hold her—forever. With a shake of his head, he muttered, "I'm scared, Jessie. That's what it boils down to. I'm scared if I reach out like I did before, I'll have you torn away from me." He shut his eyes tightly, and there was an explosion of feeling behind his next words. "I loved once and now it's gone. Losing Mary Ann and our baby damn near killed me." He opened his turbulent blue eyes and stared at her. "I can't risk loving again, Jessie. I know I don't put my feelings into words, and that's part of our problem. But the major thing is that I'm just too afraid to reach out…"

"At least you've finally told me the truth," she said in a quavery voice. "If there can't be honesty between two people in a relationship, there's nothing, anyway."

He ran his fingers through his hair with an aggravated motion. "At least we have that," he muttered. "I didn't mean to fall for you, Jessie. But from the moment I opened the car door and saw you unconscious, you grabbed my heart. I don't know how it happened or why." He shrugged tiredly, exhaustion shadowing his features. "I'm sorry. You deserve a hell of a lot better than someone like me who's crippled from too many battles in life."

She quietly approached him, as tears brimmed in her eyes, and gently placed her hand on his shoulder. "You're the very best," she whispered, "to me. That's all that counts." Jessie reached up on tiptoe and placed a kiss on his cheek. "I love you, Rafe. But don't take my admission and carry it around like guilt. I don't regret one moment spent with you, and I never will." She managed a thin smile, meeting his dark, curiously bright eyes. Rafe was close to tears himself, she realized in that shattering moment. She forced herself to release his arm and stepped away from him. "Thank you for talking with me…good night."

* * *

He couldn't sleep. Rafe got up, threw on his well-worn black terry cloth robe and padded silently out to the living room. Moonlight slanted through the windows, making the highly polished cedar floor shine beneath his feet.

Although it was July in the Rockies, the air still had a bit of a nip to it. He went to the window and stared out at the black and gray shapes of the barns and paddocks. The lowing of the Herefords and the peaceful night relaxed him to a degree. He raised his head and stared down the long hall to his left, where Jessie slept.

He had gotten up because he'd been afraid that he was going to open the door between their two bedrooms. And once he had? What would he have done? Loved her, like he wanted to…because nothing could erase the gnawing ache from his heart except her touch, her voice… He shut his eyes and rubbed his face tiredly. Why the hell couldn't he reach out? What was stopping him? He loved her.

She had been right, Rafe admitted, shoving his hands into the pockets of his robe. He was hiding behind a self-erected macho wall. Mary Ann had been willing to be a wife and mother, nothing more. She was content to allow him his abhorrent ways. Jessie wouldn't. No, she was alive and vital, unwilling to take a back seat in their relationship. A grin crossed his mouth as he recalled their heated conversation in the study about men having a tongue in their head, too. She was right, so why couldn't he begin to tell her how he felt?

Deep in thought, Rafe walked the length of the living room. Jessie brought out a kaleidoscope of emotions in him that no woman had ever tapped. He wasn't used to feeling so strongly or sharply. And in her presence that's mostly what he did, with little logic thrown in, besides. A smile of warmth glimmered in his eyes as he made his way back to his bedroom. He always thought best when he was on the back of a horse. What he needed was a moonlit ride.

Chapter 9

Rafe noticed a light on in the broodmare barn as he crossed toward the barn where the riding horses were stabled. He detoured and stepped into the cavernous shadows of the barn. Had Pinto Pete left the light on by Quilchena's stall the last time he checked on her? Normally Pete made rounds twice nightly to make sure the new foals and their mothers were doing fine. He glanced at his watch: 3:00 a.m. In all likelihood, Pete had forgotten and left the light on. Rafe wasn't angry with him; the old mustanger was at an age where he occasionally forgot something. *At thirty-five,* Rafe thought wryly, walking down the aisle, *I forget things.* He was just amazed Pete didn't forget more often.

As he drew up to the stall, Rafe felt his whole body tighten. There in the stall, with the newborn foal laying in her lap, was Jessie. The mare stood nearby, her head hanging down, her nose almost touching Jessie's shoulder. Rafe stood very still, not wanting to be discovered just yet. Jessie was dressed in a short-sleeved white blouse and jeans. Her hair had bits of straw in it, and he figured that the foal had probably taken her for a tumble in it earlier while playing with her. A smile softened his face as he watched Jessie gently run her hand down the length of the filly's silky neck and shoulder. Her gold hair lay in mussed abandon, framing her delicate face, and the light above her slanted down, creating a halo around her. She was a dream come true, Rafe thought disjointedly, fire throbbing to life in his loins. There was more color in her cheeks, and he swallowed hard, grateful that the foal had lifted her spirits.

Quilchena slowly raised her head, flicking one ear forward, her huge dark eyes focused on the stall door. Lifting her head, Jessie moved her gaze in the same direction. She had met Pinto Pete out in the barn and asked his permission to go in and see the new foal. He had smiled, tipped his hat and said yes. Her eyes registered surprise when she saw Rafe in the shadows, his hat drawn low across his forehead, his eyes pinned on her. She started awakening the foal who had been sleeping soundly with her small head between Jessie's hands.

"Stay where you are," Rafe told her softly.

Her heart skipping like a trapped rabbit's, Jessie watched as Rafe entered the stall and shut the door quietly behind him. He had a tender look burning in his eyes, and it shook her badly. She stroked the foal, who closed her long lashes, resting once again on her lap, contented. Rafe moved to her side and knelt down next to her.

"I didn't know you were up," he said, reaching out and running his fingers through the foal's silky mane.

"I couldn't sleep."

"Neither could I." He studied Jessie in the silence. Every fiber of his body screamed out in need of her. Rafe saw her lower lip tremble, and he blindly followed his feelings. He nestled her against his body.

"You're a natural mother," he told her in a husky voice. "Most foals stick to mama's side. This baby trusts you."

Jessie tried to smile as she ran her fingers lightly across the foal's forehead. "I just wanted to be near something that would give me a little affection, I guess."

Rafe nodded, understanding what she meant. He ran his fingers absently along her shoulder. "You deserve someone who can give to you in return as much as you give to them, Jessie. I wish I could."

She barely turned her head. "You can. You just don't realize it yet, Rafe."

Sadness filled him. "Do you always hope for the hopeless, Jessie?"

"Maybe I do, Rafe. I don't know anymore. I thought I understood people, but I guess I don't. Not like I want to."

He heard the despair in her voice and caressed her neck. "Nobody said living was what it was cracked up to be," he agreed.

Jessie stilled her hands over the baby. Each time Rafe touched her, it sent a prickle of pleasure straight through her. She had tossed and turned all night and had finally gotten up at 2:00 a.m., thrown on a blouse and jeans and left. She'd wanted to escape somewhere, but hadn't been sure where until she had seen the light on in the brood-mare barn and gone out to investigate. Pete had allowed her to go in and frolick with the bright-eyed little filly, who was kicking up her heels for the first time. For fifteen minutes she and the foal had played. Finally the baby had tuckered out and collapsed like a sack of potatoes onto Jessie's lap. Pete had grinned and left, saying that the filly had a second mother.

Jessie closed her eyes, allowing Rafe to pull her against his strong, hard body. Tears matted her lashes, but she refused to allow them to fall. His rough, callused hand stilled against her cheek, and she felt the moistness of his breath against her brow.

"Just let me hold you for a little while," he breathed hoarsely.

"Yes…"

"I could brain that brother of mine," Dal said in apology. She held Alessandra while Jim carried Jessie's luggage into the Denver airport. "He should have brought you here."

"It wasn't his fault, Dal," Jessie said. "I didn't want to put him through any more than we've already had to endure with each other." The fervency behind her words made both of them glance at her, and Jessie colored fiercely. She gripped Dal's free hand. "Sometimes love isn't enough, Dal," she pleaded.

"But you love each other! My God, Jessie, Jim and I went through hell, but it was our love that held us together through it all."

"Dal," Jim cautioned, "she's in enough pain right now. Don't jump on her."

Contrite, Dal apologized. "I just know you're right for Rafe. If that thick-headed, rangy longhorn of a brother of mine can't see that—"

"He can and does," Jessie defended. They stopped

at the counter, and Jim took her ticket. Gratefully she thanked him and returned her attention to Dal. "He's afraid to live again, Dal. We're so close and we both know it. But I can't do anything until he decides otherwise."

Six of the longest, most tortuous days of her life with Rafe had finally come to a merciful end. On the fourth day, using the search pattern, she had located a camp straddling federal lands and Rafe's territory. On the fifth day, law enforcement officers had closed in on the area. By that evening, a camp of fifteen survivalists had peacefully vacated the Kincaid property. From there, the FBI would take over the case, and if charges were pending, it would come from the federal government. She had done her job successfully. But it didn't give Jessie any satisfaction.

In another hour, she'd be on a plane heading East. Heading home. But this was her home, she thought, these mountains, the sharp, clear air, the range. Rafe was right—she had "country" in her soul. Perhaps her parents had been country people.

Jim came over, handed Jessie the boarding pass and gave her a smile filled with concern. "Look, stay in touch, will you, Jessie? I don't think this is over between you and Rafe. Write to us or call."

Jessie reached out, hugging first Jim and then Dal. She gave the sleeping Alessandra a kiss on the brow, marveling at the baby's delicate beauty. "I will."

"I promise I'll tell you what's going on with Rafe," Dal said, hugging her fiercely. "And get better; you look so tired and underweight…"

With a laugh, Jessie picked up her carry-on luggage

and waved. "I will. Really, you guys act as if I'm part of your family."

Jim sobered. "You are, Jessie. Give us a call when you get back to D.C. to let us know you arrived safely."

The next day, Jessie left work at noon, feeling ill. She wanted to believe it was the stress of the past week with Rafe catching up to her, but knew it was probably something more. Before she left work, she called her doctor, who told her to come in right away. She did, and was put through a barrage of tests and examined thoroughly before her doctor told her to come back the next day for the results.

In the early evening, a knock sounded on her apartment door. Who could it be? she wondered. Dressed in her cotton robe and slippers, she got up to answer it. Nick stood there.

"Jessie? How you feeling? I thought I'd drop over on my way home from work and check on you."

Embarrassed at her disheveled appearance, Jessie asked her boss in. "I'm okay, Nick. I have another doctor's appointment for tomorrow morning, to find out the results of the tests. I'll only be an hour late getting to work. I know there's a ton of work that needs to be tended to."

He handed her a small bouquet of yellow daisies and orange carnations sprigged with baby's breath. "Here, maybe these will cheer you up. Are you up to some office talk for a minute? Something rather extraordinary has happened, and it involves you. And Humphries is up in arms about it." He gave her an apologetic smile. "It couldn't wait until tomorrow."

Intrigued, Jessie asked him to sit down, holding the colorful bouquet in her hands. She sharply recalled the time Rafe had picked a handful of wildflowers and given them to her. Tearing her attention back to Nick, she tried to concentrate on the problem at hand.

"What's wrong? Wasn't my report adequate? I proved beyond any doubt that Rafe wasn't shooting those mustangs."

"No, it has nothing to do with that, Jessie. You remember I told you that old Joshua Randall had called just before you left for the Triple K?"

Jessie groaned. "Oh, God! I forgot to return his call. I promised I would first thing..." She had been miserably sick all morning, barely able to cope with the flurry of requests and the pressures put on her by Mr. Humphries.

Nick nodded and drew out a thick envelope from his breast pocket. "This came for you today after you had left. It's from Mr. Randall's executor in Casper, Wyoming."

Her eyes widened. "Executor? But—but that means—"

"Yes, Josh died the day after he placed that phone call to you. I'm sorry." He handed her the envelope. "This was addressed to Mr. Humphries. He opened it and then hit the ceiling. Go on, read it."

Tears blurred her vision as she shakily opened the envelope. Joshua Randall had been a dear man, one that Jessie had loved from a distance. His devotion to the mustangs had equalled and surpassed hers, and he'd often utilized his small ranch as a holding station for mustangs that had been wounded by angry ranchers or needed medical attention. Wiping her eyes, she sniffed. The more she read, the more confused she became.

"Nick, what does all this legalese mean?"

"The bottom line, if you don't want to wade through

all ten pages, is that Joshua Randall has willed his ranch, his entire savings and everything else to you, Jess."

Stunned, Jessie stared at her boss. "But—that's impossible!"

A small grin spread across his serious face. "That's what Mr. Humphries said. According to the Justice Department, Mr. Randall was within his rights to bequeath his ranch to anyone he wanted." He pointed to the thick sheaf of papers. "A copy of Joshua's will is in there. Isn't much to it, because the man didn't own much."

"Doesn't he have relatives? Family?" Jessie asked hoarsely, staring down at the paper in her hands.

"They're all dead or gone. Guess he never married, Jessie." He patted her shoulder. "It's all legal. You're now the owner of a five-hundred acre ranch." He rose, studying her. "The question is, what are you going to do about it? Are you going to stay here or move west?" His smile broadened. "Knowing you, you'll head west where you can help the mustangs directly. But sleep on it. All the facts, figures and financial worth is in there. I'll see you tomorrow morning."

Shocked, Jessie read through the entire ten pages, still not believing it. And then she cried hard because of Joshua Randall's kindness to her. She had never met him face-to-face; only through warm, lively phone conversations from time to time. Standing up, she crossed to the window and looked out over Washington, D.C., knowing that in her heart she wanted to go west. She went back to the couch, picked up the sheaf of papers and tried to wade through them.

According to the executor the ranch foreman, Shorty Evans, was taking care of the place and would remain on the payroll unless she wanted it otherwise. Apparently Joshua had stashed away his money over the years. The man had a large herd of Herefords that had made him that money; his mustangs never earned him a cent.

She spent the rest of the evening trying to ascertain if she could make a living on the ranch, given what Joshua had saved in the bank and in stocks. His cattle were raised on wholesome grass and without any chemicals added to their feed, the executor elaborated in the accompanying letter. Joshua's cattle were in demand not only in health-food stores, but as "clean" beef. Thirty restaurants in California bought his untainted beef, which was far healthier to consume than meat with hormones in it, and which would provide a steady income to her. Yes, she could make ends meet, providing Shorty could give her a crash course in how to run a ranch.

More tears spilled into her eyes as Jessie clutched the letter to her breast. How often had she dreamed of living on a ranch with Rafe? Her heart was breaking with pain. Now she had a ranch and her mustangs, but not the man she loved. Not the man whom she wanted to live with and love the rest of her life. With a sigh, she got up and turned out the lights in the apartment. Tomorrow was going to be a busy day: first, she'd see the doctor, and then go in to give Nick her resignation.

Doctor Nancy Csonka gestured for Jessie to sit down in her office.

"I'm glad you made it here today," she told Jessie, giving her a warm smile as she filled out the last of an examination form.

"Why?" She groaned inwardly; she didn't need some exotic virus to contend with now that she was going to be moving to Wyoming.

Dr. Csonka looked up. "You're pregnant, Jessie. Congratulations."

Pregnant! Jessie's hand flew to her belly. "W-what? I can't be! I mean, I'm infertile!"

"That's odd, because you're nearly three months along, Jessie," the doctor said as she sat back. "If my calculations are correct, you'll have your baby in early January of next year."

A fission of pure joy exploded through her, followed quickly by an icy shaft of fear. The baby was Rafe's. Their baby…her baby! What would he think? Oh, God, she didn't dare let him know. She didn't want to force Rafe into having to take her because she was carrying his child. No, if he couldn't come to her of his own accord, she didn't want their child to be the deciding factor. Anguish showed on her face. "Oh, God, Doctor…" Shakily Jessie touched her brow. "I—I thought I couldn't get pregnant. I tried for years…"

The doctor raised an eyebrow. "Tell me about it."

Jessie poured out her story, her hands resting protectively across her abdomen all the while. She didn't have a virus; it was simply morning sickness. And the thickening at her waist wasn't a weight gain; it was her baby growing inside her. And the fact that her breasts were fuller… Elation soared through her despite the shocking news.

"Well," Dr. Csonka explained carefully, "I'd say that the pressures brought on you by your husband's family probably had a great deal to do with it, Jessie. I've seen it happen before. And if Tom refused to have himself checked, you were probably missing half the puzzle, anyway. A low sperm count can make even the most fertile myrtle look barren." She looked into Jessie's dazed but glowing face and grinned broadly. "And from the look in your eyes, I think congratulations are in order."

Two weeks…two damn, miserable, lonely weeks without Jessie. Rafe walked into the cool confines of the ranch house, his white shirt clinging to his sweaty body. He glanced toward the kitchen—he wanted to sidestep Millie's fierce look because he was dusty and dirty. She didn't allow anyone to tramp through the house without first dusting themselves off. Slipping into the study, Rafe placed his cowboy hat on the desk and picked up the phone. He dialed the BLM in Washington, D.C. Pushing dark strands of wet hair off his forehead, he asked for Jessie.

"I'm sorry," the secretary said, "she's no longer working for us, Mr. Kincaid."

Shock rooted Rafe to the spot, and his eyes narrowed. "What do you mean she isn't working for you? What the hell is going on?"

"She quit work a week and a half ago, sir."

"Let me talk to her boss," he growled. Why had she quit? Where had she gone? He knew the stress of having to see him again had extracted a huge toll from her. Guilt and concern ate at him. Was she in a hospital?

"Nick Van der Meer speaking."

"This is Rafe Kincaid. I'm trying to get a hold of Jessie."

There was a moment's hesitation, then Nick said cautiously, "I'm sorry, Mr. Kincaid, but Jessie quit the BLM."

"Why?"

"We're not allowed to give out that kind of information, Mr. Kincaid. Did you have a problem that perhaps one of my other—"

"What I have to say to Jessie is personal, Mr. Van der Meer. It has nothing to do with work. Is she sick?"

"No. Look, let me give you her new phone number, and you can contact her yourself."

Rafe scribbled down the area code and phone number. It wasn't a D.C. number—it was a Wyoming area code! He wanted to ask Van der Meer more, but didn't.

"You've been helpful. Thanks," Rafe said.

Nick laughed. "If you're going to be speaking to Jessie, ask her how her mouse is. You know, she took the little fella with her and set him free? We all miss her, but wish her the very best of luck."

Rafe promised he'd pass on the message and hung up the phone. Standing up, he went to shut the door to the study before he walked to the phone again.

His hand was clammy as he dialed her number. His heartbeat accelerated as the line connected and rang.

"Bar M," a male voice said.

Rafe hesitated. A ranch? Jessie was at a ranch? He cleared his throat. "Let me speak to Jessie. This is Rafe Kincaid from the Triple K calling."

"Yeah, hold on. Miss Jessie's down by the brandin' pens. It'll be a minute."

Rafe stared at the phone, completely confused. Had she quit her job and taken another at a ranch? Why would she be down at a branding pit? She wasn't a cowboy.

Jessie ran back to the small white ranch house, her blond ponytail flying behind her. She tried to dust off her blue jeans before entering the house, to give her heart a chance to slow down. *Rafe had called.* She tried not to think about why he had called and hurried through the sparsely furnished home.

Out of breath, she picked up the phone. "Rafe?"

"Jessie? What the hell's going on? Are you all right?"

With a soft laugh, she said, "I'm fine, fine." Breathlessly, she went into the details of how her life had been transformed in the past two weeks. Unconsciously, she moved her hand to her belly; she had told no one, not even Nick, that she was pregnant. And for the next half hour, she was happy because Rafe had called without prompting. She prayed that it heralded a positive change in their relationship. After she finished with the initial explanation, she asked, "Had you called the BLM for business reasons?" She held her breath, hoping it wasn't his reason for contacting her.

Rafe's voice lowered. "No, Jessie. I called because I'm damned lonely without you. The past two weeks have been pure hell…"

She clasped the phone, as if she could reach through it and touch him. "I'm glad you called," she whispered, suddenly close to tears, aching to tell him that she was carrying their child.

Rafe cleared his throat. "Look, you're going to need help setting up house at that ranch, Jessie. How about if I bring some of the boys, and we'll get you situated? We're done with most of the bigger chores around here until fall roundup."

Was he coming out of guilt? Responsibility? Or because he loved her? Jessie wasn't sure. "Joshua has a wonderful group of ranch hands, Rafe. Everything's under control here. Shorty Evans is the foreman, and he's a good man. Right now all I'm doing is standing back and learning. Thanks for the offer, but I don't need extra men."

There was silence on the phone. "All right. Then I'm coming up to see you, Jessie."

She closed her eyes, a tremulous smile on her lips. "Yes… I'd like that, Rafe."

"Got a place where I can land a helicopter?"

"Yes. Out back of the ranch house, near a stand of cottonwoods. When are you coming?"

"When do you want to see me?"

"As soon as you can get here."

"I'll be there tomorrow morning, Jessie."

The words "I love you" nearly slipped from her, and Jessie suddenly felt lightheaded. But it wasn't from being pregnant; it was from shock and happiness. "Hurry, Rafe; I've missed you so much."

"Tomorrow morning," he promised thickly. "We have a lot to talk about."

"Yes…"

The Red Desert of Wyoming wasn't desolate to her. Three groves of sturdy cottonwood embraced the ranch house and protected it from the late summer heat of the sun. Jessie purposely stayed in the house that morning. She'd hardly been able to sleep at all the night before knowing that Rafe was coming. She had worn a pair of jeans and a loose smock because she couldn't button her denims anymore. Soon she'd have to buy some maternity clothes. Bittersweet, the closest town, was thirty miles away, down a single-lane highway that spanned the Red Desert flats of the Great Divide Basin.

All morning Jessie kept stepping out on the enclosed screened porch, waiting to hear the sound of helicopter blades announcing his arrival. The sky was a pale blue as the morning sun inched over the black silhouette of desert plain that spread before her. William Lee, her Chinese cook, smiled and gave her a sign of encouragement as he went back to the huge kitchen. William made three square meals a day for ten ranch hands and herself. He was a better cook than she was, Jessie admitted wryly.

Moving back to the living room, she busied herself with hanging wallpaper. She kept glancing at the watch on her wrist. At 9:00 a.m. she became worried, although morning meant anything between 6:00 a.m. and noon. Chafing at the bit, Jessie concentrated even more on finishing the last wall of the room. By 11:00 a.m. the papering was completed. William came in, his white apron around his waist, nodding his approval.

"Miss Jessie, you make it look like daylight indoors."

She managed a smile. "Do you like it, William?"

"Very much. The flowers bring the outside in."

The wallpaper was ivory with tiny lavender, blue and purple flowers mixed in a tasteful pattern. The effect made the room look larger and took the gloom away from the dark furnishings in it. There was no doubt a man had lived in the ranch before—everything was somber and spare. Jessie glanced toward the back door again. Had Rafe had engine trouble with the helicopter? A cold fear washed over her, and a terrible vision danced before her eyes. Rafe could have crashed…he could be dead… *No!*

Noon came and went. William looked disappointed when she didn't eat the small salad he had made especially for her. The ranch hands ate in the bunkhouse, which had been built to the east of the homestead. She sat all alone in the airy dining room, her bowl of salad the only item on the antique maple dining table that shone like rubbed glass. Had Rafe gotten cold feet? Had he backed out? Jessie squeezed her eyes shut. That was probably the real reason why he hadn't come.

Unable to stand the suspense any longer, torn between anxiety and anger, Jessie went into the library and called the Triple K. The phone rang ten times before she reluctantly hung it back up. Something was wrong; she knew it. Millie would have answered if someone had been home. Anguish shadowed her eyes. If Rafe had crashed, no one would be at the ranch house; they'd be out looking for him—or he might be in a hospital. Worse, he might have crashed somewhere in the rugged area between the Triple K and the Wyoming border. Unable to stand the bend her overactive imagination had taken, Jessie went to the kitchen.

She found William up to his elbows in soapsuds, washing lunch dishes.

"William?"

"Yes, Miss Jessie?"

"If I get any phone calls, I'll be down at the mustang corral. Come and get me, okay?"

He nodded his head. "I'll come," he promised.

The phone was ringing. Jessie dragged herself from sleep, fumbling in the darkness. She barely opened her eyes as she grasped the phone while trying to extricate herself from the tangle of sheets around her legs. The clock read 2:00 a.m.

"Hello?" she said thickly.

"Jessie?"

Her eyes widened, and she struggled into a sitting position. "Rafe!"

"I'm calling from Maine, honey. My sister Cat has been in a serious mining accident."

She tried to rub the sleep from her eyes. It had been two days since she'd expected Rafe, and she hadn't been able to get anyone at the Triple K the whole time. "Oh, Rafe, I thought—I thought something horrible had happened to you...that you'd crashed on your way up here—"

"No. We got word that Cat was inspecting an old emerald mine shaft when it caved in on her." He drew in a shaky breath. "There wasn't enough time to call you. The whole family, including Millie, flew out here."

Her head reeled with questions and answers. "How's your sister?" she asked, her voice trembling.

Rafe hesitated, exhaustion leaking through his voice. "We just got her out of the mine, and she just went into the emergency room. We're waiting to see... I wanted to call you the first chance I got, Jessie. We've been out at that mine since we landed. I rode back in the ambulance with Cat, and they sent her to the trauma unit."

She squeezed her eyes shut, hearing Rafe's pain and anxiety, and feeling it rip through herself, as if she were part of him. "Is there anything I can do?"

"I wish to hell you were here right now, Jessie." Rafe's voice shook with feeling. "I need you."

Biting down hard on her lower lip, Jessie fought back her tears. Rafe needed her! It was the first time he'd ever admitted it to her. She swallowed a lump. "I'll come if you want."

"No...there's no sense in you sitting here in this damned waiting room like the rest of us. The doctors said she has internal injuries besides busting up some ribs. We don't know anything else right now. She had a head injury, too, and we don't know how bad it is. Oh, Jessie…" He sighed heavily.

She took in a deep breath. "Then…she's in critical condition?" His sister was close to death; she sensed it through Rafe's broken tone. She felt helpless, and wished she was there to hold him and help him. Her heart ached with his, yet she was miles from where she should be— with him.

"She looks like hell. I don't know. Once the surgeons and the X-ray people put their findings together, we'll know more." In an explosion of grief, Rafe blurted out, "I love her so damn much, Jessie. Cat is like me; she's got guts and, sometimes, not enough sense. I don't know what made her walk into that worthless pit. I was there. If you'd seen the timber and flooring in that mine, you wouldn't have taken two steps into that godforsaken hole. I don't know what made her do it. Damn…"

"She's going to be all right, Rafe. I know it… I feel it. If she's like you, she's tough enough and stubborn enough to fight back, no matter what the odds are against her."

Rafe managed a strangled sound. "Cat and I are close, Jessie. She's like my shadow. All the time when we were growing up, she was my best friend. If I wanted to take a risk, Cat took it with me. She never hung back like Dal did. Once we jumped our horses across this chasm. Cat's horse landed on his knees on the other side, and she got thrown off and busted up her arm in the fall. When I ran over to help her, she was sitting there laughing through her tears, holding on to her bad arm. She's always come through, Jess, laughing and smiling…"

There was nothing Jessie could say to him in his grief, so she let him spill out everything he felt for his sister. When at last he stopped, emotionally exhausted, and apologized for rambling, Jessie whispered, "Oh, Rafe, you just don't know, do you? I know how much you love Cat, and how hard this is for you. And it's nothing you have to apologize for—you know that. Cat sounds like a beautiful person. I hope I'll meet her someday."

"Yeah. Me, too." Jessie heard the strain in his voice and imagined him running his hands through his hair. "Listen, honey, I'll let you get back to sleep. I'll call you first thing in the morning. The doctors don't know how long they'll be in surgery with her."

"All right."

"Jessie?"

Her breath caught at the emotion in his voice. "Yes?"

"I love you."

Hot, humid August dog days contributed to Jessie's exhaustion. Or was it her pregnancy? She sat beneath the stand of cottonwood in the small backyard behind the ranch. Damp bits of hair clung to her perspiring brow as she hunched over the sack of peas William had picked from the garden earlier. There was something peaceful about shelling peas, Jessie thought. A slight breeze stirred the sluggish air to life, and she sat up, stretching her tired, protesting back muscles. The nicker of horses and lowing of cows broke the noontime drowsiness.

Jessie's eyes darkened as she thought about Rafe. He said he'd try to fly up in the next day or two, but he'd been unsure because he had just returned to the Triple K. Cat was going to pull through. What was it about the Kincaids that drove them to take such risks? And yet, when it came to emotional risks, Rafe sidestepped it until recently. She never forgot the way his husky voice sounded when he told her he loved her. Had he said it out of the stress of the moment? A bittersweet feeling thrummed through Jessie, and she pressed her hand gently against her body. Soon, the doctor had promised, she would begin showing. She was carrying her baby high and still looked slim.

With a deep breath, Jessie scooped out another handful of peas and methodically began shelling them. When Rafe came, it would be the hardest thing in the world for her not to tell him that she was carrying his child. Was she strong enough not to say anything? She'd never realized what strength was until now. She knew that if she told Rafe he would automatically marry her. But it would be for the wrong reasons, and Jessie knew it. Yet, she ached to be his wife because she loved him. Only if he could overcome that hurdle of silence and reach out and love once again… Then she would tell him.

Jessie lifted her chin and stared off into the cloudless blue sky toward Colorado. What if Rafe couldn't overcome that hurdle? Her eyes turned misty with anguish. She would go on and lead her life, love her child and live on her ranch alone. Despite the aching pain in her heart, Jessie rallied. She had already been granted one miracle by being allowed to carry a baby. Was it too much to even dare for a second miracle for Rafe to love her unreservedly?

The sound of helicopter blades cutting through the thick, desultory heat punctured the afternoon air. Jessie stood, shading her eyes, trying to find the helicopter, which she knew Rafe was flying.

"He's here?" William asked, still shelling the peas.

Jessie nodded and smiled. "Yes, he's here," she answered softly. "He's here…"

Rafe took a pass over the ranch at a thousand feet,

wanting to see Jessie's spread for himself. Compared to the Triple K, the Bar M, her ranch, looked antiquated. As his practiced eye swept over the area, Rafe wondered if Jessie would break even financially at the end of every year. Probably not. The paddocks held a number of mustangs, and he could see several herds of Herefords grazing in different pastures. Unlike Colorado, this portion of Wyoming was bone dry, although a couple of small streams wound like blue ribbons through the yellowing, parched grasslands. Winter would be harsh, and he would bet that blizzard conditions would cut Jessie off from anyone for a week or two at a time. Was she prepared for that? Did she know what she was in for by assuming the duties of a working ranch? He thought not.

Looking toward the house, he spotted Jessie standing near some trees, waving to him. A smile broke out on his mouth. Even from a thousand feet, he could see her spun-gold hair. An incredible sense of relief and happiness took him by surprise as he jockeyed the helicopter to a landing on a flat area near the ranch house. Unharnessing himself, he pulled his cowboy hat back on his head and opened the door. Jessie was walking toward him in a short-sleeved pink blouse and jeans.

His smile broadened as he approached her. She was tanned and looked incredibly healthy. Any weight she had lost during her visit to the Triple K had been regained. For once Rafe didn't try to sidestep the violent emotions Jessie brought to life in him as he opened his arms to receive her.

"Rafe!" she whispered, throwing her arms around his neck and pressing herself along the length of him.

Holding her tightly, he nestled his face into the clean strands of her hair. Hungrily he kissed her damp temple, her cheek, and finally molded his mouth to her smiling lips. He drowned himself in her giving sweetness, his whole being centered on Jessie.

"God, I've missed you," he muttered, running his hands down her rib cage and settling them on her hips.

She looked deeply into Rafe's eyes and saw the love shining there. He held her away from him, a glint of humor evident in his now-relaxed face.

"You're starting to look like a rancher, Jessie. Got a tan, and your hands—" he picked them up and turned them over "—are starting to get little calluses all over them. But you look good, honey. Damn good."

She glowed beneath his inspection. "Thank you, kind sir. And you don't look too bad yourself. Come on, William has made us some lemonade." She slipped her arm around him and led him toward the house.

"This is quite a spread you inherited, Jessie," he said, gazing down at her. She was happy, Rafe realized humbly. All along, Jessie had belonged in the West, outdoors. And even more humbling was the fact that Rafe knew she belonged at his side.

"What do you think of it?" There was hope in her voice as she anxiously sought out what he thought of her place.

Several wooden chairs had been placed beneath a cottonwood. William had already brought out a pitcher of iced lemonade, and Jessie poured them each a glass as they sat down. Rafe took off his straw cowboy hat and placed it on the grass beside his chair.

"Needs a lot of work; but it's basically a good spread from what I can tell, Jessie."

"Then you like it?"

He nodded, his eyes crinkling. "Yeah, it's a nice place, Jessie."

Delighted, she leaned back. "I know it needs repairs, and I hope to get them done before winter comes." Sobering, she asked, "How's Cat doing?"

Rafe sipped the tart drink, anxious to get past the small talk. He wanted her fiercely.

Instead, he answered, "Recovering. Last time I talked to you, I think I told you she had three busted ribs and a busted-up head."

Jessie laughed. "A thick one, you said. Thank God. Is she going to come back home to recover?"

"No." He shook his head. "She'll spend another week in the hospital, and then she's heading to Texas with that guy, Donovan, I told you about. He persuaded her to go and convalesce at his place. Apparently he's a geologist, and he eventually wants to do some business with her." He grinned. "Knowing Cat, she's not going to let a close call stop her from doing what she loves."

If only you could live like that, Rafe, Jessie thought. *If only you wouldn't let the past stop you from reaching out and living once again.* Did he have the kind of courage his sister obviously possessed? She sat there, the lemonade glass clutched between her hands, knowing her fate lay with Rafe and whatever he had come to say to her.

Chapter 10

Rafe hooked the heel of his boot on the bottom rung of the fence as he stared at the mustangs that moved restlessly within the huge paddock. He heard the pride in Jessie's voice as she explained Joshua Randall's breeding program to him. The sun was low on the horizon, making him squint as he studied the well-fed wild horses.

"I discovered that Joshua kept a breeding log on his mustang mares." Jessie pointed to a stud colt at his mother's side. "That medicine hat and her baby are from the Red Desert. Joshua believed what I do, that the medicine hat is the purest form and source of wild horse blood. He kept three hundred acres to the north of here for his own private herd. I'll take that mare and her colt to that area eventually, and the blood in that colt's veins will help insure future stock of even better quality."

He glanced over at her, a smile pulling at his mouth.

"You're sounding more and more like a horsewoman every minute, Jessie." There was admiration in his tone. "And it appears you've got a solid breeding plan."

She colored beneath his compliment; Rafe wasn't one to waste praise on a plan that wouldn't work. All afternoon he'd made helpful comments when she talked about Joshua's ranching operation. Rafe had pointed out some deficits, but he'd also lauded her own ideas and efforts to institute changes for the better. Together they watched the colt rear up on his spindly legs, imitating the stallion he would one day become, and then romp around his mother.

"I just pray I can be as good as Joshua was at finding the best mustangs and save and protect them like he did."

"Jessie, you're good at anything you tackle because you care."

She tilted her head, meeting the serious expression in his intensely blue eyes. Her heart expanded with love toward him. "Rafe? How long can you stay?"

Sliding his well-worn boot off the last rung, he said slowly, "Not as long as I want to, Jessie."

"I know there must be a ton of work begging for your attention back at the Triple K, especially after your being gone so long," she agreed quietly.

Rafe noticed a couple of the ranch hands watching them. At first he had been worried that the men might give her a hard time; but from the looks of things, they respected her as boss of the operation. Jessie had the ability to be firm without rubbing a person the wrong way. He took her elbow and walked back toward the ranch house, which was in dire need of a new coat of white paint and green trim. He chafed inwardly because time wasn't his at the moment. In another two weeks fall branding of more than two thousand head of calves would get underway. The last of three hay balings would be initiated over a thousand acres of prime alfalfa and timothy pastures, which would provide food for the cattle and horses over the long winter months to come.

He guided her to the rear of the house, out of earshot and sight of the hands. What he had to say required privacy. His pulse quickened as they drew to a halt beneath the cottonwoods. Jessie's face was flushed, and she sat down on one of the chairs they had used earlier.

"This past month has been hell in just about every sense," he told her in a husky voice, holding her gaze. "First, you left, and then we almost lost Cat." Rafe shook his head and took off his hat. "I don't know which one shook me worse, Jessie. When you left, I felt a loneliness like I did after Mary Ann died. I never wanted to ever experience that feeling again." He pursed his lips. "I guess I don't like living with pain very much, Jessie."

"No one does, Rafe."

"God knows, I've given you a lot of pain."

"And a lot of happiness."

He slowly moved the hat between his fingers, studying it darkly, struggling for the words that jammed in his throat. "I want you to come back to the Triple K with me, Jessie."

Her lips parted in shock. "Back?"

Rafe gave a brisk nod. "I'm finding I can't live without you. On the phone last week, I told you two things I'd never thought I'd ever tell another woman. The first was that I needed you. I stood in that hospital hallway dying inside. All I could think about after they brought Cat into the trauma unit was calling you. I needed your voice, Jessie. You do something for me I can't explain.

You touch me in a way I've never had any woman touch me." His tone grew strained. "The second thing was… I love you. As much as I can, I do."

Tears crowded into her eyes. Jessie knew how much it had cost Rafe to admit how he felt. The urge to take him into her arms was overpowering, but she forced herself to sit quietly. "I know you love me."

He gave her a bashful look. "I have for a long time; I just didn't want to admit it."

"Why, Rafe?" They were on such tenuous ground with each other that Jessie placed her arm protectively across her belly.

Clearing his throat, he looked over her head, staring blindly toward the house. "Admitting it meant I cared. Caring meant I had to extend myself to feel again, Jessie. I was afraid then, and I am now." He wiped his perspiring brow and tried to smile. "I know I can't live without you. But I'm not sure what I can offer you, either."

"You're not offering me marriage, are you?"

He shook his head, frowning. "I—not yet. I want to make sure."

Pain shot through her, the kind that came from heartache, and Jessie clasped her hands tightly in her lap. Rafe was still afraid. He was trying to get what he wanted without having to take responsibility for his actions. They were so close…so close that she could feel him wanting to broach that last wall of fear and embrace her and the future. The lines of tension deepened on Rafe's face as Jessie slowly raised her chin and looked him in the eye.

"I can't come, Rafe. Not until you're sure of me and of yourself. Don't you see what would happen if I said yes? Do you want to cheat both of us of what might have been?"

Rafe winced outwardly. "I'm as close as I'll ever get to what you need me to be, Jessie. I've tried to change. I've tried to reconcile with the past." His blue eyes grew stormy as he met hers. "Come home with me, Jessie. I know we can make it work."

"Half of nothing is nothing, Rafe. You can't pretend to play house with our lives. We have to come to each other in honesty and with a hundred percent of our heart, soul and mind. I'm sorry… I love you so much…"

Anger snaked through Rafe, and he grimly straightened up and settled the hat back on his head. He drew the brim low, shadowing eyes that mirrored disappointment and confusion. "I don't understand what you're saying, Jessie. I love you, dammit! Come home with me, live with me. It's that simple."

Jessie tensed beneath his harsh attack. Forcing herself to look at him, she said, "There's nothing simple about your request, Rafe. You want a live-in woman, a disposable relationship. Someone you can discard if they make too many demands on you. You want my company, my love and friendship, but you're not willing to give all those things in return to me. If I married you, then that would mean you'd have to give all of yourself to me. But you can't do that right now, and I'm not going to settle for half of Rafe Kincaid. The man I marry will want to share all of himself with me."

Disbelief was etched in his eyes as he stared at her. "Thanks for telling me how you feel," he bit out. "It's always nice to know that you think I want you for nothing more than a bed warmer. I may have my hang-ups, but you've got a few of your own. I think that ex-husband of yours brainwashed you well. He drilled it into your head that you weren't any good because you couldn't bear children. And you *still* believe him, or you wouldn't be acting like this!"

Jessie stood, tears stinging her eyes. Rafe backed away, glaring at her. "No! Rafe, wait! Let's try and talk this—"

"Forget it! I tried talking to you, Jessie. We both have pasts that haunt us. And you're just as much a prisoner of yours as I am of mine. The only difference was, Jessie, I *tried* to change because I loved you. I tried to give you a measure of love." His voice lowered to a snarl. "You never changed one bit. You say you love me? I doubt it like hell, because if you had, you'd be coming home with me." Rafe's mouth drew into a tortured line, and he tried to harden his heart against Jessie as she stood helplessly in front of him. Her sable eyes were luminous with tears, and her mouth was contorted with pain. Well, he was in no less pain! Rafe spun around and began walking toward the helicopter.

She stood there in the closing heat of the day, watching helplessly as Rafe took the helicopter skyward. Tears rolled from her eyes as she watched him gradually disappear out of sight. Out of her life.

"Miss Jessie, do you want anything before I go?" William Lee stood at the entrance to the living room, decked out in his best clothes, a suitcase in each hand.

Jessie shook her head, not even trying to get up. At eight and a half months pregnant she moved carefully and slowly. "No, thank you, William. You just enjoy Christmas with your family."

He inclined his head. "I'll be back before that baby's due, but I still think you should spend Christmas in town. Doctor Novack is worried a blizzard will hit. The weather gets crazy this time of year, you know. If one comes, you could be stranded out here and—"

"William, you worry too much. I'll be fine. Doctor Novack and the midwives had said first babies are usually late and not early. We'll both be waiting until early January before Daniel decides to come into this world." Jessie walked over and patted him on the shoulder, loving him for his protective attitude toward her. Since September, William had fussed over her like a doting parent. "Now, go on. I'll see you on the thirty-first. You'd better get going, or you'll miss your train."

William gave her a guarded look, but said nothing more to persuade her. "I'll bring that baby of yours something special from San Francisco," he promised.

Shorty Evans appeared at the door after a quick knock. Frigid winter air whooshed in with him before he shut the door behind him and stepped into the living room, shaking off the snow from his boots. Nodding goodbye to William, he turned to Jessie.

"You wanted to see me, Miss Jessie?"

"Yes, come on in, Shorty." The icy blast of wind had momentarily cooled off the living room, and Jessie wrapped a pink shawl around her shoulders.

The cowhand took off his hat, his gray-and-black hair slick and damp with sweat and snow.

Jessie handed him a list of items she needed from the grocery store. "I want you and all but a skeleton crew to take the next day and half off." It was the twenty-fourth of December. Most of the men had wives or girlfriends in town, which was thirty miles from the ranch, and Jessie saw no reason for them to be standing duty at the ranch when there was no pressing business. She wanted them to spend the holiday at home, with their families, where they belonged.

"When you come back on the twenty-sixth, bring these groceries with you."

"You want me to put on a skeleton crew?" Evans looked at her disbelievingly. "The rest of us can go home?"

She smiled. "Yes. Two hands can feed the mustangs and cattle. I don't see any sense in having you boys spend Christmas at the bunkhouse when you can be with your families. Merry Christmas, Shorty."

His eyes lit up with gratefulness, and his narrow face creased into a smile. "Thank you, ma'am. But— what about you?" He motioned toward her swollen belly. "Time's gettin' near, ain't it?"

"First week in January, Shorty. Besides, you boys are only going to be gone a short time. I'll be fine."

"You've got my wife's number in case you need anything," he said helpfully. "I'll leave Dave and Mike here; they're both single and young. Their families are up in Montana."

After Shorty left, the ranch house grew serene once again. William had bought a small evergreen from town the week before and had trimmed it to perfection. Jessie sat down on her rocker, gently placed her hands across her abdomen and gazed at the tree. In the past two weeks the child had quieted within her body—normal, Dr. Novack had assured her on the last visit. According to her, the baby was now in place, getting ready to be born.

With a sigh, Jessie picked up her crocheting needle. Maud had taught her how to crochet a long time ago, and she wanted to have a small bright blue blanket finished before her baby was welcomed into the world. Her thoughts turned to Rafe, as they always did when there was a rare moment of inactivity at the ranch. Jessie's eyes grew dark with pain, and out of habit she stared at the phone. Since their disagreement, she had heard nothing from him. Dal had kept in touch, though, and had let Jessie know how angry she was with her "mule-headed" brother.

Whether she wanted to or not, Jessie felt tears forcing their way to her eyes. She shut her lids, gripping the crochet needle and resting it on her belly. *Rafe... I love you so much. Our baby is going to be born, and you don't know about it.* God, how she had been torn between telling him and remaining silent. If only he would understand that what he had asked of her wasn't fair to either of them! Dal understood. But then, Dal wasn't Rafe.

Jessie opened her eyes, blinking away the tears. Her only company since Rafe left had been her baby. Somehow, she knew it would be a boy. Long ago she'd picked out a name for him; Daniel. The hours she had spent in her web of daydreams that involved her baby were her only source of solace against the loss of Rafe, against what might have been.

"One day," Jessie told her baby, beginning to rock again, "your friends will start calling you Dan instead of Danny." A smile pulled at her lips. "Your mother will call you Daniel when you're in hot water and probably call you Danny in moments of weakness because you'll always be her little boy, no matter how old you become." Jessie stroked her stomach, believing that Dan was aware of the love she had for him. Soon, very soon, she would be able to hold him in her arms, breastfeed him and rock him to sleep in this very rocker.

She glanced beneath the tree. It was barren of gifts,

but that didn't matter. Her mustangs were a gift to her. As was the precious beauty of the West. And Joshua had given her the gift of his ranch. She was fortunate in so many ways. Her eyes misted. Rafe had given her the most precious gift of all: his love and his child. Jessie ached for him. There were times, especially when she was feeling depressed, that she had almost picked up the phone and called him to say that she'd live with him. Half of something was better than nothing. But she knew better. Those were the times when she would go to her bedroom and lie on the huge antique brass bed and cry. Cry and hold her stomach, as though she were holding her baby.

No, there was no need for any gifts under the Christmas tree this year. Dan would be her gift, and Jessie wanted nothing more. Except Rafe. A tremulous sigh came from deep within her, and she wondered if her anguish over losing Rafe had affected Dan. The baby had to hear everything; did he also feel her sadness? She prayed that he didn't; she didn't want her son to feel her grief. It wasn't Dan's fault that his parents couldn't come to terms, and he shouldn't have to bear the awful weight of pain she bore everyday.

Dal glanced at her husband as she finished placing the last of the bulbs on the tree. Rafe was standing by the picture window, his hands thrust deep into the pockets of his jeans, his back to them. They had come over in the late morning to trim the tree, an old family custom. Rafe had been moody and unpredictable and had barely spoken to anyone. She chewed on her lower lip. He was thinking of Jessie; she could feel it around him.

With a sigh of frustration, Dal continued to decorate the tree with Jim and Millie. Little Alessandra sat in her playpen, cooing delightedly at the latest toy that Rafe had gifted her with. How much should she intervene? Dal wondered. She'd always shared the letters she received from Jessie with Rafe. In those moments his entire face would change, and she could see the longing burn deep in his eyes as she related the events around the Bar M through Jessie's eyes. They were like droplets of water, sustenance to Rafe's shriveling soul, Dal thought. Why wouldn't he drive or fly up to see her? It was Christmas. The Bar M was only two hundred miles away—a short flight by helicopter or a four-hour drive. He loved her—he didn't deny it. So why was he being so damned stubborn?

Rafe excused himself with a growl and headed outdoors. He grabbed his sheepskin jacket and settled the cowboy hat on his head. Without thinking, he went to the stall that housed Jessie's Girl. The once spindly and fragile-looking black filly had grown and filled out. The look of a champion was stamped on her. Rafe stood at the entrance to the stall, and the filly nickered softly, moving over to where he stood. She thrust her velvety muzzle into Rafe's outstretched hand.

"Do you miss her, too?" Rafe asked the filly. He stood there, scratching the animal's favorite spot behind her small, fine ears, thinking of nothing else but Jessie. It was Christmas Eve. And she was alone up there. She had no family. All her friends were back East. As usual, the orphan had no one. Except him. Rafe's mouth thinned as he rested his large hand on the filly's slender neck. He couldn't stand the sense of loss any longer. How many hundreds of times had he replayed Jessie's argument to himself?

His eyes dimmed as the pressure, the need for Jessie overcame his fear of the future. He had to take the risk, no matter how frightened he was. He loved her. He needed her. The instant he made the decision, Rafe felt as if a hundred tons had miraculously slid off his shoulders. He felt lighter, almost jubilant. Giving the ebony filly a fond pat on the head, Rafe turned and strode purposefully out of the barn and back to the house.

Dal's eyes widened as she saw her brother enter the house. There was a certain set to his jaw, and a light in his eyes. "Rafe?"

He halted near the hall. "What?"

"Where are you going in such a hurry?"

Rafe held his younger sister's gaze, and there was a slight smile on his mouth. "I'm going to see Jessie. Got any objections?"

Her eyes went wide as saucers. "Jessie? You're really going to see her?"

"Yeah." He turned to Millie. "Will you pack me something to eat? I intend to drive up. The weather's too iffy for a helicopter flight."

Millie brightened instantly. "You bet!"

Dal turned to her husband, a big smile on her face, and crossed her fingers. Rafe walked down the hall toward his room to pack a bag. He wasn't planning on coming back without Jessie, and he didn't know how long that would take. But time didn't matter any more. She did.

"We interrupt this scheduled program to bring you a winter storm warning. A cold air mass from Canada is expected to sweep across Wyoming and Colorado sometime late this afternoon."

Jessie wrinkled her nose. Another storm. Already they had endured an early November blizzard that had dumped three feet of snow on the Red Desert. As she got off the couch, a cramp cut across her stomach. She froze. Labor? No, it couldn't be, Jessie thought, moving slowly toward the phone. The midwives said she'd experience a few twinges of laborlike pains as the time grew near.

Ignoring it, she continued slowly across the room. With a blizzard to hit later that day, she wanted to warn Dave and Mike. They would have to take the pickup and load it down with extra hay for the cattle on the range, north of the ranch house. After the blizzard came and dumped its two to three feet of snow, there would be no way to get to the range animals for a couple of days afterward, so if they didn't reach them now, the animals would starve to death.

Jessie glanced outside—the entire landscape was covered beneath a blanket of snow. She dialed the bunkhouse, got Dave on the phone and explained the weather situation. He promised to get Mike from the barn, and they would begin loading hay on the flatbed truck and start to deliver to the different pastures right away.

Another wave of pain radiated upward and across her belly, and she frowned, sitting back down. The baby... no, it wasn't possible. Dr. Novack had said Dan would be born in three weeks. Gently rubbing her swollen abdomen, Jessie turned her mind to more important matters; a blizzard was coming. William had left enough food for the next two weeks—no problem there. Dave, the youngest hand, was a pretty fair cook and had promised to take over William's duties the day after Christmas. All she had to do was cook for the three of them until then.

More than an hour later, the shortwave radio in the study went on. Dave's scratchy voice came over it. "Unit One to Ranch. We're leavin' now, Miss Jessie."

She went to the office, picked up the portable radio and depressed the button. "Be careful out there, Dave. The sky doesn't look good."

Dave's youthful laughter floated back over the phone. "Mike says it looks like a blue norther. You ever seen one before? The sky gets a funny blue color. Take a look out the window. Unit One out. We'll be back in six hours— in time for dinner."

Jessie smiled. "It'll be waiting for you boys. Spaghetti tonight. Over and out." Her smile disappeared. A vague, unsettled feeling stalked her as she went back to the living room. She moved to the window and pulled back the pale green drapes. Dave was right—the sky was a gun-metal gray, with an almost transparent veil of an eerie ultramarine blue that heralded the encroaching front.

A blue norther. She'd heard the phrase but had never known what it meant. The entire northern and western horizon was shadowed and threatening. Jessie worried about her ranch hands. To reach all the herds at the different feeding points would take at least six hours. The truck was equipped with heavy snow tires, and carried chains, if it proved necessary. She rested her hands against the icy window, unable to shake the nervous feeling the storm was bringing with it. Unconsciously Jessie's hand went to her stomach, and she gently stroked it, as if to reassure the baby that even though terror was coursing through her, it was nothing to worry about.

Near 3:00 p.m., the first winds struck the flats. A banshee wail sounding like a scream announced the storm's presence. Jessie watched with wide eyes as the stout, stately cottonwoods in front of the ranch house bent deeply against the savage, howling wind. The sickening crack of breaking limbs sounded, and torn branches were flung across the yard. The electricity dimmed, and she turned, watching the lights flicker, then go out. Muttering, Jessie walked across the room. Although it was only midafternoon, she could barely see through the gloom. Fortunately Joshua had had a number of kerosene lamps, and she went around, lighting them in each of the major rooms of the house.

At 5:00 p.m. the blizzard struck. Jessie tried calling the truck, worried that Dave and Mike would be caught out in the open by the storm. She had heard stories of men dying out in the cold, and as she tried again and again to raise them, her anxiety rose. The temperature in the house dropped a good five degrees, and she wrapped a shawl over her shoulders, thankful that she had gas heat in the house. Rubbing her arms, she turned up the thermostat and listened to the shrieking wind.

It was dark outside, and Jessie shivered as she watched the heavy snow blanket everything on the ground. She couldn't even make out the silhouette of the cottonwoods, which sat a mere fifty feet from the house. Suddenly a cramp gripped her body. She turned, gnawing on her lower lip. False labor pains were possible and even to be expected a few weeks before the birth. She felt liquid seeping from her nipples and looked down to see a stain developing on her dark blue blouse. No, this wasn't false labor…it was real. Protectively Jessie placed both hands on her belly and shut her eyes.

Alone…always alone. All her life, she'd been forced to do everything by herself. She slowly opened her eyes. She couldn't birth her baby by herself. She had to reach her midwives in Bittersweet and Dr. Novack.

Without thinking, Jessie went to the phone and picked it up. A frisson of fear went through her—the line was dead. The storm not only was knocking out power, it was also destroying telephone lines. She replaced the receiver and turned toward the kitchen. There was a ten-year-old pickup in the garage. William had taken the new truck, which was equipped with snow tires, to the train station. Shorty was going to drive it back to the ranch from town on the morning of the twenty-sixth. No, she decided, if she got stuck or stranded in the storm before she reached town, she could freeze to death. She was better off at the ranch.

Jessie moved to the kitchen, going over all possible options and finding none. The wind howled, buffeting the house like some invisible giant hand. The entire structure shuddered beneath its impact. She didn't dare try to drive to town now; the road would be nearly impassable, and only a four-wheel drive would ever make it through. Her hands grew icy as she turned and walked back to the living room. Every five minutes a contraction came, a little longer, a little more painful than the last one.

Her only hope was Dave and Mike. Jessie went to the study and tried to raise them on the radio. All she heard was static. Were they isolated by the blizzard in some remote pasture? Had their radio stopped working, or was it just the fury of the storm scrambling her call for help to them? Frantic, Jessie paced the room, pulling the shawl tightly across her shoulders. She was warm and safe. The ranch hands could be stranded out where they might freeze to death. She stared around the deeply shadowed room. Loneliness seethed through her as never before. She was as alone as Dave and Mike, only in a worse way. What if there were complications with the birth?

No! She wouldn't allow herself to think of the negatives, of what could happen. Forcing herself to face the reality of having to birth her own child alone, she moved to her bedroom.

Jessie allowed all the information she had gathered in her Lamaze classes to surface. The two midwives who were to help her with Dan had shared their experiences with her, and she also remembered Rafe helping to deliver the foal. Clean towels, water, a pair of sharp scissors and iodine, she recalled. Being able to do something about her predicament held her fear at bay. She placed all the items on the bedstand next to her brass bed. As she stood by the footboard, her fingers wrapped around the coolness of the brass, the wind screamed outside the darkened window. Every fiber in her wished that Rafe was there. He would know what needed to be done. He might not have ever delivered a human baby, but he'd welcomed a lot of little four-footed creatures into the world. There wasn't much difference, Jessie decided, trying to hold down her panic. Act like Rafe would. Be calm. There's so sense in crying: it won't help.

As the hours slowly unwound, she held Rafe's image in her mind and heart, as never before, and it gave her the courage she knew she would eventually need.

Chapter 11

The wind tore viciously at the house, and Jessie lay on the brass bed, wondering if the structure would remain upright despite the fury of the blue norther. The old hand-wound clock ticked away on the bedstand: it was 3:00 a.m. The lone hurricane lamp on the dresser opposite the bed filled the room with patches of weak light. Long ago, her unbound hair had become soaked with perspiration, and tendrils now clung to the sides of her face and brow as she lay waiting.

After a while, she had adjusted to the unremitting contractions sweeping across her body. To a degree, Jessie reminded herself wryly, her fists knotting the bed covers on either side of her. At first, the agony had stolen her breath; she had never felt anything like it in her life. Gradually, as she lay on the bed, it was as if her body had adjusted to the knifelike pain serrating her belly, and she was able to tolerate it to a higher degree. She took in a gasp of air as another contraction hit. They were now coming every two minutes. William had been her partner in her Lamaze classes. She was as prepared as possible, except that now there would be no doctor, no midwives or William to help her birth Dan. Sadness briefly overcame her; she regretted that Rafe had not been able to share her pregnancy, or the joy she had because she carried his son. Their future.

The wind buffeted the house, and the flicker of the hurricane lamp dimmed momentarily, as if in response. Jessie closed her eyes, her dazed mind wandering back to Dave and Mike. She worried for them. Would they know how to protect themselves out there on the flats, where the wind must be howling at seventy or eighty miles an hour? The wind chill would kill them if they ever left the safety of the truck. Had they taken warm clothing? Normally the two men assigned to the feeding circuit packed a lunch, a couple of thermoses of coffee and blankets, just in case they did get stranded. That was ranch policy. It was only common sense. Had they done that? A jagged twinge cut vertically up through her, and Jessie cried out involuntarily, her back arching like a bow. She rolled slowly onto her side, sobbing for breath, holding her tender belly.

"Oh, God…" she moaned, sweat leaking into her tightly shut eyes. She tried to pull the pale pink chenille robe back across her, the only item of clothing she wore. Her breath came in ragged gasps as she was suddenly as sensitive to the pain as at the beginning of the labor. Only this time, it was as if her body had picked up the intensity of rhythm to push her baby from her as never before. Jessie lay there, no position comfortable, as wave after wave of throbbing pain struck. She knotted her fists, pressing them hard against her bared teeth, trying to somehow escape the heightened tempo of agony and pressure.

Another hour dragged by, and the room echoed with her moans and sudden cries. Headlights, barely visible because of the storm, moved across the closed drapes at the window. Jessie blinked, trying to think coherently. Dave and Mike! They had made it back! Without thinking, she weakly pushed herself upward. Her hands trembled badly as she tied the sash beneath her breasts. Taking a deep breath, she rose unsteadily to her feet. The downward pressure created more agony, and she reached out, gripping the brass footboard of the bed for balance. She had to get to the door and let them in—it was locked. They'd be freezing. They'd need the warmth of the house. Relief shattered through Jessie as she took slow, unsteady steps through the living room.

The pounding on the door reverberated through the house, heavier and more violent than even the shrieking wind. Jessie pushed the hair off her glistening face, unable to call out. Shakily her fingers closed around the lock. Just as she twisted the knob to open the door, another violent contraction consumed her. She took a wavering step back, gripping the edge of the couch, her other arm wrapped tightly around her.

The icy coldness swept into the room as the door opened and then closed. The fingers of winter enveloped Jessie, and she felt lightheaded as she fought to stay coherent against the stabbing pain. A little cry escaped her as she slowly sank to her knees.

Rafe's eyes widened in shock as Jessie clung weakly to the couch, trying to prevent herself from falling over.

He threw off his snow-laden hat and took two long strides to her side. A hundred impressions assailed him as he leaned down, his exhaustion ripped away. Her once-beautiful hair lay in long, stringy ropes around her face and shoulders. He saw the contorted cry on her lips and the waxen color of her flesh. Sweat stood out on her frozen features, and her skin glistened beneath the lamplight. His gaze moved downward, and it was as if a huge fist has smashed into his heart. She lay in a crouched position, with her arms around herself. *Pregnant! She's pregnant....*

His fingers closed around her upper arms, and he knelt at her side. "Jessie?" he rasped, anxiously taking stock of her condition. She was in heavy labor.

No! Jessie fought off the faintness. The voice reaching her dimmed awareness sounded like Rafe's voice. Pain cut savagely upward, and she couldn't even lift her head to see if she was imagining him or not. She felt arms move protectively around her, lifting her upward. Just the action of the abrupt and unexpected movement made her cry out. Jessie sagged against him, her fingers digging into the rough texture of the sheepskin coat he wore. Each step he took was pure agony riddling through her. She forced her eyes open.

Rafe worriedly stared down into her huge sable eyes; the pupils were black and dilated. He heard her call his name, a hoarse cry of disbelief, and he automatically held her a little tighter. Finding the bedroom, he carried her into it.

"It's me, Jessie. It's all right," he told her, his own voice ragged with emotion.

Jessie sobbed. It wasn't a dream! Rafe was holding her. He was here! She choked and moved her arms up to wrap them around his thickly corded neck. "Rafe... I'm...the baby's coming. I need help..." She couldn't say anymore, as the contractions ripped the breath from her. All she could do was allow the agony to wash through her like a powerful riptide.

Rafe gently placed her on the bed. He jerked off his heavy jacket and glanced around the room. His face grew tender as he sat at her side, pulling the chenille robe across her. He took her tightly fisted hands into his.

"I had to come, Jessie," he rasped. Tears stung his eyes. "The baby...he's ours, isn't he?"

Jessie bit down hard on her lip. "Y-yes...ours. Rafe, I'm in so much pain—" She cried out as another wave overwhelmed her.

"Sshh, it's all right, honey," he soothed, stroking her sweaty brow. "Try and relax. Come on, take a couple of deep breaths between the contractions. When they come, pant. You understand?"

Just the deep, lulling sound of Rafe's voice took away the panic she was feeling. Jessie clung weakly to his hand. The contraction passed. "Rafe, he's ours. I didn't know I was pregnant until I got back to D.C. the second time." She stared up into his eyes. "I love you...and I'm so scared. I—I thought I'd be alone to have our baby."

A powerful avalanche of emotions overwhelmed Rafe. In those seconds he understood everything. He took Jessie into his arms and held her carefully. "I came back," he said, his voice cracking. "I came for you, Jessie. I can't live without you. I need you. Forever." Rafe fought his fear of what could happen to Jessie. Would she end up dying as Mary Ann had? No! This time, he wasn't too late. He'd arrived in time to help her.

"I stopped hoping you'd come back. I wanted you so

badly. So many times I almost called you." Jessie sobbed. "I was willing to take anything you'd give me."

He murmured her name reverently, running his hand through her damp hair. "We'll talk later, honey. Just know that you've got all of me now, not half." He laid her back down, keeping his hand on her thin shoulder. God, she looked so pale. He winced, knowing what her courage had cost her over the four months since he'd walked out of her life. She looked like a Madonna: her skin, although pale, was translucent with radiance. Despite the pain in her eyes, he saw a fierce light of joy in them.

"How long have you been in labor, honey?"

Jessie pushed her head against the pillow, trying not to cry out. Rafe gave her strength; he gave her steadiness. "S-since 5:00 p.m. yesterday."

Rafe glanced at his watch: it was 4:00 a.m. He gave her a slight smile.

"How far apart are your contractions?"

"A minute, maybe less. They come so often…"

"You're right on time, honey."

"H-how do you know?"

Rafe eased off the bed, unsnapping the cuffs of his dark wine-colored cowboy shirt and rolling them up. "Before Mary Ann was to have our baby, I read every possible thing I could get my hands on about pregnancy, delivery procedure and postnatal care. We took Lamaze together." Satisfaction showed in his eyes as he placed a hand on either side of her head and stared deeply into her wide, frightened eyes. "Now listen to me, honey," he said. "We're going to deliver that baby of ours. We can do it, Jessie. You and I. Like the good team we are. Trust me?"

Tears formed and fled down her cheeks. Her mouth was dry, and her lips were chapped from dehydration.

She nodded. "I trust you with my life, Rafe. I—I always have…"

He leaned down to put his mouth against the damp skin of her cheek. "Let me examine you, Jessie. I've got to see how far along you are."

Was it Rafe's presence or had the bedroom turned warmer? Jessie wasn't sure. She felt secure, the panic driven to a far edge of her mind. Rafe's bulk cast a giant shadow against the wall, and she closed her eyes, fists knotted, unafraid for the first time since the labor had begun.

Rafe managed a tight smile. "You're completely dilated, Jessie. It won't be long," he murmured, giving her ankle a caress. "I'm going to wash up. I'll be back in just a moment." He covered her with a sheet and blanket. Rafe didn't fight the urge to reach out and caress her delicate jaw. Her eyes were so dark and huge. "I love the hell out of you, lady. You just hold on to that thought until I return."

When he returned to the room, he sat at her side, and Jessie clutched his hand. Rafe sponged off her taut, sweaty features, murmuring soothing words to her. "Soon, Jessie, soon. Just hang on… I love you so much…"

Her breath came in ragged wisps. "It's a boy, Rafe. I know it's a boy…"

His smile softened his hard face. "A son. That figures. Probably weighs close to a sack of potatoes, too."

Jessie managed a grimace. "I hope not! I'm too small to carry a ten-pound sack of potatoes around."

He swabbed the gleaming perspiration from the taut cords of her neck. Was the baby too large for Jessie to birth? That worried him, but he said nothing. God, he'd seen that happen in his horses and cows, and he didn't want to think about the consequences. A doctor could perform a cesarean section on Jessie, but he couldn't. He leaned down to press a kiss on her lips.

"He may be stubborn like me, but he's got his mother's ability to bend and be flexible," Rafe reassured her. Trying to take her mind off the worry he saw in her eyes, he asked, "Do you have a name for him?"

Jessie swallowed hard, holding Rafe's tender gaze. "Ever since I found out I was pregnant, I've been calling him Dan. I don't know why; I just felt so close to him with that name."

"Dan. I like the name, Jessie. It's a strong name with a streak of sensitivity in it." Rafe's mouth thinned. "His father may not have any, but at least he has your genes in him." He caressed her temple, pushing the wet strands of hair behind her ear. Jessie's eyes widened, and he saw tears gather in them.

"You like Daniel? You really do?" It meant so much to her to make Rafe feel a part of the joy of sharing their child; they had missed out on so much in the past months of separation from each other.

"I love his mother. Why wouldn't I like the name she chose?"

Jessie shut her eyes tightly, and a scream lodged in her throat as a battering wave of pain rolled through her. "R-Rafe!"

He quietly got up. "It's time, Jessie," he told her softly. "You're ready to deliver that son of ours into my hands."

A bucking, quivering contraction bore down through her, and Jessie groaned. She could do nothing but home in on Rafe's deep voice, which soothed and guided her as he kept one hand on her hip and the other awaiting their baby as she pushed down hard. Her heartbeat pounded like a hollow drum in her heaving breast, and her breath was ragged and shallow as she felt her baby move with each powerful contraction.

"I see him, Jessie…dark hair…" Rafe's voice choked into the warming silence that wove about them. Tears glittered fiercely in his eyes as he divided his attention between Jessie and the dark-haired baby that was inching out into a world of welcoming love.

Jessie cried out, her back taut like a bow, her fingers wrapped into the blankets, twisting them. Black dots danced before her eyes, but she pushed down with all her diminishing strength. Sweat ran into her eyes, stinging them. Rafe called to her, his voice soothing to her frenzied state. And then the pressure disappeared, and Jessie knew she had given birth. She fell back, her thoughts barely coherent, upon hearing Rafe's exclamation of joy. A broken smile pulled at her mouth as she lay there, feeling a deluge of triumph neutralize all of her discomfort and pain.

Rafe held the tiny, wrinkled infant in his hands. For a stunned moment he could only stare at his son as the baby opened his mouth to draw in his first breath of life. And then, with the practice that came from delivering hundreds of calves and foals, he quickly swabbed the mucous from his son's nose and mouth and dried him off. Tears ran down the stubble of his cheeks as he cut the cord and disinfected it with iodine. After gently washing the baby and Jessie, and cleaning up the afterbirth, Rafe lifted Dan and brought him to the woman he loved so fiercely.

"Look," he coaxed brokenly, laying Dan on her belly. "Jessie, it's a boy. A beautiful baby boy."

Jessie opened her eyes as Rafe placed him on her. Instinctively she embraced her baby, and then she looked up at Rafe. He was crying. But they were tears of joy and wonder as he looked down at her.

"He didn't even cry out," Rafe whispered, touching Dan's drying black hair.

"Why should he?" she asked faintly, smiling. "He was wanted and loved. Look…"

Rafe watched as his son opened his eyes for the first time. His tiny face was a healthy pink color, and his eyes were a dark blue. The smile on Rafe's mouth grew. "My hair and eyes." And then he gently drew Jessie into his arms, their son laying between their hearts. "God, I love you so much, Jessie," he said thickly, raining a shower of kisses over her face.

Exhaustion moved through her, and Jessie was content to be held, feeling Dan begin to squirm about, moving his legs and arms. With a soft laugh she leaned upward, her lips parted, wanting to share Rafe's undisguised joy. She closed her eyes as his mouth molded tenderly to her lips, and she tasted his maleness, his love, as if for the first time. This was the Rafe she had known was there all along. Fulfillment flowed through her as she drank thirstily of the kiss that gave all of himself to her in that one gesture.

Dan fussed and Rafe drew back, looking down at his son. "I think he wants to suckle," he told her. Rafe got up, placed all the pillows he could find behind Jessie, and guided her into a slight sitting position. He found a small blue crocheted blanket and wrapped the baby in it. Then he sat on the edge of the bed, watching as Jessie placed their child to her breast for the first time. An incredible sense of peace stole through him as he watched that rosebud-shaped mouth suckle hungrily at her dusky nipple. He touched Dan's hair, marveling at its silky feel, marveling that life had been so good to him after so many years of hell. A fertile year, Rafe thought, remembering Maud's philosophy.

Jessie smiled contentedly and closed her eyes. In a sleepy voice, she murmured, "Imagine what he'll be like once the milk starts flowing. He'll probably eat enough for three people."

Rafe chuckled and caressed her hair, which was in need of a good washing and brushing. He'd help her with it tomorrow if the electricity came back on. "Dan's going to take after me in that department. He must weigh close to eight pounds, honey."

"An eight-pound sack of potatoes," Jessie agreed, laughter in her voice. Her arms were weary and her lids felt weighted down. Dan stopped suckling her breast, and she sighed. "Rafe?"

He took the baby from her arms. "I know, honey. You need to rest. I'll take care of Dan."

She barely opened her eyes as she said, "There's a bassinet over there...in the corner. And diapers in the pantry."

Rafe laid the infant down on the bed and then helped her get comfortable. "Right now," he whispered huskily, "all I want to do is hold my son and watch you sleep. I'll take care of everything. Just close your eyes, honey."

Tiredness like none other she had ever experienced drugged her. Rafe's callused hand rested against her cheek, and she nuzzled into his palm. "I love you, Rafe." She slurred the words. "I never stopped loving you..."

Dawn filtered weakly through the curtains. The last of the blizzard had blown away. Gray light sieved through the pale yellow panels, relieving the shadows from the room. The faint smell of kerosene hung in the air, and the lamp flickered away on the dresser. Jessie's hand lay near her head and her face was tranquil as she slept. The storm had passed, Rafe thought. He sat in the rocker near the bed, rocking his sleeping son. Everything he had lost had been given back to him. He had Jessie's undying love for him. She had given him a baby. His eyes still stung from the tears he had shed earlier. Whatever old wounds he had carried, whatever fears he'd had, had all been washed away by the baby he held gently in his arms.

He saw Jessie stir, and he quietly rose. He placed his son in the bassinet that he had moved near the bed. Tucking the baby in, he focused his attention on Jessie and sat down on the edge of the bed. Rafe placed a hand on her shoulder, thinking how fragile she looked. Her sable eyes were cloudy with sleep as she raised them to him.

"I'm not dreaming?" she croaked.

Rafe shook his head, giving Jessie a tender smile as he threaded his fingers through her hair. "Not a dream. I'm here, and you had our baby. Dan's still sleeping. How do you feel?"

"Like I was in a car wreck," she admitted, closing her eyes.

"Thirsty?"

She nodded and opened her eyes. His love for her was evident on his face as he slipped his arm beneath her shoulders and propped her up against him. He pressed the lip of a glass to her mouth.

"Drink all you can. It's orange juice," he told her. "Right now you need sugar to get back some of your strength." Then amusement crept into his deep voice. "That son of ours is going to wake up and want milk.

You've got to keep drinking a lot of liquids, Jessie, to keep up with his demands."

The sweet, cold orange juice soothed her raw throat and sated her initial thirst. When she finished a second glass, she closed her eyes and nestled her head beneath Rafe's solid jaw.

"Dan's all right?"

"Yes. He's like any spunky, newborn foal, honey. All he wants to do is either eat or sleep." He kissed her hair. "How do you feel?"

"Better." Miraculously so, Jessie thought. Although she felt tender and bruised, she felt an emotional vitality. "I never realized how much pain there would be."

"You bore up under it well," Rafe said with pride in his voice.

She wrinkled her nose. "I don't call screaming bearing up very well."

"Most women do scream and cry—it's normal."

Jessie moved her hand across the wrinkled cotton front of Rafe's shirt. "Tell me everything, Rafe. How did you get up here?"

He smiled, holding her close. She was so small against him, and yet so strong. "On Christmas Eve, the family got together to trim the Christmas tree at the ranch. I couldn't stand watching Dal and Jim smile at each other and know how much they loved—" He faltered. "God, I was jealous, Jessie. I wanted what they had. I knew I could have the same thing with you if I could only get past my own damn fear."

Caressing his face, she asked, "What made you decide to come to us, Rafe?"

He took a deep breath and then expelled it. "I couldn't stand being in the same room with them while they trimmed the tree, so I went for a walk. I ended up in the broodmare barn and found myself in front of Jessie's Girl's stall. She came bouncing up to me, nickering and nuzzling me. And I thought of you. You were the same as that little filly, Jessie—trusting, giving and making no demands on me except to allow her to love me." He kissed her temple. "It all fell into place in that instant, honey. I can't explain it; it was as if someone had finally taken off the blinders I was wearing, and I understood what you'd told me under the cottonwoods."

Silence settled around them, and Rafe inhaled her scent, resting his jaw on her hair. His tone softened. "Looking back on what I demanded of you makes me see it was stupid, Jessie. I had no right to come marching up here and expect you to come and live with me like I did. You were right. I wanted you without the responsibility."

Jessie opened her eyes. "Because you were afraid, Rafe. Not because you couldn't handle the responsibility of a marriage. You've already proven that once before."

"I know that—now, Jessie. I expected everything of you and nothing of myself. Some part of me knew you were more flexible and unafraid to take the emotional risks, so I thought it was a pretty logical request to make of you." Self-deprecating amusement tinged his tone. "I can see now my logic was flawed as hell."

"That's over," Jessie whispered, slowly sitting up. She framed his dark, shadowed face between her hands. "You came back on your own to us; that's all that counts."

Rafe nodded, drowning in her warm, loving gaze. "I came back to ask you to marry me, Jessie. I can't live without you. I don't want to. My fear of never having you outweighed my fear of living again." His eyes were suspiciously bright. "Will you marry this mule-headed, stubborn old cuss of a cowboy?"

Tears tightened in her throat. "I'd want nothing more."

Rafe murmured her name, and there was a prayer on his lips as he blindly embraced her, holding her tightly against him. "God, I love you so much, Jessie. So much…"

The electric power was restored later that morning. Christmas music filled the living room as Jessie slowly rocked Dan in her arms. A smile hovered on her lips as she floated in a cocoon of happiness. The storm had long since passed, and Rafe had discovered that her short-wave radio needed new batteries. He had gone out to the bunkhouse and found some and had finally been able to contact Dave and Mike. After locating the two stranded hands by radio, he'd promised to rescue them shortly. After letting Jessie know they were all right, he helped her take a shower and wash her hair. Then he hurried out to rescue the stranded men.

Dave and Mike's expressions when they tramped into the house were priceless. Jessie was in the rocker, dressed in her sapphire velour robe, with Dan fidgeting happily in her arms when they entered. The men removed their hats, lowered their voices and looked across the room at her in awe. Rafe told them to take off their coats and get comfortable. He went to the kitchen to fix them all something to eat while the young men remained with Jessie. For all their large size and gruff talk, they touched Dan's outstretched fingers with exquisite gentleness. Their smiles and the pride in their eyes told Jessie everything. They treated her with a bit of wonder and awe, too, and whispered how much Dan looked like Rafe.

Christmas dinner was spent in their enthusiastic company. William had stored plenty of leftovers in the refrigerator, and Rafe was no slouch at whipping up a hearty meal. They all ate in the living room around Jessie and her baby. The Christmas tree lights blinked radiantly in the corner, adding to the festive atmosphere. After the hands had had coffee and cake for dessert, they left to feed the animals in the paddocks and barn, then called it a night. By then Dan was hungry, and Jessie sat in the rocker feeding him while Rafe washed the dishes.

Drying his hands on a towel, Rafe stood at the entrance to the living room. Jessie had closed her eyes, and his son was nestled deep in her arms. Joy rose in him, and he quietly walked over to them. She opened her eyes as he crouched down in front of her and rested his hands on her slender thighs.

"You've got to be tired," he said, placing the towel across his shoulder. "Come on, let's get you both to bed."

With a nod, Jessie relinquished Dan to him, and with Rafe's help, she stood. She was exhausted and leaned against him as he slid his arm around her waist.

"It's been a wonderful day," she told him, walking slowly with him toward the bedroom.

"Every day will be better than the last," he promised her. "If we're lucky, the phone will be in working order by tomorrow morning, and we can call Dr. Novack."

"And your family."

He chuckled indulgently. "Wait until Dal hears about this. She's going to go crazy."

Jessie carefully sat down and watched as Rafe placed Dan in the bassinet. His undisguised love took her breath away. All their anguish and struggles had been worth it. She slipped the robe off, revealing the white flannel gown she wore.

"Alessandra now has a playpen partner," she agreed with a weary smile.

"They'll be inseparable," Rafe said, helping her into the bed. He shut off the light and leaned down, his face bathed by light spilling through the doorway to the hall. "Go to sleep, Jess. I'll be in a little later."

The pleasant thought of Rafe sleeping with her sent another jolt of warmth through her. "Hurry," she whispered. "I need you beside me."

He kissed her gently, reveling in the soft texture of her lips beneath his. Jessie needed him—it was the first time she had told him that. Although she was strong in ways he wasn't, it made him happy to know that she needed his strength and support also. "I won't be long, honey. I've got one more item to attend to, and then I'll be in to hold you all night long."

Jessie was awakened by Dan again, only this time it was eight in the morning. He had demanded a feeding at three, too. She groggily sat up, rubbing her eyes. Rafe was gone, but she could smell bacon frying as she got up to feed Dan. After she'd changed his diaper, Jessie carried her son out into the living room. She saw slats of sunlight filtering through the gray, scudding clouds and smiled.

"Oh…"

She turned. Rafe stood in the doorway, a breakfast tray in his hands. He looked crestfallen. He had obviously planned to serve her breakfast in bed, and Jessie's heart melted with love.

"I'll still eat it, Rafe. Thank you."

He grimaced and placed the tray on the couch. "I was going to surprise you."

"Dan woke me up first." She handed Rafe his son and sat down on the couch. This morning her appetite was back, and she hungrily ate the two eggs, rasher of bacon and two slices of whole wheat toast.

"Looks like the frigid spell's over," Rafe said. "If we get lucky, the telephone people'll send crews out, and maybe we'll be able to make calls later today."

"I think Millie, Dal and Jim will welcome your news as if it were a Christmas gift, Rafe."

Rafe raised one brow, nodding toward the tree. "Speaking of Christmas gifts, it looks like Santa Claus left a late one for you last night."

Jessie lifted her head and stared over at the gaily decorated tree. Sure enough, she saw a small red foil-wrapped gift beneath the tree. Her eyes lit up with genuine amusement. "Is it for me?"

Rafe gave a nonchalant shrug and got up, with Dan making contented tiny noises in his arms. "Don't know. Let me go see." He crouched down and retrieved the package. "Yep, it's got your name on it." He walked over and handed it to her.

Jessie's smile broadened, and she put the tray on the coffee table so Rafe could sit next to her when she opened the small gift. "You didn't have to get me anything, Rafe. I have you and Dan. What more could a woman want?"

He settled back, a pleased expression on his face. "Open it and see," he coaxed, his voice suddenly thick with emotion.

With trembling fingers Jessie removed the red foil

and the white satin ribbon that bound the gift. Her eyes widened as she opened the latch on the dark green velvet case. Inside was a band of gold with three vertical rows of diamonds. She touched the ring reverently; tears sprang to her eyes.

"Do you like it?"

"Y-yes, it's beautiful, Rafe."

"Like you." He cleared his throat, and his anxious gaze never left her flushed features. "I bought it in July, just before I came up here the first time. I didn't want the usual diamond engagement ring that would set high because I knew you'd be outdoors and probably working by my side, and I was afraid it would get ripped or torn off. I had a jeweler in Denver make it for me from a design I had in mind. I wanted something that sparkled like a million small suns; the same way you make me feel when you're with me. There's twelve diamonds there, Jessie; one for each month of the year, to remind you that I'll love you every day of every month of the year."

She stroked the sparkling ring. "And each of these rows of diamonds stand for how many children we'll have." Her eyes grew misty as she searched his face. "I love the ring, Rafe. It's beautiful—like your heart, which you've hidden until now."

Rafe leaned over and sealed her whispered words with a long, searching kiss meant to tell her of his love, which he still couldn't put into words and which would probably never be put into words, but he could tell her in this way. Brushing the tears from her cheeks, he managed a tremulous smile of his own. "Knowing the way I feel about you, we'll probably end up with a half a dozen just like this one." Reverently he stroked his son's cheek.

Jessie slipped her arm around Rafe, and held him and her son close. "They'll be a reflection of our love for each other," she whispered. "A measure of our love..."

* * * * *

Joan Johnston is the *New York Times* and *USA TODAY* bestselling author of more than fifty novels with more than fifteen million copies of her books in print. She has been a director of theater, drama critic, newspaper editor, college professor and attorney on her way to becoming a full-time writer. You can find out more about Joan at joanjohnston.com or on Facebook at Joan Johnston Author.

Books by Joan Johnston

Hawk's Way: Jesse
Hawk's Way: Adam
Hawk's Way: Faron
Hawk's Way: Garth
Hawk's Way: Carter
Hawk's Way: Falcon
Hawk's Way: Zach
Hawk's Way: Billy
Hawk's Way: Mac
Hawk's Way: Colt

Visit the Author Profile page
at Harlequin.com for more titles.

HAWK'S WAY: BILLY

Joan Johnston

Chapter 1

Cherry Whitelaw was in trouble. Again. She simply couldn't live up to the high expectations of her adoptive parents, Zach and Rebecca Whitelaw. She had been a Whitelaw for three years, ever since her fifteenth birthday, and it was getting harder and harder to face the looks of disappointment on her parents' faces each time they learned of her latest escapade.

This time it was really serious. This was about the worst thing that could happen to a high school girl. Well, the second worst. At least she wasn't pregnant.

Cherry had been caught spiking the punch at the senior prom this evening by the principal, Mr. Cornwell, and expelled on the spot. The worst of it was, she wasn't even guilty! Not that anyone was going to believe her. Because most of the time she was.

Her best friend, Tessa Ramos, had brought the pint

bottle of whiskey to the dance. Cherry had been trying to talk Tessa out of spiking the punch—had just taken the bottle from Tessa's hand—when Mr. Cornwell caught her with it.

He had snatched it away with a look of dismay and said, "I'm ashamed of you, young lady. It's bad enough when your behavior disrupts class. An irresponsible act like this has farther-reaching ramifications."

"But, Mr. Cornwell, I was only—"

"You're obviously incorrigible, Ms. Whitelaw."

Cherry hated being called that. *Incorrigible.* Being *incorrigible* meant no one wanted her because she was too much trouble. Except Zach and Rebecca had. They had loved her no matter what she did. They would believe in her this time, too. But that didn't change the fact she had let them down. Again.

"You're expelled," Mr. Cornwell had said, his rotund face nearly as red as Cherry's hair, but not quite, because nothing could ever be quite that red. "You will leave this dance at once. I'll be in touch with your parents tomorrow."

No amount of argument about her innocence had done any good, because she had been unwilling to name her best friend as the real culprit. She might be a troublemaker, but she was no rat.

Mr. Cornwell's pronouncement had been final. She was out. She wasn't going to graduate with the rest of her class. She would have to come back for summer school.

Rebecca was going to cry when she found out. And Zach was going to get that grim-lipped look that meant he was really upset.

Cherry felt a little like crying herself. She had no idea why she was so often driven to wild behavior. She only knew she couldn't seem to stop. And it wasn't going to do any good to protest her innocence this time. She had been guilty too often in the past.

"Hey, Cherry! You gonna sit there mopin' all night, or what?"

Cherry glanced at her prom date, Ray Estes. He lay sprawled on the grass beside her at the stock pond on the farthest edge of Hawk's Pride, her father's ranch, where she had retreated in defeat. Her full-length, pale green chiffon prom dress, which had made her feel like a fairy princess earlier in the evening, was stained with dirt and grass.

Ray's tuxedo was missing the jacket, bow tie, and cummerbund, and his shirt was unbuttoned halfway to his waist. He was guzzling the fourth can of a six-pack of beer he had been slowly but surely consuming since they had arrived at the pond an hour ago.

Cherry sat beside him holding the fifth can, but it was still nearly full. Somehow she didn't feel much like getting drunk. She had to face her parents sometime tonight, and that would only be adding insult to injury.

"C'mon, Cherry, give us a li'l kiss," Ray said, dragging himself upright with difficulty and leaning toward her.

She braced a palm in the smooth center of his chest to keep him from falling onto her. "You're drunk, Ray."

Ray grinned. "Shhure am. How 'bout that kiss, Cher-ry?"

"No, Ray."

"Awww, why not?"

"I got thrown out of school tonight, Ray. I don't feel like kissing anybody."

"Not even me?" Ray said.

Cherry laughed at the woeful, hangdog look on his

face and shook her head. "Not even you." Ray was good fun most of the time. He drank a little too much, and he drove a little too fast, and his grades hadn't been too good. But she hadn't been in a position to be too picky.

She had dreamed sometimes of what it might be like to be one of the "good girls" and have "nice boys" calling her up to ask for dates. It hadn't happened. She was the kind of trouble nice boys stayed away from.

"C'mon, Cher-ry," Ray said. "Gimme li'l kiss."

He teetered forward, and the sheer weight of him forced her backward so she was lying flat on the ground. Cherry was five-eleven in her stocking feet and could run fast enough to make the girls' track team—if she hadn't always been in too much trouble to qualify. But Ray was four inches taller and forty pounds heavier. She turned her head away to avoid his slobbery, seeking lips, which landed on her cheeks and chin.

"I said no, Ray. Get off!" She shoved uselessly at his heavy body, a sense of panic growing inside her.

"Awww, Cher-ry," he slurred drunkenly. "You know you want it." His hand closed around her breast.

"Ray! No!" she cried. She grabbed his wrist and yanked it away and heard the chiffon rip as his grasping fingers held fast to the cloth. "Ray, please!" she pleaded.

Then she felt his hand on her bare flesh. "No, Ray. No!"

"Gonna have you, Cher-ry," Ray muttered. "Always wanted to. Know you want it, too."

Cherry suddenly realized she might be in even worse trouble than she'd thought.

Billy Stonecreek was in trouble. Again. His former mother-in-law, Penelope Trask, was furious because he had gotten into a little fight in a bar in town and spent the night in jail—for the third time in a year.

He had a live-in housekeeper to stay with his daughters, so they were never alone. He figured he'd been a pretty damned good single parent to his six-year-old twins, Raejean and Annie, ever since their mother's death a year ago. But you'd never know it to hear Penelope talk.

Hell, a young man of twenty-five who worked hard on his ranch from dawn to dusk all week deserved to sow a few wild oats at week's end. His ears rang with the memory of their confrontation in his living room earlier that evening.

"You're a drunken half-breed," Penelope snapped, "not fit to raise my grandchildren. And if I have anything to say about it, you won't have them for much longer!"

Billy felt a burning rage that Penelope should say such a thing while Raejean and Annie were standing right there listening. Especially since he hadn't been the least bit drunk. He'd been looking for a fight, all right, and he'd found it in a bar, but that was all.

There was no hope his daughters hadn't heard Penelope. Their Nintendo game continued on the living room TV, but both girls were staring wide-eyed at him. "Raejean. Annie. Go upstairs while I talk to Nana."

"But, Daddy—" Raejean began. She was the twin who took control of every situation.

"Not a word," he said in a firm voice. "Go."

Annie's dark brown eyes welled with tears. She was the twin with the soft heart.

He wanted to pick them both up and hug them, but he forced himself to point an authoritative finger toward the doorway. "Upstairs and get your baths and get ready for bed. Mrs. Motherwell will be up to help in a minute." He had hired the elderly woman on the spot when he heard her name. She had proven equal to it.

Raejean shot him a reproachful look, took Annie's hand, and stomped out of the room with Annie trailing behind her.

Once they were gone, Billy turned his attention back to his nemesis. "What is it this time, Penelope?"

"This time! What is it every time? You drove my Laura to kill herself, and now you're neglecting my grandchildren. I've had it. I went to see a lawyer today. I've filed for custody of my granddaughters."

A chill of foreboding crawled down Billy's spine. "You've done what?"

"You heard me. I want custody of Raejean and Annie."

"Those are my children you're talking about."

"They'll have a better life with me than they will with a half-breed like you."

"Being part Comanche isn't a crime, Penelope. Lots of people in America are part something. Hell, you're probably part Irish or English or French yourself."

"Your kind has a reputation for not being able to hold their liquor. Obviously, it's a problem for you, too. I don't intend to let my grandchildren suffer for it."

A flush rose on Billy's high, sharp cheekbones. He refused to defend himself. It was none of Penelope's business whether he drank or not. But he didn't. He went looking for a fight when the pain built up inside, and he needed a release for it. But he chose men able to defend themselves, he fought clean, and he willingly paid the damages afterward.

He hated the idea of kowtowing to Penelope, but he didn't want a court battle with her, either. She and her husband, Harvey Trask, were wealthy; he was not. In fact, the Trasks had given this ranch—an edge carved from the larger Trask ranching empire—as a wedding present to their daughter, Laura, thereby ensuring that the newlyweds would stay close to home.

He had resented their generosity at first, but he had grown to love the land, and now he was no more willing to give up the Stonecreek Ranch than he was to relinquish his children.

But his behavior over the past year couldn't stand much scrutiny. He supposed the reason he had started those few barroom brawls wouldn't matter to a judge. And he could never have revealed to anyone the personal pain that had led to such behavior. So he had no excuses to offer Penelope—or a family court judge, either.

"Look, Penelope, I'm sorry. What if I promise—"

"Don't waste your breath. I never wanted my daughter to marry a man like you in the first place. My granddaughters deserve to be raised in a wholesome household where they won't be exposed to your kind."

"What kind is that?" Billy asked pointedly.

"The kind that doesn't have any self-respect, and therefore can't pass it on to their children."

Billy felt his stomach roll. It was a toss-up whether he felt more humiliated or furious at her accusation. "I have plenty of self-respect."

"Could have fooled me!" Penelope retorted.

"I'm not letting you take my kids away from me."

"You can't stop me." She didn't argue with him further, simply headed for the front door—she never used the back, as most people in this part of Texas did. "I'll see you in court, Billy."

Then she was gone.

Billy stood in the middle of the toy-strewn living

room, furnished with the formal satin-covered couches and chairs Laura had chosen, feeling helpless. Moments later he was headed for the back door. He paused long enough to yell up the stairs, "I'm going out, Mrs. Motherwell. Good night, Raejean. Good night, Annie."

"Good night, Daddy!" the two of them yelled back from the bathtub in unison.

Mrs. Motherwell appeared at the top of the stairs. "Don't forget this is my last week, Mr. Stonecreek. You'll need to find someone else starting Monday morning."

"I know, Mrs. Motherwell," Billy said with a sigh. He had Penelope to thank for that, too. She had filled Mrs. Motherwell's head with stories about him being a dangerous savage. His granite-hewn features, his untrimmed black hair, his broad shoulders and immense height, and a pair of dark, brooding eyes did nothing to dispel the image. But he couldn't help how he looked. "Don't worry, Mrs. Motherwell. I'll find someone to replace you."

He was the one who was worried. How was he going to find someone as capable as Mrs. Motherwell in a week? It had taken him a month to find her.

He let the kitchen screen door slam and gunned the engine in his black pickup as he drove away. But he couldn't escape his frenetic thoughts.

I'll be damned if I let Penelope take my kids away from me. Who does she think she is? How dare she threaten to steal my children!

He knew his girls needed a mother. Sometimes he missed Laura so much it made his gut ache. But no other woman could ever take her place. He had hired a series of good housekeeper/nannies one after another—it was hard to get help to stay at his isolated ranch—and he and his girls had managed fine.

Or they would, if Penelope and Harvey Trask would leave them alone.

Unfortunately, Penelope blamed him for Laura's death. She had been killed instantly in a car accident that had looked a whole lot like a suicide. Billy had tried telling Penelope that Laura hadn't killed herself, but his mother-in-law hadn't believed him. Penelope Trask had said she would see that he was punished for making Laura so miserable she had taken her own life. Now she was threatening to take his children from him.

He couldn't bear to lose Raejean and Annie. They were the light of his life and all he had left of Laura. God, how he had loved her!

Billy pounded his fist on the steering wheel of his pickup. How could he have been so stupid as to give Penelope the ammunition she needed to shoot him down in court?

It was too late to do anything about his wild reputation. But he could change his behavior. He could stop brawling in bars. If only there were some way he could show the judge he had turned over a new leaf...

Billy didn't drive in any particular direction, yet he eventually found himself at the stock pond he shared with Zach Whitelaw's ranch. The light from the rising moon and stars made a silvery reflection on the center of the pond and revealed the shadows of several pin oaks that surrounded it. He had always found the sounds of the bullfrogs and the crickets and the lapping water soothing to his inner turmoil. He had gone there often to think in the year since Laura had died.

His truck headlights revealed someone else had discovered his sanctuary. He smiled wistfully when he realized a couple was lying together on the grass. He felt a stab of envy. He and Laura had spent their share of stolen moments on the banks of this stock pond when the land had belonged to her father.

He almost turned the truck around, because he wanted to be alone, but there was something about the movements of the couple on the ground that struck him as odd. It took him a moment to realize they weren't struggling in the throes of passion. The woman was trying to fight the man off!

He hit the brakes, shoved open his truck door, and headed for them on the run. He hadn't quite reached the girl when he heard her scream of outrage.

He grabbed hold of the boy by his shoulders and yanked him upright. The tall, heavyset kid came around swinging.

That was a mistake.

Billy ducked and came up underneath with a hard fist to the belly that dropped the kid to his knees. A second later the boy toppled face-forward with a groan.

Billy made a sound of disgust that the kid hadn't put up more of a fight and hurried to help the girl. She had curled in on herself, her body rigid with tension. When he put a hand on her shoulder, she tried scrambling away.

"He's not going to hurt you anymore," he said in the calm, quiet voice he used when he was gentling horses. He turned her over so she could see she was safe from the boy, that he was there to help. Her torn bodice exposed half of a small, well-formed breast. He made himself look away, but his body tightened responsively. Her whole body began to tremble.

"Shh. It's all right. I'm here now."

She looked up at him with eyes full of pain.

"Are you hurt?" he asked, his hands doing a quick once-over for some sign of injury.

She slapped at him ineffectually with one hand while holding the torn chiffon against her nakedness with the other. "No. I'm fine. Just…just…"

Her eyes—he couldn't tell what color they were in the dark—filled with tears and, despite her desperate attempts to blink the moisture away, one sparkling teardrop spilled onto her cheek. It was then he realized the pain he had seen wasn't physical, but came from inside.

He understood that kind of pain all too well.

"Hey," he said gently. "It's going to be all right."

"Easy for you to say," she snapped, rubbing at the tears and swiping them across her cheeks. "I—"

A car engine revved, and they both looked toward the sound in time to see a pair of headlights come on.

"Wait!" the girl cried, surging to her feet.

The dress slipped, and Billy got an unwelcome look at a single, luscious breast. He swore under his breath as his body hardened.

The girl obviously wasn't used to long dresses, because the length of it caught under her knees and trapped her on the ground. By the time she made it to her feet, the car she had come in, and the boy she had come with, were gone.

He took one look at her face in the moonlight and saw a kind of desolation he hadn't often seen before.

Except perhaps in his own face in the mirror.

It made his throat ache. It might have brought him to tears, if he had been the kind of man who could cry. He wasn't. He thought maybe his Comanche heritage had something to do with it. Or maybe it was simply a lack of feeling in him. He didn't know. He didn't want to know.

As he watched, the girl sank to the ground and dropped her face into her hands. Her shoulders rocked with soundless, shuddering sobs.

He settled beside her, not speaking, not touching, merely a comforting presence, there if she needed him. Occasionally he heard a sniffling sound, but otherwise he was aware of the silence. And finally, the sounds he had come to hear. The bullfrogs. The crickets. The water lapping in the pond.

He didn't know how long he had been sitting beside her when she finally spoke.

"Thank you," she said.

Her voice was husky from crying, and rasped over him, raising the hairs on his neck. He looked at her again and saw liquid, shining eyes in a pretty face. He couldn't keep his gaze from dropping to the flesh revealed by her tightened grip on the torn fabric. Hell, he was a man, not a saint.

"Are you all right?" he asked.

She shook her head, gave a halfhearted laugh, and said, "Sure." The sarcasm in her voice made it plain she was anything but.

"Can I help?"

"I'd need a miracle to get me out of the mess I'm in." She shrugged, a surprisingly sad gesture. "I can't seem to stay out of trouble."

He smiled sympathetically. *I have the same problem.* He thought the words, but he didn't say them. He didn't want to frighten her. "Things happen," he said instead.

She reached out hesitantly to touch a recent cut above his eye. "Did Ray do this?"

He edged back from her touch. It felt too good. "No.

That's from—" *Another fight.* He didn't finish that thought aloud, either. "Something else."

He had gotten a whiff of her perfume. Something light and flowery. Something definitely female. It reminded him he hadn't been with a woman since Laura's death. And that he found the young woman sitting beside him infinitely desirable.

He tamped down his raging hormones. She needed his help. She didn't need another male lusting after her.

She reached for an open can of beer sitting in the grass nearby and lifted it to her lips.

Before it got there, he took it from her. "Aren't you a little young for this?"

"What difference does it make now? My life is ruined."

He smiled indulgently. "Just because your boyfriend—"

"Ray's not my boyfriend. And he's the least of my problems."

He raised a questioning brow. "Oh?"

He watched her grasp her full lower lip in her teeth— and wished he were doing it himself. He forced his gaze upward to meet with hers.

"I'm a disappointment to my parents," she said in a whispery, haunted voice.

How could such a beautiful—he had been looking at her long enough to realize she was more than pretty— young woman be a disappointment to anybody? "Who are your parents?"

"I'm Cherry Whitelaw."

She said it defiantly, defensively. And he knew why. She had been the talk of the neighborhood—the "juvenile delinquent" the Whitelaws had taken into their home four years ago, the most recently adopted child of their eight adopted children.

"If you're trying to scare me off, it won't work." He grinned and said, "I'm Billy Stonecreek."

The smile grew slowly on her face. He saw the moment when she relaxed and held out her hand. "It's nice to meet you, Mr. Stonecreek. I used to see you in church with your—" She cut herself off.

"It's all right to mention my wife," he said. But he knew why she had hesitated. Penelope's tongue had been wagging, telling anyone who would listen how he had caused Laura to kill herself. Cherry's lowered eyes made it obvious she had heard the stories. He didn't know why he felt the urge to defend himself to her when he hadn't to anyone else.

"I had nothing to do with Laura's death. It was simply a tragic accident." Then, before he could stop himself, "I miss her."

Cherry laid a hand on his forearm, and he felt the muscles tense beneath her soothing touch. She waited for him to look at her before she spoke. "I'm sorry about your wife, Mr. Stonecreek. It must be awful to lose someone you love."

"Call me Billy," he said, unsure how to handle her sympathy.

"Then you have to call me Cherry," she said with the beginnings of a smile. She held out her hand. "Deal?"

"Deal." He took her hand and held it a moment too long. Long enough to realize he didn't want to let go. He forced himself to sit back. He raised the beer can he had taken from her to his lips, but she took it from him before he could tip it up.

"I don't think this will solve your problems, either," she said with a cheeky grin.

He laughed. "You're right."

They smiled at each other.

Until Billy realized he wanted to kiss her about as bad as he had ever wanted anything in his life. His smile faded. He saw the growing recognition in her eyes and turned away. He was there to rescue the girl, not to ravish her.

He picked a stem of sweet grass and twirled it between his fingertips. "Would you like to talk about what you've done that's going to disappoint your parents?"

She shrugged. "Hell. Why not?"

The profanity surprised him. Until he remembered she hadn't been a Whitelaw for very long. "I'm listening."

Her eyes remained focused on her tightly laced fingers. "I got expelled from high school tonight."

He let out a breath he hadn't realized he'd been holding. "That's pretty bad, all right. What did you do?"

"Nothing! Not that I'm innocent all that often, but this time I was. Just because I had a whiskey bottle in my hand doesn't mean I was going to pour it in the punch at the prom."

He raised a skeptical brow.

"I was keeping a friend of mine from pouring it in the punch," she explained. "Not that anyone will believe me."

"As alibis go, I've heard better," he said.

"Anyway, I've been expelled and I won't graduate with my class and I'll have to go to summer school to finish. I'd rather run away from home than face Zach and Rebecca and tell them what I've done. In fact, the more I think about it, the better that idea sounds. I won't go home. I'll… I'll…"

"Go where?"

"I don't know. Somewhere."

"Dressed like that?"

She looked down at herself and back up at him, her eyes brimming with tears. "My dress is ruined. Just like my life."

Billy didn't resist the urge to lift her into his lap, and for whatever reason, she didn't resist his efforts to comfort her. She wrapped her arms around his neck and clung to him.

"I feel so lost and alone," she said, her breath moist against his skin. "I don't belong anywhere."

Billy tightened his arms around her protectively, wishing there was something more he could do to help. He crooned to her in Comanche, telling her she was safe, that he would find a way to help her, that she wasn't alone.

"What am I going to do?" she murmured in an anguished voice. "Where can I go?"

Billy swallowed over the knot in his throat. "You're going to think I'm crazy," he said. "But I've got an idea if you'd like to hear it."

"What is it?" she asked.

"You could come and live with me."

Chapter 2

Cherry had felt safe and secure in Billy Stonecreek's arms, that is, until he made his insane suggestion. She lifted her head from Billy's shoulder and stared at him wide-eyed. "What did you say?"

"Don't reject the idea before you hear me out."

"I'm listening." In fact, Cherry was fascinated.

He focused his dark-eyed gaze on her, pinning her in place. "The older lady who's been taking care of my kids is quitting on Monday. How would you like to work for me? The job comes with room and board." He smiled. "In fact, I'm including room and board because I can't afford to pay much."

"You're offering me a job?"

"And a place to live. I could be at home evenings to watch the girls while you go to night school over the summer and earn your high school diploma. What do you say?"

Cherry edged herself off Billy's lap, wondering how he had coaxed her into remaining there so long. Perversely, she missed the warmth of his embrace once it was gone. She pulled her knees up to her chest and wrapped her arms around the yards of pale green chiffon.

"Cherry?"

Her first reaction was to say yes. His offer was the simple solution to all her problems. She wouldn't have to go home. She wouldn't have to face her parents with the truth.

But she hadn't lived with Zach and Rebecca Whitelaw for four years and not learned how they felt about certain subjects. "My dad would never allow it."

"A minute ago you were going to run away from home. How is this different?"

"You obviously don't know Zach Whitelaw very well," she said with a rueful twist of her lips. "If he knew I was working so close, he'd expect me to live at home."

"Not if you were indispensible to me."

"Would I be?" she asked, intrigued.

"I can't manage the ranch and my six-year-old twin daughters all by myself. I'm up and working before dawn. Somebody has to make sure Annie and Raejean get dressed for school and feed them breakfast and be there when they get off the school bus in the afternoon." Billy shrugged. "You need a place to stay. I need help in a hurry. It's a match made in heaven."

Cherry shook her head. "It wouldn't work."

"Why not?"

"Can I be blunt?"

Billy smiled, and her stomach did a queer flip-flop. "By all means," he said.

"It's bad enough that you're single—"

"I wouldn't need the help if I had a wife," Billy interrupted.

Cherry frowned him into silence. "You're a widower. I'm only eighteen. It's a toss-up which of us has the worse reputation for getting into trouble. Can you imagine what people would say—about us—if I moved in with you?" Cherry's lips curled in an impish grin. "Eyebrows would hit hairlines all over the county."

Billy shook his head and laughed. "I hadn't thought about what people would think. We're two of a kind, all right." His features sobered. "Just not the right kind."

Cherry laid her hand on his arm in comfort. "I know what you're feeling, Billy."

"I doubt it."

Cherry felt bereft as he pulled free. He was wrong. She understood exactly what he was feeling. The words spilled out before she could stop them.

"Nobody wants anything to do with you, because you're different," she said in a quiet voice that carried in the dark. "To prove it doesn't matter what anyone else thinks, you break their rules. When they look down their noses at you, you spit in their eyes. And all the time, your heart is aching. Because you want them to like you. And respect you. But they don't."

Billy eyed her speculatively. "I guess you do understand."

For a moment Cherry thought he was going to put his arm around her. But he didn't.

She turned to stare at the pond, so he wouldn't see how much she regretted his decision to keep his distance.

"I've always hated being different," she said. "I was always taller than everyone else, thanks to my giant of a father, Big Mike Murphy." When she was a child, her father's size had always made her feel safe. But he hadn't kept her safe. He had let her be stolen away from him.

"And I don't know another person with hair as godawful fire-engine red as mine. I have Big Mike to thank for that, too." Cherry noticed Billy didn't contradict her evaluation of her hair.

"And your mother?" Billy asked. "What did you get from her?"

"Nothing, so far as I can tell," Cherry said curtly. "She walked out on Big Mike when I was five. That's when he started drinking. Eventually someone reported to social services that he was leaving me alone at night. They took me away from him when I was eight. He fell from a high scaffolding at work the next week and was killed. I think he wanted to die. I was in and out of the system for six years before the Whitelaws took me in."

"I'm sorry."

"It doesn't matter now."

"Doesn't it?" Billy asked.

Cherry shrugged. "It's in the past. You learn to protect yourself."

"Yeah," Billy said. "You do."

Billy had inherited his six-foot-four height and dark brown eyes from his Scots father. His straight black hair and burnished skin came from his Comanche mother. They had been killed in a car wreck when he was ten. He had developed his rebellious streak in a series of foster homes that treated him like he was less than human because he wasn't all white.

He opened his mouth to share his common experiences with Cherry and closed it again. It was really none of her business.

"Too bad you aren't looking for a wife," Cherry mused. "That would solve your problem. But I guess after what happened, you don't want to get married again."

"No, I don't," Billy said flatly.

"I certainly wasn't volunteering for the job," Cherry retorted. Everyone knew Billy Stonecreek had made his first wife so unhappy she had killed herself. At least, that was the story Penelope Trask had been spreading. On the other hand, Billy Stonecreek had been nothing but nice to her. She couldn't help wondering whether Billy was really as villainous as his mother-in-law had painted him.

They sat in silence. Cherry wished there was some way she could have helped Billy. But she knew Zach Whitelaw too well to believe he would allow his daughter to move in with a single man—even if she was his housekeeper. Not that Zach could have stopped her if she wanted to do it. But knowing Zach, he would find a way to make sure Billy changed his mind about needing her. And she didn't want to cause that kind of trouble for anybody.

"Having you come to work for me wouldn't really solve my biggest problem, anyway," Billy said, picking up the beer can again.

Cherry took it out of his hand, set it down, and asked, "What problem is that?"

He hesitated so long she wasn't sure he was going to speak. At last he said, "My former mother-in-law is taking me to court to try and get custody of my daughters. Penelope says I'm not a fit parent. She's determined to take Raejean and Annie away from me."

"Oh, no!" It was Cherry's worst nightmare come to

life. She had suffered terribly when she had been taken from her father as a child. "You can't let her do that! Kids belong with their parents."

Cherry was passionate about the subject. She had often wondered where her birth mother was and why she had walked away and left Cherry and Big Mike behind. Cherry had died inside when the social worker came to take her away, and she realized she was never going to see Big Mike again. It was outrageous to think someone could go to court and wrench two little girls away from their natural father.

"You've got to stop Mrs. Trask!" Cherry said. "You can't let her take your kids!"

"I'm not *letting* her do anything!" Billy cried in frustration. His hands clenched into fists. "But I'm not sure I can stop her. Over the past year I haven't exactly been a model citizen. And I haven't been able to keep a steady housekeeper. Especially once Penelope fills their ears with wild stories about me."

Billy made an angry sound in his throat. "If Laura hadn't died... Having a wife would certainly make my case as a responsible parent stronger in court."

"Isn't there somebody you could marry?"

"What woman would want a half-breed, with a ready-made family of half-breed kids?" Billy said bitterly.

Cherry gasped. "You talk like there's something wrong with you because you're part Comanche. I'm sure you have lots of redeeming qualities."

Billy eyed her sideways. "Like what?"

"I don't know. I'm sure there must be some." She paused and asked, "Aren't there?"

Billy snorted. "I've been in jail for fighting three times over the past year."

Cherry met his gaze evenly and said, "Nobody says you have to fight."

"True," Billy conceded. "But sometimes…"

"Sometimes you feel like if you don't hit something you'll explode?"

Billy nodded. "Yeah."

"I've felt that way sometimes myself."

"You're a girl," Billy protested. "Girls don't—"

"What makes you think girls don't get angry?" Cherry interrupted.

"I guess I never really thought much about it. What do you do when you feel like that?"

"Cause mischief," Cherry admitted with a grin. Her grin faded as she said, "Think, Billy. Isn't there some woman you could ask to marry you?"

Billy shook his head. "I haven't gone out much since Laura died. When I haven't been working on the ranch, I've spent my time with Raejean and Annie. Besides, I don't know too many women around here who'd think I was much of a catch."

Cherry sat silently beside Billy. Her heart went out to his two daughters. She knew what was coming for them. She felt genuinely sorry for them. For the first time in a long time she regretted her past behavior, because it meant she couldn't be a help to them.

"I wish we'd met sooner. And that I had less of a reputation for being a troublemaker," Cherry said. "If things were different, I might volunteer to help you out. But I'm not the kind of person you'd want as a mother for your kids."

Billy's head jerked around, and he stared intently at her.

Cherry was a little frightened by the fierce look on his face. "Billy? What are you thinking?"

"Why not?" he muttered. "Why the hell not?"

"Why not what?"

"Why can't you marry me?" Billy said.

Cherry clutched at her torn bodice as she surged to her feet. "You can't be serious!"

Billy rose and grabbed her by the shoulders, which was all that kept her from running. "More serious than I've ever been in my life. My kids' lives depend on me making the right choices now."

"And you think marriage to me is the right choice?" Cherry asked incredulously. "We're practically strangers! I barely know you. You don't know me at all."

"I know plenty about you. You understand what it feels like to be different. What it feels like to lose your parents. What it feels like to need a parent's love. You'd be good for my kids. And you could really help me out."

"Why me?"

"I'm desperate," Billy said. "I thought you were, too."

Cherry grimaced. Why else would a man choose her except because he was desperate? And why else would a woman accept such a proposal, unless she were desperate, too?

"Are you ready to go home and face your parents and tell them you got expelled and that you aren't going to graduate?" Billy demanded.

"When you put it that way, I... No. But marriage? That seems like such a big step. Make that a *huge* step."

"It doesn't have to be a real marriage. It can be strictly a business arrangement. We can stay married long enough for you to finish the high school credits you need and maybe take some courses at the junior college. When you figure out what you want to do with the rest of your life, we could go our separate ways."

"Couldn't I just be your housekeeper?"

Billy shook his head. "You've said yourself why that wouldn't work."

"But marriage is so...permanent."

"It would be if it were for real. Ours wouldn't be."

"Are you suggesting we tell people we're married but not really go through with it?"

He considered a moment. "No, we'd have to get married, and as far as I'm concerned, the sooner the better."

Cherry's heart bounced around inside her like a frightened rabbit. She pressed a fistful of chiffon hard against her chest, as though she could hold her heart still, but it kept right on jumping. "You want to get married right away? This week?"

"As soon as we can. We could fly to Las Vegas tonight."

"Fly?"

"I've got a pilot's license. We can charter a small private plane for the trip. Would you mind?"

"I guess not," Cherry said, overwhelmed by the speed at which things were moving.

"The more I think about it, the more I like the whole idea. Getting married would certainly spike Penelope's guns."

Cherry gnawed on her lower lip. "If you're looking for someone who'd be an asset in court, maybe you ought to reconsider taking me as your wife. My reputation's almost as bad as yours."

"You're a Whitelaw," Billy said. "That means something around this part of Texas."

"An adopted Whitelaw," Cherry reminded him. "And I'm not so sure my parents wouldn't change their minds if they had the chance."

Billy smiled. "I think we can make this arrangement

work for both of us. How about it, Cherry? Will you marry me?"

If Cherry had been anybody except who she was, she would have said no. Any rational person would have. It didn't make sense to marry a virtual stranger, one who had reportedly made his previous wife miserable. But Cherry wasn't thinking about Billy or even about herself. She was thinking about his two innocent little girls. If marrying Billy would give them a better chance of staying with their father, she really didn't think she had any other choice.

"All right, Billy," she said. "I'll marry you."

Billy gave a whoop of joy, swept her up into his arms, and whirled her in a dizzying circle, sending chiffon flying around her.

"Put me down, Billy," she said, laughing.

He immediately set her on her feet. When she swayed dizzily, he reached out to steady her.

The feel of his strong, callused hands on her bare shoulders sent an unexpected quiver skittering down her spine. She knew she ought to step away, but Billy's dark eyes held her spellbound.

"Okay now?" he asked, his voice rasping over her.

"I'm fine." She shivered, belying her words.

"You must be getting chilly." He slipped an arm around her shoulder that was warm and supportive… and possessive.

She shivered again as he began walking her toward his pickup. Only this time she realized it had nothing to do with the cold.

As Billy held open the pickup door she said as casually as she could, "This will be a marriage in name only, right?"

He closed the door behind her, slid over the hood, got into the cab, and started the pickup before he answered, "That's right."

She gave a gusty sigh of relief as the engine roared to life. "Good."

"We don't even have to sleep in the same bed," Billy said as he headed back toward the main road. "You can have the room my housekeeper will be vacating. If I feel the urge for some feminine comfort, I can get what I need from a woman in town."

"Wait a minute," Cherry said. "I don't think I'm going to want my husband satisfying his lustful urges in town."

"I won't really be your husband," Billy reminded her.

"As far as my parents and neighbors and friends are concerned, you will be."

Billy eyed her cautiously. "What do you suggest?"

"Couldn't you just…not do it."

"I'm a man, not a monk," Billy said.

Cherry pursed her lips thoughtfully. "Then I suppose I'd rather you come to me than go to some other woman."

"This is starting to sound like a real marriage," Billy said suspiciously. "I was looking for a temporary solution to both our problems."

"Oh, you don't have to worry about me falling in love with you or anything," Cherry reassured him. "I don't believe in happily-ever-after."

"You don't?"

Cherry shook her head. "Except for the Whitelaws, I've never met any married couples who really loved each other. But I can see where it would be unfair to expect you to give up sex for who knows how long. Only, if you don't mind, I'd rather we had a chance to get to know each other a little better before…you know…"

"Maybe this marriage thing isn't such a good idea, after all," Billy said. "You're just a kid, and—"

"I may be only eighteen," Cherry interrupted, "but I've lived a lifetime since my father died. You don't have to worry about me. I've been in and out of a dozen foster homes. I've spent time in juvenile detention. I've survived the past four years in a house with seven other adopted brothers and sisters. I've come through it all with a pretty good idea of what I want from life. I'm plenty old enough to know exactly what I'm doing."

"I doubt that," Billy said. Maybe if he hadn't been so panicked at the thought of losing Annie and Raejean, he would have taken more time to think the matter over. But marriage to Cherry Whitelaw would solve so many problems all at once, he accepted her statement at face value.

"All right, Cherry. We'll do this your way. I won't go looking for comfort in town, and you'll provide for my needs at home."

"After we get to know one another," Cherry qualified.

"After we get to know one another," Billy agreed.

He turned onto the main highway and headed for the airport. "Will your parents worry if you don't show up at home tonight?"

"It's prom night. I was supposed to be staying out all night with some friends of mine and have breakfast with them tomorrow. In fact, if you'll stop by my friend's house, I've got an overnight bag there with a change of clothes."

"Good. That'll leave us about twelve hours to get to Las Vegas and tie the knot before we have to face your parents."

Cherry pictured that meeting in her mind. *Good grief,* she thought. *The fur is going to fly.*

Chapter 3

The wedding chapel in Las Vegas was brightly lit, even at 3:00 a.m. To Cherry's amazement, they weren't the only couple getting married at such an ungodly hour. She and Billy had to wait ten minutes for an elderly couple to complete their vows before it was their turn. The longer they waited, the more second thoughts she had. What had she been thinking? Zach was going to be furious. Rebecca was going to cry.

The image she conjured of two identical cherubic six-year-old faces was all that kept her from running for a phone to call Zach and Rebecca to come get her. She tried to recall what Billy's twins looked like from the last time she had seen them at church. All she could remember were large dark eyes—like Billy's, she realized now—in small, round faces.

What qualities had they gotten from their mother? Cherry tried to remember how Laura Trask had looked the few times she had seen her. Did the twins have delicate noses like hers? Determined chins? Bowed lips? Had they remained petite like their mother, or become tall and raw-boned like their father?

"If you keep chewing on your lip like that, you're going to gnaw it right off."

Startled, Cherry let go of her lower lip and turned to find Billy behind her.

"Here," he said, handing her a bouquet of gardenias. "I got them from a vendor out in front of the chapel. I thought you might like to carry some flowers."

"Thank you, Billy." Cherry took the bouquet with a hand that shook. "I guess I'm a little nervous."

"Me, too," he admitted.

Cherry wished he would smile. He didn't.

"The bouquet was a lovely thought." She raised it to her nose and sniffed. And sneezed. And sneezed again. "I must be—*achoo!*"

"Allergic," Billy finished, the smile appearing as he retrieved the bouquet from her and set it on an empty folding chair. "Forget the flowers. There are blooms enough in your cheeks for me."

"You mean the freckles," Cherry said, covering her cheeks with her hands. "I know they're awful, but—"

Billy took her hands in his and kissed her gently on each cheek. "They're tasty bits of brown sugar. Didn't anyone ever tell you that?"

Cherry froze as a memory of long ago came to mind. She was sitting on Big Mike's lap at the supper table. He was alternately taking bites of vanilla ice cream and giving her ice-cold kisses across her nose and cheeks, making yummy sounds in his throat and saying, "Your freckles sure taste sweet, baby."

Her throat tightened with emotion, and she looked up, half expecting to see Big Mike standing in front of her.

But it was Billy, his brow furrowed as his dark eyes took in the pallor beneath her freckles. "Are you all right? You look like you're about to faint."

Cherry stiffened knees that were threatening to buckle. "I've never fainted in my life. I don't expect to start now."

"Are you folks ready?" the minister asked.

"Last chance to back out," Billy whispered to Cherry.

The sound tickled her ear, but she managed to stifle the inappropriate giggle that sought voice. This ridiculous wedding ceremony was serious business. "I'm not backing out. But if you've changed your mind—"

"I haven't," Billy interrupted her.

He tightened his grip on one of her hands and released the other, leading her down the aisle to the makeshift pulpit at the front of the room.

Throughout the ceremony, Cherry kept repeating two things over and over.

Those little girls need me. And, *This is the last time I'll be disappointing Zach and Rebecca. Once I'm married, I won't be their responsibility anymore.*

She was concentrating so hard on convincing herself she was doing the right thing that she had to be prompted to respond when the time came.

"Cherry?"

She turned and found Billy's eyes on her. Worried again. *And I won't be a burden to Billy Stonecreek, either,* she added for good measure. "What is it, Billy?"

"Your turn to say I do."

Cherry gave Billy a tremulous smile and said, "I do."

It was more of a croak, actually, but when Billy smiled back, she knew it was all right.

"Rings?" the minister asked.

"We don't have any," Billy replied.

The minister pulled open a drawer in a credenza behind him, and she heard a tinny clatter. To Cherry's amazement, the drawer was full of fake gold rings.

"Help yourself," the minister said.

Cherry watched Billy select a plain yellow band and try it on her finger. Too small. The next was too big. The third was also a little loose, but because she wanted the awkward moment over with she said, "This one's fine, Billy."

"That'll be ten dollars extra," the minister said.

She saw the annoyed look that crossed Billy's face and pulled the ring off. "I don't need a ring."

Billy caught it before it could drop into the drawer and put it back on her finger. He caught her chin and lifted it so she was forced to look at him. "I'm sorry, Cherry. I should have thought of getting you a ring. This is so…"

Cheap? Tawdry? Vulgar? Cherry knew what he was thinking, but couldn't bring herself to say it, either. "Don't worry about it, Billy. It doesn't matter."

"You deserve better."

"It's not a real marriage. I don't need a real ring," Cherry said quietly so the minister wouldn't overhear.

Billy let go of her chin. He opened his mouth as though to speak and closed it again. Finally he said, "I guess you're right. This one will have to do. Shall we get this over with?"

They turned back to the minister, and he finished the ceremony. "You may kiss the bride," the minister said at last.

It wasn't a real wedding, so Cherry wasn't expecting a real kiss. To her surprise, Billy put his hands on either side of her face and murmured, "The ring is phony, but at least this can be real."

Cherry had done her share of kissing. Experimenting with sex was an age-old method of teenage rebellion. She thought she knew everything there was to know about kissing and sex. It was no big deal. Boys seemed to like it a lot, but she didn't understand what all the fuss was about.

Something odd happened when Billy Stonecreek's lips feathered across hers. An unexpected curl of desire flitted across her belly and shot up to her breasts. Her hands clutched fistfuls of his Western shirt as his mouth settled firmly over hers. His tongue traced the seam of her closed lips, causing them to tingle. She opened her mouth, and his tongue slipped inside for a quick taste of her.

She made a sound in her throat somewhere between confusion and protest.

His hand slid around to capture her nape and keep her from escaping.

Cherry wasn't going anywhere. She was enthralled by what Billy was doing with his lips and teeth and tongue. She had never felt anything remotely like it. Before she was ready, the kiss ended.

She stared, bemused, into Billy's hooded eyes. His lips were still damp from hers, and she didn't resist the impulse to reach out and touch.

His hand clamped around her wrist like a vise as her fingertips caressed his lips. "Don't." His voice was harsh, and his lips pressed flat in irritation.

Cherry realized her reaction, her naive curiosity, must

have embarrassed him. The kiss had merely been a token of thanks from Billy. He didn't want anything from her in return.

She had told him she didn't want to be touched until they knew each other better. But she had touched him. She had set the ground rules, and then she hadn't followed them.

It wasn't a real marriage. She had to remember that.

There were papers to sign and collect before they could leave. The minister was in a hurry, because two more couples had arrived and were awaiting their turns. Minutes after the ceremony ended, she and Billy were back in the rental car they had picked up at the airport.

Billy finally broke the uncomfortable silence that had fallen between them. "I don't know about you, but I could use a few hours of sleep before we fly back. We have the time. Your parents won't start missing you until noon."

"I must admit I feel exhausted," Cherry said. But she wasn't sure whether it was fatigue or a delayed reaction to their strange wedding. She had never wanted to get married, but that didn't mean she hadn't fantasized about having a grand wedding. She had imagined wearing a white satin gown with a train twenty feet long, having at least three bridesmaids, and hearing the wedding processional played on an immense pipe organ. This ceremony had fallen far short of the fantasy.

"Regrets?" Billy asked.

Cherry stared at him, surprised at his intuitiveness. "Were my thoughts that transparent?"

"I can't imagine any woman wanting to get married the way we did. But drastic situations sometimes require drastic solutions. In this case I believe the end—we're now legally husband and wife—justifies the means."

Cherry hoped Zach would see the logic in such an argument.

The hotel Billy chose was outlined in pink and white neon and advertised a honeymoon suite in the center of a pink neon heart. "At least we're sure they've got a honeymoon suite here," Billy said with a cheeky grin.

Cherry laughed breathlessly. "Why would we need a honeymoon suite?"

"It's probably going to have a bigger bed than the other rooms," Billy said. "It'll be more comfortable for someone my size."

"Oh," Cherry said.

"That almost sounded like disappointment," Billy said. "I agreed to wait until you're ready to make it a real marriage. Are you telling me you're ready?"

"No, Billy. I'm not."

He didn't say anything.

"Are you disappointed?" Cherry asked.

"I guess grooms have fantasies about their wedding nights the way brides have fantasies about their weddings," Billy conceded with a grin. "Yeah. I suppose I am. But I'll survive."

Cherry wondered if Billy was remembering his first wedding night. She knew she looked nothing like Laura Trask. She wasn't the least bit petite. Her hair wasn't golden blond, and she didn't move with stately grace. She had a million freckles that speckled her milk-white skin and frizzy hair that changed color depending on the way the sun struck it. She had a small bosom that had no freckles at all and absolutely no intention of letting the groom find that out for himself tonight. No, this was not a night for fulfilling fantasies.

She followed Billy inside the hotel with the overnight bag she had picked up at her friend's house, so they weren't entirely without luggage. She pressed the ring tight against her fourth finger with her thumb so it wouldn't slip off. She stood at Billy's shoulder while he registered and got a key card for the door.

They took the elevator to the top floor and found the honeymoon suite at the end of the hall. Billy used the key card to open the door.

Before she could say anything, Billy picked her up and carried her over the threshold. She was wearing the jeans and T-shirt she had put on to replace the torn chiffon dress and she could feel the heat of him everywhere his body touched hers.

Her arm automatically clutched at his shoulder to help him support her weight, but she realized when she felt the corded muscles there, that he didn't need any help. He carried her over to the bed and let her drop.

She bounced a couple of times and came to rest. "Good grief," she said, staring at the heart-shaped bed. "How do they expect two people to sleep on something shaped like this?"

He wiggled his eyebrows. "I don't think they expect you to sleep, if you know what I mean." He dropped onto the bed beside her and stretched out on his back with his hands behind his head on one of the pillows. "It's nowhere near as big as it looked in neon, either."

Cherry scooted as far from him as she could, but although there was plenty of room for two pillows at the top of the bed, the bottom narrowed so their feet ended up nearly touching.

Billy toed off one cowboy boot, then used his stockinged foot to shove off the other boot. He reached for the phone beside the bed. "I'll ask for an eight o'clock wake-up call," he said. "That'll give us time to fly back before noon."

Cherry was wearing tennis shoes, and she reached down and tugged them off with her hands and dropped them on the floor. She lay back on the pillow with her legs as far on her side of the bed as she could get them, which was a few bare inches from Billy's feet.

Billy reached over and turned out the lamp beside the bed. It should have been dark in the room, but the neon lights outside bathed the room in a romantic pink glow.

"Do you want me to close the curtains?" Billy asked.

"It's kind of pretty."

Which might make a difference if they wanted to watch each other while they made love, Cherry thought, but wasn't going to matter much when they closed their eyes to sleep. But she noticed Billy didn't get up to close the curtains.

"Good night, Cherry," Billy said, turning on his side away from her. "Thanks again."

"Good night, Billy," Cherry said, turning on her side away from him. "You're welcome."

She lay there in uncomfortable silence for perhaps five minutes before she whispered, "Are you asleep, Billy?"

Cherry felt the bed dip as he turned back toward her.

"I thought you were tired," he said.

"I am. But I'm too excited to sleep. It's not every day a girl gets married."

She stiffened when she felt one of his hands touch her shoulder and slide down to the small of her back.

"Don't get skittish on me, woman. I'm just going to rub your back a little to help you relax."

His thumb hit her somewhere in the center of her back, and his hand wrapped around her side.

Cherry gave a luxuriant sigh as he massaged her tense muscles.

"Feel better?"

"Yes." She was impressed again by his strength. And his gentleness. And wondered how his hand would feel caressing other places on her body.

Cherry sought a subject they could discuss that would get her mind off the direction it seemed to be headed. "Could you tell me a little bit about your daughters?"

"Raejean and Annie are just finishing the first grade. Their teacher has had a devil of a time telling them apart."

"Do they look that much alike?" Cherry asked.

Billy chuckled. "Sometimes they try to fool me. But it isn't hard to tell them apart once you get to know them. Raejean carries herself differently, more confidently. She looks at you more directly and talks back more often. Annie is kinder, sweeter, more thoughtful. She follows Raejean's lead. When the two of them team up, they can be a handful."

"Have you had a lot of trouble with them?"

His hand paused for a moment, then resumed its disturbing massage. "A little. Just lately. I think they're missing Laura as much as I am."

He rubbed a little harder, as though he had admitted something he wished he hadn't.

"Were you expecting twins when they were born?"

Cherry felt his hand tighten uncomfortably on her flesh. She hissed in a breath, and his hand soothed the hurt.

"The twins were a complete surprise. They came early, and for a while it was touch and go whether Laura and the girls would all make it. They did, but there were complications. The doctor said Laura couldn't have any more children."

"You wanted more?"

"I didn't care one way or the other. But Laura did."

Abruptly his hand left her back, and he rolled away from her. "Go to sleep, Cherry."

Apparently their conversation was over, leaving her with a great deal of food for thought.

The twins missed their mother. Like he did.

Cherry could do something to replace the loss in the twins' lives. She could be a mother to Billy's little girls. Of more concern was the temptation she felt to ease Billy's sorrow. There were dangers in such an undertaking. She had to remember this was a temporary marriage. It was safer to let Billy cope with his loss on his own.

On the other hand, Cherry never had chosen the safe path. As she closed her eyes again, she saw the four of them smiling at one another…one happy family.

Billy stared at the neon outside the window, willing himself to sleep. But he couldn't stop thinking about his new wife.

The wedding kiss had surprised him. In the fluorescent light of the wedding chapel, Cherry Whitelaw had looked like anything but a radiant bride. Her blue eyes had been wide with fright and her skin pale beneath a mass of orange freckles. He'd had significant second thoughts about the marriage. And third and fourth thoughts, as well. All his thoughts came back to the same thing. She needed his help. And he needed hers.

He had been proud of her for getting through that awful ceremony—including the last-minute search for a ring that would fit—with so much dignity. That was why he had offered her the kiss, not because he had been wondering what her lips would taste like. When she had reached out to him afterward, he had stopped her because that wasn't part of their deal, not because he had been shocked at the way his body had gone rock-hard at her touch. Just thinking about it caused the same reaction all over again.

Billy swore.

"Billy? Is something wrong?"

"Nothing's wrong, Cherry. Go to sleep."

He closed his eyes, determined to get some rest, but a picture of her breast half revealed by the torn chiffon bodice appeared behind his eyelids.

He opened his eyes and stared at the neon again. Who would have thought he would find a freckle-faced redhead so erotically exciting? Or that his new wife would be off-limits for heaven knew how long? Billy heaved a long-suffering sigh. It was going to be one hell of a marriage.

His eyes slid closed again as sleep claimed his exhausted body.

Billy was having a really spectacular dream. He had a handful of soft female breast, which just happened to belong to his new wife. Her eyes were closed in passion, and as he flicked his thumb across her nipple, he heard a moan that made his loins tighten. He lowered his head to take her nipple in his mouth. It was covered by a thin layer of cotton. He sucked on her through the damp cloth and felt her body arch toward him. Her hands threaded into his hair...and yanked on it—

Billy came awake with a jerk. "What the hell?"

Cherry was sitting bolt upright in bed with her hands

crossed defensively under her breasts. A damp spot on her T-shirt revealed that he hadn't been dreaming.

It shouldn't have surprised him. His last thoughts before drifting to sleep had been about Cherry. No wonder his body had been drawn to hers during the night. He shoved a hand through hair that was standing on end and groaned. "God, Cherry, I'm sorry. I was dreaming."

She eyed him suspiciously.

"I swear I didn't know what I was doing."

That made her look crestfallen.

"Not that it isn't exactly what I'd like to be doing at this moment," he said.

She gave a hitching breath that was almost a sob. "We agreed to wait."

"Yeah, I know," Billy said. "I don't suppose you've changed your mind."

She hesitated so long he thought maybe she had. Until she shook her head no.

Billy looked at the clock. It was only six. But he didn't trust himself to lie back down beside her. "I can't sleep anymore. How about if we head for the airport?"

"All right," she said.

He started pulling on his boots and felt her hand on his shoulder. He froze.

She cleared her throat and said, "I liked what you were doing, Billy. It felt…good. I wanted you to know that. It's just…"

He shoved his foot down into the boot and stood. He had to get away from her or he was going to turn around and lay her flat on the bed and do something he would be sorry for later. "I know," he said. "We agreed to wait."

She had a brave smile on her face. And looked every bit her youthful age.

What on earth had possessed him to marry her?

It was a silent flight from Las Vegas to the airport in Amarillo. And an even more silent truck ride to the Stonecreek Ranch. Billy pulled up to the back door of a large, two-story white clapboard house and killed the engine. The blue morning glories he had planted for Laura were soaking up the midday sun on a trellis along the eastern edge of the porch.

"We're home," Billy said. His throat tightened painfully. They were the same words he had spoken to Laura—how many years ago?—when they had moved into this house.

Suddenly he realized he couldn't go back into Laura's house right now with a new wife. It was still too full of Laura. He needed a little time to accept the fact that she really was gone forever.

"Look, why don't you go inside and introduce yourself to Mrs. Motherwell, my housekeeper. I just realized I was supposed to pick up a load of feed in town this morning. I'll be back in an hour or so."

Cherry was staring at him as if he had grown a second head. "You want me to go in there without you?" she asked.

"Just tell Mrs. Motherwell you've come to replace her. I'll explain everything to the kids when I get back." When Cherry continued sitting there staring at him, he snapped, "Changed your mind already?"

His new wife looked sober and thoughtful. There were shadows of fatigue beneath her eyes. "No. I'm determined to see this through." She gave him one last anxious look before she left the truck. "Don't be gone long."

"I won't."

Billy resisted the urge to gun the engine as he backed

away from the house. Once he hit paved road he headed the truck toward town. He hadn't gone two miles when he saw flashing red and blue lights behind him. He glanced down at the speedometer and swore. He swerved off the road and braked hard enough to raise a cloud of dust.

He was out of the truck and reaching for his wallet to get his driver's license when he saw the highway patrolman had a gun in his hand that was pointed at him.

"Freeze, Stonecreek, or I'll blow your head off."

Billy froze. "What the hell's the matter with you?"

"Put your hands up. You're under arrest."

"Arrest? For what?"

"Kidnapping."

It took a full second for the charge to register. *Kidnapping?* Then he realized what must have happened and groaned. "Look, Officer, I can explain everything."

"You have the right to remain silent," the officer began.

Billy's lips pressed flat. He had married Cherry Whitelaw in the hope of solving his problems. Instead he had jumped right out of the frying pan into the fire.

Chapter 4

Cherry stared at the back door of Billy's house—now her home, too—trying to work up the courage to go inside, wondering, absurdly, if she should knock first.

She turned and stole a glance at Billy's rugged profile as he drove away, pondering what it was about him she had found so beguiling. He had rescued her, listened to her troubles, and shared his in return. She had felt his desperation and responded to it. Now he was her husband. She twisted the cheap gold ring that confirmed it wasn't all a dream, that she was, indeed, Mrs. Billy Stonecreek.

Good grief. What had she done?

Cherry had gone off half-cocked in the past, but the enormity of this escapade was finally sinking in. Surely it would have been better to face Zach and Rebecca and explain the truth of what had happened at the dance. How was she going to justify this latest lapse of common sense?

She felt a surge of anger at Billy for abandoning her at the door. It wouldn't have taken long to introduce her to Mrs. Motherwell and explain the situation. So why hadn't he done it?

Maybe because he's having the same second thoughts as you are. Maybe in the cold light of day he's thinking he made a bad bargain. Maybe he's trying to figure out a way right now to get out of it.

If the back door hadn't opened at that precise moment, Cherry would have turned and headed for Hawk's Pride.

But it did. And Cherry found herself face-to-face with Penelope Trask.

"I saw you standing out here," Mrs. Trask said. "Is there something I can do for you?"

"I, uh… Is Mrs. Motherwell here?"

"She packed her bags and left this morning."

Cherry stood with her jaw agape, speechless for perhaps the first time in her life. Had Mrs. Trask already managed to gain legal custody of Billy's children? Had their marriage been for naught? She wished Billy were here.

"Don't I know you? Aren't you one of those Whitelaw Bra—" Mrs. Trask cut herself off.

Cherry knew what she had been about to say. The eight adopted Whitelaw kids were known around this part of Texas as the Whitelaw Brats, just like Zach and his siblings before them, and Grandpa Garth and his siblings before that. Cherry had done her share to help earn the nickname. She was proud to be one of them.

She met the older woman's disdainful look with defiance. "Yes, I'm a Whitelaw Brat. You have a problem with that?"

"None at all. But if you're looking for your missing

sister, she isn't here. I have no idea what my no-account excuse for a son-in-law has done with her." She started to close the door in Cherry's face.

Cherry stuck her foot in the door. "Wait! What are you talking about?"

A flare of recognition lit Mrs. Trask's eyes. "Oh, my God. You're the girl, aren't you? The one Billy kidnapped." She stuck her head out the screen door and looked around. "Where is he? I have a few things to say to him."

"Kidnapped?" Cherry gasped. "I wasn't kidnapped!"

"Your parents reported you missing late last night."

"Why would they think I was with Billy?"

"Your date wrapped his car around a telephone pole, and when he kept mumbling your name the police called your parents, thinking maybe you'd been thrown from the car. At the hospital, the boy told your father that he'd left you at the stock pond with Billy, after my son-in-law ran him off with his fists.

"Your father couldn't find you at the stock pond, and when he came looking for you here in a rage, Mrs. Motherwell called me. Your father seemed bent on strangling someone before the night was out."

Probably me, Cherry thought morosely.

"Of course I came right over," Mrs. Trask said. "All I could tell your father was that I wouldn't put it past my reckless son-in-law to kidnap an innocent young woman."

"Mrs. Trask, I wasn't kidnapped."

"I suggest you go home and tell that to your father. He told the police Billy must have kidnapped you, because you'd never go off on your own like that." Mrs.

Trask smirked. "Of course, that was before he found out you'd been expelled from school earlier in the evening."

Cherry groaned.

"You're in an awful lot of trouble, young lady. Where have you been? And where's Billy?"

Cherry put a hand to her throbbing temple. Zach and Rebecca must be frantic with worry. And disappointed beyond belief. She didn't want to think about how angry they were going to be when they heard what she had done.

"May I please use your phone?" It was her phone now, so she shouldn't have to ask. Except, this didn't seem the right moment to announce that she and Billy had run off to Las Vegas to get married.

Mrs. Trask hesitated, then pushed the screen door open wide. "Come on in, if you must."

As soon as Cherry's eyes adjusted to the dim light in the kitchen, she saw Raejean and Annie standing together near the table.

They wore their straight black hair in adorable, beribboned pigtails, and stared at her with dark, serious brown eyes. Their noses were small and their chins dainty, like their mother, but they had high, sharp cheekbones that reminded her of Billy. They were tall for six-year-olds and dressed exactly alike in collared blouses tucked into denim coveralls and white tennis shoes.

"Hello, Raejean," she said, addressing the child who had her arm wrapped comfortingly around the other's shoulder.

The child's eyes widened in surprise at being recognized. Then she said, "I'm not Raejean, I'm Annie."

The other twin's mouth dropped open, and she glanced

at her sister. Then she turned to Cherry, pointed to her chest with her thumb, and said, "I'm Raejean."

"I see," Cherry said. They were both missing the exact same front tooth. No help there telling them apart. Billy had said Raejean was the confident one, so Cherry had assumed it was Raejean who was giving comfort to her sister. But maybe she had been wrong.

"I need to use your phone," she said, moving toward where it hung on the kitchen wall.

Cherry felt the girls watching her while she dialed.

"We don't need another housekeeper," the twin who had identified herself as Annie said. "We're going to stay at Nana's house until Daddy gets home."

Cherry felt her heart miss a beat. She turned to Mrs. Trask and said, "Billy went into town for supplies. He should be back any time now. There's no need to take the girls anywhere."

"I'll be the best judge of that," Mrs. Trask said. "Go upstairs, girls, and finish packing."

The twins turned and ran. Cherry heard their footsteps pounding on the stairs as the ringing phone was answered by her sister, Jewel. Of her seven Whitelaw siblings, Jewel was the sister closest to her in age. Jewel had been adopted by Zach and Rebecca when she was five—the first of the current generation of Whitelaw Brats.

It had taken Cherry a while to straighten them all out, but now she could recite their names and ages with ease. Rolleen was 21, Jewel was 19, she was 18, Avery was 17, Jake was 16, Frannie was 13, Rabbit was 12, and Colt was 11.

Of course Rabbit's name wasn't really Rabbit, it was Louis, but nobody called him that. Jewel had given him the nickname Rabbit when he was little, because he ate so many carrots, and the name had stuck. Colt was the only one of them who had been adopted as a baby. The rest of them had all known at least one other parent before being abandoned, orphaned, or fostered out.

"Is anybody there?" Jewel asked breathlessly. "If this is the kidnapper, we'll pay whatever you ask."

"It's me, Jewel."

"Cherry! Where are you? Are you all right? Are you hurt?"

"I'm fine. I'm at Billy Stonecreek's ranch."

"So he did kidnap you! I'll send Daddy to get you right away."

"No! I mean…" Cherry had turned her back to Mrs. Trask and kept her voice low thus far, but she figured there was no sense postponing the inevitable. "Billy didn't kidnap me. Last night we flew to Las Vegas and got married."

She was met with stunned silence on the other end of the line. Which was a good thing, because Mrs. Trask gave an outraged shriek that brought the two little girls back downstairs on the run.

"Nana! Nana! What's wrong?"

"I have to go now, Jewel," Cherry said. "Tell Zach and Rebecca I'm okay, and that I'll come to see them soon and explain everything."

"Cherry, don't—"

Cherry hung up the phone in time to turn and greet the twins a second time. Again, she identified the twin taking the lead as Raejean, which meant the one standing slightly behind her was Annie. "Hello, Raejean. Hello, Annie."

"I'm Annie," Raejean contradicted.

Before Annie could misidentify herself as Raejean,

Mrs. Trask snapped, "Don't bother trying to tell them apart. They're identical, you know."

"But—" From Billy's descriptions of them it was so obvious to her which twin was which. Couldn't Mrs. Trask see the difference?

"What's wrong, Nana?" Raejean asked. "Why did you scream?"

Mrs. Trask's face looked more like a beet or a turnip than a human head, she was so flushed. It was clear she wasn't sure exactly what to say.

"Your grandmother was just excited about some news she heard," Cherry said.

"What news?" Annie asked.

"It's a surprise I think your Daddy will want to tell you about himself when he gets home," Cherry said.

"We're not going to be here that long," Mrs. Trask retorted. "The girls and I are leaving."

"Not until Billy gets back," Cherry said firmly. "I'm sure Raejean and Annie want to wait and say goodbye to their father." Cherry turned to the girls and asked, "Don't you?"

Raejean eyed her consideringly, but Annie piped up, "I want to wait for Daddy."

Mrs. Trask made an angry sound in her throat. "I hope you're happy now," she said to Cherry. "My grandchildren have had a difficult enough time over the past year, without adding someone like you to the picture."

Cherry reminded herself that Mrs. Trask was always going to be Raejean and Annie's grandmother. Throwing barbs now, however satisfying it might be, would only cause problems later. Zach and Rebecca would have been astounded at her tact when she spoke.

"I'm sorry we surprised you like this, Mrs. Trask. I

know Billy will want to explain everything to you himself. Won't you consider waiting until he returns before you leave?"

"No."

Of course, there were times when being blunt worked best. Cherry crossed to stand beside the twins. "I'm sorry you have to leave, Mrs. Trask. The girls and I will have Billy give you a call when he gets home."

Cherry saw the moment when Mrs. Trask realized that she had been outmaneuvered. She wasn't going to make a quick and easy escape with Billy's children. Cherry was there to stand in her way.

Billy chose that moment to pull open the screen door and step into the kitchen.

Annie and Raejean gave shrieks of joy and raced into his wide open arms. He lifted them both, one in each arm, and gave them each a smacking kiss. "How are my girls?" he asked.

Raejean answered for both of them.

"Some man got mad at Mrs. Motherwell because she didn't know where you were and Nana came and Mrs. Motherwell packed her bags and left and Nana said we should pack, too, and go live with her until you came back home, only this lady came a little while ago and said you were coming home really soon and we had to wait for you because you have a surprise for us. What's our surprise, Daddy? Can we have it now?"

Cherry had watched Billy's narrowed gaze flicker from his daughter to Mrs. Trask and back again as Raejean made her breathless recital. When Raejean got to the part about a surprise, his gaze shot to her, and she thought she saw both panic and resignation.

"What are you doing back here so soon?" Mrs. Trask said. "I was told you were going into town for supplies."

"I got stopped by the police long before I got there and arrested for kidnapping," Billy said.

"Then why aren't you in jail?" Mrs. Trask demanded.

Billy's lips curled. "I showed them my marriage license."

"Who got kidnapped, Daddy?" Annie asked.

"Nobody, sweetheart," Billy replied. "It was all a big mistake."

"Then, can we have our surprise now?" Annie asked.

He knelt down and set them back on their feet. Keeping an arm around each of them, he said, "The surprise is that you have a new mother."

Annie's brow furrowed. "A new mother?"

Raejean frowned. "Our mother is in heaven."

"I know that," Billy said in a sandpaper-rough voice that made Cherry's throat swell with emotion. "I've married someone else who's going to be your mother from now on."

Raejean and Annie looked at each other, then turned as one to stare with shocked, suspicious eyes at Cherry.

Raejean's head shot around to confront her father. "Her?"

Billy nodded.

Raejean jerked free and shouted, "I don't want another mother! Make her go away!" Then she ran from the room.

Annie's eyes had filled with tears and one spilled over as she stared at Raejean's fleeing form. Cherry willed the softhearted child to accept her, but Annie paused only another moment before she turned and ran after her sister.

Cherry met Billy's stricken gaze. She felt sick to her stomach. The two charming and innocent little girls she had married Billy to save from harm, didn't want anything to do with her.

"You're a fool, Billy," Mrs. Trask said, grabbing her purse from the kitchen counter. "I don't know what you hoped to accomplish with this charade, but it won't work. I'm more convinced than ever that my grandchildren belong with me." She gave Cherry a look down her nose. "I'll see you both in court."

She made a grand exit through the doorway that led to the front of the house. Cherry and Billy stood unmoving until they heard the front door slam behind her.

"She's right," Billy said. "I always intend to do the right thing, but somehow it turns out wrong."

"This wasn't wrong, Billy. If I hadn't gotten here when I did, Mrs. Trask would have taken the children and been gone before you returned. At least Raejean and Annie are still here."

"And angry and unhappy."

"We can change that with time."

"I hope so. It won't help much to argue in court that I've got a wife to take care of my children, if my children hate her guts."

"We have a more immediate problem," Cherry said.

"What's that?"

"Zach Whitelaw."

"What about him?"

"He's going to kill you on sight."

Billy gave a relieved laugh. "Is that all? I thought it was something serious."

"Don't joke," Cherry said. "This is serious. Three years ago a boy tried to force himself on Jewel at a Fourth of July picnic. I'll never forget the look in Zach's eyes when Jewel stood crying in his arms, her face bruised and her dress torn. He took a horsewhip to the boy and nearly flayed him alive. Both families kept it quiet, but you know how that sort of thing gets around. None of us girls has ever had any problems with boys since then.

"That's why it surprised me when Ray... If Ray hadn't been drunk, he would never have done what he did."

"And we wouldn't be where we are today," Billy said. "I won't let any man whip me, Cherry. If your father tries—"

"I'm only telling you all this so you'll understand why I have to go home and explain all of this to him by myself. Once he understands I was willing and—"

Billy shook his head. "We go together, or you don't go at all."

"Zach's going to be furious with me."

"All the more reason for us to go together. You may have been his daughter yesterday, but you're my wife today. No man is going to threaten my wife. Not even her father."

Cherry stared wide-eyed at Billy. She supposed she should have told him that no matter how angry Zach got with her, he would never raise a hand to her. In the past she had been sent to her room without supper, or been forced to spend a day alone thinking about the wisdom of a course of action. But the Whitelaws had always used reason, rather than force, to teach their children right from wrong.

Billy wouldn't have to defend her, but she reveled in the thought that he was willing to do so. Of more concern to her was the possibility that the two men might provoke one another to violence. She already knew that Billy liked to fight. Zach would be more than willing to give him one.

"I'll let you come with me on one condition," she said.

"What's that?"

"We bring the girls with us."

Billy frowned. "What purpose would that serve?"

"Zach won't be able to fight with you—or yell at me—if he's busy meeting his new grandchildren."

"Raejean and Annie don't even like you. What makes you think they'll take to your father?"

"Trust me. Zach Whitelaw could sell snow in Alaska. He'll have Raejean and Annie eating out of his hand in no time. Besides, we have no choice but to take them with us. Mrs. Motherwell is gone."

"I forgot about that," Billy said as he headed toward the door that led upstairs. "Damn. All right. Let me go get them. We might as well get this meeting over with."

"Billy," Cherry called after him. When he stopped and turned to her, she said, "We can still call the whole thing off."

He walked the few steps back to her and lifted her chin with his finger. "Buck up, kid. You're doing great."

Cherry felt tears prickle her eyes and blinked to keep them from forming.

Billy leaned down and kissed her mouth. His touch was gentle, intended to comfort. "I'm sorry, Cherry. I shouldn't have left you here alone and driven away. It's not easy to admit it, but I was scared."

Cherry searched his eyes. If he had once been afraid, the fear was gone now. If he had regrets, he wasn't letting her see them. She wished she knew him better as a person. Could she rely on him? Would he be there for her when the going got rough?

When he pulled her into his arms and hugged her, she felt safe and secure. She knew that was an illusion. Her father had made her feel safe, too. But they had been torn from each other. It was better not to try and make more of this relationship than it was.

Before she could edge herself away from Billy, the screen door was flung open. Billy threw her aside to confront whatever danger threatened them.

Zach Whitelaw stood in the doorway.

Chapter 5

"Daddy, don't!" Cherry cried as Zach took a step toward Billy, his hands tightened into angry knots.

Zach froze, his eyes wide with shock.

It took Cherry a second to realize she had called him "Daddy" instead of "Zach," something she had never done before. She felt confused, unsure why she had blurted it out like that, especially now, when she wasn't going to be his daughter anymore, but someone else's wife.

"Please don't fight," she said.

"Stay out of this, Cherry," Billy said, his hands curling into fists as menacing as Zach's.

"How did you get here so quickly?" Cherry said to her father. "I just got off the phone with Jewel."

"The police called me when they picked up Billy. A phony marriage license isn't going to save you from me," he snarled at Billy.

"We really are married," Cherry said, taking a step to put herself between the two men. Temporarily, it kept them from throwing punches.

Zach snorted. "In a Las Vegas ceremony? That's no kind of wedding."

"It's legal," Billy said coldly.

There was nothing Zach could say to counter that except, "Come home, Cherry. I know the situation last night must have upset you, but Rebecca and I want you to know we're on your side. We believe there must be some reasonable explanation for what happened. We can fix this problem."

"It's too late for that. Billy and I are married. I'm staying with him."

Zach glared at Billy. "You should be ashamed of yourself, taking advantage of a vulnerable child to—"

"She's no child," Billy said quietly. "She's a woman. And my wife." His hands slid around Cherry's waist from behind, and he pulled her back against the length of his body.

Cherry saw the inference Zach drew from Billy's words and actions that the two of them had done what husbands and wives do on their wedding night. By the time her father's gaze skipped to her face, she bore a flush high on her cheekbones that seemed to confirm what he was thinking. There was no way she was going to admit the truth.

She saw the wounded look in Zach's eyes before he hid it behind lowered lids.

"I didn't meant to hurt you or Rebecca," she forced past the lump in her throat.

"Why, Cherry?" he asked. "Why couldn't you trust us to be on your side? I thought…"

They were good parents. They had done everything they could to make her feel loved and appreciated, safe and secure. But they expected her to believe parents could protect their children from the evils of the world. She knew from experience that simply wasn't true. She could never trust them completely. She would never trust anybody that much again.

"I'm sorry, Zach." She saw his gaze flicker at her re-version to the less familiar, less personal title. "Please tell Rebecca—"

Zach cut her off. "You explain this to your mother. I couldn't find the words." He turned and left as abruptly as he had come.

Cherry felt her nose burning, felt the tears threaten and fought them back. She had chosen to travel this road. She had no one to blame but herself for her predicament. Crying over spilled milk wasn't going to accomplish anything.

"Thanks for sticking by me," Billy said against her ear.

"I'm your wife."

"Sometimes that doesn't mean much when parents enter the picture," Billy said bitterly.

Cherry turned in his embrace and put her arms around him to hug him, laying her cheek against his shoulder. "I'll try to be a good wife, Billy." She raised her face to his, only to find herself unexpectedly kissed.

There was as much desperation as there was hunger in Billy's kiss. Something inside Cherry responded to both emotions, and she found herself kissing Billy back.

"Hey! What are you doing to my dad?"

Cherry pulled free of Billy's grasp and turned to the

urchin who had spoken. Behind her stood the other twin, her face less belligerent, more perplexed.

"Uh…" Cherry began. She had no idea where to go from there. She expected Billy to make some sort of explanation, but he gave her a helpless one-shouldered shrug. Cherry turned back to the twins and said to the one who had spoken, "Your dad and I were kissing, Raejean. That's what married people do."

"I'm Annie," Raejean said.

"I'm Raejean," Annie dutifully added.

"Hey, you two," Billy said. "What's the big idea trying to fool Cherry?"

Raejean's chin jutted. "I don't know why you're so mad, Daddy. She isn't fooled at all." She turned to Cherry, her brow furrowed. "How do you do that, anyway? No one but Mommy and Daddy has ever been able to tell us apart."

Cherry said, "There's nothing magic about it. You're as different from your sister as night from day."

"We're twins," Raejean protested. "We're *exactly* alike."

"You look alike on the outside," Cherry conceded, "but inside here—" Cherry touched her head. "And here—" She touched her heart. "You're very different."

"I'm glad you can tell us apart," Annie said. "I don't like fooling people."

"I don't care if you can tell us apart," Raejean said. "I'm not going to like you."

"Isn't it a little soon to make up your mind about that?" Cherry asked. "You hardly know me."

"I know you want to be my mother. I don't want another mother. My mother's in heaven!" Raejean turned and headed for the stairs. She hadn't gone very far before she realized Annie hadn't automatically followed her. She turned and said, "Come on, Annie."

Annie hesitated briefly before she turned and followed her sister.

Cherry whirled on Billy the instant they were gone. "I can't do this all by myself, Billy. You're going to have to help."

"You can't blame them for being confused, Cherry. After all, the only woman they've ever seen me kissing is their mother."

"Then maybe we shouldn't let the girls see us kissing. Maybe you should keep your distance when they're around."

Billy thought about it for a moment, then shook his head. "I don't want to do that for two reasons. Penelope would be sure to notice if we never touched each other. It would be a dead giveaway that there's something fishy about our marriage."

"And the second reason?"

"I don't want my daughters to see me ignoring the woman they believe is my wife. It would give them the wrong impression of what marriage is all about."

"I see." What she saw was that Billy had all sorts of reasons for kissing and hugging her that had nothing whatsoever to do with actually loving her. But loving hadn't been a part of their bargain. She had to remind herself of the rules of this game. *Help each other out. Don't get involved. Don't start to care.* That way lay heartache.

"All right, Billy," Cherry said. "I'll play along with you where the kissing and touching is concerned. So long as we both know it's only an act, I suppose neither of us can be hurt. Now that we have that settled, I believe you need to get to town for those supplies, and I'd better get some lunch started."

Cherry turned her back on Billy, but she hadn't taken two steps toward the sink before his arms slid around her from behind again, circling her waist. Her treacherous body melted against him. She forced herself to stiffen in his embrace. "Don't, Billy," she said in a quiet voice.

"You're my wife, Cherry."

"In name only," Cherry reminded him. "We can pretend for everybody else, but I think it's best if we're honest with each other. We aren't in love, Billy. We never will be."

Billy's hands dropped away, but he didn't move. She felt the heat of his body along the entire length of her back. Her eyes slid closed, and she held herself rigid to keep from leaning back into his fiery warmth.

"If we're being honest," Billy said in a husky voice, "I think you should know I'm more than a little attracted to you, Cherry. I have been since the moment I first laid eyes on you." Billy took her by the shoulders and turned her to face him. "That's the truth."

She lifted her eyes to meet his. "That's lust, Billy. Not love."

His dark eyes narrowed, and his hands dropped away from her shoulders. "There's nothing wrong with desiring your wife in bed."

"I'm not your wi—"

"Dammit, Cherry!"

When Billy took a step back and shoved his hands into his jeans pockets, Cherry had the distinct impression he did it to keep himself from reaching for her again.

"You *are* my wife," he said through gritted teeth. "Not

forever. Not even for very long. But we most definitely are married. I suggest you start thinking that way!"

Before she could contradict him, he was gone, the screen door slamming behind him.

Billy couldn't remember a time when he had been more frustrated. Even when he had been arguing with Laura about whether or not she should try to get pregnant again when the doctor had advised her against it, he hadn't felt so much like he was butting his head against a stone wall. Deep down, he knew Cherry was right. It would be better for both of them if he kept his distance from her.

He had made up his mind to try.

Of course, that was before he stepped into Cherry's bedroom the morning after their wedding. He had expected her to be up and dressed, since he had helped her set the alarm for 5:30 a.m. the previous evening. Apparently, she had turned it off.

He found her sleeping beneath tousled sheets, one long, exquisite leg exposed all the way to her hip, one rosy nipple peeking at him, her lips slightly parted, her silky red curls spread across the pillow, waiting for a lover's hands to gather them up.

He cleared his throat noisily, hoping that would be enough to wake her. All she did was roll over, rearranging the sheet, exposing an entire milky white breast.

He swallowed hard and averted his eyes. He sat down beside her, thinking maybe the dip in the mattress would make her aware of his presence.

She slept on.

His gaze returned to rest on her face. Close as he was, he could see the dark shadows under her eyes. She must not have slept very well. He could understand that. He hadn't slept too well himself. He had resorted to a desperate act—marriage—to solve one problem and had created a host of others in the process. Not the least of which was the fact he wanted to have carnal knowledge of his new wife.

He debated whether he ought to kiss her awake. But he wasn't Prince Charming. And Sleeping Beauty had never had such a freckled face. Nevertheless, his body responded to the mere thought of pressing his lips against hers, of tasting the hot, sweet wetness of her mouth.

Billy swore viciously.

And Cherry woke with a start.

It took her a second to realize how exposed she was, and she grabbed at the sheet as she sat up and drew her knees to her chest. Her blue eyes were wide and wary. "What are you doing in here?"

"I came to wake you up. You overslept."

She glanced at the clock, then dropped her forehead to her knees and groaned. "I must have turned off the alarm."

"I figured as much when you didn't show up in the kitchen. I've already had my breakfast. I left some coffee perking for you. The kids'll be up in a little while. You probably have time for a quick shower."

Thinking about her naked in the shower had about the same effect as contemplating kissing her. Billy needed to leave, but he was too aware of what Cherry would see if he stood right now. So he went right on sitting where he was.

Unfortunately, she now had the sheet flattened against herself, and he could see the darker outline of her nipples beneath the soft cotton. He found that every bit as erotic as seeing her naked.

"Hell," Billy muttered, shifting uncomfortably on the edge of the bed.

"What's the matter?"

Billy's lip curled wryly. "I'm not used to looking at a woman in bed without being able to touch."

"Oh." She clutched the sheet tighter, exposing the fact that her nipples had become hard nubs.

Billy bolted to his feet and saw her gaze lock on the bulge beneath his zipper. He froze where he was, his body aching, his mouth dry.

He watched her until she lifted her eyes to his face. Her pupils were enormous, her lips full, as though he had been kissing her. She was aroused, and he hadn't even touched her.

"Tell me to go, Cherry." He wanted to consume her in a hurry, like ice cream on a hot day. He wanted to take his time and sip at her slow and easy, like a cool mint julep on a lazy summer afternoon.

She licked her lips, and he felt his body harden like stone.

"The girls will be up soon," Cherry reminded him. "I need to get dressed."

Heaven help him, he had forgotten all about his daughters. He shoved a distracted hand through his hair and huffed out a breath of air. "I'll be working on the range today. If you need anything…"

Cherry smiled. "Don't worry about us, Billy. We'll manage fine."

"All right. So long."

He was almost out the door when she called him back. "Billy?"

He turned and found her standing beside the bed with the sheet draped around her in a way that revealed as much as it covered. "What?" he asked, his voice hoarse from the sudden rush of desire he felt.

"You didn't kiss me goodbye."

He shook his head. "I don't think that would be a good idea, Cherry."

Before he realized what she had in mind, she closed the few steps between them and lifted her face to him. "I thought a lot about our situation last night, when I couldn't sleep," she said earnestly. "And I realized that if we're going to convince Mrs. Trask that this is a real marriage, we're going to have to act as much like a happily married couple as possible.

"Zach always gives Rebecca a kiss goodbye in the morning." She gave him a winsome smile. "So, pucker up, Mr. Stonecreek, and give me a kiss."

She didn't give him much of a choice. She raised herself on tiptoe and leaned forward and pressed her lips against his.

Billy gathered her in his arms and pulled her close as his mouth opened over hers, taking what he had denied himself only moments before. His hands slid down her naked back, shoving the sheet out of his way. Then he held her buttocks tight against his arousal with one hand while the other caught her nape and slid up to grasp a handful of her hair.

He took his time kissing her, his tongue thrusting hard and deep, and then slowing for several soft, probing forays, seeking the honey within. She made a moaning sound deep in her throat, and he gave an answering growl of passion.

When he let her go at last, she gave him a dazed look

through half-closed lids, then grabbed at the sheet that had slid down to her waist and pulled it back up to cover herself. He grinned and said, "That was a good idea. I think we'll keep it up."

It took all the willpower he had to turn and walk out the bedroom door.

Cherry watched Billy go this time without calling him back. She was still quivering from his kiss. She forced her wobbly legs to take one step, and then another, as she headed for the bentwood rocker where she had thrown her robe. She slipped it on and let the sheet drop to the floor.

She was tying her terry-cloth robe closed when she heard a knock on the door. She hurried to open it and found Billy standing there with his hat on, his hip cocked, and his thumbs in his front pockets.

"Did you forget something?" she asked.

Not a thing, Billy realized. He remembered exactly how she had looked in bed. *And you look as delicious in that robe as you did in bed.* He couldn't very well tell her he had come back just to look at her again. So he said, "I forgot to say good morning." He smiled and tipped his hat. "Mornin', ma'am."

Cherry laughed.

And then, because he was looking for an excuse to spend more time with her, he said, "I wondered if you'd like to join me for a cup of coffee before I leave."

"I should get dressed," Cherry said, tightening the belt on her robe. "The girls will be up soon."

"You're right about that." Billy searched for something else to say, because otherwise he would have no excuse to linger.

"By the way, I never got around to telling you, but

you'll need to go grocery shopping today. The ranch has an account at the store in town. I think Harvey Mills already knows we're married—I doubt there's anyone in the county who doesn't know by now—but just in case, I'll give him a call and tell him to put your name on the account. Feel free to get anything you think we'll need."

It was more than Cherry had heard Billy say at one time since she had met him at the pond. But the words had nothing to do with what he was saying with his eyes. His eyes were eating her alive. Her heart was pumping hard. Her breasts felt full. Her mouth felt dry.

She cleared her throat and said, "Shopping. Got it. Anything else?"

"Not unless you'd like that cup of coffee."

Cherry slowly shook her head. She had to send him away or she was going to invite him into her room. "I need to shower and dress before the girls wake up. Have a nice day, Billy."

"Yeah. I'll do that."

When he didn't leave, she raised a brow and said, "Is there something else, Billy?"

"If you want, I can go with you later today to see your family…to explain things."

Cherry felt a sense of relief. "Thanks, Billy. I'd like that."

"Well. I guess I'd better get started."

It took him another moment or two before he moved away from the door. She watched his sexy, loose-limbed amble until he was gone from sight, then scurried up the stairs to the shower.

However, when she reached the bathroom, it was locked. She would have to wait her turn. She leaned against the wall, a towel over her arm, one bare foot perched atop the other and waited. And waited. The door never opened.

She leaned her ear against the door, but there was no sound coming from inside. She knocked and said, "Is someone in there?"

No answer.

"Raejean? Annie?"

Nothing.

She walked down the hall to the girls' bedroom. Their unmade twin beds were empty. She checked the other doors along the hall and found an office and Billy's bedroom, but no sign of the children.

"Raejean!" she called loudly. "Annie! If you're hiding somewhere up here, I want you to come out right now!"

Nothing.

She crossed back to the bathroom door and listened intently. She thought she heard whispers. She banged on the door. "I know you two are in there. I want you to come out right now."

Nothing.

She grabbed the doorknob and yanked on it, then slammed her shoulder against the door as though to break it open. "Open up!"

Nothing.

Cherry leaned back against the wall and sighed heavily. She hadn't counted on this sort of misbehavior when she had nobly volunteered to rescue Billy's daughters from their grandmother's clutches. Right now, Mrs. Trask was more than welcome to the two of them!

Cherry smiled. Actually, she had pulled the same trick on one of her foster parents. She had spent almost two days in the bathroom before hunger finally forced her out. Which gave her an idea.

"All right, fine, stay in there. But you're going to get awfully hungry before the day is out. I'm going downstairs and make myself some blueberry pancakes with whipped cream on top and scrambled eggs and sausage and wash it all down with some hot chocolate with marshmallows."

Loud, agitated whispers.

The bathroom door opened and one of the twins stuck her head out. "Whipped cream on pancakes?"

Cherry nodded.

An identical face appeared and asked, "Big marshmallows? Or little ones?"

"Which do you prefer?"

"Little ones. Mrs. Motherwell only bought the big ones."

"Then we'll cut them into little pieces," Cherry suggested.

"All right." Annie shot out of the bathroom before Raejean could stop her and took Cherry by the hand. "Let's go."

Cherry waited to see what Raejean would do. The twin obviously wasn't happy to see rebellion in the ranks. She seemed unsure whether to stay where she was or abandon the fort. Her stomach growled and settled the matter. Raejean left the bathroom and headed down the hall toward the stairs, ignoring the hand Cherry held out to her.

Cherry realized as she followed Raejean down the stairs, Annie chattering excitedly beside her, that she might have won this battle, but the war had just begun.

Chapter 6

Breakfast was a huge success. Cherry sat at the kitchen table giving herself a pat on the back for having pleased both girls so well. Two plates had been licked clean. Annie must have eaten almost as many additional marshmallows as the two of them had cut up together for her hot chocolate. Raejean had devoured the entire batch of whipped cream. The kitchen was a mess, but Cherry would have time to clean it once the twins were at school.

"Uh-oh," Annie said.

"Daddy's going to be *really* mad," Raejean said.

Cherry followed the direction of the girls' gazes out the kitchen window and saw the school bus at the end of the lane. It paused momentarily, honked, and when no one appeared, continued on its way.

"Oh, no!" Cherry raced to the back door, yanked it open and shouted to the bus driver. "Wait!"

He didn't hear her, which was just as well, because when she turned back to the kitchen she realized the girls weren't dressed and their hair wasn't combed.

Billy hadn't asked much of her—only that she feed his children breakfast and get them to school and be there when they got home in the afternoon. She couldn't even manage that.

She looked at the clock. Seven-thirty in the morning and she was already a failure as a stepmother. Before despair could take hold, it dawned on her that elementary school surely couldn't start this early. Maybe she could still get the girls there on time.

"When do classes start?" she asked Raejean.

"Eight o'clock sharp," Raejean answered. "Mrs. Winslow gets *really* mad if we're late."

"You still have time to get there if we move like lightning," Cherry said.

She hurried the girls upstairs, but the more urgency she felt, the slower they both seemed to move. She ended up accidentally yanking Annie's hair as she shoved the hairbrush through a knot.

"Ouch!" Annie cried. "That hurt."

Cherry was instantly contrite. She had too much experience of her own with substitute parents who were in too much of a hurry to be gentle with her. She went down on one knee in the bathroom beside Annie and said, "I'm sorry, Annie. I should have been more careful. I guess I'm worried that I won't get you to school on time."

"Yeah. And Daddy will be *really* mad," Raejean reminded her through a mouthful of toothpaste.

"Spit and rinse," Cherry ordered Raejean as she finished putting Annie's hair into pigtails. "I'll get to you next."

For a moment Raejean seemed to consider putting up a fight, but she stood still while Cherry pulled the brush through her tangled hair.

"My mom always put ribbons in our hair," Raejean said.

Cherry heard the wistful longing in the complaint, but there wasn't time to fulfill any wishes this morning. "Tonight we'll see what we can find and have them ready for tomorrow morning," she promised.

It wasn't until she had dressed herself and was ushering the girls out the back door that she realized she had no idea what they were going to use for transportation. There had to be some vehicle available, because Billy had suggested she go shopping during the day. But the only thing on four wheels she saw was a rusted-out pickup near the barn.

A set of hooks inside the back door held a key attached to a rabbit's foot. She grabbed the key, shoved the girls out the door, and prayed the truck had an automatic transmission.

It didn't.

"Don't you know how to drive?" Annie asked, concern etched in her young brow.

"I can drive. I have the license to prove it."

"Then why aren't we moving?" Annie asked.

Cherry stared helplessly at the stick shift on the floor of the pickup. "I'm not sure how to get this thing into gear." She tried moving the stick, and it made an ominous grinding sound.

"If you break Daddy's truck, he's going to be *really* mad," Raejean said.

Cherry was getting the picture. If she didn't figure out something soon, she was going to be dealing with a seriously annoyed teacher when she got the girls to school and a fierce, wild-eyed beast of a man when Billy got home.

She crossed her arms on the steering wheel and leaned her head down to think. She could call her sister Jewel to come rescue her, but that was so mortifying a prospect she immediately rejected it. She felt a small hand tapping her shoulder.

"I can show you how to do it," Annie volunteered.

Cherry lifted her head and stared suspiciously at the six-year-old. "You know how to drive a stick shift?"

"Sure," Annie said. "Daddy lets us do it all the time."

Since there wasn't anyone else to show her how, Cherry said, "All right. Go ahead and show me what to do."

"Put your foot on that pedal down there first," Annie said. "Turn the key, and then move this thing here."

Cherry pushed down the clutch, turned on the ignition, and reached for the black gearshift knob. To her amazement the gearshift moved easily without making a sound. However, she ended up in third gear, didn't give the truck enough gas, and let the clutch go too fast. The pickup stalled.

"You have to follow the numbers," Raejean chided, pointing to the black gearshift knob. "See? One, two, three, four, and R."

"R isn't a number," Cherry pointed out.

"R is for reverse," Annie piped up.

Maybe Billy did let them drive, Cherry thought. At least they knew more about a stick shift than she did. "All right. Here goes."

It was touch and go at first, but she managed to get the truck into second gear, and they chugged down the lane headed for the highway. She stalled a couple of times and ground the gears more than once before she got the hang of it. But she felt proud of herself when she finally pulled into the school parking lot and killed the engine.

"We made it," she said, glancing at her wristwatch. "With five minutes to spare."

"You forgot our lunches," Raejean said.

"What lunches?"

"Mrs. Motherwell always made us a sack lunch. We're going to starve," Annie said.

"Daddy's going to be *really* mad," Raejean said.

"Maybe you could buy your lunches today," Cherry suggested.

"I guess we could," Raejean conceded.

Annie and Raejean held out their hands for money.

Cherry realized she hadn't brought her purse with her. She checked both her jeans pockets and came up empty. "Look, I'll go home and make lunches for you and bring them back to school. How would that be?"

"Okay, I guess," Raejean said.

"I don't feel so good," Annie said, her hand on her stomach.

"Probably all the excitement this morning," Cherry said sympathetically. "You'll feel better once you're settled in class. Have a nice day, Raejean. Enjoy yourself, Annie."

She watched the two girls make their way inside, Raejean skipping and Annie holding on to her stomach.

To be honest, her own stomach was churning. It had been a hectic morning. And it wasn't over yet. She had to get home, make lunches and get back, then get the kitchen and the house cleaned up before the girls got home in the afternoon.

It was a lot of responsibility for someone whose biggest problem before today was whether she could figure out her calculus homework or get the formulas right in chemistry class. The entire responsibility for the house and two lively children now rested on her shoulders. It was an awesome burden.

She should have thought of that sooner. Now that she had made the commitment, she was determined to see it through. There were bound to be a few glitches at first. The important thing was to keep on trying until she succeeded.

Of course, she wasn't going anywhere until she figured out how to get the pickup into reverse. No matter how many times she put the gearshift where she thought R ought to be, she couldn't get the truck to back up. When the final tardy bell rang, she was still sitting there.

She was going to have to call Jewel after all.

"Hey, Cherry, what's the matter?"

Cherry looked up into the sapphire blue eyes of her eleven-year-old brother, Colt. A black curl had slipped from his ponytail and curled around his ear. He was wearing tight jeans instead of the frumpy ones currently in style, and a white T-shirt and cowboy boots reminiscent of James Dean. Colt truly was the rebel in the family. But he somehow convinced everybody that doing things his way was their idea.

Cherry glanced at the empty schoolyard and said, "You're late, Colt."

He grinned. "Yeah. Looks that way."

"You don't seem too concerned about it. Zach will be—" Cherry stopped herself when she realized she was about to echo Raejean and say "*really* mad."

"Dad knows I'm late," Colt said. "Things were a little

crazy this morning because of you disappearing and all. You really did it this time, Cherry. Mom went ballistic when she heard what you did, and Dad hasn't come down off the ceiling since he got back from the Stonecreek Ranch. Are you really married to Billy Stonecreek?"

"Uh-huh."

"Neat. He really knows how to use his fists to defend himself." Colt shrugged his book bag off and did some shadow boxing. He was tall for his age, his body lean, his movements graceful. "Billy's been in three fights this year," he said. "Do you think he'd show me a few punches?"

"Absolutely not! And where did you find out all this information about Billy?" Cherry asked.

"I heard Mom and Dad talking. They're worried that Billy's a bad influence on you. They said he's gonna undo all the hard work they've done, and you're gonna end up back in trouble again."

Cherry felt her face heating. Not that she didn't appreciate what Zach and Rebecca had done for her. But she had come a long way since the days when she had habitually cut school and been ready to fight the world.

"You'd better get inside," she told Colt.

"It's all right. Mom called and told them I'd be late," Colt replied. "What are you doing here?"

"I drove Raejean and Annie Stonecreek to school."

"Why didn't they take the bus?"

"They missed the bus."

Colt grinned. "Overslept, huh? You never were very good at getting up in the morning."

"Not that it's any of your business, but I didn't oversleep. I merely lost track of the time."

"Same difference," Colt said. "So why aren't you headed back home?"

"I can't figure out how to get this damn truck into reverse."

Colt laughed. "It's easy. Press the stick down and over."

"Press down? You have to press *down* on the stick before you move it?"

"Sure."

Cherry tried it, gave the truck a little gas, and felt it move backward. "Good grief," she muttered. "Thanks, Colt. I owe you one."

"Will you ask Billy if he'll show me a few punches?"

"I'll think about it," she replied as she backed out of the parking lot. "Tell Rebecca I'll come see her tonight," she called out the window as she drove away.

It was the coward's way out to have Colt relay her message. She should have called Rebecca and told her she was coming. But she didn't want to be forced into explaining things to her mother over the phone, and she knew Rebecca must be anxious for some sort of explanation for what she had done. The truth was, she needed the rest of the day to think of one.

By the time she made it back to the ranch she was a pro at shifting gears. She parked the truck behind the house, stepped inside the kitchen, and realized it looked like a tornado had been through. What if Billy came back home for some reason and saw it looking like this?

But she didn't want to stop and clean it right now and take a chance on being late with the girls' lunches. The mess was even worse by the time she finished making sandwiches. She vowed to clean up the kitchen as soon as she returned. She was out the door half an hour later, sack lunches in hand.

When she arrived at the principal's office, Cherry was surprised to be told that Annie still wasn't feeling well. Her teacher had asked the office to call the house and have someone come and pick her up.

"I was concerned when I couldn't reach anyone at the ranch," the principal said, "so I called Mrs. Trask."

"Oh, no," Cherry groaned. "Call her back, please, and tell her it isn't necessary to come. I'll take Annie home."

"I'll try," the principal said. "But she's probably already on her way."

Cherry's only thought was to get Annie and leave as quickly as possible.

"I'm Cherry Whitelaw, Mrs. Winslow," she said when she arrived at Annie's classroom. Cherry flushed. "Except it's Stonecreek now. My name, I mean. I'm here for Annie."

"She's lying on a cot at the back of the room, Mrs. Stonecreek. Raejean insisted on sitting with her."

It felt strange to be called by her married name. Only she really was Mrs. Stonecreek, and responsible for the twins' welfare. She sat on a chair beside the cot and brushed the bangs away from Annie's forehead. "How are you, sweetheart?"

Annie moaned. "My stomach hurts."

"She ate too many marshmallows," Raejean said from her perch beside her sister.

"Marshmallows?" Mrs. Winslow asked.

"Annie had a few marshmallows with her hot chocolate this morning," Cherry said.

"How many is a few?" Mrs. Winslow asked.

Cherry hadn't counted. "Too many, I guess. Can you walk, Annie? Or do I need to carry you?"

Annie sat up, holding her stomach. "I don't feel so good."

Cherry picked her up in her arms.

"Where are you taking her?" Raejean demanded.

"Home," Cherry said.

"I'm going, too," Raejean said.

"There's no reason for you to miss a day of school," Cherry said reasonably. "I'll take good care of Annie."

"How do I know that?" Raejean demanded. "You're practically a stranger!"

"Raejean," Mrs. Winslow said. "Mrs. Stonecreek is right. There's no reason for you to leave."

"I'm going with Annie," Raejean said to Mrs. Winslow, her face flushed. "I'm not staying here alone."

"You won't be alone," Mrs. Winslow soothed. "You'll—"

"I'm going with Annie!" Raejean cried.

"Raejean—" Cherry began.

"I'm going with Annie!" she screeched hysterically.

Cherry knew the dangers of giving in to a tantrum. But in her mind's eye she saw Mrs. Trask arriving to find a scene like this and knew she was over a barrel. "All right, Raejean, you can come. I'm sorry for the trouble, Mrs. Winslow."

She turned and headed for the door with Annie in her arms and Raejean a half step behind her. She was almost out the door when Mrs. Trask showed up.

"What's the matter with my granddaughter? What have you done to her?" she demanded.

"Annie is fine, Mrs. Trask." Cherry kept moving down the hall toward the front door of the school, still hoping to escape without a major confrontation.

"Annie's sick because she ate too many marshmallows," Raejean volunteered.

"Marshmallows?" Mrs. Trask said as though what she was really saying was "Poison?"

"Annie will be fine, Mrs. Trask."

"I was afraid of something like this. You're not responsible enough to be left in charge of two little girls."

Cherry didn't want to admit Mrs. Trask might be right. She had misjudged the situation this morning, but that didn't mean she couldn't do better. She would learn. After all, nobody had practice being a parent before they actually became one.

"Thank you for coming, Mrs. Trask, but as you can see, I have the situation well in hand."

"I'm coming home with you," Mrs. Trask said.

"I don't believe that's necessary," Cherry countered. "I—"

"What's going on here?"

Cherry stopped in her tracks.

It was Billy. He didn't look *really* mad, as Raejean had promised. He looked frantic, his brow furrowed, his sweat-stained work shirt pulled out of his jeans and hanging open, revealing a hairy chest covered with a damp sheen of sweat. He was still wearing his buckskin work gloves, but he was missing his hat. He had obviously shoved an agitated hand through his dark hair more than once, leaving it awry. He looked virile and strong... and very worried.

"I stopped by the house for some tools and found you gone and a message on the answering machine that Annie wasn't feeling well. Is she all right?"

"I'm sick, Daddy," Annie cried.

For a moment Cherry thought Billy would take Annie from her. Instead he asked, "Do you need any help with her?"

"I can manage if you'll get the door to the pickup."

"I knew something like this would happen," Mrs.

Trask said to Billy as they all headed outside to the rusted pickup.

"Something like what, Penelope?" Billy said.

"Something awful."

"Kids get stomachaches, Penelope," Billy said.

"Not if parents are careful and watch what they eat."

"Look, Penelope, I appreciate you coming, but Cherry and I can handle things now."

"How can you trust that woman—"

Billy turned on his former mother-in-law, and for the first time Cherry saw the anger Raejean had threatened. "*That woman* is my wife. And I have the utmost trust in her to take the very best care possible of Raejean and Annie."

"Well, I don't."

"You don't have anything to say about it, Penelope."

"We'll see about that! The day is coming—"

Billy cut her off again. "You'll have your day in court, Penelope. Until then, I can manage my family just fine without any help from you."

Cherry was impressed by Billy's support of her. She had done nothing to deserve his trust, and yet he had given it to her. She wanted very much to prove his faith in her was well-founded. She was simply going to have to try a little harder to be responsible.

"I'll follow you back to the house," Billy said to her as he buckled Raejean into her seat belt. "Maybe we can figure out what made Annie sick."

"She ate too many marshmallows," Raejean volunteered.

"What the hell was she doing eating marshmallows at breakfast?" Billy demanded of Cherry.

"I gave them to her," Cherry confessed. "With her hot chocolate. I guess I gave her a few too many."

Billy opened his mouth and snapped it shut on whatever criticism was caught in his throat. "We'll discuss this when we get home." He turned and marched to the other truck, a pickup in much better shape than the one she was driving.

The ride home was silent except for an occasional moan from Annie. When they arrived home, Billy carried Annie inside with Raejean trailing behind him. Billy breezed through the chaos in the kitchen without a pause and headed for the stairs. Cherry followed them, feeling as unwelcome as red ants at a picnic.

She stood at the bedroom door watching as Billy tucked Annie into bed and settled Raejean at a small desk with a coloring book and some crayons. She was amazed at his patience with his daughters. Amazed at his calm, quiet voice as he talked to them. The longer she watched, the worse she felt.

Billy had needed someone to help him out. All she had done was cause more trouble. Maybe he would want out of the marriage now. Maybe that's what he wanted to discuss with her.

When he rose at last and came toward her, he indicated with a nod that she should precede him down the stairs. Cherry felt the tension mounting as she headed into the kitchen, where the peanut butter jar stood open and blobs of jelly lay smeared on the counter. A pan bearing the scraped remnants of scrambled eggs sat in the sink, along with one lined with scalded milk.

She turned to face Billy. "I can explain everything," she said.

That was when he started laughing.

Chapter 7

"What's so funny?" Cherry demanded.

"Annie eating all those marshmallows. She probably begged you for more."

"How did you know?"

"Laura and I let the twins eat too much ice cream the first time they tried it. It's hard to deny them anything when you see how much they're enjoying it. You'll learn." His expression sobered as he added, "That's what parents have to do, Cherry. They have to set limits and stand by them, for the sake of the kids."

"I'll try to do better, Billy," she replied.

Rather than say more, he merely scooped her into his arms, gave her a hug and said, "I've got to get back to mending fence. See you at supper."

It wasn't until he was out the door and gone that she realized he hadn't said a word about the sorry state of the kitchen. Cherry took a look around. There was no way he hadn't noticed. She blessed him for not criticizing, and decided to reward him with a sparkling kitchen when he next saw it.

Of course, that was before she knew what the afternoon held in store.

Grocery shopping was out of the question because Annie was in bed sick, so she took some hamburger out of the freezer to defrost for meatloaf while she cleaned up the kitchen. When she went to check on the twins, she found Annie sound asleep.

Raejean was gone.

She searched the entire house, high and low, without finding her. "She couldn't have left the house. I would have seen her," Cherry muttered to herself.

Unless she went out the front door.

Cherry found the front door open a crack.

"Oh, no, Raejean."

She was afraid to leave Annie alone in the house while she searched, but she knew she had to find Raejean before Billy came home. It was one thing to let a child overeat; it was quite another to lose one entirely. She had no choice but to call for help.

"Jewel, can you come over here?"

"What's wrong, Cherry? Should I get Mom and Dad?"

"No! I'm sure I can handle this. Would you please just come over?"

When she was home from college, Jewel helped run Camp Littlehawk, a retreat that Rebecca had started years ago at Hawk's Pride for kids with cancer. Summer sessions hadn't yet begun, so Jewel was free to come and go as she pleased.

"I'll be there in thirty minutes," Jewel said. "Is that soon enough?"

"No. But I guess it'll have to do."

"It sounds serious, Cherry. Are you sure—"

"I'm sure I can handle it with your help, Jewel. Please hurry."

The next thirty minutes were the longest of Cherry's life. Billy had shown a tremendous amount of trust in her, and she had already let him down once. She had to find Raejean before anything happened to her.

"How can I help?" Jewel asked the instant she came through the kitchen door.

With that single question, Jewel proved what a gem of a sister she was and why she was Cherry's favorite sibling. Jewel gave a thousand percent to whatever she did and never asked for anything in return.

She walked with a slight limp, a result of the car wreck that had orphaned her, and her face bore faint, crisscrossing scars from the same accident. She had mud-brown eyes and dishwater-blond curls, and looked so ordinary you wouldn't see her in a crowd. But she had a heart so big it made her an extraordinary human being.

"I'm in way over my head, Jewel," Cherry confessed. "I thought taking care of two little girls was going to be a breeze. It isn't."

"What's the problem?" Jewel asked.

"Annie's upstairs in bed sick, and Raejean's missing. I need you to watch Annie while I hunt for Raejean."

"I'll be glad to do that. Are you sure you don't want some more help hunting down Raejean?"

"I'd rather try to find her myself first. With any luck, she's hiding somewhere close to the house."

Cherry looked in the barn, which was the most obvious place for the little girl to hide. It was dark and cool and smelled of hay and leather and manure. A search of the stalls turned up two geldings and a litter of kittens, but no little girl.

She climbed the ladder that led to the loft and gave it a quick look, but there was nothing but hay bales and feed sacks, so she climbed down again. As she turned to leave the barn, she heard a sound in the loft. Several pieces of straw wafted through the air and landed on the cement floor in front of her.

"I know you're up there, Raejean," she said. "Please come down. I've been very worried about you."

Footsteps sounded on the wooden floor above her before Raejean said, "You have not! I'm not coming down till my Daddy gets home."

Cherry climbed the ladder to the loft and followed the sounds of a sobbing child to the feed sacks in the corner. Raejean was huddled there, her knees wrapped up in her arms, her stubborn jaw outthrust as she glared at her new stepmother.

Cherry sat on the scattered straw across from Raejean. "I know what it feels like to lose your mother, Raejean. I know what it feels like to have a stranger try to boss you around. I'm sorry your mother died. I'm sorry she isn't here right now. I know I can never replace her. But your Daddy asked me to take care of you and Annie for him while he works every day. Won't you let me help him?"

Raejean's tear-drenched eyes lowered as she picked at a loose thread on the knee of her coveralls. "I miss my mommy. I want my nana."

Cherry's heart climbed to her throat. She could understand Raejean's need for the familiar. In the ordinary course of things, it would have been wonderful to have the girls' grandmother take care of them temporarily. But Mrs. Trask wanted to wrench them away from their father permanently. Cherry wasn't willing to worry Raejean with that possibility, but she wasn't going to encourage Raejean's desire to run to her grandmother for solace, either.

"I'm sure your daddy will take you to visit your grandmother soon. Right now we need to go back inside and check on Annie. I invited my sister, Jewel, to stay with her while I looked for you, but I think Annie needs us."

"She doesn't need you!" Raejean retorted.

"Maybe not. But she needs you. Will you come back inside with me?"

Cherry's heart sank when the little girl said nothing. What was she supposed to do now? She couldn't very well drag Raejean down the ladder. And while she could probably let her sit up here until Billy came home, it wasn't a particularly safe place for a six-year-old.

She put a comforting hand on Raejean's shoulder, but the child shrugged it off. "Please, Raejean? I need your help with Annie."

"Oh, all right," Raejean said. "But I'm coming inside for Annie. Not for you."

Her face remained sullen as she followed Cherry inside, and she glowered when she discovered that Annie was still asleep.

"Maybe while Annie's sleeping you could help me make supper," Cherry cajoled.

"I don't know how to cook," Raejean said. "Mrs. Motherwell wouldn't let us in the kitchen, and Nana has a lady to do all her cooking."

"Would you like to learn?"

Reluctantly Raejean nodded her head.

"Let's give it a try, shall we?"

"If the emergency is over, I've got some chores I need to do this afternoon," Jewel said.

"I'll walk you to your car," Cherry said. "I'll be back in a few minutes, Raejean. Then we can get started on supper."

"When will I see you again?" Jewel asked as they headed downstairs.

"I told Colt I was going to bring the girls and Billy to meet Zach and Rebecca this evening, but I think I'd better revise that plan. Will you tell Rebecca that Annie's not well, and that we'll come visit as soon as we can?"

"Why don't you call her yourself?" Jewel urged as Cherry walked her out to her car. "I know she wants to talk to you."

"I can't face her, Jewel. Not after the way I disappointed her again."

"You know Mom and Dad are proud of you."

"Most of the time."

"You're their daughter. They love you."

"I don't know why," Cherry said with a sigh.

Jewel shook her head. "There's no rhyme or reason to loving someone. You should know that by now." She gave Cherry a hug. "Take care, Mrs. Stonecreek."

"Please don't call me that, Jewel."

"Why not? You're married, aren't you?"

"Yes." *Temporarily.* "It feels strange, that's all. It's a marriage of convenience," she confessed. "Billy needed someone to take care of his girls, and I—I couldn't face Zach and Rebecca after what happened at the prom."

"I figured it might be something like that."

Cherry could tell Jewel was curious, but Jewel didn't

ask questions. She merely smiled and gave Cherry another hug. "Call me if you need me, okay?"

As Jewel drove away, Cherry turned back to the house, to perhaps the biggest challenge of her life—being a mother to two little girls who didn't want one.

Billy entered the kitchen at dusk, after a long, discouraging day that had included a visit to a lawyer, to find utter chaos.

The open peanut butter and jelly jars were gone from the counter, replaced by catsup and a round container of oatmeal. Dirty dishes no longer sat in the sink; it was filled with potato peels. The kitchen smelled like something good was cooking in the oven. But instead of a table set for supper, he found three flour-dusted faces standing on a flour-dusted floor, laboring over a flour-dusted table.

"Hi, Daddy!" Raejean's face bore perhaps the biggest smile Billy had seen there since Laura's death. She held a rolling pin in her small hands and was mashing it across some dough spread on the table. "We're cooking."

"Hi, Daddy!" Annie's grin was equally large. She held up two flour-dusted hands, one of which held a hunk of half-eaten dough. "We're making an apple pie for you, because it's your favorite!"

Billy finally let his gaze come to rest on Cherry. She had been in his thoughts too often during the day. She had a panicked look on her face as she glanced around at the mess in the kitchen. She pointed to the dough in Annie's hand and said, "I only let her have this little bit. It's not enough to make her sick."

"I see," Billy said.

What Billy saw was Cherry reassuring him that she

had learned her lesson. That she was willing to take responsibility for being the adult when she was barely one herself.

"We're running a little late," Cherry said, rubbing her hands across the front of her jeans and leaving them flour-dusted, as well. "After we got the meatloaf and mashed potatoes prepared, there was still time before we expected you back, so we decided to make a pie."

"I see."

What Billy saw was something he had never seen when Laura was alive, and likely never would have seen, even if she had lived. Laura had never learned to cook, and she didn't pretend to be any good at it or take any joy in it. The only apple pie she had ever made for him had come from a frozen food box. Culinary expertise hadn't been high on Billy's list of requirements for a wife, so he had never minded.

Now he realized what he had been missing. To see the three of them working together to make something especially for him touched a place deep inside of him. It fed a hunger for the sort of hearth and home that he imagined others experienced, but which had been lost to him since his parents' deaths. It was an added bonus to see Raejean and Annie so happy.

A different man might have seen only the mess and not the loving gesture that had been the source of it. Billy merely said, "Would you mind if I take a quick shower before I join you? I'm a little rank after a day on the range."

Cherry looked relieved. "That'll be fine. It'll give us time to finish up here."

He started for the hall but turned around before he got there and returned to the table. He saw the wariness in Cherry's eyes, the vulnerable look that said, "What have I done wrong now?"

He brushed a patch of flour from her cheek with his thumb before he lowered his mouth to touch hers. The shock was electric. When he could breathe again, he said, "Thanks, Cherry. Homemade apple pie will be a real treat."

"I helped," Raejean said.

"Me, too," Annie added.

Billy gave each of them a quick kiss on the nose. "I can tell," he said with a smile. "You two need a shower almost as bad as I do."

He made himself leave them and go shower, even though he was tempted to stay. He had to remind himself that Cherry was only there for a little while. Long enough to keep Penelope at bay. Long enough to make sure he kept custody of his kids.

By the time he got back downstairs, the pie was in the oven and the kitchen had undergone a partial transformation. The sink was stacked high with everything that had been on the table, but the floor was swept clear, and Cherry and his daughters no longer sported a liberal dusting of flour on their faces and clothes.

"I set the table," Raejean said proudly.

"It looks great," Billy said as he eyed the knife and fork on a folded paper napkin beside his plate.

"I picked the flowers," Annie said.

A collection of blue morning glories with tiny, half-inch stems floated in a bowl of water.

"They're beautiful," Billy said as he sat down and joined them at the kitchen table. "Your mother…" His throat closed suddenly. The swell of emotion surprised him. He had thought he had finished grieving. But the senseless tragedy of Laura's death was there with him again, as though it hadn't happened a full year in the past, but only yesterday.

The two girls looked at him expectantly, waiting for him to finish. He swallowed back the lump in his throat and managed to say, "Your mother would have loved to see them there."

"It was Cherry's idea," Annie volunteered. "She said they would be pretty."

"They are," Billy agreed softly. He let his gaze slip to Cherry for the first time since he had come to the table. "Morning glories were Laura's favorite flower," he said.

"I didn't know," she replied. "I can take them off the table, if you like."

"No. Leave them there. It's all right." He had to keep on living. He had to go on despite the fact Laura was no longer with him. He fought back the anger at Laura for leaving him alone to raise their two girls. It didn't help to feel angry. Better not to feel anything.

Only, that wasn't possible anymore. Not with Cherry living in the same house. Just looking at her made him feel way too much. He wanted her. And felt guilty because of it, even though he knew that was foolish. He was still alive. He still had needs. And she was his wife.

Temporarily. And only as a matter of convenience.

That didn't seem to matter to his body. It thrummed with excitement every time he looked at her. He wondered how her breasts would feel in his hands. He wondered whether she had freckles everywhere. He wanted to see her blue eyes darken with passion for him.

He was damned glad she couldn't read his mind.

After supper, the two little girls who had enjoyed making pie were less willing to clean up the results of their handiwork.

"Mrs. Motherwell always did the dishes by herself," Raejean protested.

"Yeah," Annie added.

"Maybe so, but she isn't here anymore," Cherry said. "Now everybody helps in the kitchen."

Raejean's eyes narrowed as though gauging whether she had to obey this dictum. She glanced at her father, still sitting at the table finishing up his second slice of pie, and asked, "Even Daddy?"

Billy had been listening to the byplay between Cherry and his daughters, a little surprised that she expected the twins to help. There was nothing wrong with them learning to do their share of the chores. Of course, he hadn't expected to be included. Dishes were women's work.

Now what, smart guy? Are you going to act like a male chauvinist pig? Or are you going to provide a good example to your children and pitch in to help?

Billy rose and carried his plate to the sink. "All of us have to do our part," he said. "Even me."

It was fun.

He had never done dishes as a family project, but there were definite advantages to doing the work as a team. Like having the girls tease him with the sprayer in the sink as they stood on a chair and rinsed off the dishes before Cherry loaded them in the dishwasher. And tickling Cherry, who turned out to be the most ticklish person he had ever known.

In the past, jobs at the ranch had been divided into *his* and *hers*. Cherry made everything *ours*.

"Where did you learn all these communal work ethics?" Billy asked as they each toweled off one of the twins after their bath.

"When there are eight kids in a household, everyone has to chip in and do their part," Cherry said. "And knowing there was at least one extra pair of hands to help made every job easier."

"And more fun," Billy said, as he picked up the twins, one in each arm, and headed toward their bedroom.

"And more fun," Cherry agreed as she turned down the twins' beds.

Billy set each twin on her bed and then sat down cross-legged on the floor between them. Cherry stood against the wall, her arms crossed around herself, watching them.

"Tell us a story," Raejean begged.

"Please, Daddy," Annie wheedled.

When the twins were younger and having children was still a novelty, Billy had often told them bedtime stories. As they had gotten older and his responsibilities on the ranch had become more pressing, Laura had been the one to put the girls to bed at night. He'd had to be satisfied with looking in on them after they were already asleep. Over the past year he had allowed a series of housekeepers to enjoy this precious time with his daughters.

Billy realized that he would probably be working on the bookkeeping right now if Cherry hadn't made everything so much fun that he had wanted to stay with them rather than retire to his office to work. He was grateful to her, but he couldn't tell her why without admitting he had been lax as a parent.

It shocked him to realize that maybe Penelope was right about him. Maybe he hadn't been a very good parent for his daughters over the past year. Maybe it was time to acknowledge that being a father meant more than planting the seeds in a woman that grew into children and earning the money that put food in their mouths, a roof over their heads, and clothes on their backs.

When he finished the story and his giggling girls were tucked in and kissed on their noses, he turned at last to find Cherry and realized that sometime during the reading of the bedtime story she had left the room.

"Good night, girls," he said as he turned out the light. "Sleep tight."

"Don't let the bedbugs bite!" they recited in chorus.

Billy headed downstairs in search of Cherry, anxious to thank her for making him aware of the priceless moments he had been missing with his daughters.

He knocked on the door to her room, but she wasn't there. He searched the house and finally found her sitting in one of the two rockers on the front porch. It was dark outside, and when he turned on the front porch light she said, "Please leave it off."

"All right," he said as he settled in the second rocker. "What are you doing sitting out here in the dark?"

"Thinking."

"About what?"

"About us. About why we got married." She pulled her feet up onto the rocker seat, circled her legs with her arms, and set her chin on her knees as she stared into the darkness. "We shouldn't have done it, Billy," she said softly.

"I disagree, Cherry. Especially after today."

She lifted her head and turned to stare at him. "I would think, if anything, today proved what a rotten mother I am. I wasn't going to tell you, but Annie and Raejean missed the bus this morning, so I had to take them there and I didn't know how to drive a stick shift and I forgot to make them lunches and then I let Annie eat too many marshmallows and then Mrs. Trask showed up at school because I wasn't here to get the call from the principal, and then Raejean ran off and the kitchen was a mess and supper wasn't ready and—"

Billy stood abruptly and lifted her out of the rocker and settled her in his lap as he sat back down. He felt the tension in her body and wanted desperately to ease the misery he had heard in her voice.

"So maybe you don't have the mechanics down. But you know everything about being a mother that really counts."

"Like what?" she said, her voice muffled because she had her mouth pressed against his throat.

"Like wanting them to be happy. Like caring what happens to them. Teaching them to do their share. Showing them the pleasure of doing something nice for somebody else. And showing me how much I've been missing by letting someone else try to be both parents, instead of doing my part."

He felt her relax against him, felt her hand curl up behind his neck and thread into his hair. He liked the feel of her in his arms, liked the way she leaned on him.

"Thanks, Billy," she murmured. "I want to be a helpmate for you."

She sounded tired, half asleep. After the day she had described to him, it was no wonder. "You are, Cherry," he said, pulling her close. "You are."

He only meant to give her a kiss of comfort. His intent wasn't the least bit amorous. He tipped her chin up with his forefinger and pressed soothing kisses on her closed eyelids, her freckled cheeks, and her nose. And one last kiss on her mouth.

Only he let himself linger a bit too long.

And Cherry returned the kiss. Her tongue made a long, lazy foray into his mouth.

His body reacted instantly, turning rock-hard. He groaned, almost in pain. He wanted her. Desperately. But he had agreed to wait.

"Cherry, please," he begged.

She didn't answer him one way or the other. He had to touch her, needed to touch her. He slid his hand up under her T-shirt and let his fingertips roam the silky flesh across her belly. His thumb caught under her breast.

He reached for the center clasp of her bra, holding his breath, hoping she wouldn't ask him to stop. He felt the clasp come free and huffed out a breath all at the same time.

She made a carnal sound as his hand closed over the warmth of her breast and gasped as his thumb flicked across the rigid nipple.

His mouth covered hers, and his tongue mimicked the sexual act as his hand palmed her flesh and then slid down between her legs. He cupped her and felt the heat and heard her moan.

His mouth slid down to her throat, sucking hard at the flesh as his thumb caressed her through a thin layer of denim, making her writhe in his arms.

"Billy, no!"

He froze, his breath rasping out through his open mouth, his body aching. He didn't try to stop her when she stumbled from his lap and grabbed at one of the porch pillars to hold herself upright. Her whole body was trembling with desire—or fear, he wasn't sure which.

"I'm sorry," she said. "I can't. I'm sorry."

Then she was gone.

Chapter 8

Cherry spent the first month of her marriage trying desperately to win Raejean's and Annie's trust. And trying desperately not to think about how close she had come those first few days to making love with Billy.

She had felt warm and safe and secure in his arms. She had felt desired and cherished. She had felt the beginnings of passion—and torn herself from his embrace.

It was fear that had kept her from surrendering. Fear that she would begin to care too much. Fear that what she felt for him was illusion. Fear that what he felt for her was too ephemeral to last. If she gave herself to him body and soul, she would be lost. And when the marriage was over, she would die inside.

It was safer to keep her distance. That was the hard lesson she had learned as a child. She knew better than to trust anyone with her heart. If she gave it up to Billy, he would only break it.

But she wasn't strong enough to deny herself his touch entirely. She liked his kisses. She liked his caresses. And they were a necessary part of the charade she and Billy were playing out for the benefit of Mrs. Trask.

Of course, Mrs. Trask wasn't there each morning when Billy slipped up behind her while she was making coffee and nuzzled her neck and said in a husky voice, "Good morning, Cherry."

Mrs. Trask wasn't there when she turned and pressed herself against him, sieved her fingers into his thick, silky hair, and waited for his morning kiss.

Mrs. Trask wasn't there when Billy lowered his head and took her lips in a kiss as tender as anything Cherry had ever experienced, or when that same kiss grew into something so terrifyingly overwhelming that it left her breathless.

If Billy had asked her to yield entirely, she would likely have stopped allowing the kisses. But he seemed to be satisfied with what she was willing to give him. It wasn't until a month had passed that it dawned on Cherry that each morning Billy asked for a little more. And each morning she gave it to him.

A hand cupping her breast. The feel of his arousal against her belly. Drugging kisses that left her knees ready to buckle. Her hand pressed to the front of his fly to feel the length and the hardness of him. His mouth on her throat. Her robe eased aside, and his mouth on her naked breast.

The feelings were exquisite. Irresistible. Like Billy himself.

If physical seduction had been his only allure, she

might have resisted him more successfully. But not only was she attracted to Billy physically, she liked and admired him, as well. He was a good father, a hard worker, a considerate helpmate. Cherry knew she was sliding down a slippery slope. She was in serious danger of complete surrender.

She tried not to think about Billy during the day. It was easy for great stretches of time to involve herself with Raejean and Annie and housekeeping and the chores in the barn she had taken over for Billy. And she had started night school to earn her high school diploma, and there was always homework to be finished. Her life was full and busy, and she felt useful and satisfied.

Most of the time.

But she could feel Billy's eyes on her in the evening after supper when they spent time with the children and gave them their baths. Watching her. Waiting for her to want him the way he wanted her.

The sexual tension between them had grown palpable. Her skin tingled at the mere thought of him touching her. Her breasts ached for the feel of his callused hands. Her blood raced when she saw him come through the door each evening, his washboard belly visible through his open shirt, his sinewy arms bared by rolled-up shirtsleeves, his muscular body fatigued from a day of hard labor.

And her heart went out to him when she saw his face, his dark eyes haunted by the stress of an imminent showdown in court with Mrs. Trask. Was it any wonder she wanted to hold out her arms to him and offer comfort?

As he shoved open the kitchen screen door, her thoughts became reality. Their eyes met and held for an instant, and Cherry knew that tonight she would give herself to him. Tonight she would offer him solace, even if it meant giving up her own peace of mind.

"Hi, Daddy," Raejean said as Billy settled his Stetson on a hat rack by the kitchen door.

"Hi, Daddy," Annie echoed.

Cherry felt a tightness in her chest as she saw the smile form on his face when he lifted the girls up into his arms and gave each of them a kiss on the nose. He loved them so very much. And there was a very real danger that he would lose them.

"How are my girls?" he asked. "What are you doing to keep busy now that school's over?"

"Cherry made us work!" Raejean said.

Billy raised his eyebrows. "Oh?"

"We had to help dig a garden behind the house."

"A garden?"

Cherry met Billy's surprised look and explained, "I thought it would be nice to have some fresh vegetables." Then she realized how presumptuous it was to assume she would still be around in the fall to harvest them.

"We had to plant flowers around the edge of the garden when we were done digging," Annie said.

"What kind of flowers?" Billy asked.

"Marigolds," Annie chirped. "It was fun, Daddy."

"Did you have fun, too, Raejean?" Billy asked.

"Maybe," Raejean conceded. "A little."

Cherry knew it had been an adjustment for Raejean and Annie to find themselves suddenly responsible for chores appropriate to their ages. Before Laura's death they had been too young, and the series of housekeepers had found it easier to do the work themselves than to involve the children. Cherry had explained to Billy that she wasn't there as a housekeeper, she was there as a surrogate mother. And she could best teach the girls the things they would need to know to manage a ranching household by involving them in every aspect of what she did.

It wasn't until she had come to live with Rebecca and Zach that Cherry had been included in precisely that way in the running of a household. In previous foster homes she had been more like a maid-of-all-work. In the Whitelaw home she had been part of a family in which each member did his or her part. She had learned the satisfaction to be had from contributing her fair share.

The more she put to good use the lessons Rebecca had taught her, the more she realized how much she had learned from her, the more grateful she felt for having been adopted into the Whitelaw family, and the more guilty she felt for having run away and married Billy instead of coming home and facing Zach and Rebecca the night she had been expelled.

There was no doubt she had been a difficult child to parent. The longer she was a stepparent, the more understanding she had of the other side of the fence. And the more appreciation she had for Zach and Rebecca's endless patience and love.

She knew she ought to tell them so.

But she couldn't face them and say on the one hand how much she appreciated all the things they had taught her, while on the other she was perpetrating the deceit involved in her temporary marriage to Billy Stonecreek.

So she had found excuses to avoid visiting them and reasons to keep her family from visiting her. Except for Jewel, who knew everything, and was quick to point out that Cherry was acting like an idiot and should simply call Zach and Rebecca and confess everything.

"They'll understand," Jewel had said. "And they'll forgive. And they'll still love you as much as ever. That's what parents do."

Cherry was finding that out for herself. Raejean still resented her and complained about nearly everything Cherry asked her to do, although she would eventually do it. Annie hadn't surrendered her trust to Cherry in loyalty to Raejean.

If her marriage to Billy had been a permanent thing, Cherry would have said time was on her side. It had taken more than a year for her barriers to come down with Zach and Rebecca, but in the face of all that love, they *had* come down. She needed to win Raejean's and Annie's trust before the court hearing—a matter of weeks. A great deal depended on her finding a way to break through the little girls' stubborn resistance.

They had long since broken through hers. She loved them both dearly, enough to know it was going to hurt a great deal when she was no longer a part of their lives.

"You got a letter today," she told Billy as he set the girls back on their feet. "It looks official."

Billy's face was grim as he went to the kitchen counter where she always left the mail and sorted through it. He picked up the envelope, looked at it, and set it back down again. "It can wait until after the kids are in bed."

Cherry understood why he was postponing the inevitable. But she knew he was as aware of it sitting there all evening as she was.

He hugged the girls so hard at bedtime that Annie protested, "I can't breathe, Daddy."

She knew he was afraid of losing them. So was she.

She walked ahead of him down the stairs and instead of heading for the porch rockers to relax for a few minutes before going back to work, she headed for the kitchen. Billy followed her.

She went directly to the stack of mail, found the letter she wanted, and handed it to him. "Read it."

He tore it open viciously, his teeth clenched tight enough to make a muscle in his jaw jerk. He read silently. Without a word, he handed the official-looking letter to her. "Read it."

She read quickly. The court date had been set for July 15. Billy was asked to appear and explain certain accusations that had been made against him that he was not a fit custodian for his children.

"Three weeks," he said bitterly. "Three lousy weeks before I have to appear in court and prove I'm a fit father. How the hell am I going to do that, Cherry? Tell me that? I can't make those nights in jail go away. And you can bet Penelope will make sure the judge knows that the mother I've provided for my children is an eighteen-year-old girl who used to be a juvenile delinquent."

Cherry went white around the mouth. She hadn't expected his attack. It was useless to point out that he was the one who had suggested marriage. It didn't change the facts. "What do you want to do, Billy? Do you want to annul the marriage? Would that help, do you think?"

"Oh, God, no!" His arms closed tight around her. "I'm sorry, Cherry. I didn't mean to suggest that any of this is your fault, or that you aren't a wonderful mother. You are. Raejean and Annie are lucky to have you. Only…"

"Only I have been a juvenile delinquent."

"And I've spent a few nights in jail," Billy said. "Nobody's perfect, Cherry. We simply have to convince the judge that all that behavior is in the past. That right now we're the best possible parents for two little girls who've lost their mother, and whose grandmother is a bit misguided."

"Is that what she is?" Cherry asked, her lips twisting wryly.

"She misses her daughter, Cherry. She's still grieving. But that doesn't mean I'm going to give her my children to replace the one she lost," Billy said, his voice hard, his eyes flinty.

"Raejean still doesn't like me," Cherry pointed out. "What is the judge going to make of that?"

Billy's brow furrowed between his eyes. "I don't know, Cherry. He'll have to understand that we're all still making adjustments. He'll have to see that you're doing the best you can."

She took a deep breath and said, "I couldn't bear to see you lose them, Billy."

"I won't. I can't." He paused at the realization that the court had the power to take his children away from him before repeating, "I won't."

His arms tightened painfully around her, and she knew he was holding on to her because he was afraid of losing them. When his mouth came seeking hers— seeking solace, as she had known he would—she gave it to him.

"I need you," he said in a guttural voice. "I need you, Cherry."

"I'm yours, Billy," she answered him. "I'm all yours."

He picked her up and carried her to her room, shoving open the bedroom door with his hip and laying her on the bed. He turned on the bedside lamp and sat down beside her.

"I want to see you. I want to feel your flesh against mine," he said as he tore off her T-shirt and threw it across the room. He had her bra unclasped a second later and it was gone, leaving her bared to him from the waist up.

He stopped to look at what he had. "No freckles here," he mused as a callused finger circled her breast. "Just this rosy crest," he finished as his mouth closed on her.

Her hands tangled in his hair and held him as he suckled her. Her body arched with pleasure as his hand slipped down between her legs to hold the heat and the heart of her.

Cherry had endured weeks of teasing foreplay. Now she wanted what had been denied her. "Please, Billy. Please." She shoved at his shirt, wanting to feel his flesh against her fingertips. She reached for his belt buckle and undid it with trembling fingers and then undid the button and slid down the zipper on his jeans. Billy copied everything she did.

When her hand slid beneath his briefs to reach for him, his did the same beneath her panties.

They stopped and looked at each other and grinned.

"Gotcha," Billy said as he slid a finger deep inside her. She was wet and slick, and he added another finger to the first.

Cherry groaned.

Her gaze trailed down to where her hand disappeared inside Billy's briefs. She tightened her grasp and slid her hand up and down the hard length of him.

Billy groaned.

Their mouths merged, their tongues mimicking the sexual act as their hands kept up their teasing titillation.

Suddenly it wasn't enough. Cherry wasn't sure which of them shoved at the other's jeans first, but it wasn't long before both of them were naked. A moment after that, Billy was inside her.

They both went still.

It felt like she had found her other half. Now she was whole.

Cherry looked up into Billy's dark eyes and saw a wealth of emotion. Too many feelings. More than were safe. She closed her eyes against them.

"Look at me, Cherry," Billy said.

She slowly raised her lids and gazed at him with wonder.

He loves me, she thought. *I never dreamed... I never imagined...*

She waited for the words, but he never said them.

And she knew why. She didn't love him back. She wouldn't allow herself to love him. He knew the rules. It was to be a safe, temporary marriage.

Her eyes slid closed again as his mouth covered hers, hungry, needy. For the first time in her life she was grateful for her height, which made them fit together so perfectly that they could be joined at the hip and their mouths still meet for a soul-searching kiss. She felt the passion rise, felt her body shiver and shudder under the onslaught of his desire.

His body moved slowly at first, the tension building equally slowly, until it was unbearable, until she writhed beneath him, desperate for release.

"Please, Billy," she cried. "Please!"

She heard a savage sound deep in his throat as his body surged against hers, as he fought the inevitable climax, wanting to prolong the pleasure.

She felt her body tensing, thrusting against his, seeking the heaven he promised, until they found it, his seed spilling into her at last.

His weight was welcome, comforting, as he lowered his exhausted, sweat-slick body onto hers, their chests still heaving to gather breath to support their labored bodies, their heartbeats still pounding to carry blood to straining vessels.

Eventually, as their breathing slowed and their hearts returned to normal, Billy slid to her side and spooned her bottom against his groin. His hand curled around her breast as though it were the most natural place in the world for it to be. "Thanks, Cherry. I needed that. You," he amended.

It was more than she was willing to admit, so she remained mute. She was content to lie in his arms, saying nothing, enjoying the closeness.

It was during this quiet aftermath that she realized they had used no protection. They both knew better. Under the circumstances, a pregnancy could be disastrous. "Billy," she murmured.

"Hmm."

"We didn't use anything."

"Hmm?"

"To keep me from getting pregnant."

His stiffening body revealed his distress. "I should have asked. I should have—"

She turned in his arms and put her fingertips against his lips. "It's the wrong time of the month, I think."

"You think?"

"If there is a safe time," she amended, "this is probably it."

"Thank God," he said.

Even though she knew rationally that it was in both of

their interests for her not to get pregnant, it was still irksome to see the amount of relief on Billy's face. "I guess you don't want any more children," she said.

"It isn't that," he said. "I always wanted more kids. But Laura..."

She remembered that Laura couldn't have any more. Only, that wasn't what Billy said next.

"Laura wasn't supposed to get pregnant because it was dangerous."

She felt him shudder and a thought occurred to her. "Are you saying she got pregnant anyway?"

He paused so long she didn't think he was going to answer her. At last he said, "Yes."

"What happened? To the baby, I mean?"

"She miscarried. Twice."

He pulled her close so his chin rested on her head, and she couldn't see his eyes. But she could feel him trembling and hear his convulsive swallow.

"The second time it happened I told her that if she didn't stop trying to get pregnant, I'd refuse to sleep with her anymore. I didn't want to take the chance of losing her. She meant too much to me, more than any baby ever could."

Another swallow.

"She was furious with me. She said she had promised me a houseful of kids, and she knew I couldn't be happy with just the twins. I told her the twins were enough. But she didn't believe me.

"The truth was, she had this insane idea that a woman who couldn't have kids wasn't a real woman. She refused to stop trying to get pregnant, despite the risk to her health. So I told her I was through arguing. I wasn't going to sleep with her again until she changed her mind and agreed to be sensible."

He shuddered.

"She went stomping out of the house, furiously angry, and got into the car. And…and she was killed."

"Oh, my God," Cherry breathed. "And you're not really sure whether it was an accident, or whether she killed herself on purpose, is that it?"

"She wouldn't kill herself. Not because of something like that. She wouldn't. It was an accident."

Cherry wasn't sure who he was trying to convince, himself or her.

"All Penelope saw the year before she died was Laura's despondency over the first miscarriage," Billy continued. "Penelope knew we'd been arguing a lot around the time of Laura's death, although she didn't know what we'd been arguing about. Laura didn't tell her about the miscarriage—probably because she knew her mother would be on my side."

"Why didn't you tell Mrs. Trask what had happened?" Cherry asked.

"It was none of her business!" Billy retorted. "It was between me and my wife."

"Maybe if she understood why—"

"It's over and done with now."

"Perhaps if you explained—"

"Laura's dead. There's no bringing her back."

And he wasn't sure he wasn't to blame, Cherry realized. No wonder he had gotten into so many fights in the year since Laura's death. He had been in pain, with no way of easing it. Because he would never know for sure what had happened.

"It wasn't your fault she died," Cherry said quietly.

"How do you know that?" he snarled.

"You were right. It wasn't safe for her to continue getting pregnant. You had to take a stand."

"I should have found some other way to say no."

"Hindsight is always better. You did the best you could at the time."

"That's supposed to make me feel better?"

She leaned back to look into his troubled eyes and saw the need in him to strike out against the pain. There were other ways of easing it. She laid her hand against his cheek and said, "You're a good man, Billy. You never meant for her to be hurt. Whether it was an accident…or not… Laura was responsible for what happened."

"I want to believe that," he said. "I try to believe that. But…"

"Believe it," she whispered as her lips sought his.

His arms surrounded her like iron bands, and his mouth sought hers like a thirsting man who finds an oasis in the desert. He was inside her moments later, needing the closeness, needing the comfort she offered, the surcease from endless pain.

She held him in her arms as he loved her and crooned to him that everything would be all right. That he was a good man and a good father and he shouldn't blame himself anymore for what wasn't his fault.

He spilled himself inside her with a cry that was almost anguish. He slipped to the side and pulled her to him, holding her close with strong arms that promised always to keep her safe.

She knew it was wrong to trust in him. He would betray her in the end. Unfortunately, the heart doesn't always obey the dictates of the more reasonable head.

I love him, she thought. And then, *I can't love him. I shouldn't love him. I'd be a fool to love him.*

They fell asleep, their bodies entangled, their souls enmeshed, their hearts confused.

Chapter 9

Over the next three weeks the twins sensed the growing tension in Billy, and their behavior grew worse instead of better. Cherry tried to be understanding, but she was under a great deal of pressure, as well, since she had to study for night school finals, which she couldn't afford to fail.

Things came to a head the day before the court hearing, when Cherry asked Raejean for the third time to take her cookie and juice snack back to the kitchen to eat it.

"I don't have to do what you say," Raejean said. "You're not my mother!"

"I'm the one in charge," Cherry replied, using her last ounce of patience to keep her voice level. "And I say you have to get that juice out of the living room. If it spills in here, it'll ruin the furniture."

Cherry couldn't imagine what had possessed Laura to

put silk and satin fabrics in a ranch living room. It wasn't a place to look at; they actually lived in it. If it had been up to her, she would have put protective covers on the furniture long ago to save the delicate fabrics from everyday wear and tear. When she had broached the subject to Billy, he had said, "We live here. If the furniture gets dirty, it gets dirty."

Cherry didn't figure that included spilling grape juice on white satin. So she insisted, "Take that juice into the kitchen, Raejean. Now!"

"Oh, all right!" Raejean huffed. "Come on, Annie. Let's go."

"I'm watching Sesame Street," Annie protested from her seat beside Raejean on the couch.

Raejean pinched her. "Come on. If I have to go, you have to go."

"Raejean," Cherry warned. "Leave Annie be. Take your glass and go."

Raejean shot Cherry a mutinous look as she snatched at the glass on the end table, accidentally knocking it over—right onto the arm of the couch.

The two of them stared, horrified, as the grape juice soaked into the white satin, leaving a huge purple blotch.

"Oh, no!" Cherry cried. She looked for something to sop up the mess, but there was nothing handy. And by then the couch had soaked up the juice like a sponge.

"It's all your fault," Raejean cried, tears welling in her eyes. "If you hadn't been yelling at me, I wouldn't have spilled it."

"Daddy's going to be *really* mad," Annie whispered as she abandoned Sesame Street to ogle the growing stain.

"Go to your room," Cherry said. "Both of you!"

"I didn't do anything," Annie protested.

"We don't have to do what you say!" Raejean said. "Do we, Annie?"

Annie looked uncertain, and Raejean pinched her again.

"Ow!" she said. "Stop it, Raejean."

"Stop it, both of you!" Cherry cried. She knew she had lost control, but she wasn't sure how to get it back. "Apologize to your sister, Raejean."

"I don't have to. Tell her, Annie. Tell her Nana's going to be taking care of us from now on, so we don't have to do what Cherry says anymore."

Cherry couldn't believe what she was hearing. "Who said your grandmother's going to be taking care of you from now on?"

"Nana did."

"When?" Cherry said.

"When she called on the phone."

"When was that?" Cherry demanded.

"This morning, when you were in the shower. She said that after tomorrow she's going to be taking care of us, and we'll get to play in her pool and Grampa's buying us a new dollhouse and we won't have to do chores anymore, either," she announced.

Cherry stared at Raejean, aghast. She didn't know what to say. The little girl had no idea what Mrs. Trask really intended. She didn't seem to realize that going to live with her grandmother meant leaving her father for good. And Cherry had no intention of frightening her by explaining it.

She was furious with Mrs. Trask but resisted the urge to criticize her in front of her granddaughters. She was way out of her depth and drowning fast. She needed help.

To Cherry's surprise, the name and face that came to mind wasn't Billy's. Or even Jewel's. It was Rebecca's.

She wanted her mother.

"Let's go," she said suddenly.

"Go where?" Raejean asked suspiciously.

"To see your other grandmother."

Both girls stared at her with wide eyes.

"We have another grandmother?" Annie said.

"Uh-huh. You sure do."

"Who is she?" Raejean asked. "Where does she live?"

"Her name is Rebecca Whitelaw, and she lives on a ranch called Hawk's Pride. It isn't far from here. Shall we go? It's either that, or go to your room. You choose."

There was no contest, and Cherry wasted no time getting the girls into the pickup and driving to the adobe ranch house at Hawk's Pride that she had called home for the previous four years. Since Camp Littlehawk was under way, she knew where to look for Rebecca. Sure enough, she found her working with the novice riders at the corral. Raejean and Annie raced ahead of her to stand gaping at the lucky horseback riders.

"That's good, Jamie," Rebecca encouraged, one foot perched on the lowest rung of the wooden corral. "Let the pony know who's boss."

"I suppose that's good advice for parents dealing with children, too," Cherry said as she joined Rebecca.

"Cherry! What a wonderful surprise! Ted, would you watch the children for a few minutes while I speak with my daughter?"

Cherry noticed that Ted was on crutches. That didn't surprise her. Rebecca often found people in need and offered them a helping hand. Cherry was sure Ted was great with kids or horses or both. It always worked out that way. Rebecca's faith in people had never been proven wrong. It was that same goodheartedness that had led Rebecca to rescue a rebellious fourteen-year-old juvenile delinquent and adopt her as her own.

"I'd like you to meet your new granddaughters," Cherry said as Rebecca took the few steps to reach the twins. They were standing on the bottom rail of the corral with their arms hanging over the top.

"Raejean, Annie, I'd like you to meet your Grandma 'Becca." 'Becca was what Jewel had called Rebecca when Jewel was a child. It was also a fond nickname Zach used when he was teasing her. And it was the first thing that came to mind when Cherry searched for a name the little girls could use to address their new grand-mother.

Raejean and Annie turned lively black eyes on Re-becca.

"Are you really our grandmother?" Raejean asked.

"Yes," Rebecca said with a smile.

"Are you going to give us cookies and milk, like Nana?" Annie asked.

"I'll even help you bake the cookies, if you like," Re-becca said. "If you'll tell me which one of you is which."

"I'm Annie," Raejean said. "And this is Raejean," she said, pointing to her shyer twin.

"Raejean," Cherry warned.

"Aw, Cherry." She hesitated before admitting, "I'm really Raejean, and this is really Annie."

"Pleased to meet you both," Rebecca said. "It's going to be fun having grandchildren come to visit."

"Will you let us ride horses, too?" Raejean asked, eye-ing the children on horseback enviously.

"Would you like to ride one now?"

Raejean's and Annie's faces lit up as though they had been given the key to heaven. "Oh, yes!" they said in unison.

It didn't take long to get ponies saddled and send the girls into the ring with the other children to be supervised by Ted.

As soon as the twins were settled, Rebecca said, "All right, Cherry. Spit it out. What's wrong?"

"Everything," Cherry admitted. She felt like crying suddenly. The whole weight of the world had been on her shoulders for the past seven weeks, and it was as though with that one admission she had shifted the burden to her mother.

"Tell me about it," Rebecca said.

And Cherry did. About why she and Billy had married and the awful wedding and the twins' resentment, how Mrs. Trask was manipulating the children's feelings, and how scared she was that Billy would lose his children.

"What about you? Would it hurt you to lose them?"

Cherry hadn't even let herself think about the possibility. When she did, she felt a terrible ache in her chest. "Yes. Oh, yes. I'd miss them terribly. As much trouble as they are, I love them dearly."

Rebecca smiled. "So what can I do to help?"

Cherry shoved a hand through her tumble of red curls and let out a gusty sigh. "I'm not sure. Could you and Zach just be there in court tomorrow? Would that be possible?"

"Oh, darling, of course we'll be there. Is that all? Are you sure there isn't something else I could do to help?"

"I think you've already done it," Cherry said.

"Done what?"

"Taught me to believe in love again."

"Oh, darling…"

Cherry saw the tears in her mother's eyes and felt her throat tighten until it hurt. "I owe you so much… Mother." She gave a sobbing laugh and said, "There, I said it. Mother. Oh, God, why did I wait so long?"

It had taken being a mother herself to understand the tremendous gift Zach and Rebecca had given her. She could hardly see Rebecca through the blur of tears, and when she blinked, she realized Rebecca had her arms open wide. She grasped her around the waist and held on tight.

Cherry refused her mother's invitation to stay for dinner. "Billy and Zach—Daddy—aren't comfortable enough around each other yet. I'd rather give them time to get to know each other better before we show up for supper."

"All right. Whatever you think best. You can count on us to be in court tomorrow to support you both."

"Thanks, Mother. That means a lot."

"I wasn't sure before that you were ready for marriage and all its responsibilities," Rebecca said. "This visit has reassured me."

"That I'm ready for marriage?"

"That you're ready for whatever life offers. Be happy, Cherry. That's all I can ask."

Cherry smiled. "I'll try, Mom."

"Mom. I like that," Rebecca said. "Mom feels even better than Mother."

"Yeah, Mom," Cherry agreed with a cheeky grin. "It does."

Cherry spent the rest of the afternoon floating on air. She had never felt so confident. She had never been so certain that everything would turn out all right. Her youthful optimism remained firmly in place until Billy was late arriving home for supper. She waited an hour for him before she finally fed the girls and sent them upstairs to play.

She put a plate of food in the oven to stay warm while she cleaned up the kitchen. She still wasn't worried. Billy had been late once or twice before when some work had needed to be finished before dark.

But sundown came and went without any sign of Billy.

Cherry told herself, as she bathed the twins, that there was probably some good reason for the delay. Maybe he was working hard to make up for the fact he would be in court all day tomorrow. Maybe the truck had broken down and he had needed to walk home.

Maybe he had an accident. Maybe he's lying hurt or dying somewhere while you've been blithely assuming everything is fine.

Cherry silenced the voice that told her disaster had struck. Nothing could have happened to Billy. He was strong and had quick reflexes, and he knew the dangers of the kind of work he did. He was fine.

But he was very late.

Cherry read the girls two bedtime stories, thinking he would show up at any minute to tease and tickle them and kiss them good-night.

"Where's Daddy?" Raejean asked when Cherry said it was time to turn out the light.

"Isn't he coming home?" Annie asked.

"Of course he's coming home. He just had some errands to run. As soon as he arrives, he'll come and kiss you good-night. Go to sleep now."

She turned out the light and was almost out of the room when Raejean whispered, "Is Daddy going away?"

Cherry turned the light back on. Both Raejean and Annie stared back at her with frightened eyes. *Damn Mrs. Trask and her phone calls,* Cherry thought. She crossed and sat beside Raejean and brushed the bangs away and kissed her forehead reassuringly.

"Your daddy isn't going anywhere. He'll be right here when you wake up in the morning."

"Nana said Daddy might be going away," Raejean confessed. "I don't want him to leave."

"Neither do I," Annie whimpered.

"Oh, my dear ones," Cherry said. She lifted a sobbing Raejean into her arms and carried her over to Annie's bed, then slid an arm around each girl and rocked them against her. "Don't worry. Everything's going to be fine. Your Daddy's not going anywhere. And neither am I."

"Are you going to be our mother forever?" Annie asked.

Cherry was struck dumb by the question. She realized the folly of her promise that she wasn't going anywhere. She and Billy had a temporary marriage. She had no right to presume he would want it to continue any longer than necessary to convince the court to let him keep his children.

She was forced to admit the truth to herself.

She didn't want the marriage to end. She wanted to stay married to Billy. She wanted to be the twins' mother forever. All she had to do was convince Billy to let her stay.

When he showed up. If he ever did.

"Why don't we ask your daddy when he comes home

if it's all right with him for me to be your mother forever," she answered Annie at last. "Would that be all right?"

"I guess," Annie said. "If you're sure he's coming home."

"I'm sure," Cherry said.

That seemed to assuage the worst of their fear, and she managed to get them tucked in again. As she was turning out the light, Raejean said, "Cherry?"

"What is it, Raejean?"

"I don't want you to leave, either."

Cherry smiled. "Thanks, Raejean. That means a lot to me."

She rose up on one elbow and said, "I'm sorry about spilling grape juice on the couch. You don't think Daddy came home and saw it while we were gone and got *really* mad, do you?"

Her heart went out to the child. "No, Raejean, I don't think it's anything you did that's making your father late getting home. I'm sure he's been delayed by business. Go to sleep now. Before you know it, he'll be waking you up to kiss you good-night."

As she was closing the door, Cherry heard Annie whisper, "That's silly. Why is Daddy going to wake us up to kiss us good-night?"

"So we'll know he's home, dummy," Raejean explained scornfully.

"Oh," Annie whispered back. "All right."

Cherry headed downstairs hoping that Billy would arrive to fulfill her promise and waken the twins with a kiss.

As the night passed and he didn't return, she began to worry in earnest. The worst thing was, she had no idea where he might have gone. She made up her mind to wait until midnight before she called the police to report him missing. That's when the bars in town closed.

Not that she believed for one second that he had gone to a bar. Not with everything on the line the way it was. Not with everything he did subject to intense scrutiny in the courtroom. Not as determined as he was to keep custody of his children in the face of his mother-in-law's clutching grasp for them.

She sat in the dark on the front porch step, waiting for him to come home. At five minutes before midnight she saw a pair of headlights coming down the dirt road that led to the house. Her heart began to pound.

Surely it was Billy. Surely it was him and not someone coming to tell her he had been hurt.

The vehicle was headed for the back of the house, moving too fast for safety. She ran through the house, turned on the back porch light and slammed her way out the back door. She was there when the pickup skidded to a stop.

When she saw it was Billy's truck, she released a breath of air she hadn't realized she had been holding. The relief turned quickly to anger when Billy stepped out of the truck and she saw his face. One eye was swollen almost closed and his lip had a cut on one side.

"You've been fighting!" She gasped as he began to weave his way unsteadily toward her. "You're drunk!" she accused. "How could you, Billy? How could you?"

"I'm not drunk!" he said. "I've just got a couple of cracked ribs that are giving me hell."

She quickly moved to support him. "What happened? Where have you been? Who did this to you?"

She felt him slump against her. "Aw, Cherry, I don't

believe I let this happen. Not the day before I have to go to court. The judge'll never understand."

"Forget the judge. Explain this to me."

"I went to town to get some supplies at the hardware store and ran into that Ray character, the one who took you to the prom."

"Ray did this to you?" she asked incredulously.

"Him and three of his friends."

"But why?"

"It doesn't matter why. Or it won't to the judge. All he'll see is that I've been fighting again. Lord, Cherry, I hurt. Inside and out."

"Come on in to the kitchen and let me bind your ribs," Cherry said. "Maybe I can get the swelling down in your eye, so it won't look so bad tomorrow."

"Maybe I can say I'm sick and get a postponement," Billy suggested.

"Is it possible the Trasks won't find out about the fight? Did the police come?" she asked.

"They were there," Billy said.

"But you weren't arrested?" Cherry said. "That must mean something. I mean, that you weren't at fault."

"I wanted to fight, all right," Billy said flatly. "And I'd do it again."

"Don't say things like that. You can't keep getting into fights, Billy. Not if you want to keep custody of your girls. What could be so important it was worth risking your girls to fight about?" she demanded.

He didn't answer her, but that could have been because he was too busy hissing in a breath as she administered antiseptic to the cuts on his face. She eased the torn shirt off his shoulders and saw the bruises on his ribs. They must have kicked him when he was down.

"Where have you been all night, if you weren't in a bar somewhere drinking?" Cherry asked.

"I went to the stock pond to sit and think," he said.

"While you were thinking, did it occur to you that I'd be worried," Cherry asked archly.

"I'm sorry, Cherry. I lost track of the time."

He sat stoically while she strapped his ribs. But the light had gone out of his eyes. He had already given up. He had already conceded the battle to Penelope.

"You aren't going to lose tomorrow," she said to him. "You can tell the judge a bull stomped you, or—"

Billy snorted. "Stomped on my eye? Forget it, Cherry. You know as well as I do that my fight with Penelope is over before it's begun."

"I refuse to accept that!" Cherry snapped back. "You're a good father. You love your children, and you provide a stable home for them."

"That isn't enough."

"What more can the judge ask?" Cherry demanded.

Billy reached up gingerly and brushed his hair out of his eyes. "I don't know. You can believe there'll be something Penelope can offer that I can't."

"There's *nothing* she can give them that you can't," Cherry said fiercely. "And there's something you can give them that no one else can."

"What?"

"Love. A parent's love. Don't discount it, Billy. It's a powerful thing."

She saw the doubt in his eyes. He wanted to believe her, but he was afraid to let his hopes get too high. She lowered her lips to his, tender, as gentle as she had ever been. She brushed at the hank of hair that had fallen once more on his forehead. "You're going to win, Billy. Believe it."

He took her hand and pressed her palm against his lips. "Thanks, Cherry. I needed to hear that."

But she saw he didn't completely believe it. He believed this was the beginning of the end. He believed he was going to lose his children. That he was going to lose her. She could feel it in the way he clung to her hand.

She pulled herself free, unwilling to indulge in his despair.

"The girls were worried about you," she said as she scurried around fixing an ice pack for his eye. "I promised them you would wake them up to kiss them goodnight so they would know you got home all right."

"I'll go do that now," he said, groaning as he got to his feet, the ice pack pressed against his eye.

"Don't fall coming back downstairs," she said.

He turned and looked at her. He was in no condition to make love to her, and for a second she thought he was going to refuse to come back downstairs and join her in bed. But he nodded his head in acquiescence.

"I'll be down in a few minutes."

Cherry hurried to finish her ablutions and ready herself for bed before Billy came to her room. The sexiest nightgown she owned was a football jersey, and she quickly slipped it over her head. She was naked underneath it.

She pulled the covers down and slipped under them to wait for him. She left the light burning, because she knew he liked to watch her as they made love.

It didn't take her long to realize, once Billy entered her room and began undressing himself, that he needed help.

She got out of bed and came to him, sick at heart at this reminder of the fight that might cost him his children.

She took her time undressing him, kissing his flesh as she exposed it. Shoulders. Chest. Belly. She sat him down and pulled off his boots and socks and made him stand again so she could unbuckle his belt and unzip his jeans and pull them off. By the time he was naked, he was also obviously aroused.

"Lie down," she coaxed. "You're hurt. Let me do all the work."

She had never said she loved Billy in words. But she showed him with her mouth and hands and body. She eased herself down on his shaft, and when he arched his body into hers, said, "Lie still. I'll move for both of us."

She did, riding him like a stallion, never giving him a rest, until both of them were breathing hard and slick with sweat. She pushed him to the brink, brought him back, and took him there again. Until at last she rode him home.

He was already asleep, his breathing deep and even, by the time she slipped to his side, reached over to turn out the light, and snuggled against him.

"You'll win, Billy," she whispered into the darkness. "You have to win. Because I love you and Raejean and Annie. And I can't bear to give you up."

She felt his arm tighten around her.

At first she was terrified because she thought he must have heard her. Then she realized it was a reflexive move. He had reached for her in his sleep and pulled her close.

"You're not going to lose me, Billy," she murmured against his throat. "I'm not going anywhere."

His body relaxed, and she closed her eyes to sleep.

Chapter 10

The day of the hearing dawned fly-buzzing hot, as though to deny the cloud of disaster that loomed over their heads. In the bright sunshine Billy's face looked even worse than it had the night before. His left eye was swollen nearly shut, and the myriad bruises had taken on a rainbow of colors—pink, yellow and purple. He walked stiffly up the courthouse steps, like an old man, an occasional wince revealing what even that effort cost him in pain.

Cherry had put on a simple, flowered cotton dress with a Peter Pan collar she often wore to church. It made her look every bit as young as she was. Billy was dressed in a dark suit that fit his broad shoulders like a glove and made him into a dangerous, imposing stranger.

The twins bounced along beside them in matching dresses and pigtails, chattering like magpies, excited by the prospect of going on a picnic after the court hearing was over. Cherry chattered back at them, putting on a cheery false front to prove she wasn't as frightened as she was.

She and Billy had exchanged very few words since waking that morning, but their eyes had met often, communicating a wealth of information.

I feel awful.

I can see that. You look like you got stomped by something mean.

What if I say something wrong? What if I can't convince the judge to let me keep my kids?

Everything will be all right.

What if it isn't? What will I do?

I'm here for you, Billy.

I'm scared, Cherry.

So am I.

I'm glad you're here with me.

He reached out to take her hand, clutching it so tightly it hurt, as they entered the courtroom. The instant the twins saw their grandparents sitting at a table at the front of the courtroom with two men dressed in expensive suits, they went racing down the aisle to greet them.

"Hi, Nana," Raejean said, giving her grandmother a hug. Mrs. Trask wore a sleek designer suit that shouted wealth, her short-cropped, silvery-white hair perfectly coiffed.

"Hi, Grandpa," Annie said, getting a sound hug from her grandfather. Mr. Trask sported a double-breasted wool blend suit, his pale blond hair cut short on top and trimmed high over his ears.

The adults exchanged not a word, but their eyes spoke volumes.

Animosity from Mrs. Trask.

Antagonism from Billy.

Anguish from Cherry.

"Raejean. Annie. Come sit over here," Billy ordered.

Reluctantly the girls left their grandparents and came to sit beside Billy and Cherry across the courtroom.

Billy's attorney had already suggested that Billy compromise with Mr. and Mrs. Trask and give them partial custody of the children. The lawyer had warned that with their duo of legal experts, the Trasks would very likely win full custody if Billy insisted on fighting them in court.

"Are you ready, Mr. Stonecreek?" Billy's lawyer asked as Billy and Cherry joined him.

"I'm ready." Billy knew his lawyer believed they were fighting a lost cause. But he wasn't willing to give up his children without clawing for them tooth and nail.

Billy turned to find the source of a small commotion at the back of the courtroom. "Cherry, look."

Cherry looked and felt tears prickle behind her eyes. Her whole family was trooping into the courtroom. Zach and Rebecca, Rolleen, Jewel, Avery, Jake, Frannie, Rabbit, and Colt. She knew what it meant at that moment to be part of a family. They were there for her.

"Thank you," she mouthed.

Her mother smiled encouragement. Zach nodded. Colt grinned and gave her a thumbs-up, while Jewel mouthed back, "We're with you, Cherry."

At that moment the judge entered the courtroom, and the bailiff called, "All rise."

Cherry stood and reached for Billy's hand as he reached for hers. They stood grim-lipped, stark-eyed, waiting for the worst, hoping for the best.

"In the interest of keeping this hearing as open and

frank as we can get it," the judge began, "I think the minor children should wait outside. Is there someone who can take care of them?"

Jewel popped up in back. "I will, Your Honor."

"Very well. The children will leave the courtroom and remain outside until I call for them."

"Why do we have to leave, Daddy?" Raejean asked, her brow furrowed.

"Because the judge said so," Billy answered.

"I don't want to go," Annie said, clinging to Cherry's skirt.

"It's all right, Annie," Cherry said. "It's only for a little while. We'll all be together again soon."

She hoped.

Cherry prayed that the girls wouldn't make a scene in front of the judge, proving Cherry and Billy couldn't control their children. To her immense relief, they allowed Jewel to take their hands and lead them from the courtroom.

"This is a hearing to decide whether Mr. Stonecreek's two minor children should be taken away from him and given to their grandparents," the judge began solemnly. "I would like the petitioners to explain in their own words why they are seeking custody of their grandchildren."

"It's simple, Your Honor," Mrs. Trask said as she rose to her feet. "Billy Stonecreek is an inadequate and irresponsible parent who is doing irreparable harm to my grandchildren by neglecting them. He also happens to be a drunken brawler without an ounce of self-respect. It's a well-known fact that his kind can't hold their liquor."

"His kind?" the judge inquired.

"Billy Stonecreek's mother was an Indian, Your Honor," Mrs. Trask replied disdainfully.

The judge's brows arrowed down between his eyes, but all he said was, "Please continue."

"My former son-in-law has instigated several free-for-alls over the past year since my daughter's death, for which he has been repeatedly jailed. As you can plainly see from the condition of his face, he hasn't reformed his behavior over time.

"He has subjected my granddaughters to a series of housekeepers who come and go. His latest act of idiocy was to marry an eighteen-year-old high school dropout, who was a juvenile delinquent herself."

Billy had remained silent during Penelope's attack on him. When she started on Cherry, he couldn't sit still for it. "Wait one damn minute—"

"Sit down, Mr. Stonecreek," the judge admonished. "You'll have a chance to speak your piece."

Penelope shot Billy a smug smile and continued. "This pitiful excuse for a father doesn't have the time, money, or inclination to give his children the things they need. On the other hand, Mr. Trask and I are ready, willing, and able to provide a secure and stable home for our grandchildren."

"Is there anything else?" the judge asked.

Mrs. Trask hesitated before she said, "I believe Billy Stonecreek is responsible for my daughter, Laura's, death, Your Honor."

The judge raised a disbelieving brow.

"He didn't kill her with his bare hands," Mrs. Trask said. "But he made her so unhappy that…that she took her own life."

Cherry bounced up and said, "That's not true, Your Honor!"

The judge made a disgruntled sound. "Young lady—"

"Please, Your Honor. You have to let me speak," Cherry pleaded.

The judge turned to Mrs. Trask and said, "Are you finished, Mrs. Trask?"

"I am, Your Honor." She sat down as regally as a queen reclaiming her throne.

"Very well, then. Proceed, Mrs. Stonecreek."

"It simply isn't true that Billy is responsible for Laura's death."

"Cherry, don't," Billy muttered.

Cherry looked Billy in the eye and said, "I have to tell them, Billy. It's the only way."

When he lowered his gaze, she turned to face the judge. "Laura Stonecreek didn't commit suicide, Your Honor. She was involved in a tragic automobile accident. She was unhappy, all right—because she wanted to have more children, but wasn't medically able to carry another child to term. On the day she had her fatal accident, Laura miscarried a child for the second time."

An audible gasp could be heard from the other table.

"Billy didn't want her to take the risk of getting pregnant anymore. When Laura left the house that day she was despondent, but not because Billy didn't love her enough. It was because he loved her too much to take the chance of losing her by getting her pregnant again.

"Billy Stonecreek is the most gentle, most kind, and considerate man I know. He's a wonderful father to his girls, and they love him dearly. If you could only see him with them, giving them a bath, reading a story to them, kissing them good-night. They trust him to take care of them always. It would be a travesty to separate them."

"What you say is all to the good, Mrs. Stonecreek," the judge said. "But I'm concerned about your husband's propensity to physical violence. I'm especially concerned to see his condition today. I would think he would have avoided this sort of behavior, when he knew he would be appearing before this court."

Cherry felt miserable. Billy had refused to tell her why he had gotten into another fight. And he had said he would do it again. She could understand the judge's point. There was nothing she could say to defend Billy, except, "He's a good man, Your Honor. He loves his children. Please don't take them away from him."

"Excuse me, Your Honor."

Cherry turned at the sound of her father's voice. Zach was standing, waiting to be recognized by the judge.

"What is it, Zach?"

Cherry was surprised to hear the judge call her father by his first name until she remembered what Billy had said when he married her. The Whitelaws were well known around this part of Texas. It appeared Zach had a personal acquaintance with the judge.

"I can explain the cause of Billy's most recent altercation, if the court will allow it."

The two lawyers conferred hastily at the Trasks' table before one rose to say, "I object, Your Honor. Mr. Whitelaw has no standing to get involved in this case."

"I'm the grandfather of those little girls, too, Your Honor," Zach said. "My daughter hasn't adopted them yet, but that's only a formality. I know she loves them as though they were already her own."

Cherry's throat thickened with emotion.

"I see no reason why I shouldn't allow Mr. Whitelaw to make his point, Counsel," the judge said. "Especially in light of the consequences if I rule against Mr. Stonecreek. I'd like to hear an explanation for this most recent fight—if there is one. Go ahead, Zach."

"First let me say that I did not initially approve of my daughter's marriage. I thought she was too young, and I knew Billy Stonecreek's reputation for getting into trouble. I thought he would be a bad influence on her."

Cherry felt her heart sinking. Nothing her father had said so far was the least bit helpful to Billy. In fact, it was as though he had dug the hole deeper.

"However," Zach said, "I've since changed my mind. I did enough checking to find out that my son-in-law is a hardworking, church-going man who spends most of his free time with his children. With three notable exceptions—all occurring since his wife's tragic death— he has been an outstanding citizen of this community.

"Although my son-in-law chose to start those three fights over the past year in bars, no one I talked to has ever seen him the least bit drunk. He has never hurt anyone seriously, and he has always paid for whatever damages there were. I know that doesn't excuse him entirely."

"Or at all," the judge interjected. "What I'd like to know is why Mr. Stonecreek started those fights."

"Only Billy himself knows the answer to that question. If I were guessing, I'd say he was a young man in a lot of pain and looking for a way to ease it."

"Then he chose the wrong way," the judge said. "All this is very interesting, but it doesn't explain why he was fighting within days of this hearing."

"To defend his wife's honor," Zach said.

Cherry's glance shot to Billy. He lowered his gaze to avoid hers, and a flush spread high on his cheekbones.

"I'm listening," the judge said.

"I was in Estes's Hardware Store yesterday when

Billy came in. He picked up what he needed and went to the counter to pay. Ray Estes stood at the register and began making abusive, slanderous comments about my daughter, Cherry, in front of several other men, friends of Ray's, who were also waiting for service.

"Billy asked Ray to stop, but Ray continued provoking him, saying things to sully my daughter's reputation that no man could stand by and let another man say about his wife. Even then, Billy didn't throw the first punch.

"He told Ray he didn't want to fight, that he knew Ray was only mad because of what had happened the night Billy had kept him from assaulting Cherry. Billy said he would forget the insults if Ray would say he was sorry and hadn't meant what he'd said. Billy wanted the words taken back.

"Ray called Billy a coward, said he only fought men who were drunk. Even then, Your Honor, Billy kept his hands to himself. His fists were white-knuckled, but he didn't launch a blow.

"That's when Ray shoved him backward, and one of Ray's friends tripped him so he fell. Ray came over the counter and kicked him hard, while he was down. That was when Billy came up swinging. Ray's friends held his arms, so Ray could go at him. That's when he got the black eye.

"To tell you the truth, Your Honor, I took a few swings at those fellows myself. So you see, Billy tried to avoid a fight. He only got involved when it was a clear matter of self-defense."

Cherry gave her father a grateful look as he sat down, then met Billy's dark-eyed gaze. She reached for his hand under the table and clasped it tight. "Oh, Billy," she whispered. "Why didn't you tell me?"

"I shouldn't have let Ray provoke me," Billy muttered. "But I couldn't let him get away with saying those ugly things about you. I couldn't, Cherry."

She squeezed his hand. "It's all right, Billy. Surely the judge won't blame you now that he's heard the truth."

"I'll concede Mr. Stonecreek may have been provoked beyond endurance in this case," the judge said, confirming Cherry's hope. "The courts have conceded there are such things as 'fighting words' to which a man may respond justifiably with violence. And I'll take into consideration your suggestion that Mr. Stonecreek's other forays into fisticuffs may have been motivated by something other than drunkenness," the judge said.

"However," he continued, "I am concerned by several of Mrs. Trask's other accusations. Especially those concerning Mrs. Stonecreek's past behavior and her ability to function as a capable mother to two little girls."

"I'd like to speak on my wife's behalf, if I may," Billy said, rising to face the judge.

"Very well, Mr. Stonecreek," the judge replied.

"My daughters are lucky to have someone as wonderful as Cherry to be their mother," Billy said. "I feel myself fortunate to have her for my wife. Cherry was expelled from school for something she didn't do. Since then, she's taken care of Raejean and Annie during the day and gone to school every night to make up the classes she needs for graduation. I have every confidence that she'll complete her education with high marks and receive her diploma."

"I wasn't questioning your wife's intelligence," the judge said gently. "I'm more concerned about her maturity, her sense of responsibility, the example she'll set for the children."

Cherry saw Billy's Adam's apple bob as he swallowed hard. She wished she had led a different life. What could he say to defend her? She had been a troublemaker all her life. There was some truth in everything Mrs. Trask had said about her.

"I think Cherry's actions speak for themselves. My daughters are happy, healthy, and well-adjusted. Cherry treats them as though they were her own flesh and blood. You see, Your Honor, she knows what it feels like to lose your parents at a young age. She knows how important it is to make a child feel safe and secure and loved. That's what Cherry offers my children. Unconditional love. There's nothing more important to a child than knowing they're loved, is there, Your Honor?"

The judge cleared his throat. "Yes, well, that's true, of course."

"But, Your Honor," Mrs. Trask protested, seeing the tide shifting. "The same young woman whose merits Billy is extolling spent time in a juvenile detention facility. The fact remains, she was expelled from school. And she's only eighteen years old!"

"I will take all of that into consideration, Mrs. Trask," the judge promised. "Does anyone have anything further to say? Very well. I will need some time in chambers to deliberate this matter. I'll have a decision for you shortly. Court is recessed."

"All rise," the bailiff commanded.

Cherry rose on shaky legs and grabbed hold of Billy's hand for support. They had done all they could—which seemed precious little—to convince the judge they would be good parents. But was it enough?

One thing had become clear to Cherry. It wasn't only

the children she was afraid to lose. She was afraid of losing Billy, too.

He had only married her temporarily to have a mother for his children. What role would there be for her in his life if his children were taken from him? Would she only be a painful reminder of what he had lost?

Cherry looked into Billy's eyes, all her fears naked for him to see. *Do you love me, Billy? If it weren't for the children, would you still want me for your wife?*

And found the reassurance she sought.

His love was visible in the reassuring warmth of his gaze, in the way he held firmly, supportively, to her hand, in the way he had defended her in court.

Without a word, Billy rose and pulled her into his embrace. His arms closed tight around her. "Don't leave me, Cherry," he whispered in her ear.

"I'm not going anywhere," she promised.

"I want us to be together forever."

"Forever? But—"

"No matter what happens here today, I want you with me. I love you, Cherry."

"I love you, too, Billy."

They held each other tight, offering strength and solace, parting only as the twins came hurtling down the aisle to greet them. Raejean leapt into Billy's arms, while Cherry scooped up Annie.

"Jewel says we have lots of aunts and uncles and cousins," Raejean announced. "Zillions of them!"

Cherry laughed. "Not quite that many."

"How many?" Annie asked.

"I don't know, exactly," Cherry said. "But lots."

"Can we go on a picnic now?" Raejean asked.

"Not yet," Billy said. "Soon."

"We have to go home first and change our clothes," Cherry reminded her.

"Can we leave now?" Annie asked. "Is the judge all done?"

"Almost," Cherry said. "He wants to think about things a little while before he makes up his mind."

"Makes up his mind about what?" Raejean asked.

Cherry and Billy exchanged a tormented glance.

Makes up his mind about whether to take you away from us.

Billy's heart had been thundering in his chest ever since the hearing began. He felt himself on the verge of panic, and the only thing he had to hang on to was Cherry's hand. So far, he had protected his daughters from knowing about the desperate courtroom struggle that would decide their future.

This morning, as he and Cherry had sipped coffee together at dawn, he had decided that even if the Trasks won custody, he would do his best to make the transition as amicable as possible. Surely the judge wouldn't deny him visitation rights, and he would continue to have a strong and loving relationship with his children.

Only, if there was one thing Billy had learned in this life, it was that there were no guarantees. He was terrified the judge would rule against him. He was terrified the Trasks would try to bar him from all contact with his children.

Right now he felt like taking Raejean and Annie and Cherry and running as far and as fast as he could. Fortunately, Cherry's family came to the rail that separated the spectators from the litigants, all of them talking at once, making escape impossible, even if he had succumbed to the urge.

He felt a hand on his shoulder and turned to find Zach Whitelaw standing behind him.

"I want to thank you for your words of support, sir," Billy said.

"It was my pleasure, son. I never had a chance to congratulate you on your wedding. I expect you to take good care of my daughter."

Billy would have answered if his jaw hadn't been clenched to keep his chin from quivering with emotion. Instead, he gave a jerky nod.

"The judge is coming back already, Dad," Colt said. "Wasn't it supposed to take longer?"

It had already been too long, as far as Billy was concerned, although he realized it had only been a matter of minutes since the judge had left the courtroom.

"We'd better get back to our seats," Zach said.

Billy was afraid to send his daughters away, afraid they weren't going to be his when he saw them again.

"All rise," the bailiff said.

Jewel was leading the children out of the courtroom when the judge said, "The children can stay."

Billy exchanged a quick look with Cherry and quickly gathered Raejean and Annie into the circle of his arms in front of him.

Cherry gave him a quavery smile. "Surely it's a good sign that the judge let them stay," she whispered as she slipped her arm around his waist. It was questionable who was supporting whom.

When the judge sat, Billy and Cherry sat, each of them holding one of the twins on their laps. They could hear the clock ticking as the judge shuffled papers.

Finally he looked up and said, "The circumstances of this case are unique. The grandparents of these children have a great deal to offer them, not the least of which is the experience to be gained with age. The children's father has shown a lack of judgment on occasion that makes his suitability as a parent questionable."

Billy's heart felt like it was going to pound right out of his chest. *He's going to give them to Penelope. I'm going to lose my children.*

"However," the judge continued, "the law favors the natural parents of a child over any other custodian. And there are other factors evident here that I believe have to be considered in my decision."

What is your decision, dammit? Billy raged inwardly.

"I've decided to leave custody of the minor children with their father," the judge announced.

Shouts of joy and clapping erupted behind Billy.

"I want quiet in the court," the judge said, pounding his gavel.

Billy was too stunned to move, his throat too tight to speak. He saw Cherry through a blurred haze of tears. She was laughing and crying at the same time.

"We won, Billy. We won!" Cherry sobbed.

"What did we win, Daddy?" Raejean said.

"Did we get a prize?" Annie asked.

"Quiet in the court," the judge repeated.

"Shh," Billy said to the girls. "Let's listen to the judge."

He was more than willing to listen, now that he knew his children were his to keep.

"There will be those who question my decision in light of the evidence heard here today about the actions of the children's father and stepmother. They have made mistakes in the past. However, they both seem dedicated to rectifying their behavior.

"So I have based my decision not on what either of

them might have done in the past, but on what I saw here in this courtroom today that bodes well for the future.

"Seldom have I seen two individuals more supportive of each other, or more apparently devoted to each other. These children will have what too few children have these days—two parents who love and respect one another. I am convinced that these two young people are capable of providing a stable, healthy and happy home for the two minor children. Good luck to you both. Court is dismissed."

"All rise," the bailiff ordered.

Billy's knees were rubbery when he stood, and he slipped an arm around Cherry to keep himself upright. He realized he was grinning as he accepted the congratulatory slaps of the Whitelaws.

"Can we go on a picnic now?" Raejean asked.

"Soon," Cherry promised with a hiccuping laugh that was choked by tears of joy.

"Can Nana and Grampa Trask come, too?" Annie asked.

Billy looked across the room at the bitter face of Mrs. Trask and realized he only felt sorry for her. She had lost her daughter. Now she had lost her grandchildren, too. Because it would be a cold day in hell before he let her near his children again.

He felt Cherry's hand on his arm.

"The girls need their grandparents, Billy," she said. "And Mr. and Mrs. Trask need their grandchildren."

Billy struggled to be generous. He was still angry. And still afraid that the Trasks might yet find some way to take his children from him. But Cherry was right. Raejean and Annie loved their grandparents. It would be cruel to take them away. For their sakes, he had to forgive what the Trasks had tried to do.

"Why don't you go ask Nana and Grampa Trask if they'd like to come on our picnic with us?" Billy said to Raejean and Annie.

Billy pulled Cherry close against him as they watched the girls skip across the room to invite Penelope and Harvey Trask to join their picnic. Billy met Penelope's startled glance when she heard what the girls had to say. He saw her hesitate, then shake her head no and say something to the children.

Moments later the girls returned and Raejean said, "Nana says maybe next time."

Billy exchanged one last poignant look with Penelope before she turned away. Then he glanced down at Raejean and ruffled her hair. "Next time," Billy said.

Cherry met his eyes, her gaze proud and supportive, and said, "Next time for sure."

"Let's go home," Billy said as he reached for Cherry's hand. She reached out for Annie, and he reached out for Raejean. They walked out of the courtroom hand in hand in hand in hand, a family at last.

* * * * *

SPECIAL EXCERPT FROM

⊞HARLEQUIN®

ROMANTIC suspense

*Parting ways broke both attorney Simone Black's
and Dr. Paul Reilly's hearts. Now Paul desperately
needs Simone's help when he discovers something
fatally wrong in the medications provided by a major
pharmaceutical company. Can these two find
their way back to each other while bringing down
a very powerful enemy?*

Read on for a sneak preview of
Reunited by the Badge,
the next book in Deborah Fletcher Mello's
To Serve and Seduce *miniseries!*

"I appreciate you coming," he said.

"You said it was important."

Paul nodded as he gestured for her to take a seat. Sitting down, Simone stole another quick glance toward the bar. The two strangers were both staring blatantly, not bothering to hide their interest in the two of them.

Simone rested an elbow on the tabletop, turning flirtatiously toward her friend. "Do you know Tom and Jerry over there at the bar?" she asked softly. She reached a hand out, trailing her fingers against his arm.

Her touch was just distracting enough that Paul didn't turn abruptly to stare back, drawing even more attention in their direction. His focus shifted slowly from her toward the duo at the bar. He eyed them briefly before turning his attention back to Simone. He shook his head. "Should I?"

"It might be nothing, but they seem very interested in you."

Paul's gaze danced back in their direction and he took a swift inhale of air. One of the men was on a cell phone and both were still eyeing him intently.

"We need to leave," he said, suddenly anxious. He began to gather his papers.

"What's going on, Paul?"

"I don't think we're safe, Simone."

"What do you mean we're not safe?" she snapped, her teeth clenched tightly. "Why are we not safe?"

"I'll explain, but I think we really need to leave."

Simone took a deep breath and held it, watching as he repacked his belongings into his briefcase.

"We're not going anywhere until you explain," she started, and then a commotion at the door pulled at her attention.

Don't miss
Reunited by the Badge *by Deborah Fletcher Mello available October 2019 wherever Harlequin® Romantic Suspense books and ebooks are sold.*

www.Harlequin.com

Copyright © 2019 by Deborah Fletcher Mello

HRSEXP0919

Need an adrenaline rush from nail-biting tales
(and irresistible males)?

Check out **Harlequin Intrigue®**,
Harlequin® Romantic Suspense and
Love Inspired® Suspense books!

New books available every month!

CONNECT WITH US AT:

Facebook.com/groups/HarlequinConnection

 Facebook.com/HarlequinBooks

 Twitter.com/HarlequinBooks

 Instagram.com/HarlequinBooks

 Pinterest.com/HarlequinBooks

ReaderService.com

**ROMANCE WHEN
YOU NEED IT**

SGENRE2018R

SPECIAL EXCERPT FROM

◆ HARLEQUIN®
™

I N T R I G U E

*Waking in the middle of a war zone, Jane Doe
has no memory of who she is or who she can trust.
When she meets former elite Force Recon member
Gus Walsh, she finds that trusting him is her only
chance at finding answers.*

Read on for a sneak preview of
Driving Force,
the fourth installment of the thrilling
Declan's Defenders *series by* New York Times
and USA TODAY *bestselling author Elle James.*

CHAPTER ONE

She struggled to surface from the black hole trying to suck
her back down. Her head hurt and she could barely open her
eyes. Every part of her body ached so badly she began to
think death would be a relief. But her heart, buried behind
bruised and broken ribs, beat strong, pushing blood through
her veins. And with the blood, the desire to live.

Willing her eyes to open, she blinked and gazed through
narrow slits at the dirty mud-and-stick wall in front of her.
Why couldn't she open her eyes more? She raised her hand
to her face and felt the puffy, blood-crusted skin around
her eyes and mouth. When she tried to move her lips, they
cracked and warm liquid oozed out on her chin.

Her fingernails were split, some ripped down to the quick,
and the backs of her knuckles looked like pounded hamburger

meat. Bruises, scratches and cuts covered her arms.

She felt along her torso, wincing when she touched a bruised rib. As she shifted her search lower, her hands shook and she held her breath, feeling for bruises, wondering if she'd been assaulted in other ways. When she felt no tenderness between her legs, she let go of the breath she'd held in a rush of relief.

She pushed into a sitting position and winced at the pain knifing through her head. Running her hand over her scalp, she felt a couple of goose egg–sized lumps. One behind her left ear, the other at the base of her skull.

A glance around the small cell-like room gave her little information about where she was. The floor was hard-packed dirt and smelled of urine and feces. She wore a torn shirt and the dark pants women wore beneath their burkas.

Voices outside the rough wooden door made her tense and her body cringe.

She wasn't sure why she was there, but those voices inspired an automatic response of drawing deep within, preparing for additional beatings and torture.

What she had done to deserve it, she couldn't remember. Everything about her life was a gaping, useless void.

The door jerked open. A man wearing the camouflage uniform of a Syrian fighter and a black hood covering his head and face stood in the doorway with a Russian AK-47 slung over his shoulder and a steel pipe in his hand.

Don't miss
Driving Force *by Elle James,*
available October 2019 wherever
Harlequin® books and ebooks are sold.

www.Harlequin.com

Copyright © 2019 by Mary Jernigan

HIEXP0919

Love Harlequin romance?

DISCOVER.

Be the first to find out about promotions, news and exclusive content!

f Facebook.com/HarlequinBooks

y Twitter.com/HarlequinBooks

◉ Instagram.com/HarlequinBooks

p Pinterest.com/HarlequinBooks

ReaderService.com

EXPLORE.

Sign up for the Harlequin e-newsletter and download a free book from any series at **TryHarlequin.com.**

CONNECT.

Join our Harlequin community to share your thoughts and connect with other romance readers!
Facebook.com/groups/HarlequinConnection

⬢H HARLEQUIN®
™

**ROMANCE WHEN
YOU NEED IT**

HSOCIAL2018